Also by
J. D. Rinehart

◆ BOOK TWO ◆

The Lost Realm

J. D. RINEHART

CROWN OF THREE

♦ **BOOK ONE** ♦

ALADDIN

New York   London   Toronto   Sydney   New Delhi

ALADDIN

An imprint of Simon & Schuster Children's Publishing Division

1230 Avenue of the Americas, New York, New York 10020

First Aladdin paperback edition February 2016

Text copyright © 2015 by Working Partners Limited

Cover illustration copyright © 2015 by Iacopo Bruno

ALADDIN is a trademark of Simon & Schuster, Inc., and related logo is a registered trademark of Simon & Schuster, Inc.

For information about special discounts for bulk purchases, please contact Simon & Schuster Special Sales at 1-866-506-1949 or business@simonandschuster.com.

The Simon & Schuster Speakers Bureau can bring authors to your live event. For more information or to book an event contact the Simon & Schuster Speakers Bureau at 1-866-248-3049 or visit our website at www.simonspeakers.com.

Book design by Laura Lyn DiSiena

The text of this book was set in Oneleigh Pro.

Manufactured in the United States of America 0116 OFF

2 4 6 8 10 9 7 5 3 1

The Library of Congress has cataloged the hardcover edition as follows:

Rinehart, J. D.

Crown of three / by J. D. Rinehart. — First Aladdin hardcover edition.

p. cm.

Summary: "Toronia, a kingdom composed of three realms, is wracked with civil war. King Brutan rules with an iron fist. The kingdom's only hope comes in the form of Brutan's illegitimate triplets, prophesied to kill the king and rule together in peace. Separated at birth and scattered throughout the realms, the triplets face a desperate fight to secure their destiny."—Provided by publisher.

[1. Fantasy. 2. Kings, queens, rulers, etc.—Fiction. 3. Triplets—Fiction. 4. Brothers—Fiction. 5. Prophecies—Fiction.] I. Title.

PZ7.1.B6Cr 2015

[Fic] —dc23

2014023578

ISBN 978-1-4814-2443-1 (hc)

ISBN 978-1-4814-2444-8 (pbk)

ISBN 978-1-4814-2445-5 (eBook)

Special thanks to Graham Edwards

For Y. K.

In Toronia, realm of three,

A tempest has long raged.

By power's potent siren call,

Weak men are enslaved.

Too much virtuous blood has spilt

In this accursed age.

When the stars increase by three

The kingdom shall be saved.

Beneath these fresh celestial lights,

Three new heirs will enter in.

They shall summon unknown power,

They shall kill the cursed king.

With three crowns they shall ascend,

And true peace, they will bring.

—Gryndor, first wizard of Toronia

PROLOGUE

Melchior stood in the courtyard of Castle Tor, his wrinkled face turned up to the heavens. A million stars burned above him. Their light was old and cold, but Melchior's eyes were older.

Long ago, before the stars had kindled, the sky had been a barren, empty place. Beneath its shadow, the earth and the sea had been filled with darkness and strange magic.

Long ago, things had been different.

Melchior closed his ancient eyes and tried to summon a picture of that long-lost time and place. But his memory failed him. The past was gone.

Even a wizard cannot remember everything, he thought.

When Melchior opened his eyes again, the sky had changed.

Directly overhead, framed by the hard stone of the castle

battlements, three new stars blazed. The first was tinted faintly green, the second red, and the third gold. Each of them alone was brighter than anything else in the sky. Together they formed a tiny triangular constellation hanging in the blackness like an impossible jewel.

"The prophecy," whispered Melchior.

His back—which had been bent—straightened. The weight of long years fell away. His gnarled fingers tightened on his staff. He turned and ran toward the tower steps, his worn yellow cloak spreading behind him like wings. He shot past the kitchens. In an open doorway, framed by orange oven light, a servant stood frozen in the act of throwing out the slops. As the white-haired wizard sprinted past, the young man dropped the copper pot, sending it clattering onto the flagstones.

Melchior took the steps two at a time. The stone stairs wound around the outer wall of the castle's central keep. The wizard's bare feet slapped on the narrow stone treads.

At an open doorway three floors up, he darted inside the tower. A dizzying series of passages carried him deep into the castle interior. The corridors were dark and deserted. With King Brutan's army busy fighting the rebels at Ritherlee, Castle Tor was all but empty. Melchior muttered arcane words and the tip of his staff sputtered with cold fire, lighting his path.

Ducking beneath a low arch, the wizard charged into a wide, circular chamber from which a spiral staircase rose. Beneath the stairs, on a rickety wooden table, three tallow candles were burning. Coincidence or another sign?

Melchior didn't believe in coincidence.

"Hey! Who goes there?" A round-bellied guard levered himself off the bench on which he'd been dozing. "You can't see Kalia. I've got orders, me."

Without breaking stride, Melchior spun his staff in his hand. The fire at its tip became a circle of light. The light looped over the guard's head, where it contracted instantly to form a shining halo. As soon as the light touched the man's brow, his eyes rolled back in their sockets and he slumped to the floor.

Melchior glanced through the window. The three stars were in clear view. The guard probably hadn't noticed them, but sooner or later somebody would and the alarm would be raised.

Melchior had lived for more years than he could count. Never had time felt so precious.

He bounded up the two hundred and ten steps to Kalia's chamber. Counting the steps was something he did without thinking. For Melchior, all magic was numbers. *Measure the world and you will be its master.* This was what he knew, and what he taught, although he was well aware that his spells were not the only way to wield power.

There was much more to magic than mere numbers.

At the top of the staircase was a stout oak door. Melchior crashed through it. Beyond was a large room with a high ceiling. Flames flickered in an open hearth. Tapestries lined the walls. A connecting corridor took him past a polished table and a single chair, into a chamber containing a four-poster bed draped with silk.

On the bed sat a woman. Her face was flushed. Her long, red-gold hair was tangled and matted with sweat.

"They have their father's eyes," she said.

Melchior stopped in his tracks. He knelt at the side of the bed and placed his staff on the coverlet. The light at its tip faded to nothing. The wizard's breathing was soft and slow, even though he'd just run the length of the castle.

"Three," he said.

"Yes," Kalia replied.

On the bed before her were three bundles. At a glance, each might have been just a pile of laundry. But Melchior knew better.

He leaned forward, parting the flannel cloth and peering inside the bundles, one after the other. Inside each he saw a newborn baby. Each child was pink like its mother, and bore a dusting of her red-gold hair on its head. Each had eyes as black as the night sky.

"The prophecy." Melchior pointed to the window, beyond which the three stars were just rising into view.

"All the time I was carrying them, I kept telling myself it wasn't true," said Kalia. "Even now, I can hardly believe it."

"This has nothing to do with belief," Melchior said gently. "This is fate. For a thousand years, Toronia has known only war. Here"— he spread his hands before the babies—"here at last lies the promise of peace."

"But sending them away . . . Melchior, it's just so hard."

"Fate gives us no quarter, Kalia." He pointed a finger at the window. The stars were already climbing toward the middle of the sky. "Three stars for three children, just as the prophecy foretold. Kalia, the king will see the stars too. I can no longer keep your children secret."

Kalia turned her distraught face toward the newborns. "I've only just brought them into the world. How can I let them go?"

"If you do not let me take them, your babies will die."

The words hit home. Melchior hated himself for being cruel. *But if we do not act swiftly, all will be lost.*

"He wouldn't," she said.

"He would. You know better than anyone what the prophecy says. Triplets will be born to the king. They will kill their father and rule in his place. Only when they have taken the throne will Toronia know peace." He gestured toward the three babies. "What do you think King Brutan will do when he sees them? Do you think they will live to see the dawn?"

Kalia clutched Melchior's hand. "Then take me, too!"

"Kalia, I . . ."

Footsteps thundered on the stairs outside. Swords rang against the stone walls. A voice bellowed, unmistakable.

"King Brutan is here!" Melchior gave a silent curse. They'd waited too long! There was no other way out of the chambers. They were trapped.

Seizing his staff, the old wizard ran his sensitive fingertips down the runes carved into its age-worn surface. His fingers danced, playing the staff like a musical instrument, though it made no sound. He counted the beat of the silent song he was making, hoping he would finish it in time.

Four men, dressed in the bronze armor of the King's Legion, marched into the bedchamber. No sooner had they entered than a fifth man, taller and broader than the rest, forced his way through their ranks. He wore only a light sleeping robe, and his black hair and beard were disheveled, but still King Brutan was more imposing than any of his soldiers.

Kalia gasped and clutched her sweat-damp nightdress about her neck. "Brutan!" she cried. "I can explain. . . ."

"Explain?" Brutan's voice boomed through the bedchamber. "Can you explain that?" He pointed through the window, where the three stars were riding high. Kalia said nothing.

The king took a step closer to the bed. His broad brow was filmed with sweat. His black eyes were wide and wild. "You lied. You said there would be one child. But omens do not lie."

He bent over the three bundles. Kalia clutched his arm but he threw her off. She fell back on the bed, sobbing. Brutan seized the blanket in which the first baby was wrapped and ripped it open.

Staring at what lay inside, the king grunted.

He opened the second bundle and grunted again.

Slowly, Brutan peeled apart the third tiny bundle of flannel, looking long and hard at what lay revealed.

He grunted once more.

Melchior stepped forward. His hands gripped his staff, his fingers carefully placed.

"As you can see, sire," he said, "the children were not meant for this world."

On the bed, the three newborn babies lay for all to see. Their arms and legs were splayed out. Their skin was blue and wrinkled. Their eyes were closed. Their little chests were motionless.

"Dead?" said Brutan.

Raising her head, Kalia screamed.

Melchior bowed. "Stillborn," he said. "That is why I was summoned here—to see if my magic could help. Alas, I was too late."

"And the prophecy?" said Brutan.

"Has failed."

A long silence followed, broken only by Kalia's sobs as she threw herself over her dead babies. Then Brutan began to laugh.

"Failed!" he cried. "Failed! Was there ever a finer moment than this, Wizard? Well, was there?"

"No," Melchior replied. "This is a fine moment indeed."

Brutan seized Kalia's hair and yanked her head back. He planted his lips on hers. When she tried to pull away, he twisted her hair until she cried out. Finally he shoved her aside.

"If you ever lie to me again," he hissed, "I will burn you for the witch you are." He pointed to the babies. "Take them as far away from me as possible. That is an order. Do you understand, Wizard?"

"Perfectly, sire," Melchior replied.

As soon as Brutan and his legionnaires had left, Melchior released his grip on his staff. The hot wood cooled. Something like an exhaled breath wafted through the bedchamber, although the air didn't move.

Immediately the skin of the babies transformed from blue to healthy pink. The wrinkles plumped out. One after the other, their little chests heaved. Their eyes opened. So did their mouths.

"Hush," said Melchior, waving his hand. "Don't cry, little ones. Don't cry."

One after the other, the little mouths closed. Three pairs of black eyes stared up at the wizard, wide and unafraid. Kalia gathered up the babies and hugged them to her, tears coursing down her cheeks.

"Forgive me," said Melchior. "It was the only way."

"It's better than we could have hoped for," said Kalia, hitching in her breaths between sobs. "He thinks the prophecy has come and gone. They'll be safe now, won't they? Only . . ."

"Yes?"

Kalia looked down sadly at the three newborns. They gazed back at her. "You're right—I can't go with them. If I do, Brutan will know something is wrong. He'll come after me and . . ."

"What will you do?"

Kalia's eyes grew hard. Melchior sensed her strength, and hoped at least a little of it had flowed into her children. They would need it.

"It's not up to me anymore. It's up to you, Melchior. Take them. Send them away. Send them where Brutan will never find them."

She lifted the first child, a boy, and kissed his forehead. "You are Tarlan," she whispered. Hands trembling a little, she handed him to Melchior.

The second child was a girl. Kalia kissed her cheek. "Elodie, my daughter."

The third child was a boy. Kalia kissed the tip of his nose and said, "Your name is Agulphus."

By the time the three babies were secured safely inside Melchior's capacious robes, Kalia's tears were flowing freely again.

"These names I bind to you, my loves," she said. "It's all I have to give. I'm sorry. No child deserves your fate. Be strong, all three of you, and be true to yourselves. I hope one day we can . . ." She turned away, unable to speak further.

"My lady?" said Melchior.

"Go, Melchior. Before I change my mind."

And he did.

The great south wall of Castle Tor stood tall and dark against the pale dawn sky. Melchior slipped through the shadow of the postern gatehouse—the least used of all the entrances to the castle—toward three men on horseback.

All three were staring up at the slender tower rising from the castle's southeast corner. A wisp of yellow smoke lingered at the top: the last remnant of the beacon Melchior had lit to summon the riders. Sending the signal without being spotted had been difficult; waiting for dawn to come, and the men to arrive, had been agonizing.

Fate is hard.

As one, the three men tore their gazes from the beacon and fixed their eyes on Melchior.

"We are ready," said the first man. He was thickset, broader even than King Brutan, with a deeply furrowed brow. But behind the perpetual frown, his eyes were kind.

Without speaking, Melchior reached into his robes and drew out a small, white bundle. He handed it to the man.

"I will take the boy to my home in Yalasti," the rider said. "The cold will make him strong."

"That is well, Captain Leom," said Melchior. He handed a second bundle to a tall man mounted on a glossy gray charger. "And you, Lord Vicerin?"

"She will live as one of my own family," Vicerin replied. "She will want for nothing."

Melchior presented the third child to the remaining rider, a gray-haired knight wearing battered armor. The warhorse he rode was scarred and ancient.

"Will you keep him safe, Sir Brax?"

"I know a tavern," said the old knight. "It is hidden deep in the Isurian woods. The boy will not be found."

The three horsemen turned their steeds and galloped into the dawn. At the end of the castle track, the road widened, taking them out across the great Idilliam Bridge and into the kingdom beyond.

Melchior watched them dwindle and merge to a single moving dot. When they reached the far end of the bridge, each rider chose his different path and the dot broke into three again. The dust kicked up by the horses' hooves thickened and spread. By the time it had cleared, they had vanished.

Weariness spread through Melchior's limbs. He felt old again, old and empty.

Have I done the right thing?

He hoped so. Triplets were unusual in Toronia. If they remained together, sooner or later Brutan would discover them, and all would be lost. Their only chance was to grow up in separate corners of the kingdom. If they survived, fate might one day bring them together again.

And once together, they might at last take the crown.

Melchior trudged back up the path to the castle. Just before passing through the gate, he paused long enough to look up at the sky. Most of the stars had faded. Three alone remained.

"You are Toronia's only hope," he whispered, and went inside.

ACT ONE

Thirteen Years Later

CHAPTER 1

Gulph stared at the crowd. An ocean of faces surrounded him, some expectant, some bored. There must have been hundreds of spectators—perhaps even a thousand—all dressed in finery the like of which Gulph had never seen. They filled the tiered seats of the Toronian Great Hall. Gulph used to daydream about playing to such a large audience but had never imagined that, when the time came, it would be as a captive of the king.

He inhaled, his empty belly gurgling at the tang of roasted pork wafting from trays carried by wandering servants. He listened to the low rumble of the audience as the king's guests murmured to each other, shifted in their seats, waved their fans against the heat. He watched airborne dust move through rays of light pouring down from the gold-tinted windows in the roof. Was it possible to make glass from gold? Gulph didn't know.

"Get on with it!" called a voice from the uppermost row of seats. *Not as if we've got any choice,* Gulph thought.

He bowed low, bending forward at the waist until his nose touched the tip of his left shoe. He waited as a ripple of amusement moved through the crowd. Then he stood up straight again, paused, and bent over backward. This time the crowd gasped. Gulph's spine folded over on itself. Gripping his ankles with his hands, he stuck his head through his legs and forced himself to grin his biggest grin.

With his body contorted in this seemingly impossible fashion, Gulph trotted from one end of the sand-covered floor to the other. On the way he passed Pip, who was juggling a selection of apples and pears and hopping from foot to foot. As Gulph circled her, she dropped him a wink, but there was no mistaking the sadness in her brown eyes. The other members of the Tangletree Players looked on and clapped their hands. The jester, Sidebottom John, went one step further by standing on his hands and jangling the bells attached to his ankles.

The crowd took up the applause. By the time Gulph had returned to the center of the hall, many of the audience were on their feet. He planted his hands on the floor and flipped his legs over his head. Landing on his feet, he bowed again, this time to the royal box.

King Brutan and Queen Magritt were unmissable in their

crimson robes. The king stroked his beard, expressionless. The queen dipped her head, but, instead of a smile on her face, Gulph thought he saw a frown.

A cloud cast its shadow overhead and the golden light faded. Suddenly Gulph saw the Great Hall for what it was: a once-grand chamber grown old and tired. Paint was peeling from the thick supporting columns, and the uniforms of the various servants and orderlies were patched and in ill repair.

Castle Tor might have been the heart of the kingdom, but the heart was sick.

There was a particular face in the royal box Gulph wished he'd never set eyes on: that of General Elrick. This pompous military man with the face of a weasel looked very pleased with his place beside the king and queen, and took every opportunity to chatter to them, seemingly oblivious to their obvious dislike of him.

It was Elrick who'd brought the Tangletree Players to Idilliam. Weary from the war, he'd clearly been delighted to discover Gulph and his troupe of wandering entertainers performing for Brutan's soldiers in the nearby forests of Isur. He'd promised them riches and full bellies, warm quarters, and the king's protection.

The reality had been different. General Elrick had paraded the players before the king as spoils of war, then introduced them to their new home—one freezing cell between all twelve of them. Life on the road—sleeping under hedges wondering where their next meal was coming from, or whether they'd wake to find their throat being cut by some wandering ruffian—had been hard. But as far as Gulph was concerned, at least he had been free.

As an encore, Gulph went into a series of backflips. The crowd roared. After every flip, he paused and took another bow, exploiting the extraordinary flexibility of his body to the limit . . . and taking the opportunity to throw another glance at Queen Magritt.

Every time he looked at her, her expression grew more ferocious. *Stare at me all you like. I'm used to it.*

Many people saw Gulph's contortionist skills as a kind of deformity, along with his bulging eyes and the crook in his back. But this was different.

So intense was the queen's glare that, on his final backflip, Gulph stumbled. Ankles tangled, he fell heavily on his backside in a puff of dust. Laughter pealed through the audience.

Queen Magritt rose to her feet. Her fists were clenched. On her cheeks, bright red spots stood out like beacons against her pale skin. The king raised his hand to pull her down but she shook him aside.

"Take him out of my sight!" she shrieked, pointing directly at Gulph. Instantly the crowd fell silent. Gulph stared at the queen, bewildered, as her words echoed through the Great Hall. "This . . . this malformed monster will bring nothing but ill fortune to the realm."

"But, Your Majesty . . ." said General Elrick, rising to his feet.

The king shoved him down, then turned to regard his queen with one bushy eyebrow raised quizzically.

"The Vault of Heaven!" said Queen Magritt. Astonished cries rose from the audience. She waved a group of legionnaires forward. "Take him there. Take him there now. I won't have him in my sight a moment longer!"

As the soldiers strode toward him, Gulph looked up at the shocked faces of his friends.

"They won't take you!" called Sidebottom John.

"Tangletree stays together," said Willum, the bright-eyed piper. He ran toward Gulph; after a moment's hesitation, the other players followed suit.

Pip, the juggler, was much closer than the rest. Seizing Gulph's hand, she hauled him to his feet.

"What's the Vault of Heaven?" said Gulph, dazed.

"I don't know." Pip's hold turned into an embrace. "I won't let them take you, Gulph!"

The legionnaires reached Gulph before the rest of his friends. Grabbing Pip, they shoved her aside. As they surrounded Gulph, she beat against their backs. The rest of the Tangletree Players halted, uncertain in the face of such force.

"Get back," said Gulph, anxious for Pip's safety. "You can't help me!"

"Yes, I can!" Pip replied.

She raced across the arena to the royal box. Skidding to a halt, she fell to her knees before the king.

"Please, sire, I beg you," she cried. "Show my friend mercy. He only wants to entertain you. He's done nothing wrong."

The king leaned forward, smiling. "Such loyalty toward such a grotesque creature." His grin became a scowl. "Do you know what happens to little girls who question a royal command?"

Peering past the heads of his captors, Gulph watched in horror as a legionnaire struck Pip square in the chest with the blunt end of his spear. Pip fell backward onto the sandy floor.

"Leave her alone!" shouted Gulph, trying to force his way through the legionnaires. "I don't care where you take me. Just leave my friends alone!"

Hands clamped around Gulph's arms and shoulders. He struggled in vain as Queen Magritt beckoned to a tall, gray-haired man dressed in the bronze armor of the King's Legion.

"Captain Ossilius," she said. "Come to me."

The crowd hushed as she murmured to the legionnaire. Giving up the struggle, Gulph waited. He listened to the blood thumping in his ears.

When the queen had finished speaking, Captain Ossilius nodded and marched over to Gulph. The soldiers fell back, leaving Gulph standing alone and exposed.

"Will you defy me, boy?" said Captain Ossilius.

Gulph stared into the man's eyes. He looked tired and a little sad.

Gulph glanced at Pip, who was being helped to her feet by Sidebottom John. A pair of legionnaires loomed over them.

"No, sir," he said. He had no idea why this was happening—or even what had happened. He just knew that to save his friends he had to obey.

"Very well," said Captain Ossilius. Seizing Gulph's arm, he dragged the young contortionist out of the Great Hall. As they passed the royal box, King Brutan turned his rage on General Elrick.

"You fool!" the king bellowed as the general cowered. "How dare you upset my queen? The day is ruined!"

His voice was drowned out by the clamor in Gulph's head. *The Vault of Heaven*, he thought wildly, wondering what his destination could be. The name was strangely beautiful but did nothing to lessen his fear.

Outside the castle, the narrow streets were packed with peasants putting up rickety tables and erecting makeshift stalls. Captain Ossilius hauled Gulph through the labyrinth without saying a word. The captain's grip on his arm was like iron.

I can't wriggle my way out of this one.

As they passed a vegetable stall, a woman behind it threw a cabbage at Gulph. It struck him on the side of the head and slid onto his shoulder in a mass of pulpy, rotten leaves. The stench was overwhelming; so was Gulph's misery. He tugged at his captor's arm, wanting to explain to the stallholder that he wasn't a criminal, that it was all a mistake.

Then he saw that all the vegetables on the stall were rotten, not just the one the woman had thrown. He realized the clothes for sale in the adjacent stall had been thrice mended and were ready to fall apart. Even through his despair, Gulph saw that Idilliam was not a happy place.

Turning a corner, they left the market and entered an open yard. Here Captain Ossilius stopped.

"We are here," he said.

Gulph didn't understand. He'd been expecting some kind of prison, but all he could see was a forest of tree trunks stripped of their branches. They rose from the cobbled yard like the legs of some enormous beast.

"What . . . ?" he began. Then he looked up.

The trunks were stilts. Perched on top of them was what looked like a gigantic bird's nest. It appeared big enough to contain the entire Great Hall, where the Tangletree Players had just been performing.

What Gulph had thought were branches were in fact iron bars, bent and woven into an intricate mesh. Between them he saw the occasional flicker of an orange flame. But for the most part, the nest's interior was utterly black.

"Come, boy," said Captain Ossilius.

A narrow set of steps led up through the massive stilts. Suspended from creaking ropes, the steps swayed as they climbed. At the top was a square iron door. Beside it was a row of rusted gibbets—small metal cages each just big enough to hold a man.

Captain Ossilius thrust Gulph inside one of the gibbets and snapped the lock shut. Taking a key from his pocket, he opened the door and disappeared inside the iron nest.

Gulph stared through the bars he was standing on, to the ground below. It was a very long way down. He looked sideways into the next gibbet and saw a pile of bones.

Was this it? Was he to be left here to die of thirst and starvation? And for what? Because the sight of his deformed body offended the queen?

Gulph pinched his eyes shut. He would not cry.

The door clanged open. Someone fumbled with the gibbet's lock. Gulph opened his eyes to see Captain Ossilius standing before him. He searched the man's face for some sign of hope.

"Forgive me," said the captain, and Gulph's heart lifted. It had all been a mistake after all! But Ossilius said, "I had to restrain you while I made arrangements. Come!"

The captain's hand clamped once more around Gulph's arm. He was dragged through the door and into darkness. The door slammed shut, and out of the black void ahead came a gravelly voice.

"Ah, here you are," it said. "Welcome to the Vault of Heaven."

CHAPTER 2

A wave of hot air washed over Gulph, thick with the stench of smoke and sweat. Somewhere in the distance, people were shouting and screaming, their voices ringing off the woven bars that made up the Vault's walls.

"What is this place?" he said.

"Be quiet," said Captain Ossilius as he marched Gulph down a long, winding corridor. Orange light bloomed ahead; the nearer they got to it, the louder the uproar became.

"It's the Vault," came the same coarse voice that had greeted him.

Looking back, Gulph saw a short, fat man hurrying behind them. A huge bunch of keys jangled at his prodigious waist, and sweat sprayed from his bald head.

"What's . . . ?" he began, but his words trailed away as they reached the end of the corridor and emerged into a vast, echoing chamber. Directly ahead was the source of the light Gulph had glimpsed: a giant sphere of metal pierced through with countless circular holes from which tongues of flame licked out. This brazier hung suspended from cables and swung slowly, spitting sparks over the uneven floor.

The walls! They're moving!

Blinking, Gulph slowly understood what he was seeing. They weren't walls at all, but cages crammed full of people. A spider's web of iron bars, intricately knotted together, behind which squirmed a tangle of arms and legs and writhing bodies. The prisoners of the Vault of Heaven.

"Any more questions?" growled the fat man, breathing rotten meat and garlic into Gulph's face. "The Vault looks crowded, don't it? But there's always room for a little one."

He pulled Gulph away from Captain Ossilius and dragged him past the brazier toward a cell in which the shrieking prisoners were packed like fish in a barrel. As they approached, a scrawny man wearing only rags around his waist thrust a pipe-thin arm through the bars.

"Give us the freak!" he shouted. "We'll look after him!"

"Freak's more skinny than you, Shankers!" cackled a woman with hair like a rat's nest.

"Looks like a frog with them bulging eyes," called another.

"Frog's legs for dinner," said the man called Shankers. "Frog's legs! Frog's legs!"

The other prisoners took up the chant. Gulph dug in his heels and tried to free himself from the guard, but the fat man's grip was even stronger than that of Captain Ossilius.

"Back from the bars!" he bellowed. "Wretched rebels, the lot of you! Think you can fight the crown? Look at you now! You make me want to puke!"

The fat man raised his arms. The keys dangled from one hand; Gulph dangled from the other. The tremendous heat thumped inside his head. He wanted to scream. Scream and run. Then he noticed the bars weren't as closely spaced as he'd first thought. Once inside, there was a chance he'd be able to squeeze back out.

If I survive long enough.

"Stop!" Suddenly Captain Ossilius was there, planting himself squarely in front of the cage. He glared down at the man, his face like stone. "You have your orders, Blist. Now carry them out!"

Blist's round face quivered with uncertainty. "I thought you was jesting."

"I never jest. And you will call me 'sir.'"

"But . . . the Black Cell? You don't mean it. Sir."

Ossilius bent close. "These are not my orders, Blist. These are the orders of the queen herself. Shall I explain to her that you would not carry them out?"

"No, sir," said Blist. His eyes, which up to now had been

shining, turned cold and dead. "I would no more betray the queen than a captain of the Legion."

"Very well. Discharge your duty, jailer, and I will discharge mine."

Captain Ossilius swung on his heels and marched away. As he passed into the exit corridor, he paused and looked back at Gulph. He opened his mouth, about to speak, before changing his mind and stepping out of the Vault, into the dazzling day outside.

"Can you put me down, please?" said Gulph. "My arm hurts."

Blist's other hand clenched around the bunch of keys, and for a moment, Gulph thought the jailer would drive them into his face. Then the fat man's shoulders slumped, and he lowered Gulph to the floor.

"Not another sound from you, you little freak," he growled, before dragging Gulph back past the brazier and into a narrow tunnel that wound upward in a tight spiral. As they climbed, the sounds of screaming faded, although the heat increased. By the time they reached the top, Gulph's whole body was slick with sweat.

Before them was a low door. Without speaking, Blist selected a long, black key from his bunch and jabbed it into the lock. He twisted it, and with a drawn-out screech, the door opened. Releasing his grip on Gulph's arm, the jailer delivered a tremendous kick to the small of his back. Gulph tumbled through the doorway, rolling instinctively and coming up on his feet.

The door slammed shut. The key rattled in the lock and Blist's heavy footsteps echoed briefly before melting into the background roar of the prison.

Gulph turned slowly, taking in his surroundings. The room was awkward, with an uneven floor and oddly angled walls . . . but it was a room, not a cell. A desk stood in one corner, covered in books and scrolls, beside which an oil lamp flickered.

High above, the ceiling was a steep slope of iron beams; Gulph felt as though he'd stepped into a strange metal attic. There were no windows, and the only daylight filtered in a thin stream from a slit between two of the rafters. Opposite the desk was a chair with embroidered cushions, and a simple bed piled high with blankets. On the floor was a thick rug.

Something rushed out of the shadows beside the bed: a billowing shape topped by a pale face.

A ghost!

Clapping his hand to his mouth to stifle a scream, Gulph backed away, tripping on the edge of the rug and nearly falling. The shape emerged fully into the light, revealing itself to be not a ghost at all but a tall boy dressed in a flowing gray robe. His skin was whiter than any Gulph had seen, and his pale blue eyes were wide. But he was grinning.

"Welcome," the boy cried, extending trembling hands. "Oh, welcome!"

Gulph had retreated as far as the door. There was nowhere else to go. The boy was a little older than him, and although he looked sickly, he carried himself with an air of confidence.

"Who are you?" said Gulph.

"I'm Nynus. What's your name?"

"Gulph."

The grin became manic. "Pleased to meet you, Gulph. You've no idea how happy I am to have company again. I've been locked in this cell since I was six and . . ." The boy's face collapsed suddenly into grief. "Ten years. Can it really be that long?"

"Cell?" said Gulph. "You call this a cell?"

"I suppose it could be worse." The grin was back, the gloom having left Nynus as quickly as it had come. "But I do get bored reading the same old books, and pacing the same old circle."

Gulph smiled back uneasily. "Well, it's luxurious compared to the rest of this place." His eyes strayed over the fine needlework of Nynus's robe, the gold trim at the hems. "So how does this work? Are you rich or something?"

"Yes." Nynus nodded happily.

"Oh. All right. But I'm not. I don't understand why they've put me in here too. Queen Magritt ordered it, but . . ."

"Well, I'm only here because King Brutan doesn't like me. I've done nothing wrong."

"That doesn't sound very fair."

"It isn't. But there's nothing I can do about it."

The smile had vanished again and all the energy seemed to drain from Nynus's body. He looked even paler than when he'd first jumped out of the shadows. Gulph had never seen anyone look sadder or more wretched.

"I'm sorry," he said. "It must be terrible, being shut away from your family all these years."

Nynus shrugged. "I don't even remember what they look like." He started humming what sounded like a lullaby. At the same time, his hand crept up to his face and started stroking his cheek.

Gulph shifted awkwardly. Should he try to comfort him, and tell this strange, pale boy that he knew what it was like to grow up without a family? With a shiver, he wondered if this place would eventually make him like Nynus too.

A drop of water landed on Gulph's cheek. He looked up at the slit in the rafters. The daylight had turned gray—a cloud passing in front of the sun, he supposed. More water splashed on his upturned face; outside, it was raining.

Hope stirred inside him.

"Have you ever tried to escape?" he said.

Before Nynus could reply, Gulph went over to the desk and swept the books onto the floor.

"Hey," said Nynus. "My books!"

"The world's full of books," said Gulph. "I'll show you."

Gulph climbed on top of the desk he'd cleared. Lodging his fingers into the woven strands, he started up the iron wall. It was hard work, like trying to climb a tree with only the rough texture of the bark to cling to, but his joints were strong and supple and soon he was halfway up. The wall was smoother here, forcing him to contort his body and stretch his arms beyond the reach of any normal boy in order to find the next handhold. Each time he performed another impossible maneuver, he heard Nynus gasp, and felt a warm glow of pride. The other prisoners had called him a freak. If only they could see what a freak could do.

At last he reached the place where the wall met the sloping roof. Hanging like a spider, he pressed his face against the narrow slit in the rafters and peered out. The smell of sewage wafted in.

Below stretched the crowded streets of Idilliam. Beyond them, at the city's edge, loomed the craggy rock known as the High Peak, which Pip had pointed out to him on the day they arrived.

"From the top of the High Peak," Pip had said, "you can see all three realms of the kingdom. I wish we could go up there!"

The memory of that moment stung Gulph's eyes even more than the rain. He wondered if he'd ever see Pip again.

Near the High Peak was the great Idilliam Bridge: a huge stone structure spanning the chasm between the Toronian capital and the vast green forests of Isur. It felt like a lifetime since the

Tangletree Players had crossed that bridge on their way into the city. Yet it was merely five days. Now the bridge promised escape and freedom, but it was impossibly distant. Gulph couldn't see how he'd ever reach it.

One step at a time.

He studied the roof outside. Just below the slit through which he was peering, a network of gutters met above a fat waste pipe. The top of the pipe was open; it was from here that the bad smell was emanating. The pipe ran at a steep angle down the side of the Vault of Heaven.

All the way to the ground.

The door to Nynus's cell rattled. Heart racing, Gulph scrambled back down the wall, releasing his grip and leaping the last few feet to the floor. Just as he landed, a slot in the bottom of the door swung open and a fat hand shoved two battered metal bowls into the room. One contained a steaming pork chop, two potatoes, and a mound of cabbage. The other was filled with a nameless gray slop.

Unable to stop himself, Gulph said, "Are we supposed to fight over dinner?"

A second slot opened at eye level and Blist glared through. "Know your place, freak," said the jailer. "Nothing in my orders about giving you special treatment. It's not like you're a prince, is it?"

"Of course I'm not a prince!" Gulph shouted, but already the door slots were shut. He turned to Nynus. "What was he talking about? What's this got to do with—?"

To his astonishment, his cell mate was bowing. "Prince Nynus, at your service. I'd ask you to kiss my hand, but I think we've got past that, don't you?"

"Prince . . . Do you mean you're the son of . . . ?" Shock made it hard to string the words together. "But what are you doing locked up here? You said the king ordered it, but isn't he . . . ?"

"My father? Yes, he is. He's also completely mad. He's convinced everyone's out to steal his throne."

"Why?"

"Who knows? Maybe it's because he stole it in the first place. When I was six, he got it into his head that I'd be the next one to try, so he had me locked up. Mother—I mean, the queen—had no choice but to go along with it, but she does what she can to make life comfortable for me." Nynus's eyes widened. "That's why you're here! She sent you to be my companion!"

Beaming, Prince Nynus clasped his arms around Gulph and hugged him so hard his feet left the floor. Gulph endured the embrace, bewildered that a deformed contortionist from a traveling circus should have found himself mixed up in a royal family feud. And what must it be like for Nynus, being at its center?

Gulph didn't even remember his father or mother, but Nynus's only memory of his parents was the day they locked him away.

No wonder he's ended up like this.

Still smiling, Nynus put down Gulph and picked up the bowls of food.

"Shall we share?" he said brightly.

CHAPTER 3

B lack le . . ."

The words died on the frost witch's blue lips. A shudder ran the length of her body. One of the elk hides slipped aside, exposing a white, bony wrist and a hand like a spider.

Tarlan replaced the fur blanket and stroked the old witch's brow. Her skin was colder than the ice that lined the mouth of the cave. Reaching up, he pulled down another hide from the wall and draped it over her motionless form.

"Don't try to speak, Mirith," he said. "Just rest."

He grabbed a stick and poked it into the fire. The flames rose a little before sinking back to a feeble flicker. Soon he'd have to fetch more wood. But he couldn't leave Mirith like this. She looked so small, so weak. Just like a baby.

Seeing her this way, Tarlan felt momentarily dizzy, as if time had stood still—or folded over on itself. Was this how he had looked to Mirith, thirteen years earlier, when she'd found him as a helpless baby, abandoned in the icy wastes of Yalasti? When she'd picked him up, taken him in, cared for him as he'd grown.

Just like a mother.

A clay pot was lodged in the embers at the edge of the fire. In it was the dregs of the broth Tarlan had prepared the previous night. He dipped a bowl into the pot and scooped out the steaming food.

Slipping his free arm under Mirith's shoulders, he eased her into a sitting position. It shocked Tarlan how little she weighed. For the first time, it occurred to him that she might die. The realization filled him with terror. The thought that followed was even worse.

It was his job to care for her. If she died, it would be his fault.

"Here," he said, pressing the edge of the bowl to her mouth. "Try to drink."

Mirith shook her head. With more strength than she'd mustered for several days, she lifted one trembling hand from beneath the elk hides and pushed the bowl away.

"Black . . ." she began, before lapsing into a fit of coughing.

"What? Black what?"

"Lea . . . Black leaf."

Tarlan cursed himself for not understanding sooner. "Black leaf? You want me to get some? Is it medicine? Will it help you?"

Mirith nodded. Tarlan thought he could hear the bones in her neck creaking.

He put down the bowl and lowered her back onto the bed. Springing to his feet, he snatched up his robe and threw it over his shoulders. The dizziness came again. This was the same robe he'd been wrapped in when Mirith had found him. Now he'd grown tall enough to wear it without the hem brushing the floor of the cave.

Bending, he kissed Mirith's brow. Her eyes were closed. He held his cheek close to her lips, reassuring himself she was still breathing. Then he seized his hunting spear and strode out of the cave.

The instant he was on the ledge, the icy Yalasti wind slammed him back against the sheer rock wall. Tarlan forced himself to stand against its blast. He'd known this wind all his life, and was more than a match for it. He wrapped his cloak tightly around him, the warmth of its black velvet defying the cold white wilderness surrounding him.

Cupping his hands around his mouth, Tarlan tipped back his head and shrieked. His scream sliced like a knife through the gale. When his breath was gone he paused, breathed in, then shrieked again.

On the third call, the thorrods came.

They swooped out of the low cloud, just as if they'd been waiting for Tarlan's call. Perhaps they had. The gold feathers on their wingtips fluttered as they dropped toward the ledge. The dawn light glanced off their huge, hooked beaks. Long talons opened and closed. They resembled gigantic eagles, but the intelligence in their eyes was more than birdlike.

Reaching the level of the ledge, the four enormous birds began to circle. The flock's leader, Seethan, turned his gray head toward Tarlan. Most thorrods were as big as horses. Seethan was bigger than two.

"Something wrong," said the huge bird. His voice sounded like splintering wood.

"Mirith's sick," Tarlan shouted in the thorrods' tongue, into the wind. "It's getting worse. I have to bring her black leaf. If I don't, I'm afraid—" The words choked in his throat. "I'm afraid she'll die."

"East forest," said Seethan, soaring back up to hover above the other birds. His wings cast great moving shadows over the ledge.

"Kitheen!" called Tarlan.

A thorrod the size of a pony landed on the ledge before him. Extending his open hand like a wing, Tarlan allowed Kitheen to touch it with the tip of his lethal beak: the gesture of trust between thorrods.

"Will you stay here?" said Tarlan. "Keep guard?"

Kitheen said nothing, simply hopped past Tarlan and took up station in front of the cave, his feathers—black but for those golden wingtips—plumped against the wind.

Tarlan bunched the hand he'd extended into a fist. At once, a third thorrod left formation and flew just beneath the level of the ledge. Timing his jump to perfection, Tarlan leaped onto her back, thrusting his legs down behind her wings and seizing the thick ruff of feathers around her neck. Of all the thorrods, Theeta alone had golden feathers from head to tail.

"You're the one who found me in the forest, Theeta," he said. "You're the one who brought Mirith to me. You saved me and . . . and now we must save her. Fly fast, as fast as you can!"

Theeta carried him low over the snow-covered landscape. Seethan and white-breasted Nasheen flew just ahead, their slipstream making it easier for her to carry her load.

Away from Mirith's mountain retreat, the wind was less violent, but the air was no less cold. They passed village after village, each filled with houses cut from the ice. Smoke rose from countless fires as the men and women who lived there made their stand against the endless Yalasti winter.

A dark blur on the horizon grew rapidly in size. Soon they were flying over the great eastern forest. Theeta swooped over the towering cinderpines. The lower trunks of these majestic trees were bare of branches, but each carried a broad canopy of glossy green leaves at the very top. The leaves were coated with flammable resin, which local villagers harvested to burn in their winter fires.

Tarlan tried to peer down through the canopy, but the leaves were too thick. "Where's the black leaf?" he said.

"Low," Theeta replied. "On trunks."

"There," called Nasheen, dipping her beak. "Gap."

Theeta dived toward a space in the canopy. Tarlan ducked his head and closed his eyes as his gigantic steed plunged through the leaves and into the clear space beneath.

When Tarlan opened his eyes, the whole world had changed. Above him, instead of the clear blue sky, was a glowing green ceiling. All around him were the stiff, straight trunks of the cinderpines. Tarlan clung to Theeta's feathers as she weaved her way between them. Had his mission not been so desperate, he might have whooped with excitement.

"Here," said Theeta.

Clinging to the trunk of a particularly massive tree was a plant that was all curling tendrils and drooping leaves. Black leaves.

"That's it!" cried Tarlan. "Get nearer!"

Theeta hovered as close to the tree as she was able. Tarlan stretched out, grabbing handfuls of the leaves and stuffing them into a pocket within his cloak. They stood out in sharp contrast to its bloodred lining.

Seethan, who had followed them down through the canopy, flew out from behind the vast trunk.

"Men," the old bird hissed. "Many."

Looking down, Tarlan saw a line of mounted hunters making their way through the trees. They were riding not horses but elks. The huge antlers of these great winter beasts nodded steadily as their riders drove them on through the snow. The riders had antlers too, sculpted from wood and fixed to their helmets.

"Elk-men!" said Theeta.

Tarlan's heart sank. Mirith had warned him about these merciless hunters who roamed the forest, not just hunting for food but chasing down and slaughtering anything that would run, simply for the sport of it.

Including people, he thought grimly.

A cry rose up from below. Suddenly the line of elks was fanning out. Faces looked up. Mouths opened and began to shout. An arrow shot past Tarlan's face, then another.

"Quick, Theeta!" he cried. "Time to go."

The giant thorrod wheeled in the air, screeching. Down on the ground, one of the hunters had dismounted and was running along the line of elks with a burning brand. As he passed each of his comrades, he used the brand to light the tip of a waiting arrowhead.

"Go!" called Seethan. His silvery wingtips blurred as he angled into a steep dive, heading straight toward the hunters. Six men drew their bows and fired at him. The old thorrod darted through the lethal onslaught, and the burning arrows slammed into the canopy above.

The resin-coated leaves exploded into flame. Fire leaped from one treetop to the next, quicker than Tarlan's eye could follow it. Within seconds, the entire roof of the forest was ablaze.

Fire above. Hunters below. No way out!

Shrieking, Theeta beat her mighty wings against the searing air and raced through the trees. Burning embers fell all around. Whenever they landed on her feathers, Tarlan beat them away. But the trees closed in, forcing Theeta to double back and fly straight toward the waiting hunters.

As they approached, one of the men stood up on the back of his elk steed and brandished a spear. "You tame the thorrods!" he shouted. "Witch boy! Your birds will feed us for a month!"

"Nobody catches the thorrod!" Tarlan yelled back, waving his own spear in fury. But the words caught in his throat.

How are we going to get out of this?

"This way!" It was Nasheen, dropping down in front of the gasping Theeta and leading the way toward a distant gap in the trees. The three thorrods sped toward it, Seethan bringing up the rear. The hunters followed, spurring on their elks with harsh cries and angry kicks. Burning arrows flew past, some falling harmlessly into the snow, others striking the trees and starting new blazes.

"Nearly there!" cried Tarlan as the gap opened up before them. Then, from behind came a dreadful scream.

Turning, Tarlan saw Seethan's great wings falter and fold, saw the old thorrod tip over onto his back. Saw the burning arrow jutting from his chest. As Seethan plunged toward the snow, flames engulfed him. By the time he hit the ground, his whole body was on fire.

Theeta faltered, letting out an anguished screech of her own. Below, the leader of the elk-men spurred his mount over Seethan's burning body and drew back his spear, aiming it upward, directly at Theeta's heart. Before Tarlan could bring his own spear to bear on the enemy, another arrow shot through the air directly in front of Theeta's face. He tugged at her feathers and she rolled aside. The arrow whipped past her beak, slicing through the upper part of Tarlan's right arm.

Pain seared through him. Losing his grip, he slipped from Theeta's back and plummeted toward the ground. As the white hump of a snowdrift rose up to meet him, all he could think of was Mirith, cold and alone in the mountain cave.

He'd failed her after all.

CHAPTER 4

I t's entirely the wrong color," said Elodie, tossing aside the sample of blue silk she'd selected from the market stall.

"What do you mean?" sighed Lady Sylva Vicerin. "It's blue, isn't it?"

"But it's not the right blue. I want something more . . ." Elodie waved her hand impatiently.

"Like the sky?"

"No."

"Like a river?"

"No."

"Like what then, Elodie?"

"I'll know it when I see it!"

Elodie marched across the castle court to another row of stalls.

A strong breeze caught the bolts of silks and linens, turning them into pennants. Sylva scurried in her wake.

"What about this one?" Sylva suggested, pointing to a roll of sapphire cloth on a nearby stall.

"It's cotton," said Elodie, curling her lip. "Don't you want me to look nice at the banquet? Do you want Lord Vicerin to look like a miser?"

"My father says he might have to cancel it," said Sylva.

"*What?*" This was terrible news. Vicerin banquets were grand affairs, meticulously planned and talked about far and wide. Elodie had been dreaming about it for weeks. "He can't do that. The seamstresses are waiting to start on my dress. They've only got three days to make it and—"

"Elodie, I'm sorry. For once, my father has other things on his mind."

"What do you mean?" Elodie found it hard to imagine anything more important than a banquet.

Sylva led her into a quiet space between two stalls. "Don't tell anyone, but I heard Father say the king's army has reached the Northwood Dale."

"Oh, that's leagues away. Anyway, don't we have people out there to stop them?"

"Yes. But Father says that the crown troops already control lots

of the main borderways. He thinks our allies are spread too thinly."
Sylva's gray eyes were serious. "Elodie, these traders were lucky
to get through—next month, there may be no market at all. Who
knows, if the fighting goes on much longer, Castle Vicerin itself
might be under siege."

Elodie looked up at the red stone walls and the battlements running along the top. The stalls huddled beneath them seemed very
small. For all the color and noise, the market looked ramshackle,
as if it had been set up in haste, and might be taken down at any
moment. Several of the traders even wore light armor; Elodie didn't
recall ever seeing that before. Did they really think King Brutan's
men would bother attacking a few trestle tables?

"I don't know why everyone worries so much," she said. "We're
safe enough here. Anyway, Lord Vicerin always sets things right."

She picked up a length of shimmering turquoise silk and draped
it around her neck. "What do you think? Is it too green?"

"I think we've been out here long enough," said Sylva, grabbing the silk and replacing it on the stall. The stallholder—a
hungry-looking man with eager eyes—watched them closely.
"My father wanted us back before midday."

"I'm not leaving until I have my silk. Go home if you don't like
shopping. I don't need a chaperone."

Sylva sighed in frustration. Despite her irritation, Elodie couldn't
help sympathizing. Sylva no more wanted to be her protector than

Elodie wanted to be protected. She liked Sylva and wished their relationship could be simpler.

I wish you really were my sister, she thought.

Elodie made her way along the row of stalls. As usual, Sylva shadowed her, matching her step for step. When Elodie went left, Sylva went left. When one stopped, they both stopped.

It was infuriating.

Elodie picked up her skirts and began to run, darting through the maze of stalls. She passed barrows laden with fresh produce harvested from the great fields of Ritherlee: potatoes and carrots and succulent greens. A large cart creaked under the weight of countless barrels filled with beer or molasses or both. Down one alley, sides of meat swung like great pendulums.

"Elodie!" came Sylva's cry. "Wait for me!"

Turning a corner, Elodie saw Lord Vicerin's daughter hurrying clumsily toward her on her fine shoes, her face red and anxious.

"Catch me if you can!" She laughed and dodged behind a stall piled high with pewter bowls and goblets.

The longer the pursuit went on, the more Elodie found it amusing . . . and ridiculous. Although Elodie's identity was a secret to all but the immediate Vicerin family, the truth was she was the daughter of King Brutan and thus destined, one day, to rule over all Toronia. Why else would Lord Vicerin be fighting the crown but for the right to put his adopted daughter on the throne? Did

Sylva really think Elodie would run away from a destiny like that?

If only they would let me go, then they'd realize I want to stay.

A flash of color stopped Elodie in her tracks. It was yet another silk stall, stacked high with bolts of fabric finer than any she'd seen. Running her fingers over the cloth, she dismissed one roll after another. This one was too coarse, this one too pale, this one too dark. . . .

"Is this all you have?" Elodie called to the old woman who ran the stall. She was busy serving a tall man in an elegant court outfit and ignored her. Affronted, Elodie put a hand on her hip. "I said—"

"Stop it!" said a voice in her ear. "Stop being such a greedy little brat!"

Whirling around, Elodie found herself staring straight into the flushed face of Sylva.

"How dare you speak like that to your future queen!" she snapped. She wanted to shake Sylva, or slap her. What had possessed Sylva to say such a thing? Why would she even think it?

And why had the words stung so badly?

"Hush, Elodie," said Sylva. "Mind what you say. Nobody can know who you truly are."

"Mind my tongue? Is that it? Well, perhaps you should mind yours before calling me a brat!"

"Brat?" said Sylva, looking confused. "Who called you a brat?"

"You did. You said—"

"Elodie, I didn't say anything. I just came up and you snapped at me. Who were you talking to?"

Just for a second, the hubbub of the market died away, leaving Elodie alone in a bubble of silence. Her ears throbbed. She stared at Sylva's pink, earnest face and saw only simple concern. Then the bubble burst, and the world rushed in again.

"I thought I heard someone," Elodie muttered.

They made their way back through the stalls toward the south end of the market, where they'd first begun. Elodie was suddenly tired of shopping. Maybe the silk there hadn't been too bad, after all.

As they walked, she cast surreptitious glances into the shadows between the stalls. This wasn't the first time she'd heard a strange voice. Once, she'd been sitting in the grand Vicerin banqueting hall and an old man had whispered in her ear. But there had been no old man there. Another time, she'd heard laughter in the rose garden below her private chambers. At night, voices called to her from behind the dresses in her closet.

If Sylva worried about people learning that her adopted sister was a princess, Elodie had a far greater fear: that Lord Vicerin would find out she heard voices and decide she was mad. As soon as he knew the truth, he would send her away.

Isn't that what you do with people who are insane?

Might that not be what her real mother had done, all those

years ago, when she'd discovered there was something wrong with her daughter?

Soon they found themselves back in front of the very first stall they'd looked at. Elodie pointed out the closest roll of blue. "This one," she said dully to the stallholder. All her excitement about finding the correct shade had melted away with the mysterious voice.

While Elodie was searching in her purse for the right coins, a red-haired girl appeared from behind a nearby tent. She was tall and looked just a few years older than Elodie—perhaps the same age as Sylva. Her long skirt rippled in the breeze, and the high sun flashed off something hidden beneath: a short metal sword in an open scabbard strapped to her thigh. Staring straight at Elodie, the girl walked toward them.

Elodie put her purse away.

"What's the matter?" said Sylva.

"Something's wrong," said Elodie. Heart racing, she grabbed Sylva's hand. "Come on." Her other hand went instinctively to the emerald dangling on its gold chain around her neck, fingers clasping the green gem as they always did when she was nervous.

"Aren't you going to buy the silk?" said Sylva.

The approaching girl pulled her hair away from her face. Her eyes flicked sideways. Following her gaze, Elodie spotted a young man in a green tunic lurking beside a nearby ale tent. As the girl tossed her hair, he gave an almost imperceptible nod.

Without warning, the fabric stall tipped forward, spilling rolls of material across the ground. Elodie's silk unfurled in a billow of bright blue. A food stall went over, and suddenly people were shouting. Someone picked up a cabbage and lobbed it into the crowd. A wooden bowl flew like a discus. Scuffles broke out.

Sylva's grip tightened on Elodie's hand . . . then was suddenly snatched away. At the same instant, a fat man appeared from nowhere and barged into Elodie, nearly knocking her off her feet. By the time she recovered her balance, she was adrift in an ocean of bodies, her companion nowhere to be seen.

"Sylva!" she shouted, suddenly frightened.

Elodie tried to force her way through the throng. Where had they all come from? Then she heard a sound that chilled her blood: the unmistakable *sschink* of a sword being drawn.

Had Sylva been right after all? Was the king's army even now storming the gates of Castle Vicerin?

"Elodie!"

Sylva's face appeared, wide-eyed with fear. An instant later she had vanished, swallowed by the crowd. Elodie pushed against the press of people, ducking as missiles flew over her head. But Sylva was gone.

A man's hand gripped her wrist. She screamed but nobody listened. She tugged but the fingers were locked tight. The man started to haul her through the crowd. All she could see of him was a broad back clad all in green. Was it the same man she'd seen lurking by the tent? She tried to struggle, but he was too strong.

Kidnap-and-rescue, Elodie thought, remembering the favorite game she'd played years earlier as a child, when Sylva's older brother Cedric had dragged them both through the nursery and into a pirate's den made of bedsheets and boxes. She wanted desperately to believe this was all just make-believe, that the man before her would spin around to reveal Cedric's broad smile and laughing eyes.

But Cedric had gone to war, and she was no longer a child.

And this was no game.

They reached the edge of the market square, where a coach was waiting. The coach looked shabby, with mud-splattered wheels and long scratches in the wooden panels, but the four white horses standing in the traces looked fit and fresh and ready to race the length of the kingdom.

Seeing the coach filled Elodie with fresh terror. So kidnap it was. But as for rescue . . .

"Let me go!" she shouted, struggling anew to free herself. "Don't you know who I am? If you so much as dirty my dress, Lord Vicerin will have you hanged from the lynchtower!"

Ignoring her outburst, the man opened the door to the coach and tried to push her up the steps and inside. Elodie planted her feet wide and put all her strength into resisting him. Just as she thought she was winning, a second pair of hands in the small of her back shoved her unceremoniously into the coach. The door slammed shut, leaving her staring through a tiny slot of a window at the girl with the red hair. Elodie tried to turn the handle, but it refused to move. The door was locked. She was trapped.

A whip cracked and the coach lurched forward. Elodie pressed her face to the little window and screamed.

"Call out the guard! I'm being abducted! Help me! Somebody help!"

Blank faces went past in a blur. Elodie screamed again, not using words this time but simply howling her despair.

Nobody heard.

The coach slowed as it turned the corner leading to the main castle gate . . . and suddenly Sylva was there. She'd thrown off her heels and was sprinting barefoot after the coach, running so fast she was actually gaining on it. She no longer looked scared but angry and determined.

"Sylva!" Elodie yelled. "Help me!"

For a moment, she thought Sylva was going to catch up. Then the whip cracked again and Elodie was thrown against the hard wooden bench at the back of the coach. Her head hit the bulkhead and, briefly, her vision flashed white.

By the time she got back to the window, Sylva was gone. Even the castle was gone. The coach was on the high road, speeding down the long, steady slope toward the wide plains of East Ritherlee. Out in the fields, farmhands toiled, unaware of her plight.

Each time she saw someone, Elodie banged on the door of the coach and shouted through the tiny window. But they were either too far away or lost in their toil. Her frustration turned to anguish as the crop-filled fields gave way to meadows dotted with cattle and sheep. Their dumb lack of concern was somehow worse than the inattentiveness of the farmhands, and the tears that had been building inside Elodie since leaving the castle finally burst from her.

Elodie wept until she could weep no more. Exhausted, she threw herself onto the hard bench. The sound of the road tracked the coach's every turn as it swayed this way and that. Soon it would meet the Great Way, which ran all the way north to the Isur Bridge and into the forest lands beyond, stopping only when it reached Idilliam and the castle of King Brutan.

That she'd been captured by the king's forces she had no doubt. Somehow, Brutan had learned of her identity and ordered her to be brought in. What would he do with his daughter now that he had her in his power? Elodie had no idea. Lord Vicerin had always told her that King Brutan was a tyrant, jealous and cruel, who would do anything to maintain his iron grip on the throne of Toronia.

Even if it means killing the rightful heir.

The coach sped on through the Ritherlee fields. Every league she traveled, and every tear she shed, carried Elodie farther from Castle Vicerin, her home.

Farther from her dreams of becoming queen.

CHAPTER 5

What do you see?" Prince Nynus called up. He was crouched in the corner of the cell with his arms wrapped around his knees, rocking slowly backward and forward.

"Nothing," Gulph hissed back. "It's night. And we should keep our voices down."

Actually, with his head pressed into the slot in the roof, Gulph could see quite a lot: the long, faint shadows cast by the crescent moon over the city rooftops; the flicker of fires behind a thousand tiny windows; the stars like sparks in the night sky.

Idilliam looks so beautiful.

Gulph crammed his head through the slot. It was so tight that, for a horrible moment, he thought he was stuck. What a sight he'd be for the jailer in the morning: a reckless boy hanging from the rafters by his head, arms and legs dangling like limp rope. He wriggled and pushed and, finally, forced his head through. He took a deep breath, expecting cool, fresh air . . . but he'd forgotten how close he was to the sewer pipe. The stench was indescribable.

Nynus called again from the cell, but now his voice was muffled. Gulph drew his head back inside, popping it out of the tiny aperture like a cork from a wine bottle.

"Do you need more light?" said Nynus. He'd moved to stand beside the desk and was waving the oil lamp from side to side. The moving light cast strange shadows on his pale face.

"Just hold it as high as you can. And hold it still." Gulph didn't have the heart to tell the prince it was making no difference whatsoever. "Is he still snoring?"

Both boys fell silent, listening. For a moment, Gulph heard nothing. Then, very faint, there came a sound like a distant sawmill, rising and falling in regular rhythm.

"Like a baby," said the prince.

"That doesn't sound like any baby I ever met. If we can hear it all the way up here, imagine what's it's like in the room with him."

"Perhaps he'll wake himself up!" Nynus's face pinched with alarm. Dropping the lamp on the table, he scurried back to the corner.

"Never mind. If Blist is asleep, he's not interested in what we're up to. This is our chance, Nynus. Are you ready?" There was no reply. "Are you ready, Nynus?"

The boy looked up with a fresh and dreadful clarity in his eyes. "I've been ready for ten years, Gulph."

Turning his attention back to the roof, Gulph thrust his free hand through the slot. He was using his other hand—and his bare feet—to cling onto the cell wall, just as he had earlier.

Once his hand was outside, and with his arm fully extended, he gave the odd little shrug that he knew would dislocate his shoulder. The bone jumped out of its socket with practiced ease, allowing him to angle his neck unnaturally close to his collarbone. Thus contorted, he was able to feel around on the roof.

His finger touched cold slates, still damp from the afternoon rain. The edges were soft, and crumbled to the touch. Perfect.

Gulph drew his arm back inside.

"How are you doing that?" said Nynus. His bloodless face, upturned and lit by the flickering lamplight, looked paler than the moon.

"Good news," said Gulph, ignoring the question. "Soon you won't be a prisoner anymore. Throw me one of those dishes."

Smiling, Nynus obeyed. Gulph freed a foot and caught the spinning bowl in his toes, causing the prince's grin to broaden even further. Contracting his stomach muscles, Gulph curled his body to bring the foot up past his head. He used his toes to jam the bowl through the slot, ready to be received by his waiting hand.

Having secured his grip on the cell wall again, Gulph used the bowl's sharp metal edge to chisel away at the soft slates surrounding the hole. As the slot widened, moonlight cascaded down to flood across Nynus's face. White worry had replaced the prince's smile.

"You will come back for me, won't you?" he said. He sounded as plaintive as he must have done as a little boy on the day he'd been locked away.

"Why wouldn't I?" said Gulph.

"I've been on my own for so long. I don't want to be alone ever again."

"We're friends now, you and me." How long was it since anyone had said such a thing to this wretched boy? "I'll come back. I promise."

Once he'd finished widening the hole, Gulph let the bowl fall down onto the bed, popped his shoulder back into place, and slithered easily out onto the roof. Poised on all fours, he scanned his surroundings. Braided iron watchtowers rose from the sloping roof at regular intervals. Gulph saw no movement in the lamplit nests that topped them, but he couldn't take any chances. He would have to be quick.

Scuttling like a spider, he hurried to the edge of the roof and peered down. Below the guttering, the woven wall of the Vault of Heaven plunged down into deep shadow.

Gulph's night vision was good, and it didn't take him long to find a bar narrow enough to grip. Swinging his legs over the edge of the roof, he lowered himself hand over hand until he'd reached the level of the cells. A little more searching located a gap between the bars that was big enough for him to slide through . . . just as he'd thought.

Landing softly on his bare feet, Gulph stopped, suddenly conscious of the madness he'd undertaken.

He'd been locked up, by order of the queen, with an undesirable prince of the realms.

He'd promptly escaped.

And where had he escaped to?

Another cell, this one packed to bursting point with the snoring, snuffling scum of the city. If any one of them woke up, Gulph was dead.

Slowly, silently, Gulph picked his way across the cell. In the darkness, the sleeping forms of the prisoners slumped like sacks in a cellar. Several times, his naked toes brushed an outstretched hand or a lolling face. The slightest contact set his pulse racing, and he had to bite his lip so as not to cry out.

At last he reached the other side of the cell. Just as he was about to slip through the bars and out into the corridor, a guard ambled past. Gulph froze, limbs tensed, mouth clamped shut over his breath. It was too late to retreat.

Don't move a muscle!

The guard passed by, turned a corner, and vanished from sight.

Gulph let out a long, slow breath, and eased his slender body through the bars and into the wide space between the cells. The brazier loomed over him like a giant's plaything. Round lids had been dropped over most of the ventilation holes, damping down the fire for the night; those that were still open revealed a sullen interior where red coals pulsed with heavy light.

He stopped, listened. The faint sound of snoring rose over the soft crackle of embers in the brazier. Following the sound, Gulph made his way to the far end of the row of cells, where a short corridor led to a small, boxy room. Drapes embroidered with hunting scenes hung from the iron walls, a crude attempt to make the room seem homely.

In the middle, sprawled on a sagging chair, was Blist. With both hands he clasped an empty beer bottle to his enormous belly, which shook as he breathed. His head was tilted back and his mouth was wide open, revealing black and yellow teeth. Brown drool had run down his cheek, staining the shoulder of his jacket.

I was right. That snoring is really loud.

Gulph edged closer. Blist's huge bunch of keys dangled from his belt, clear to see and within easy reach. The black key that opened the door to Prince Nynus's cell jangled softly against its neighbors.

Crouching beside Blist's chair, he cupped his left hand underneath the keys, then closed the fingers of his right hand completely around them, holding them still and muffling any sound they might make.

What next, Pip? he thought, wishing his friend were here beside him.

Pip's response was no more than an echo in his head. But imagining she was with him in this awful place gave Gulph the strength he needed.

"Remember what I showed you?" Pip seemed to say. *"Back in that village in Isur, when we needed coins to buy bread?"*

Gulph remembered only too well. The Tangletree Players had spent months traveling through Isur before they'd been caught up in the fighting and captured. Some days the audiences had been appreciative, and they'd eaten well. Most of the time they'd been close to starvation.

I remember. A vivid memory came to Gulph: the day when Pip had shown him how to pick the pockets of the wealthy, distracting them for long enough to dip a hand in a money pouch or lift a purse from a belt.

"It's all about speed and silence," said Pip's voice. *"Rehearse the move in your head, then just do it. Above all, be confident."*

With his right hand still holding the keys tightly, Gulph studied the clasp by which they were attached to Blist's belt. If he turned the key ring just *so*, and pulled it *thus*, the clasp should open smoothly.

The snoring stopped. Gulph's blood turned to ice as Blist shifted his tremendous bulk on the seat, leaning so far sideways that Gulph was convinced the jailer would fall off the chair, squashing him flat. The bottle jerked, squirting warm beer into Gulph's face. The chair teetered, two legs off the floor, on the verge of tipping completely over.

Then it rocked back. Blist's belly sagged, and the snoring started again, louder than ever.

Quickly, Gulph reached forward with his left hand and seized the clasp, turning it just *so*, and pulling it *thus*. The thick metal parted, a spring contracted, and, with the faintest of clicks, the bunch of keys was released.

His fist closed tight on his prize, Gulph rose smoothly and, without looking back, made his exit. All the way down the corridor, he was convinced Blist would wake, discover the keys were missing, and come rampaging after him. Never mind the queen's orders; if the jailer found he'd been robbed, he'd tear Gulph limb from limb.

But the snoring continued, fading a little as Gulph ascended the spiral tunnel leading to Nynus's cell. Plunging the black key into the lock, he opened the door to find Nynus waiting for him on the other side. The young prince was hopping from one foot to the other. In his arms he carried a pile of books.

"I knew you'd do it!" Nynus exclaimed. "I knew it!"

"Shh! And don't count your eggs before they're laid. We're not out yet. What are you doing with those books?"

"I can't leave them behind. What will I read?"

"Where we're going, you won't be doing much reading."

"Why? Where are we going?"

Gulph convinced Nynus to leave all the books except one (a thin volume he clung to with fanatical devotion), then led the boy back down the tunnel until they reached a narrow side passage. Gulph ducked his head inside and sniffed.

"This way," he said.

"Really?" said Nynus. "There's a dreadful smell."

"Exactly."

The passage was short, and opened into a small chamber filled with the stench of rotting meat and sewage. Moonlight filtered through a large grille in the ceiling, illuminating a low wall with a square door set in the middle.

"What's behind the door?" said Nynus, clutching the book to his chest.

"If I'm right," said Gulph, "freedom."

He pulled the handle and the door swung open, revealing a

black abyss. Impossible though it was to believe, the smell grew ten times worse.

"Ugh!" said Nynus, his voice muffled as he clamped his hand over his nose and mouth. "What is it?"

"Sewage pipe. I spotted it from the roof." Gulph paused. "Wait. Listen."

"I don't hear anything."

"That's what worries me."

Gulph strained his ears, hoping he was wrong. But he wasn't. The snoring had stopped.

"I think . . ."

He stopped as sounds finally began to filter down the passage: shouts, the drawing of swords, the hurried thud of footsteps.

"Blist's woken up!" Gulph wished he'd had the presence of mind to take only the key to the Black Cell, and not the whole bunch.

"He might not be coming this way," said Nynus.

They listened. The sounds of the commotion grew steadily louder.

"Or he might want to check his most precious prisoner first," said Gulph.

Before Nynus could respond, Gulph shoved him into the sewage pipe. Then, holding his breath, he swung his legs over the lip of the hole and plunged after him.

The descent was fast and foul. The pipe's interior was smooth and coated with greasy liquids that lubricated his passage down to the ground. Gulph didn't like to think what those liquids were. He just kept his hands pressed to his chest, closed his eyes and mouth, and fell.

The pipe spat him out into a pool of noxious sludge. As he landed, Gulph slapped his hands down on the surface of the foul-smelling liquid, to stop his head from going under. Waves rolled lazily to the pool's far side, where a bubbling whirlpool drew the sewage down into some unseen outlet. Overhead, the Vault of Heaven was a huge nest of knitted iron, perched impossibly on its wooden stilts. Torches darted to and fro behind its woven walls: the hunt was on.

"Over here!" What seemed to be a monstrous brown troll was crouched on the edge of the pool, its misshapen hands reaching out for Gulph. "Before you're sucked under!"

The troll wiped a hand across its face, revealing the familiar features of Prince Nynus, otherwise unrecognizable beneath his coat of dripping sludge. With his other hand, he grabbed Gulph's collar and helped him clamber out.

"I lost my book." Even through the filth, the look of desolation on the young prince's face was clear to see. "It was a story about a good king and an evil wizard. It was my favorite."

"We'll get you more books," said Gulph. He tossed Blist's keys into the sludge, where they landed with a sticky *plop* and sank from sight.

Prince Nynus grabbed Gulph's hands. To Gulph's astonishment, he seemed to have already forgotten the book and was laughing, his teeth bright against the noxious brown slime still covering his face. Gulph found the boy's lightning changes of mood dizzying.

"You're right!" Prince Nynus cried, leading him in a clumsy imitation of a waltz. "We're free! We did it. *You* did it. I'll never forget this, Gulph. Never!"

Gulph couldn't imagine how it must feel to taste freedom after ten whole years in a cell. He knew they had to keep running, get away from the sewage pool before the guards caught up with them. But for now he let the prince spin him around, filthy and stinking beneath the watchful crescent moon.

CHAPTER 6

Keeping to the shadows, Gulph and Nynus crept through the winding streets of Idilliam. Timber-framed buildings loomed over them, their upper stories leaning in so far that their roofs almost touched. They passed workshops and stores, and humble homes; everywhere the windows were unlit and the doors were closed against the night. Jagged rooflines sliced the moonlight into knife-thin beams, through which the two boys flew like ghosts.

At first, Gulph was content to let the prince lead the way, but it soon became apparent that Nynus had no more idea of where they were than he did.

"I think we might be lost," said Nynus, halting at the edge of a little square where seven narrow streets met. In the middle of the square was a well. A bucket swung from a rusted chain, squeaking in the silence of the night. "I can't believe how much the city's changed since Father put me away."

"Don't you recognize anything?" said Gulph, glancing anxiously back over his shoulder.

"Yes. No. Sort of. It's just that half the windows are boarded up, and all the gutters are leaking. And everything's so *filthy*."

Gulph stared at Nynus's sludge-caked clothes. Nynus stared back.

Both boys burst out laughing.

A man dressed in rags emerged from a doorway and stumbled across the square, muttering to himself. With every step, he took a swig from an earthenware jar. When he reached the well, he leaned over the stone parapet and vomited into its depths, then continued toward the boys, drinking as he came.

Gulph pulled Nynus into a dark alley beside a stone-walled building, out of the man's sight. A sign on a door read, LAUNDRY. Beneath it was a smaller sign, hastily handwritten. It said, CLOSD TIL FURTHR NOTIS. From somewhere nearby came the sound of running water. As the drunk staggered past, Gulph realized the man was talking not to himself but to the jar of liquor.

"Terr'ble times," mumbled the man. "Terr'ble. Still . . . I've got you. M'only friend. You and me. Terr'ble times." Cradling the jar like a baby, he disappeared into the night.

"Come on," said Nynus, tugging Gulph's sleeve.

"Wait." Gulph ventured to the end of the alley, where a broken pipe jutted from the side of the laundry building. Water poured from it in a steady stream and ran down a gutter set deep in the cobbled ground.

Stepping under this impromptu faucet, Gulph allowed the water to soak him, rubbing away the sticky sewage clinging to his clothes and body. By the time he'd finished, he was cold and not exactly clean.

At least I feel human again.

"We need a proper plan," he said as Nynus took his turn under the water. "We've run away from the prison. Now we need to decide what we're running toward."

"What do you mean?" said Nynus, scraping muck from his robe.

"You said it yourself. Idilliam is a mess—and every member of the King's Legion will be after us. Why would we want to stay here?"

Nynus shook his head. "I'm not leaving on my own. My mother always said that if you cross the Idilliam Bridge, you take your life in your hands. The world outside is wild."

"It's not so bad. And you wouldn't be alone. You'd be with me. And my friends."

"What friends?"

"The Tangletree Players. They must be somewhere in the castle. If we can find them, we can all escape the city together. If we can only get over the bridge and back to Isur, everything will be all right." Gulph hesitated as the frown deepened on the prince's face. "I'm not saying it isn't hard, trying to make a living out there, but at least we'll be free."

Nynus stepped out from under the water, dripping.

"Stop this talk, Gulph," he said. "Stop it now. We're going to see the queen. Both of us."

"The *queen*? Are you crazy? She's the one who had me locked up in the first place."

"But not me. My mother loves me, Gulph. She sent you to help me, and when she finds out you actually helped me escape . . . well, she'll love you, too."

It was tempting to believe him, but Gulph was unconvinced. Had Queen Magritt really foreseen this, or had she put Gulph in the cell simply as a plaything to keep her son distracted?

"I don't know," he said.

"You said your friends are in the castle," said Nynus, clapping his hands on Gulph's narrow shoulders. His grip was uncomfortably tight, but Gulph endured it. "My mother is there too. So, you see, we're going the same way. We have to stick together, Gulph. We simply have to. That's what's brought us this far."

"I suppose so."

"So you won't leave me?" The prince's grip tightened further, his fingers digging painfully into Gulph's flesh. "You promise?"

"I promise."

Gulph followed Nynus into the square. Jumping up onto the well's low parapet, the prince scanned each of the seven streets in turn.

"This one!" he said at last, pointing down one a little wider and straighter than the others. At the far end rose a high stone wall: one of the ramparts of Castle Tor. "I don't know why I didn't spot it before. I'll bet you anything you like the castle hasn't changed. Come on."

Beaming, Nynus trotted down the street toward the castle. Gulph trudged behind. While they'd been in the alley, the moon had set, robbing the world of its silver light. In the east, dawn was beginning to paint the sky red, the color of approaching fire.

The castle wall was a vast, rising shadow. While Nynus stared up at the bleak slate-colored stonework, Gulph searched in vain for a doorway.

"There's no way in," he said, returning to the prince's side. The sun was rising, dispersing the gloom around the rampart, and he felt anxious and exposed. The only thing stopping him from fleeing the city right now was the certainty that his friends were still trapped inside the castle.

"Up there," said Nynus, pointing to a small window set high into the wall. Yellow candlelight flickered inside it. "I think that's my mother's private quarters."

"How does that help us?"

"We can climb up there."

Gulph ran his hands over the stone wall, feeling the deep pits and crevices of its age-worn surface. "I could probably do it. But what about you? I still say we should look for . . ."

But Nynus had already clambered on top of a pile of logs stacked against the wall. Spitting on his palms, he started climbing up hand over hand. The prince's speed surprised Gulph; his clumsiness worried him.

"Slow down," said Gulph, beginning his own ascent. "Let me lead."

He climbed past Nynus, not thinking about what he was doing, content to let his clever fingers and toes find their own holds in the wall. It was just like when he was performing for a crowd: his mind stopped thinking altogether and his body simply did what it had been built to do.

Soon he was thirty feet off the ground, with a dizzying view across the city. To the south rose the High Peak and the bridge over the chasm, with its promise of escape.

Never mind all that, Gulph. Just keep climbing.

"Watch me," he called down, pitching his voice as softly as he could. "Put your hands and feet where I do."

He'd just begun to believe they were going to make it when he heard a yelp from below. He looked down just in time to see Nynus's hands detach from the wall. For an instant the prince seemed to float, his pale face staring straight up at Gulph, suddenly terrified.

Nynus fell.

He hit the pile of logs with a splintering crash. The logs scattered, spilling the prince to the ground and rolling across the cobbles toward a nearby tavern. They struck the hitching rail and clattered to a halt, tangled like ninepins.

"Nynus!" hissed Gulph. He scampered back down the wall. "Nynus! Are you all right?"

"Do you think anyone heard?" Nynus groaned.

Gulph was already at his side. Before he could answer, two men appeared from the shadows. They wore bronze armor overlaid with crimson tunics—the colors of the King's Legion—and carried long broadswords. The swords were unsheathed, and shone despite the darkness.

"Who goes there?" said the first legionnaire, brandishing his blade. Leather boots creaking, his companion strolled around behind the two boys, cutting off their escape.

"We're sorry," blurted Gulph, quelling his panic. "We'll, uh, clear up the mess."

The soldier regarded the scattered logs. Each was the size of a small oak tree. He snorted and strode toward the two boys.

Every nerve in Gulph's body was screaming. *We should have gone to the bridge when we had the chance*, he thought, wondering if they might be able to lose the soldiers in the maze of alleys behind the tavern.

"Don't you know who I am?" said Nynus, planting his hands on his hips.

Gulph stared at him, horrified. He'd been hoping the soldiers wouldn't realize they were the ones who had broken out of the Vault of Heaven.

The legionnaire's smile turned to a look of confusion. Then his companion cried, "By the stars, Tomas—it's them!"

Without waiting for the first soldier to react, Gulph bolted toward the tavern. He'd gone two steps before a strong hand closed on his collar.

"Well, doesn't this save us a runaround?" said the legionnaire called Tomas.

Gulph struggled, desperate to escape, stopping only when his captor held a sword blade under his nose.

"Don't give me reason to kill you, little one," said the man. "No one would miss you—you're not the one who's a prince."

Gulph had no choice but to let his body go limp. The disappointment was bitter in his mouth—they'd been so close.

The other legionnaire gripped Nynus's arm. Gulph and the prince were marched around a corner and through a narrow doorway, Gulph wincing as Nynus continued to babble.

"Think about what we can offer you," he said. "I am Prince Nynus, the son of the king and the rightful heir to the crown of Toronia. Let me go—let *us* go—and you will be well rewarded."

"Be quiet, boy," said Tomas.

The legionnaires led them through winding passages, stopping when they reached a small room where haunches of meat hung from metal hooks. The room was cold and filled with the faint, sweet smell of curing meat.

"We're under the butchery," whispered Nynus.

Tomas led the boys between the hanging carcasses. Gulph shuddered each time he brushed against one of the cold slabs of flesh. On a shelf was a pile of sheep's heads, stripped of their skin, eyeless, the ghastly skulls staring at them with the vacancy of the dead.

Is that how we'll end up? Gulph thought in horror. *Is that why they've brought us in here?* Beside him, Nynus had stopped talking, his face even paler than usual.

Reaching the other side of the chamber, Tomas shoved aside a butchered pig to reveal a wooden door. He opened it, and between them the two legionnaires flung Gulph and Nynus inside. Before either boy could pick himself up, the door had been slammed shut. There was a solid click as a key was turned in the lock.

Gulph took in their surroundings. They were in a room no bigger than the Black Cell. A set of bunk beds stood against one wall; leaning against another was a low desk on which a pair of candles burned. There were no windows, and the room smelled of rats and damp.

"I think we were better off in the Vault of Heaven," said Gulph. All the same, it was strangely convenient that this room should have been waiting for them. Stranger still that its entrance was hidden in a butcher's pantry.

"I think you may be right." Nynus's pale eyes were wide and scared. "Did you see their tunics? Those soldiers are men of the Legion. The King's Legion." He reached a shaking hand to his own face, stroking the cheek. "Oh, Gulph. When they come back, my father will be with them!"

The key clicked in the lock once more and the handle turned. Nynus gave a yelp. Mouth dry, Gulph backed against the desk, knocking it so that one of the candles sputtered and died.

Grabbing the smoking candlestick, Gulph held it in front of him like a sword.

You won't take me without a fight!

Two figures loomed in the dark doorway.

"Mother!" cried Nynus. He lunged toward the first figure, then checked himself, the joy on his face dissolving into uncertainty. "Mother?"

Queen Magritt opened her arms and smiled through sudden tears. "My boy," she said. "My dear, poor boy."

She gathered him up, hugging him tight and enveloping him in her long, voluminous dress. While the prince sobbed against her breast, she stared over his head and straight into Gulph's eyes.

Gulph realized he was still brandishing the candlestick. He supposed he looked foolish, but he couldn't bring himself to lower it. The last time he'd seen the queen, she'd called him a malformed monster and had him locked up in the most hateful place he'd seen in his life.

And yet . . . Queen Magritt looked different from the way he remembered her from the arena: less regal, somehow softer. Kinder. Had it all been a ruse after all? Had her cruel words really been part of a complex plot to deliver a savior to her son?

To his astonishment, she smiled at him.

Putting down the candlestick, Gulph gave a cautious nod.

The queen's companion stepped into the light of the remaining candle, and Gulph gasped. It was Captain Ossilius, the very man who'd taken him to be locked up in the Vault of Heaven.

"You are a resourceful young man," the captain said. He touched one finger to his temple: a small salute. Not quite able to believe what was happening, all Gulph could do was stare at him.

At last Queen Magritt released her hold and stood away from her son. She gazed at him long and hard, as if unable to believe what she was seeing.

"My boy," she said again. Then she turned to Gulph. "The

minute I saw you performing at court, I knew you were the one. Clever. Agile. I knew if anyone could help my son escape that terrible place, it was you. So I thank you, truly, with all of my heart."

"You're welcome," said Gulph. "Although, I'm not sure I really understand. . . ."

"I know. I'm sorry for what I said to you yesterday. I called you some terrible things. But it was just an act. You understand acting. I had to make it look real; otherwise the king would have become suspicious. You see that, don't you?"

It was strange, having a queen plead forgiveness. But not really any stranger than everything else that had happened to Gulph since he'd arrived in Idilliam.

"I don't . . . I mean, I think I understand," he stammered. "And I suppose . . . it all came out for the best."

Bending a little, the queen kissed his cheek. Her lips were soft, and her breath held a faint scent of strawberries. She was a little older than Gulph had first thought, with tiny lines crowding the corners of her eyes. A little sadder, too.

Not for the first time, he wondered what his own mother had looked like.

"My men have been watching for you all night," said Captain Ossilius, closing the door softly behind him. "We thought you would come to the castle, and had this room prepared. You will be safe here. Nobody will find you."

"What about Blist?" said Gulph. "I stole his keys. I don't think he'll be very happy."

"He'll be happy enough with the purse of silver I'll give him," said Ossilius. "He'll keep his silence."

"Or lose his head," said Queen Magritt, so abruptly that Gulph flinched.

While she'd been talking to Gulph, Nynus had retreated to the corner of the room. He was crouched there now, rocking back and forth and looking exactly like the lost, forgotten boy Gulph had first met in the Vault of Heaven. Queen Magritt went over to him.

"Now, my darling son," she gushed, "we must make plans. You'll be safe here for a while, but I do not intend for you to remain a prisoner any longer than is necessary, however comfortable the cell."

She pulled Nynus onto his feet.

"First, King Brutan," the queen went on. "I hate him for locking you up. I want you to know that, Nynus, and I want you to believe it. Your imprisonment was none of my doing. You do believe it?"

"I do, Mother," Nynus replied.

"Good. But you are not the only one Brutan betrayed." Her lip curled a little, and she clasped her hands to still the trembling that had overtaken them. "There is also the matter of Kalia. What he did with that witch . . . his affair . . . I will never forgive him for that. Never! To choose her over me . . ." She stopped, swallowed, went on. "So. Plans. You must take the throne, Nynus. It is yours by right, and by all I hold dear, it will be yours in truth. King Brutan will be brought down, and you will take his place!"

She stopped, breathing hard in the sudden silence.

"Your mother has the Legion's support in this," said Captain Ossilius. "Brutan's reign of terror must end."

Gulph stared at them. Nynus might have been Brutan's heir, but surely they didn't believe this wretched boy was fit to rule? Gulph couldn't imagine Nynus in charge of a puppy, let alone a kingdom.

But the idea seemed to appeal to the prince. His shoulders—broader than Gulph's, but hardly muscular—were squared, and his chin jutted with newfound pride.

"I . . . I'll be a good king," said Nynus, nodding seriously. "I will be merciful to my father. He will have his own castle—a small one—in the Toronian hinterlands. He can live out his days there."

"Whatever you choose," said the queen.

"And the Thousand Year War," said Nynus, warming to his subject. He held up a hand as if he were giving a speech to an eager crowd. "I'll end it. My people need peace. There will be fine foods for everyone, and parties every night, and I'll ride through the realms so everyone can see their king." He whirled around and clapped Gulph on the back. "And you, Gulph, will be at my side the whole time. My chief courtier! I wouldn't be here if it wasn't for you!"

Gulph didn't know what to say. He was growing used to the speed with which Nynus changed his mood, but this was extreme, even for him: from downtrodden prisoner to future king, all in the blink of an eye.

"Nynus is quite right," said Queen Magritt. "When he sits upon the throne, you must be by his side. You are such a good friend to us, Gulph."

Gulph ran his hand over his acrobat's clothes, soiled and ragged at the seams. His becoming a courtier was even more ridiculous than Nynus becoming king. And yet . . . If Magritt was right, and it somehow came true, things would be different. No more jeers, no more sly comments about his appearance, no more laughter behind his back. It was an incredible thought.

The others were watching him expectantly. "Of course, Nynus," Gulph said. "I'd be honored."

There was a gentle knock at the door. Half drawing his sword, Captain Ossilius eased it open a crack. Gulph heard muttered words, then the door opened fully to admit a young blond woman wearing a white apron and carrying a tray of food. Instead of the Vault's metal bowls, there were porcelain plates; instead of tough meat and gruel, there was shining fruit and bread so fresh it was steaming.

"This is Limmoni," said the queen. "Apart from myself and

Captain Ossilius, she is the only other person who knows you are here. She will bring you food each day and keep your room clean. If you want to send me a message, give it to Limmoni."

Snapping her fingers, the queen ushered Captain Ossilius farther into the room.

"And now, let us make them look respectable," she said.

"Yes, Your Highness," said Ossilius. He took a bag from his shoulder and emptied a heap of clothes onto the bottom bunk. Nynus gasped and ran his hands over the finely woven fabric.

"Later, Limmoni will bring water so you can wash," said the queen, with a slight sniff of distaste, "but let us at least dress you smartly. You first, Nynus. Limmoni—please escort our guest outside until it's his turn."

Limmoni put down the tray and led Gulph back into the butchery. He flinched as he brushed against the pig carcass that hid the door; Limmoni squeezed his hand.

"Don't fear the dead," she said. She was smiling, but the expression didn't look entirely comfortable on her face. The dim light seemed to strike her brow and cheeks at odd angles. Gulph had the peculiar sensation that he was seeing her from many directions at once.

"Here," she said, producing an apple from the pocket of her apron. "These are wonderful."

Gulph took the bright green fruit and bit into it. Juice ran down his chin; he'd never tasted anything so delicious.

Under her breath, Limmoni said, "They are using you."

Gulph stopped chewing, not sure he'd heard her correctly. "Pardon?"

"The queen used you to rescue her son."

"I know."

"She will have need for you again. Soon. Do not trust her. Do not trust any of them."

Gulph swallowed, nearly choking on the unchewed apple. As he coughed, he felt Limmoni slip something into his hand.

"This is yours," she whispered. "Keep it close to you. And keep it hidden. It is your friend." She tilted her head. Light cascaded down the strange angles of her face. "So am I."

She began to slip away through the rows of carcasses.

"Wait!" called Gulph. "Won't they ask where you've got to?"

Limmoni looked back at him over her shoulder. "Their memory that I was here is already fading," she said. "Be careful, Gulph." And she was gone.

Gulph blinked in confusion. What was that supposed to mean? He turned her name over in his mind. *Limmoni.* Who was she? Why was she trying to help him?

He opened his hand to reveal a coil of gold chain, on which

hung a green gemstone. The jewel was curiously shaped, smoothly faceted on one side but jagged on the other, as if it were not a whole gem, but only part of one. It was strange and beautiful, just like the young woman.

She said she was my friend.

He slipped the chain around his neck, tucking it under his acrobat's clothes to ensure it was hidden. When his turn came to change, he would do it in private. He was sure nobody would object.

He knocked on the door. As Queen Magritt called for him to come back inside, Limmoni's words echoed in his head.

Do not trust her. Do not trust any of them.

CHAPTER 7

Thud. Thud. Thud.

The chopping sound was sharp, repetitive, hypnotic. It penetrated Tarlan's dream, pulling him up from a deep, dark ocean filled with vague sensations of flying. And falling.

He opened his bleary eyes, and the darkness was replaced by a white glare. The light was too much, and he raised his hand to shield his eyes, but his hands wouldn't obey him. He tried again, this time feeling the coarse tug of the ropes that bound his wrists behind his back.

Thud. Thud. Thud.

Gradually his eyes adjusted. White clouds filled his vision, racing on a gale through gray sky. Around him, white walls rose. A castle? Tarlan blinked and saw that the walls were made not of stone but ice, enormous sharp-edged slabs stacked one on top of another to form crude towers and bastions.

Thud. Thud. Thud.

Bunching his stomach muscles—and ignoring the pain from the wound in his shoulder—Tarlan sat up. His vision blurred and for a moment he thought he was going to faint. Then it cleared, revealing a crowd of fur-clad men and a corral filled with huge antlered creatures. To the side, large joints of meat sizzled over a blazing fire. The smell was rich and tantalizing, and Tarlan's mouth began to water.

Thud. Thud. Thud.

The elk-hunters were crowded around something Tarlan couldn't quite see: a heap of something red and silver piled in the snow. As he watched, they parted, and he saw at last where the chopping sound was coming from.

The thing piled in the snow was Seethan. The once mighty thorrod was now a bloody mass of flesh and burned feathers. One of the hunters was hacking at the corpse with a huge ax, slicing off hunks of meat and handing them to his companions, who carried them to the fire.

The meaty smell curdled in his throat. Anger came in an instant, like storm clouds rolling over a mountain.

Seethan is dead.

"Leave him alone!" he bellowed. He yanked at his bonds, but

the more he tugged the tighter they became. He kicked his feet in the snow, trying to pick himself up. He shouted again, and the shout became first a sob, then an incoherent cry of rage.

The hunter who'd been cutting up Seethan's corpse strode over to Tarlan, swinging his ax. As he walked, the huge wooden antlers adorning his helmet nodded back and forth. Two men accompanied him; their helmets were bare.

"Pick him up," said the man with the ax.

Tarlan continued to roar and wriggle, but the men were strong, and his body still ached after its fall through the trees. Worst of all was the wound in his shoulder, where the burning arrow had opened a deep gash. He remembered everything about the fight in the forest—faced with the remains of Seethan, he could hardly forget. He could only hope the other thorrods had escaped and returned to Mirith.

Mirith . . .

Is she even still alive?

When it became clear he wasn't going to escape, Tarlan forced his muscles into stillness. With more difficulty, he managed to suppress his rage. It boiled inside him, volcano hot. He savored the feeling. When the chance came to vent his anger, he'd make these men pay for what they'd done.

"The bird is dead," said the hunter. He wiped the blood-covered head of his ax on the thick furs covering his body. He wore an iron torque around his neck, a dented metal thing that was half necklace, half breastplate. Tarlan supposed he was their leader. Very well. He would be the first to die.

"He wasn't a bird," said Tarlan. "He was a thorrod."

The elk-leader shrugged. "Times are hard. The king has forgotten Yalasti and its people. We must take what we can, and this *bird* will feed my men for many days." He held out a fistful of dripping flesh. "Care for a bite?"

Tarlan hawked back saliva and spat in his face. One of the men holding him cuffed his head, hard, twice. Laughing, the elk-leader lifted his ax and pressed the blade against Tarlan's throat. Tarlan flinched, not at the touch of the cold metal, but at the unspeakable sensation of Seethan's blood running down his neck.

"If you're friends with the thorrods," the elk-leader said, "you're no friend to me. I don't like witch boys. I was going to keep you, but now . . . I've changed my mind."

He gave a curt nod to his companions, who braced themselves against Tarlan, ensuring there was no chance of escape. The elk-leader drew back his ax. The blade flashed white, reflecting the racing clouds, the blank ice walls. Tarlan set his face in a snarl; he wasn't going to let this brute see he was scared.

The ax reached the end of its arc. The elk-leader paused, grinned, and swung it toward Tarlan's exposed throat.

As he prepared to die, Tarlan could think of only one thing.

I'm sorry, Mirith. I've failed you.

There was a sudden gust of cold wind, and a shadow passed over them.

The ax flew past Tarlan, missing his neck completely and spinning erratically through the air to land in a distant mound of snow. The elk-leader's hand was still gripping the wooden haft; the rest of his arm went with the weapon too, torn off at the root.

The elk-leader grunted and raised his remaining hand to the red pulp of his shoulder. Blood jetted in a fountain, staining the snow crimson. The shadow came again, and the wind, and this time Tarlan saw what had caused it: a great gold bird, flying fast and low, almost too fast to be seen.

"Theeta!" he cried.

The thorrod's beak snapped shut on the elk-leader's waist, slicing him in two. Beating her enormous wings, Theeta pulled out of her dive and tossed the top half of his body out and over the walls of ice. The man's legs crumpled to the ground.

One of Tarlan's captors released his grip. Tarlan shoulder-charged the other; free at last, he started running through the snow toward the fallen ax.

Theeta's shadow returned, along with another. Tarlan looked up to see Nasheen wheeling down from the sky. With her white breast, she was almost invisible against the clouds. Her beak was wide open, ready to attack. The long feathers on her outstretched wings rippled like liquid gold. Like Theeta, she made no sound whatsoever.

If the thorrods were attacking in silence, on the ground all was noise and motion. Men and women scattered, shouting instructions, banging weapons against shields. In the corral, the elks reared up, hooting their distress.

The shadows of the thorrods swept over the crowd, back and forth in an endless round. Long talons slashed down, biting deep into the hunters' bodies as the birds snatched them up, one after the other, and flung them against the walls of the ice fort. Shouts became screams, and simple confusion became utter chaos.

Through it all, the giant thorrods were silent.

Reaching the ax, Tarlan dropped to his knees in the snow. Ignoring the gory mess of the elk-leader's severed arm, he tried to twist his body, intending to use the blade to cut through his bonds. But the ax head was buried, and the pain in his right arm was very bad; try as he might, he couldn't wrestle it free.

"Let me."

With a soft *plump*, Theeta landed in the snow beside him. Wings spread protectively over him, she lowered her cruel beak to his wrists and snipped through the rope with gentle care.

"There!" One of the hunters had spotted them. Unslinging a

bow from her back, a woman rushed toward Tarlan, nocking an arrow on the string as she ran.

Before Tarlan could move, Nasheen was there, diving vertically at astonishing speed to pound the bow woman into the snow, then lifting off again, her talons dripping blood.

"Come," said Theeta, nudging Tarlan with her beak.

"Hold on!"

Tarlan went to the woman's crushed remains and snatched up her bow, along with a quiver of arrows. A man appeared from a swirl of snowflakes, shrieking and brandishing a long sword. Without thinking, Tarlan fished an arrow from the quiver, drew the bow, and shot him through the throat.

"Come!" said Theeta again.

Tarlan needed no further encouragement. More hunters were hurrying through the snow toward him, led by a veritable giant wearing a helmet no less impressive than that of their former leader.

Grabbing a handful of Theeta's feathers, he scrambled onto her back. Pain stabbed his body in a dozen different places.

"Fly, Theeta!" he said. "Let's get out of here."

Theeta was airborne before the words had left his mouth. On the far side of the fort, Nasheen was attacking a line of hunters who'd climbed with bows and arrows to the top of the ice wall, clearly hoping to down the thorrods by firing on them from above.

Nasheen flew the entire length of the battlements, raking her claws through their ranks. By the time she reached the far end, they all lay dead in the snow.

Theeta flew one final circle over the fort. White snow and ice ran red with the blood of the elk-hunters; worse by far was the sight of poor Seethan's butchered body. As she passed for the last time above the elder thorrod's remains, Theeta let out a keening cry.

"We'll mourn him later," said Tarlan, tugging at the feathers on her neck. "Right now, we've got to get back to Mirith, or this will all have been for nothing."

As they sped from the fort on its lonely, snow-covered hilltop, Nasheen dropped in front of Theeta, calming the air with her slipstream. They flew swiftly, passing back over the icebound villages of Yalasti toward Mirith's mountain retreat.

Soon the terrain grew rockier, and the mountain rose before them, its peak shrouded in fog. Tarlan was about to urge even greater speed when a dark shape emerged from the low cloud.

"Kitheen!" he shouted. "I told you to stay with Mirith!"

Kitheen said nothing, simply puffed out his black breast and took the lead, hurrying them up the mountain to a narrow canyon near the entrance to Mirith's cave.

A figure lay in the snow at the canyon entrance.

Mirith!

Tarlan leaped from Theeta's back even before the giant thorrod had touched down. He landed hard in the snow, picked himself up, and stumbled to Mirith's side. Cradling her head in his lap, he wiped snow from her eyes and lips; cold as their surroundings were, her skin felt as hot as a furnace.

"What were you thinking?" he said. "Why didn't you stay in the cave?"

"Needed . . . find you," the frost witch croaked. Her voice rustled like paper, barely audible over the distant howl of wind deep in the canyon.

"I'm here," said Tarlan. Suddenly he remembered what he'd gone for in the first place. He rummaged in his cloak. Only two of the precious black leaves that had cost them so dearly remained. When had he lost the rest? It didn't matter.

Hands shaking, he held up the leaves.

"What do I do? Crush them? Boil them? Make a paste? Tell me!"

Mirith's hand was steady as it closed over his. It had no more strength than a snowflake.

"Black leaf . . . soothes pain . . . nothing more . . ."

"But . . ."

"Hush. I sensed it."

"What? Sensed what?"

"You . . . Seethan . . . elk . . ." With a soft grunt, she tried to sit up. "Tarlan, you are . . . in danger. The elk-hunters will . . . will not rest. You are their prey now. You must . . . must leave Yalasti."

"Not without you!" Tarlan's tears froze on his cheeks, hard little beads of grief.

"I am dying."

"No!"

"Take . . . this." Mirith drew a gold chain from under her cloak. Hanging from the chain was a shard of green gemstone. It spun, glittering, and Tarlan was momentarily entranced.

"What's this?" he said.

"Show it to Melchior. . . . He will know what to do. . . ."

"Melchior? Who's he?" The name sounded familiar, but Tarlan was captivated by the jewel. Yet he was reluctant to take it, or even touch it. To do so would be to accept that Mirith was going to die.

"Melchior is an old friend. . . ."

The jewel turned, catching the icy light. The name turned too, inside Tarlan's racing thoughts.

"A wizard," he said slowly. "Melchior was a wizard. You told me stories."

Mirith nodded, her breath rasping as she tried to speak. "Yes," she managed to gasp at last.

"There are no wizards. You told me they grew too old and time left them behind."

"All but one. All but . . . Melchior."

Tarlan looked away. His heart was too full for his head to work properly. "Who is he, Mirith? What do you mean me to do?"

Mirith said nothing. When Tarlan looked back, she was staring at the sky with eyes that had already glazed over white with ice. The frost witch's body slowly stiffened in Tarlan's arms, losing the heat of the fever that had finally claimed her life. Her skin turned the dazzling blue of winter frost, growing transparent and seeming to shine with an inner light. From somewhere far away, Tarlan seemed to hear a long, sad sigh.

Gently he lowered her into the snow. She lay there, sheer and glittering, as if sculpted from the ice she'd loved her whole life.

The green jewel hung from her icy fingers, sparkling and enticing.

Tarlan sat for a long time in the snow, heedless of the cold leaching into his body. His thoughts wandered. He wanted to cry more tears, but it seemed his body had forgotten how. He just felt numb.

After a while, Theeta's feathers fell over him as the huge thorrod snuggled against his back. The warmth of her massive body, and her soft, sad cawing, revived him a little.

"What should I do, Theeta?" he said. "If Mirith wants me to go, then I must. But where? If all the men of the outside world are like those elk-hunters, I'd rather stay here with you."

He stroked Theeta's feathers. If only he could fly, like the thorrods. Fly away from everything.

"Hunters!" said Nasheen, her hoarse voice breaking into his reverie. "Coming!"

Peering past Theeta's beak, Tarlan saw a line of flares on the horizon. Were they coming this way? It was hard to tell.

"Are you sure it's them?" he said. Nasheen didn't reply; nor did Tarlan really need to ask. The thorrods' eyes were a thousand times keener than his. If she said the hunters were on their way, then it was true.

"Mirith was right." He eyed the dangling jewel. "She was always right, about everything."

Tugging the gold chain gently from Mirith's frozen hand, he tucked it safely inside his cloak. At once, countless tiny cracks appeared in the frost witch's body, racing from head to toe in an eye blink. With a soft, powdery *crack*, it shattered to blue dust. The wind picked up the dust and blew it up from the canyon and out over the mountain.

"Good-bye, Mirith," murmured Tarlan.

"Come," said Theeta, nudging him.

"No." Tarlan turned to the enormous bird. His friend. "I go. You stay."

Theeta regarded him with her deep, black eyes. "Why?" she said at last.

Tarlan was startled. He'd never known a thorrod to ask a question before. Their minds were simple and solid, filled only with facts.

"Because . . ." He faltered; he hadn't expected this to be so hard. "Because you've already lost Seethan. And . . . if I'm to leave Yalasti, I'll have to cross the Icy Wastes. It's too dangerous. I can't ask you to come with me."

Theeta stepped back and planted her talons wide in the snow. She puffed out her chest and spread her wings. Breath steamed from her beak. She was a statue of living gold, warm and vital in the barren winter landscape.

"Not ask," she said. "I come."

At last the tears came. Tears for Mirith, tears for Seethan. Also tears for the thorrod before him, his loyal friend.

Oh, Theeta, I hope I never have to grieve for you.

"We come," said Nasheen, dropping lightly from the sky to land at Theeta's side. Then Kitheen was there too, characteristically silent, but nodding his agreement all the same. The three thorrods towered over him, an impenetrable wall of feathers.

"I suppose it's no use arguing," said Tarlan. His right arm throbbed, and his heart ached. But he also felt joy, that he had such friends at his side.

Using his good arm, he pulled himself onto Theeta's back. She waited while he settled himself into the ruff of feathers behind her neck, then opened her wings and lifted into the sky. Nasheen and Kitheen followed, and together the three thorrods carried Tarlan away from the mountain, toward the Icy Wastes.

CHAPTER 8

Elodie awoke to a harsh rattling sound coming from under the wheels of the coach. The bench she was lying on vibrated beneath her, nearly tossing her onto the floor. She threw out her hands for balance and tried not to be sick.

How long had she been traveling? Sunlight cast a dusty beam through the coach's narrow window; she couldn't believe she'd slept through the night, so this had to be the same day. Peering out, she saw the sun was low in the west. It would soon be night.

The coach was speeding over a bed of wooden planks. Below— far below—was a vast swathe of blue she took at first to be the ocean (not that she'd ever seen the sea). Then she saw distant banks; no ocean then, but a river.

To the south, the land she'd left behind was green and gentle, a familiar terrain of field and meadow and rolling dales. Ritherlee, her home. Ahead and to the north was the biggest expanse of forest she'd ever seen. Trees jostled like teeth in a crowded jaw, biting into the sunset sky.

Isur!

The coach crossed from the wooden planks onto a solid stone deck. And still the bridge went on. Elodie had heard the Isurian River was wide, but this was beyond all reckoning. At this rate, it would be dark before they reached the other side.

I wish this bridge would go on forever, she thought, staring down at the water. A white boat was moving against the current, far below. It looked impossibly small.

Staying on the bridge would mean she'd never reach Isur, so she couldn't be carried from there into Idilliam, to experience whatever dreadful fate King Brutan had in store for her. But it would also mean she'd never see Ritherlee again.

Just the thought of home filled her with grief. If only she could exchange this cold, hard coach for the pillow-filled warmth of her tower chamber. What she wouldn't give to be sat at Lord Vicerin's table right now, dining on the finest meats and laughing along as the conversation flowed through the room.

Yet with Elodie's sadness came hope.

They won't let me go so easily. They'll search and search until they find me. I know they will!

A chiding voice came and went on the breeze:

If they think you're worth it.

Elodie shivered. With a stab of regret, she recalled Sylva's determined expression as her young chaperone had tried to chase the coach. Why had Elodie been so mean to her? She wished she could return to the start of the day and do everything differently.

The coach sped on, and Elodie dozed again. When she next awoke, it had stopped. All was still. She heard distant conversation, the crackle of fires, the faint ringing of metal against metal. She sat up in panic. Where was she?

Through the tiny window Elodie saw that the coach had stopped in a clearing filled with tents. Thick forest rose to meet a purple sky. Fires blazed; men and women bustled to and fro, carrying food and weapons, chopping wood; a small group practiced with swords, the sound of their mock combat like a steel song in the gathering dusk.

The door opened. Elodie shrank back into the corner of the bench, instinctively clutching the green jewel at her throat. A face appeared: the young man who'd captured her.

"Stay away from me," she snapped.

The man executed a small bow. He was older than Elodie; about twenty, she thought. A long scar extended in a fine pink strip from his hairline down the left side of his jaw. "I am Fessan," he said. "You are welcome here, Princess Elodie."

What? How does he know?

Confused and astonished, Elodie got up and stood in the doorway of the coach. At the sight of her, everyone stopped what they were doing. Eyes grew wide. Mouths opened. Several people bowed, like Fessan; some even dropped to their knees. Elodie stared. These people had kidnapped her, so why were they behaving like this? It didn't make sense.

"Let me help you down." Fessan took her arm, but Elodie shook him away.

"Keep your filthy hands off me."

Hitching up the skirts of her dress, which had been badly torn in the scuffle in the market, she descended the steps with as much haughtiness as she could muster.

"Now," she said coolly, "how do you know who I am? What do you want with me?"

"There is much I need to tell you, Princess," said Fessan. "Come!"

He began to walk away from the coach to a large tent near the edge of the forest. Its green canvas—the same color as Fessan's tunic—made it hard to see against the trees. Elodie hesitated, wondering if she could bolt into the forest, but the watching people made her dismiss the idea. Instead, she followed Fessan into the tent.

Inside, it was sparsely furnished, with rough wooden seats made from crates. In one corner stood a barrel filled with large rolled-up sheets of parchment. An oil lamp hung from a metal post driven into the ground. Elodie wrinkled her nose at the fumes it was giving off.

"Please, sit down." Fessan gestured toward a pile of furs. He carried himself with the same easy confidence Elodie was used to seeing in Lord Vicerin's soldiers. A military man, sent by King Brutan to bring her to Idilliam? Yet Elodie sensed that underneath he was nervous. Well, if he wasn't working for Brutan, she could guess what he and his rabble in their awful tents and tattered clothes were after. She should have realized from the start.

"I prefer to stand," she said, eyeing the furs with disgust. "Just hurry up and tell me how much you want."

"How much . . . What do you mean?"

"How much ransom. You obviously need the money, living out here like this in these . . . tents. Well, I won't pretend my adopted father isn't rich, but I should warn you: If you push him too far you'll regret it."

"We do not want Lord Vicerin's money."

Elodie didn't believe him. "Oh, then I suppose you've brought me all the way out here just to kill me?"

Fessan's cheek twitched, causing the long scar to writhe. "*Kill* you? Whatever . . . why would you think that?"

Elodie made a show of looking around the tent. "I'm surprised King Brutan didn't come to finish the job himself. I suppose he didn't want to get his hands dirty."

Fessan frowned. "I'm not going to kill you, Princess. Quite the opposite. I am . . . we have not been sent by the king. We are Trident."

"Trident?" Elodie was confused. The only tridents she knew were the three-pronged harpoons carried by Lord Vicerin's guard during special ceremonies in the castle.

"We are an independent troop. Practically an army now." Fessan's chest swelled a little. "The king does not know we exist. We are based here in the Weeping Woods, which means we can . . ."

So you're mercenaries. Elodie's confidence ebbed a little. Such people were likely to be unpredictable. But at least it meant they understood the value of gold coin.

"I understand. You're not going to kill me. You're just going to hand me over. Well, whatever price King Brutan has put on my head, I can assure you Lord Vicerin will pay double."

"That will not be necessary."

Is he smiling? Elodie felt off balance. Had she been reading this conversation all wrong?

"I demand you release me!" She knew her cheeks were burning, but she was powerless to prevent it.

"And where will you go?"

"That's none of your business!"

"You are not a prisoner here, Princess Elodie."

"I demand that you . . . What did you say?"

"You are not a prisoner."

Elodie stared. "But . . ."

"I promise you, when you know the truth, you will want to stay."

"The truth?" Elodie said weakly.

"Are you sure you don't want to sit down?"

Fessan stepped around the lamp on its post. With the light playing on just the right side of his face, the scar was invisible. It occurred to Elodie that he was handsome.

"Please," she said, "just tell me what's going on."

Fessan took a deep breath. "Very well. We have scouts at Castle Vicerin. They've been watching you for some time. The Vicerins want to put you on the throne. . . ."

"I know that."

". . . but only temporarily. Lord Vicerin is ambitious, Princess, and wants the throne for himself. To get it, he will use you. Then he will throw you away. I'm sorry, I know this is hard for you to hear."

Elodie felt her face flushing again. "I don't believe you."

"Trident is pledged to restore the rightful heirs to the throne. Already we have you. More scouts are searching for your brothers. Once you are reunited, we will depose King Brutan and the three of you will take the throne, just as the prophecy has foretold."

Fessan crossed the tent to a crude desk on which a green flag lay, neatly folded. He lifted the flag and let it fall open. On it was an image of a three-pronged spear. Around the spear were three crowns.

"This is our banner," he said. "We carry it for you, Princess Elodie. For all of you. So you see, you are not our prisoner at all." He sank to one knee. "We are your servants."

Pain thumped inside Elodie's head. She pressed her hands to her temples, trying to ease the throbbing.

"Prophecy?" she said. "What are you talking about? I don't have any brothers. I am to be queen—just me! Lord Vicerin told me this; he *promised* me."

"Lord Vicerin lied to you," said Fessan, rising to his feet. He folded the flag and replaced it on his desk. "I am sorry. I know this must be confusing for you."

Elodie shook her head violently. "No. There isn't any prophecy. My father would have told me. You're the one who's lying!"

"I have told you the truth."

"So you say!"

"Forgive me, Princess Elodie. It grieves me to upset you, but I cannot see you deceived. Is it not better to know the truth?"

"Who are you to say what's best for me?"

Fessan covered the distance to her in two long strides. "You have been cruelly deceived, Princess Elodie. Can you not see what Lord Vicerin wants you to be?"

"A queen?"

"No. A puppet."

"*What?*" Anger flashed through Elodie. "My father loves me. He would never do that—never. How dare you!"

"I'm sorry, Princess. It's the truth."

"Will you stop saying that!" Elodie snapped.

Fessan opened his mouth as if to speak, but then his gaze passed behind her. Elodie turned to see the red-haired girl from the marketplace. A huge bear-skin cloak hung from her shoulders, a row of teeth dangling from the hood. Through the matted folds, Elodie could see a sword swinging against the girl's bare legs. She looked fit and lean.

"Excuse me," the girl said. "I didn't mean to disturb you. Are you ready, Princess?"

Elodie didn't feel ready for anything. She straightened her dress and tried to summon the confidence she'd carried with her into the tent.

"What do you want?" she said.

"I'm Palenie. I'm to train you."

"Train me?" Elodie's sense of disconnection grew. Was she to have lessons here now? How could she learn about history and painting, and how to walk into a room with her back straight and her head held high, from these peasants who lived in the woods? "Train me in what?"

"In the sword," said Fessan. "The throne is yours, Princess Elodie. But I am afraid you will have to fight for it."

Palenie's tent was even more spartan than Fessan's: just two heaps of furs and a pile of weapons. So different from Elodie's chambers back at Castle Vicerin. She felt a sudden wrench in her stomach.

Could those things Fessan said about Lord Vicerin be true? Even if they were, she desperately wished she were home again.

As she'd followed Palenie across the clearing, she'd been acutely aware of the faces watching her pass, their expressions open and curious . . . and somehow possessive. Fessan had told her she wasn't a prisoner. So why did she still feel as if she'd been kidnapped?

"This one's yours," said Palenie, spreading out a silvery blanket stitched together from fox pelts. "That one's mine." She pointed to a heavy black fur. Like her cloak, it must once have belonged to a bear.

"I have to sleep on a dead animal?"

"Sorry. I suppose it's not what you're used to. But it gets cold out here. You'll be glad of the warmth."

"No—I mean what do we *sleep* on?"

Palenie looked at her with something like pity. "The ground."

Elodie swallowed the sob building in her throat. She wasn't going to let this stranger see her cry. In case her expression betrayed her feelings, she bent over and started fiddling with the rip in her skirt.

"Look, these are for you," said Palenie. She arranged a pile of clothes on the fox blanket. "Tunic. Leggings. Boots. That dress won't last a day out here, I'm afraid." She laid a hand on Elodie's arm. "Princess, why don't you get changed and have some rest? You'll need to be fresh for your training tomorrow."

"Do you really expect me to use a sword?" Elodie picked through the clothes. Everything was green, stitched from coarsely woven cloth.

"Sword. Spear. Bow and arrow." Palenie's voice was soft. "Look, Princess. I'm sorry. I know this is tough, but taking the throne is going to be hard. You need to be able to handle yourself."

Somehow the kindness was worse even than what Fessan had said to her. Fighting against the tears, Elodie pushed past Palenie. She pulled back the tent flap, waiting for her new chaperone to block her way, just as Sylva would have done. Instead, Palenie just said:

"Be careful out there."

"Aren't you going to stop me?"

"You're not a prisoner."

"So you're just letting me leave?"

"I'm telling you not to stray far. Whatever you do, don't go into the trees."

"I suppose you're going to tell me they're full of bears?"

"Where do you think my cloak came from? But it's not that. There are worse things than bears in the Weeping Woods."

Something trickled down Elodie's spine: a touch like icy water. But she swept out of the tent. "I'll take my chances!" she called back.

In the clearing the fires still blazed, but many of the people she'd seen earlier had vanished. She supposed they were inside their own tents, perhaps eating. At the thought of food, her stomach growled.

She ignored it. There would be time enough to eat once she'd made her escape from this forsaken place.

Tall trees surrounded the clearing on all sides. In the dusk they looked almost black. The sun had sunk out of sight, but the western sky was still flaming red. Elodie set it to her right, so that she was facing south: the direction she'd come from. That way lay Ritherlee. That way lay home.

How far is it? Is it even possible to walk such a distance?

She marched to the tree line. On the way, she passed a tent in which she heard two people arguing.

"What does he know about being commander?" a man grumbled. "He's barely older than a squire. I don't trust him."

"Be quiet, Stown," said a woman. "You don't want him to hear you talking like that."

"I hope he does. He keeps telling us it's time to fight, but what does he know? That girl is just going to get in the way."

He means Fessan, Elodie thought. *And me. Well, I won't be in their way any longer. I never asked for any of them to fight for me—and I don't want them to.* Pulling her torn dress up from around her ankles, she stepped into the Weeping Woods.

CHAPTER 9

Almost immediately, Elodie lost all sense of direction. Dense firs enveloped her, rearing up on every side like silent giants. The darkness intensified, shadows transforming into thick black forms, as if the night itself were coming alive. The noises of the camp died away, leaving Elodie alone with the soft sounds of her own footfalls.

The ground was a mossy carpet that rose and fell in a series of shallow ditches and low ridges. In the corner of her eye, she could have sworn she saw it rippling, like the surface of the great river she'd crossed earlier that day. Questing needles snagged her dress, and branches seemed to move of their own accord, reaching out to block her path.

Except there was no path.

Elodie stopped. She looked left. She looked right. Every direction was the same.

"The road leads where it will."

The voice came from behind her. She whirled around, heart racing, eyes wide in the darkness. There was nobody there.

Trident had carried her far from home, far from everything that was familiar. Yet even here in the Weeping Woods of Isur, the wretched voices were still with her. Would she ever be rid of them?

"Oh, be quiet!" Elodie snapped at the trees.

She stumbled on, using her hands to force her way through the mass of hanging needles. Thick bracken rose up, as if it were trying to hold her back. She waded through the undergrowth toward an opening in the trees, and broke through at last into a small glade.

She stood, panting, her dress in ribbons, her hands scratched and bleeding, head tilted back to look up at the stars. Was she still facing south?

In the glade, someone was sobbing.

But of course nobody was there.

Despair crept over Elodie. She sank to the ground as the sobbing grew louder. Another voice drifted down from the branches over her head, chanting what sounded like a marching song. A third voice hissed something in a language she didn't understand. More voices joined in, until Elodie was surrounded by groans and sighs, whispered taunts and pleas.

The noise built and built until she couldn't stand it anymore, and she got to her feet, running across the glade and back into the forest. If only she could run fast enough, maybe she could leave them behind.

"Shut up!" she shouted at the branches as she crashed through them. "Just leave me alone!"

Elodie ran blindly, driving her way through the trees, until she could run no more. She stopped again, her breath like a knife in her throat, her scratched face wet with tears. Around her, the firs had given way to trees that were older and more gnarled. Giant, twisted oaks loomed over slender stands of hazel and willow. In the tortured bark of their ancient trunks, Elodie thought she could see faces.

One face moved.

She shrieked, stumbling backward. The face's two eyes blinked. A man stepped out from behind a holly bush. He wore a battered leather jerkin with a dagger hanging from his belt. His face was covered with grime.

"Stay away from me!" Elodie yelled. "My father will kill you if you don't!"

She looked frantically for an escape route, but the forest was as pathless as ever. The trees loomed, trapping her with this sudden stranger.

Then she saw it wasn't quite a man, but a boy about her own age. Beneath the dirt, the line of his jaw was smooth and, perhaps, handsome.

He looked as shocked as she felt.

Elodie took a deep breath, then another. Slowly and deliberately, she smoothed her hands down her dress and over her hair, which had fallen from its braids and hung tangled around her face. What must she look like?

"Will you help me?" she said, still gasping a little for breath.

The boy said nothing.

"I was taken by the people who call themselves Trident. Do you know them? I've . . . decided to leave. I want to go to Ritherlee. Can you show me the way?"

Elodie bit her tongue. Had she said too much? Yet the boy's face was kind.

At last the boy spoke. "I cannot leave the woods," he said. His voice was thin and somehow musical.

"Oh." It wasn't the response Elodie had expected. "Why not?"

"I cannot leave the woods, but you may stay. I will protect you." He bowed, lowering his curly head.

A single gust of wind blew down through the trees, cutting

through the tattered remnants of Elodie's dress. She shivered.

"I suppose I should wait until morning," she said.

"I will protect you," the boy repeated. "My name is Samial."

"I'm Elodie."

"Please, follow me."

Samial turned and began to walk toward a cluster of willow trees. Elodie followed, grateful to have found a friend in such a dreadful place. Someone who treated her as she deserved, even though he couldn't possibly know who she was.

"Do you live here in the woods?" she said as she followed the boy. He moved effortlessly through the trees, almost seeming to glide, finding a path where Elodie was certain no path existed. Best of all, as long as she remained in his footsteps, the trees didn't snare her anymore, as if they knew to keep their distance.

"I am here with my knight," Samial replied. "I am squire to Sir Jaken. My lord fought under the banner of King Morlon in the War of Blood, many years ago. He and the others of his banner have remained here ever since." Elodie knew what had happened only too well; the Thousand Year War, of which the War of Blood was just a part, had been one of her tutor's favorite lessons. Elodie was revolted by the story of how her father had killed his own brother, King Morlon, and stolen the crown of Toronia.

She looked around, seeing the trees in a whole new light. Could this dismal forest really be home to a banner of venerable knights opposed to King Brutan? The War of Blood might have been fifteen years ago, but such a force would still be far more impressive than Fessan's motley tribe.

"How long have you been with Sir Jaken?" she asked. "Since I was eleven," Samial replied. "Sir Jaken's home lies in Idilliam. As long as Brutan remains on the throne, he can never go home. And nor can I."

The romance of it made Elodie smile. *A boy squired to an exiled knight!* What was more, if Sir Jaken and his banner hated Brutan so much, surely they would fight for her. *I'd much rather have them on my side than stupid Trident.*

She was about to ask more, but at that moment Samial jumped down a bank onto a wide track running between the trees. He looked up, holding out his hand to help her down, and on his face was a look of such sadness that she stilled her tongue.

She reached out for him, but to her surprise he snatched his hand away again before she could touch it.

"What is it?" she asked, scrambling down the bank herself. He was far ahead now, a lonely figure slipping from one shadow to the next, like a character from a romantic story of old.

"No matter," he said in his lilting way.

The track wound in a gentle curve, taking them back through the fir trees to the edge of the Weeping Woods. Here, Samial stood aside, allowing Elodie to hurry past.

"Is this your camp?" she said, spotting flames flickering beyond the trees. She rushed out into the clearing, only to stop short. Above the campfires and tents flew a banner she recognized. On it was the image of a trident, surrounded by three crowns.

Her fists clenched. She turned on Samial, suddenly furious. "You tricked me! How *dare* you!"

"I said I would protect you," Samial told her. "I could not leave you to sleep on the cold ground, to be found by wolves and bears. Do not run from Trident. You are safe with them."

For the first time since they'd met, he smiled. It transformed his face, happiness shining through the dirt like a beacon. Despite herself, Elodie felt her anger simmer and die away.

The smell of cooked meat wafted toward her on the night breeze. Her stomach grumbled, reminding her how hungry she was.

"Was that a bear?" said Samial, his grin turning mischievous.

"You know it wasn't." Elodie sighed. "I suppose you're right, Samial. I'll stay here—for now, at least."

"Then be safe, Elodie."

Samial turned and headed back into the Weeping Woods, seeming not so much to retreat as to melt into the shadows.

"Wait!" Elodie called. "Can I come and see you again?"

The boy's face lingered, hovering like a lamp in the darkness.

"I will be here," he said.

CHAPTER 10

"We should ask Limmoni for another lamp," said Gulph.

Nynus stopped in the middle of the chamber. Gulph was glad he'd brought Nynus's endless pacing to a halt. How many times could a person walk from one side of a small room to the other?

"Who's Limmoni?"

Gulph blinked. The mysterious young woman had said the others would forget her visit to the chamber. *How did she do that?*

"Oh, I think your mother said she was her servant," he said.

Nynus shrugged. "Why do we need another lamp?"

"There's no window. It's dark in here."

Nynus started pacing again, hands clasped tight behind his back. "It's fine," he muttered. "Darkness can bring a light of its own."

Nynus hadn't slept all night, and his behavior was beginning to worry Gulph. Every time he'd awoken, the prince had been pacing and murmuring. Gulph had caught the odd phrase—something about "doing wrong" or "righting wrongs"—but what had struck him most of all had been the empty look on Nynus's face. He supposed the prince was disoriented after his long imprisonment.

I wish I could help you, Nynus, Gulph thought.

The chamber door opened and Queen Magritt walked in. Watery light poured around her, filtered from a skylight that had been opened high in the butcher's storeroom. Gulph inhaled sharply, as if he could breathe in the light. The feel of it on his face was wonderful.

"Close the door!" said Nynus, flinching. He backed away from it, raising his hands to shield his eyes.

Leaving the door ajar, the queen held up a large hessian sack. "This is the day, my son," she said.

"I told you to close the door!"

The queen's face stiffened. "After today, all doors will be open to you. But the choice is yours. Would you be king or not?"

Nynus held his body taut for a moment, then relaxed. "I'm sorry, Mother. I didn't sleep well. I haven't slept properly for years. Forgive me."

"There is nothing to forgive."

She smoothed his face with her gloved hand and Nynus's eyelids half closed. *So that's where he gets it from,* thought Gulph, remembering the prince's cheek-stroking habit. *Magritt probably did that before he was locked up.*

Gulph smothered a flash of envy. What had happened to his own mother? Had she ever comforted him like that? Sometimes he wondered if she'd abandoned him, as disgusted by his deformities as so many others had been.

He cleared his throat. "Begging your pardon," Gulph said, eyeing the door. "Does this mean you're going to let us out?"

"You speak as if you are a prisoner. But to answer your question, yes. Today, everything will change. And you, my little trouper, will have an important part to play."

"I will?"

The queen drew what looked like an animal skin from the sack. She shook it out, and it unfurled into a gaudy costume of red fur and orange frills. Copper claws jangled on a series of interlocking straps and belts. Perched on top was a mask that was half bird, half lizard. It was both beautiful and terrifying; Gulph couldn't decide whether he wanted to run from it or put it on.

"You will wear this," said the queen, as if she'd read his mind. "Nobody will know you behind the mask. Here, let me help you."

They are using you. Limmoni's words echoed in his head as

Magritt helped him step into the costume. It was hot and heavy; Gulph started sweating almost immediately.

"What am I?" he said, shrugging the furs up over his shoulders. "I mean, what am I supposed to be?"

"The bakaliss," said Queen Magritt. She turned the mask over in her hands. Its scaly surface contrasted with her soft white gloves. "It is one of the oldest legends of Toronia."

"I read that story," said Nynus. He turned on Gulph, his face suddenly ferocious. "It was in that book that got spoiled."

Gulph stared at him, startled. "I . . . I'm sorry about your book," he said.

Nynus's snarl turned instantly to a grin. "I'm only teasing you. When I'm king, I'll have all the books I want."

Gulph smiled weakly back. If anything, Nynus's mood swings seemed to be getting worse since their escape. "So what's this story?" he said lamely.

"The bakaliss was a serpent that slept under a mountain," said Nynus. "One day a king came to kill it. But the serpent woke."

"What happened then?"

"The serpent bit off the king's head," said the queen, "and swallowed it whole."

She pressed the mask over Gulph's face. He shuddered: The story hadn't ended quite the way he'd expected. Even worse, wearing the mask felt a little like entering another prison.

It's just a costume, he told himself. If doing his old job was the most Magritt would ask of him, maybe he needn't heed Limmoni's warning after all.

Peering out through the mask's narrow eye slits, he watched as the queen carefully lifted a small crown from the sack. Like the claws hanging from his waist, it was made of copper, though she handled it as if it were made of fragile crystal.

"Take this," she said, slipping it gently into a pouch hidden inside the costume's furs. "Keep it hidden until the time comes to use it."

"Use it for what?"

"You will perform with your friends, the Tanglewood Players."

"Tangletree."

"You will keep the mask on at all times. Nobody must see your face. When the performance ends, you will place the crown on King Brutan's head. That will be the signal."

"Signal?"

"That his reign is over. Will you do this for me, Gulph? Will you do it for us?"

The crown pressed against Gulph's chest, hard and unyielding. He didn't know what to say.

Do not trust her.

Nynus's white face appeared in front of the mask, bright with excitement. "You're such a true friend," said Nynus. "Just think, when I'm on the throne you'll have everything you ever wanted:

money, a grand chamber of your own. And your friends. I'll look after them, too. You saved me, Gulph," he went on. "Why would I not repay my debt?"

Gulph hesitated. It was such a silly thing: to put a fake crown on the head of a king. He imagined it was Pip asking. Would he refuse her such a request? Of course not: She was his friend, and that was what friends did. And yet . . .

"He'll do it," said Magritt. "Won't you, Gulph?"

Her eyes were steely. Unease pooled in the bottom of Gulph's stomach as he realized the queen didn't plan on allowing him to refuse.

Come on, Gulph, play along. You know how to do that, at least.

He forced a laugh. "Of course I will!" he said brightly. For good measure he gave a spin, the claws of the costume rattling.

"Very good," said the queen with a thin smile. "Now, we must be quick. The banquet begins shortly and you must be in your place. We must all be in our places."

"Wait," said Nynus. "His hands."

"What about my hands?"

Magritt and Nynus exchanged a glance.

"Of course," said the queen quickly. "Hands are like faces. People recognize them. Your friends will know you if we don't cover them up. Here." She peeled off her long silk gloves and handed them to Gulph. He pulled them on, bunching the fine material up inside his sleeves.

"All right," he said. "I'm ready."

Nynus's beaming smile appeared through the eye slits. "Oh, I can't wait to see their faces," the prince cried. "A bakaliss has come to Idilliam!"

The banqueting hall lay deep inside the castle. It was very grand, its walls and columns encrusted with ornate carvings and filigrees of gold. High at one end, on a minstrel's gallery, a small band of pipers played. Polished tables ran the entire length of the hall, piled high with food. From where he stood near the kitchen doors, it seemed to Gulph that he could hear them groaning under the weight. More tables filled the hall's central space. Seated around them were people wearing rich clothes, laughing and chatting. The swing doors beside him were in constant motion as countless bustling servants carried out trays of breads and wine and steaming meats. The smell of the food, and the rumbling chatter of the crowd, and the weight of the bakaliss costume, all conspired to make Gulph feel dizzy.

Queen Magritt and Nynus were nowhere to be seen.

"Are you all right?"

Someone tugged at Gulph's furs. He turned clumsily and found himself staring straight into the upturned face of Pip. She looked so sweet and familiar, with her freckled face and her patchwork outfit of blue and green, that it was as much as Gulph could do not to throw his arms around her. But the queen's orders had been clear.

"Yes," he said, adopting a gruff tone that would, he hoped, fool his oldest friend.

"It's just that, well, you were swaying a bit. I thought you were going to faint. I bet it's hot in there."

"Yes." It was all Gulph dared to say.

"I suppose they sent you to make up our numbers. I was wondering if . . . Well, we lost someone. He was, um, taken away to somewhere they call the Vault of Heaven. You don't know anything about it, do you?"

"No."

"It's just . . . I'm worried about him."

Even through the mask's eye slits, Pip's anguish was plain to see. Gulph wanted to strip off the costume, to explain to her everything that had happened to him, and that it would be all right.

Instead, he told himself that he had no choice but to follow the plan. As soon as King Brutan was brought down and Nynus was on the throne, he and Pip would be reunited. Until then, he just had to be patient.

The pipers stopped playing. Horns sounded a fanfare. Servants scattered to the four corners of the hall, and a hush descended over the throng. Everyone stood.

King Brutan strode in.

He was tall and broad, a big man for a big hall. At his side walked Queen Magritt, dressed all in crimson. Would the king see she was no longer wearing her gloves? Gulph doubted it. Brutan didn't look like the kind of man who noticed such things.

The royal couple walked between the tables to the platform that held two thrones, a table already crammed with food in front of them. Brutan helped Magritt into the smaller one, then took the Toronian throne, sculpted with eagles and lions, for himself. As he sank down onto the blood-colored cushions, another fanfare echoed through the hall, and the rest of the diners seated themselves again.

King Brutan ripped the leg from a roasted pheasant and raised it over his head.

"Let us eat!" he roared, cramming the meat into his mouth.

"We're on," said Pip. "Follow me. And try to keep up!"

As they trotted to their places before the king's table, a small band of minstrels appeared in a gallery overlooking the hall. A drumbeat began; a fiddle player took up the rhythm and suddenly the entire hall was filled with raucous music. Grinning through a mouthful of half-chewed meat, Brutan started thumping the table.

Pip began to dance, the bells on her outfit ringing merrily. Around her, the other members of the Tangletree Players launched into their routines of juggling and mime. Gulph watched dumbly for a moment, temporarily lost.

"Do something!" hissed Pip as she cavorted past.

Snapping out of his reverie, Gulph spread his arms and skipped down the hall. The diners roared, apparently pleased to see this creature of legend come to life. When he reached the royal table, he clicked his shoulders out of their sockets, preparing to perform one of the impossible contortions that always went down so well.

He stopped. Nothing would give him away more quickly than one of his usual moves. Spinning wildly, he restored his bones to their proper places and started doing backflips instead. The weight of the costume made it difficult, but his wiry body was strong.

"Faster! Faster!" roared the king, banging the table again.

Gulph complied, forcing extra speed from his sweating limbs. Each time he returned to an upright position, it seemed the king's mouth was stuffed with more food, his cloak was more stained with wine, and the servants scurrying around him were more bent and afraid.

I bet no one will miss him, thought Gulph. *Toronia can't be any worse off with Nynus on that throne instead.*

As Gulph continued with his antics, he spotted a tall figure taking up station beside the throne platform. It was Captain Ossilius, scanning the room with keen eyes. Behind him, a whole troop of legionnaires stood at attention in their shining bronze armor. More soldiers had appeared down the length of the banqueting hall.

One of the legionnaires in Ossilius's troop was shorter than the others. His helmet covered most of his face, leaving exposed only a pale, beardless jaw.

Nynus.

The time to act was nearly here.

The music reached a crescendo. Gulph accelerated his pace, turning the backflips into stationary cartwheels. The red furs flapped against his legs; the copper claws clashed like swords. The crowd cheered.

With a final rattle of drums, the music crashed to a halt. With a rousing cheer, the Tangletree Players formed themselves into a line and bowed before the king. Gulph was only dimly aware of them concluding their act. He'd been performing in a world of his own.

Silence descended on the banqueting hall. Through the mask, Gulph saw that Captain Ossilius was staring straight at him. Slowly, the captain nodded his head, the tiniest movement.

After his acrobatics, Gulph's heart was racing. Now it started to hammer. Sweat poured down his face, dripping into his eyes. In a fog, he stepped up onto the platform. Brutan's laughter was loud, and his breath was terrible. The king's face was a red blur.

Reaching inside his costume, Gulph pulled out the copper crown. He raised his gloved hands above his head and turned a slow circle. The diners cheered. The king guffawed.

"King Brutan!" Gulph cried, no longer caring who recognized his voice. "It is not enough to be king of Toronia!"

Through the film of sweat, Gulph saw Brutan lower his brow into a deadly frown.

"What did you say?" he rumbled ominously.

"I say that you are also the king of merriment!" cried Gulph, dancing round the table to the throne. Now the crown was poised directly above the king's head.

Brutan looked up at the crown. Gulph's vision cleared at last, and their eyes locked.

"And I say so too!" shouted Brutan, squirming on the throne like a little boy about to receive a treat.

Hands shaking, Gulph placed the crown on his head.

The crowd erupted. Gulph stepped back. The uproar continued, but nobody moved.

Gulph looked at Captain Ossilius. What was going on? With the signal given, surely the legionnaires should draw their weapons and lead the king away. Wasn't that how it was supposed to work? Why wasn't anything happening?

What had he done wrong?

A choking sound came from the throne. Brutan clutched at the sides of his head. Then his hands dropped to his throat. His eyes bulged. His red face turned purple, thick veins throbbing at his temples. His tongue lolled from his mouth, swelling visibly, like a balloon.

The cheering subsided. People started to scream. Servants and courtiers rushed to the throne, some of them clambering over the table in an effort to reach the king quickly.

Horrified, Gulph took a faltering step backward. The costume seemed suddenly twice as heavy, the sweat on his body twice as slick. Something was terribly wrong.

Captain Ossilius barked a command and the legionnaires moved, spreading out across the floor with fast efficiency, holding back the throng and blocking the exits.

Foam bubbled from Brutan's mouth. His arms thrashed, throwing off the servants who were trying to hold him down.

Where the crown touched his head was a ring of bubbling flesh, as if the copper had been dipped in fire just before Gulph had set it in place.

In fire or . . . in poison.

Gulph tore off the gloves and threw them down; they lay coiled on the wine-soaked floor like dead snakes. Suddenly he understood why Nynus had insisted he wear them. As the realization came, Brutan reared up from the throne, his swollen mouth gaping in a silent scream. The servants fell away, their expressions confused and distraught.

Queen Magritt stood slowly and took her husband's twitching arm.

"Yes, my dear," she said with soft menace. "The time has come for you to leave the throne for good. But do not worry. There is someone here ready to take your place."

Nynus appeared at her side. He'd removed his helmet. His pale face was contorted into what Gulph supposed was a smile. It looked more like the cold and haunted grin of a skeleton.

Gulph looked again at the gloves strewn on the floor. This was what the queen had planned all along. And Nynus, his friend, had known too. Everything he'd said about wanting to spare his father, giving him his own castle in which to live out the rest of his life. . . .

All lies.

Limmoni had been right.

With a final, agonized gasp, King Brutan fell dead across the table. The poisoned crown rolled from his head and toppled to the floor, where it spun and spun, ringing like a metal coin for what seemed like hours, until it finally settled to a stop. Silence fell again, and all was still.

One thought thundered inside Gulph's head. *I have killed the king.*

CHAPTER 11

Gulph's mouth was dry. His heart juddered as if it were pumping hot sand around his veins. Wind howled in his head like a wolf. He'd felt fear before, but never anything like this. It was as if his entire body—no, his entire *being*—was shriveling to nothing.

They will kill me, he thought.

Stricken with panic, he staggered backward through the crowds of confused and frightened people. Nobody paid him any heed; some even seemed to stare right through him. How could they be so blind to someone in such an absurd costume?

His stumbling feet tripped on a pile of fallen dinner plates, and he fell. A split opened in the furs he was wearing, and his beaked and scaly mask slipped. He threw it aside, starting to tear off the whole hideous costume. Had dressing him as a king-killing monster been Magritt and Nynus's idea of a joke?

"What's happening?" The voice was Pip's. She was right beside him, fallen too, and gazing up at the confused activity around the throne. She blinked, and seemed to see Gulph for the first time.

"You!" she cried. "Gulph! It's you!" Her eyes were wide with surprise.

"Pip! I've so much to . . ." Gulph broke off. The expression on Pip's face wasn't surprise after all. It was horror.

She was staring at the remains of his costume. "What have you done?"

"Wait, Pip. Let me explain."

But she was hurrying away. He set off after her until her way was blocked by a fallen table. She backed against it, shaking her head.

"Don't come any nearer."

Gulph stopped and held out his hands. *The hands of a killer.* "Pip, please, just let me—"

She was shaking. "I thought you were my friend! How could you? You . . . you're a murderer!"

"I didn't . . . Pip, I'm still me. I'm still Gulph."

"No, you're not. Get away from me!"

Cries rose from the end of the hall. A gap opened in the crowd of servants and courtiers, creating a clear line of sight to the platform. The table had been pushed aside to reveal the throne. Nynus was sitting on it, his white face bright and alert. Beside him, one hand resting lightly on his shoulder, stood his mother.

"The king is dead!" cried Queen Magritt. "May the new king live long! Kneel now before him! Kneel before Nynus, king of Toronia!"

Something like a wave passed down the length of the hall as, one after the other, everyone present dropped to one knee. The servants surrounding the throne did so with fearful expressions on their faces; many of the courtiers too looked afraid, although some looked pleased; the majority of the diners simply looked stunned.

The wave reached the spot where Gulph and Pip were crouched. Gulph shuffled himself into a kneeling position, and was relieved to see Pip do the same. What else could they do?

At Magritt's command, several of Captain Ossilius's legionnaires dragged Brutan's body from the table and spirited it away out of sight, treating it with no more care than one of the sides of beef in the butcher's store. Waving her arms, the queen cleared the last lingering servants from the platform, leaving herself and her son alone in their place of honor.

"Toronia is broken," she said, her voice echoing around the enormous hall. "King Nynus will rebuild it. He will crush the rebel forces with his strength. With his wisdom, he will make new laws to ensure that Toronia will never again be divided. Heed his first command as your sovereign."

The watching assembly listened in silence. Some shifted awkwardly, clearly uncomfortable on their knees. But their king hadn't yet given them permission to stand.

"The king's command concerns a witch called Kalia," Magritt continued. "Kalia seduced King Brutan, and corrupted him. Thirteen years ago she bore him three children—triplets indeed."

Gasps rose up. Some of those watching turned to each other and started whispering. Gulph heard several mutter the word "prophecy." It made him think of the Prophecy Song, an old tune he'd heard in the taverns of Isur, bawled by drunks at the end of a night. How was that connected with what he'd been forced to do to King Brutan?

Nynus raised one hand. Silence fell.

"Be quiet!" he called, his voice thin and clear. "Listen to what my mother has to say."

"Brutan was deceived," the queen went on. "Kalia tricked him into believing these thrice-cursed brats had died at birth. Then, years later, a man was brought to him, a pathetic drunkard who went by the name of Sir Brax.

"Although Sir Brax's mind was ruined by drink, on one point he was very clear: the three children were still alive."

More gasps. Gulph glanced at Pip. She held her slender body taut, not looking at him, just staring straight ahead at Queen Magritt and the new king.

"Kalia confessed the truth," said the queen. "In the end. But where the triplets were, she would not tell. Even when she was tied to the stake and set aflame, her mouth remained sealed. Their whereabouts is a mystery."

The gasps turned to cries. Gulph couldn't tell if people were outraged that Kalia had been burned to death or concerned that these three children still wandered the kingdom.

"Silence!" roared Nynus, standing from the throne. His face was red, like that of a child about to have a tantrum. "The next person who interrupts will find themselves in the Vault of Heaven. Do I make myself clear?"

Nobody made a sound.

"No doubt many of you are thinking about the prophecy," said the queen. "King Nynus says to you now that the prophecy is proved false! According to the legend, Brutan's death would be caused by one of these wretched triplets. But as you have seen for yourselves, it is Nynus, my son, and the one true heir to the throne of Toronia, who brought him down. So here is the truth of it: Nynus is king, and as for this so-called prophecy"—she paused, scanning the hall with glittering eyes—"it has no more life in it than Brutan himself."

Except you didn't have the guts to do it yourselves, Gulph thought bitterly. The plan might have been set in motion by Queen Magritt, and Nynus might be the one to benefit from it, but Gulph's were the hands that had set the crown on the head of the king.

"But a thread remains untied," said the queen. "Or, to be precise, three threads. As long as these three brats remain alive, they will attract all those opposed to the fair rule of Toronia. Rebels, ingrates, and criminals, all will flock to their call. Unless we wish the current conflicts to escalate into an all-consuming war, they must be eliminated."

"There will be rewards," said Nynus, spreading his hands generously. "Rich rewards. Anyone who brings me the head of one of these wretched triplets will receive great wealth and a permanent place in my court." His eyes found Gulph's, and fixed on them. He gave him one of his beaming smiles. "Indeed, all those who serve the crown will find themselves in my favor."

A knot tightened in Gulph's stomach. He wanted to turn and run, but instead, he forced an answering smile onto his face.

Nynus's voice rose to a shout. He took a step forward, scanning the banqueting hall with narrowed eyes. "You of the King's Legion—close the shutters. I would not have sunlight in this place!"

Captain Ossilius, who had taken up station beside the throne, frowned at this odd request. However, Gulph knew exactly what was going on inside Nynus's head. Ten years inside the Vault of Heaven. Ten years without sunlight. Without companionship. None of this was really Nynus's fault. Was it any wonder the boy's mind had turned as dark as the cell in which he'd been incarcerated?

Captain Ossilius's obvious puzzlement didn't stop him obeying the command of the new king of Toronia. Under his direction, two soldiers hurried to opposite sides of the hall and turned the large cranked handles that operated the roof shutters. Slowly the shutters descended, canvas unfurling over long wooden slats. Shadows slid over the crowd, plunging the banqueting hall into a dim twilight.

Gulph waited with the rest of the assembly, but both Nynus and his mother had spoken their fill. Guards opened the doors and began to usher the diners away; servants were dispatched to clear the tables. Slowly, silently, the banqueting hall began to empty.

He looked around for Pip, but she'd gone. He returned to the kitchen doors, where he'd first bumped into her, but neither she nor any of the Tangletree Players were anywhere in sight.

Disconsolate, Gulph turned a slow circle, scanning the hall for a familiar face. But despite the crowd, he was alone.

"This way," whispered a voice.

Startled, Gulph spun around. One of the doors was just swinging closed. He pushed through it and into a long room filled with steam. The figure of a woman darted across his vision, beckoned, and disappeared down a corridor . . . but not before flicking her face in his direction.

Limmoni!

Gulph hurried after her. The corridor twisted and turned, delivering him finally into a small vaulted room. Wooden chests were stacked high against one wall, piles of linen against the other.

Limmoni stood in the middle of the room. As he entered, she took a step toward him, moving with an easy grace. Her servant's clothes flowed strangely against her body as she moved. "Have you heard of the wizard Melchior?"

Gulph frowned. He knew the name from the stories Sidebottom John used to tell around the fire, back in Isur. "Yes. But I thought all the wizards were—"

"I am Melchior's apprentice." Limmoni's eyes were a deep violet, their softness a curious contrast to the sharp, angular lines of her face. Her gaze seemed to bore through him. "Or rather, I was, until he disappeared. Now the time has come for me to find him again. He must be told about Nynus."

Gulph's head swam. "You're . . . a magician?" So that was how she'd faded from the minds of Magritt and Nynus—magic.

Limmoni nodded.

He sat heavily on one of the chests. Belatedly, he shrugged off the remnants of the ridiculous bakaliss costume. It pooled on the floor, the red fur spreading on the flagstones like blood.

"What's all this got to do with me?" he said. "Why did you give me this jewel? I mean, why bother? I'm just a nobody. You know what I'm really worth? The cost of a barrel of ale! Yes! That's how I came to be with the players. My father swapped me for a cask of Isur's finest brew—"

"He was not your father," said Limmoni.

"I was lucky they didn't leave me in a ditch there and then. . . . What? What did you say?"

"The man who gave you away. He was not your father."

"How do you . . . ? Who was he?"

"He was your protector. A duty he utterly failed to fulfill. His name was Sir Brax."

Gulph blinked. "Queen Magritt talked about a knight called Sir Brax."

"It was the same man."

For an instant, the strange sensation of dryness washed over Gulph again. His pulse pounded against his temples. His skin felt cracked and old. Limmoni peered at him, her eyes narrowed in curiosity.

Gulph ran his hands down his face. His thoughts were a storm.

"Sir Brax was my protector. Are you saying . . . Limmoni, are you saying that he . . . that I was . . . am one of the children from the prophecy? One of the triplets?" He swallowed. "The son of King Brutan?"

Limmoni clasped her hands behind her back. "Yes, Gulph. It is true. That gem I gave you? It is but one of three, just as you are but one of three who will rule Toronia."

"How did you get it?" Gulph's hand went to the green jewel. It felt suddenly heavier around his neck. No wonder.

It is filled with fate.

"Melchior gave it to Sir Brax to guard with you, but he sold it to a pawnbroker. But I followed his tracks and recovered it. I have been keeping it ever since."

Gulph held out the green gem on its long, gold chain. It felt more than merely heavy. It felt toxic. *Poison.* "I don't want it! I don't want this jewel, or the crown. . . . I don't want any of it! I just want things the way they were."

"Hiding away from the war? Being laughed at?" There was no malice in Limmoni's voice, just simple truth.

"You might not think it was much of a life, but it was better than this!"

"Gulph, I am sorry, but you have no choice. You cannot deny your destiny."

"I don't care about destiny."

"But destiny cares about you. What Magritt and Nynus made you do to Brutan was terrible, but it had to be done. He was meant to die by your hand."

At this, Gulph stared at her, shaking, breathing hard.

"You will be safe here, for a time," said Limmoni. "But you must continue to let Nynus believe you are his friend. Everything depends on that."

"I could just run."

"He would follow. He would have you killed."

Gulph shook his head with vigor. "He wouldn't. He's my friend."

"But his mother is not," said Limmoni gently.

"So it's stay and live. Or leave and die. Is that what you're saying?"

"Yes."

All the strength left Gulph's body. His arm dropped to his side. He felt completely spent.

"What happens next?" he said.

"The future is a mystery, Agulphus, even to me."

"What did you call me?" Strange as it was, the name she'd used seemed to echo in his head, as if he'd heard it spoken long ago.

"Agulphus. It is your true name, the name of a king."

A shiver ran down Gulph's back.

"Hear me now," Limmoni went on. "Change is coming— coming like the winter wind. We cannot change the weather, Agulphus. But we can stand before the storm."

Footsteps sounded in the corridor outside. Gulph turned to look. A shadow was moving toward him.

"Limmoni . . ." he began, looking back. But she'd already gone.

"Gulph?" The voice belonged to Nynus. "Gulph! I know you're there. I saw you scurry away. Are you trying to avoid me?"

With shaking hands, Gulph slipped the chain over his neck and tucked the jewel under his tunic.

"I'm in here, Nynus," he called. Then he added, "I mean, Your Majesty."

The footsteps grew louder.

My half brother! Gulph's mind bent in an effort to accommodate the truth. The thought made him feel sick. If only Sir Brax hadn't been a drunkard, if only he hadn't been found by the Tangletree Players, if only they hadn't been captured and brought to Idilliam. . . .

If only.

The sickness receded, leaving just three thoughts drifting through Gulph's head. Three.

My name is Agulphus.

My future is bound by fate.

And:

I have killed the king, my father.

Nynus's white face appeared at the door.

"Ah, there you are, Gulph. Thought you could get away from me, eh?"

Somehow, from somewhere, Gulph found a smile.

"Me, King Nynus?" he said. "I'm not going anywhere."

ACT TWO

CHAPTER 12

Tarlan stared down at the featureless white landscape rolling past below Theeta's wings. How long was it since he'd last seen a village? A day? Two? He didn't know. The freezing air had numbed his mind as well as his body. His injured arm ached, despite the black leaf he'd rubbed on it.

I thought Yalasti was cold. It's nothing compared to the Icy Wastes.

Wind gusted down from the north, blasting directly into Tarlan's face. It was the same wind they'd been fighting against all the way here. At first, its bitter touch had scoured his cheeks; now he couldn't feel it at all. The wind blew over his tangled hair, his black robe, but neither hair nor robe moved: both were frozen solid.

Tarlan could hear something: a vague, chattering sound. Tiny dancing shapes materialized in the air ahead of him, like fireflies or falling stars. They were beautiful. Fighting the lethargy that had overpowered his limbs, Tarlan reached toward the glittering cloud, but it was still far, far away.

"Storm," said Theeta.

"Always storm," said Nasheen, weaving in the air to their left.

Kitheen, as usual, said nothing.

Tarlan tried to remember what Mirith had told him about the Icy Wastes. But his thoughts were frozen, just like his hair and cloak. All he knew was that it was a dangerous place, and that few who ventured there ever returned.

The glittering shapes grew bigger and more beautiful. Tarlan still had no idea what he was looking at. But he couldn't ignore the thorrods' unease.

"Take me down," he said. "You've come far enough. I'll go on alone. There's no need for you to risk your lives for me."

"We fly," said Theeta.

Tarlan bowed his head. These giant birds were his dearest friends. But he couldn't bear the thought of leading them into danger.

"I'll be all right," he said. "It's what Mirith would have wanted."

"Thorrod is sky," said Nasheen.

"What do you mean?"

Nasheen's golden head twitched with frustration. When he was younger, Tarlan had thought the thorrods stupid. Now he knew that beneath their simple language lay profound wisdom.

"Sky above," said Nasheen. "Land below. Thorrod is sky. Mirith is land."

"But Mirith is dead." Tarlan pressed down his grief in his efforts to understand what Nasheen was trying to say.

"Yes, yes," said the thorrod, tossing her head. "Now Tarlan is Mirith."

"Sky needs land," said Theeta gently. "Thorrod needs Tarlan."

"It is," added Nasheen. Tarlan waited for her to complete the statement, then realized she'd said everything she wanted to say.

It is.

The loyalty of these majestic birds took his breath away. Wherever he went, they would follow.

If it weren't for Mirith, I'd never have known you, he thought with a pang of grief.

Tarlan had a sudden sense of his own place in the great flow of history. The thorrods were old, he knew that, and Mirith had told him there had been frost witches in the mountains of Yalasti for thousands of years. He had no doubt the alliance between the two extended far, far back in time.

"Then I say to you now that Tarlan needs thorrod. As you are mine, so I am yours. I will be here for you, always. I will never let you down."

The glittering shapes turned out to be ice crystals, torn up from the winter landscape and whirled into a frenzy by the howling wind. As the thorrods flew into the storm, Tarlan hunched over, burying his head as best he could under his frozen cloak. When the ice penetrated his defense—as it frequently did—it cut like a thousand tiny knives.

The veil of cloud and flying ice swallowed the sun. It was like flying into the thickest—and deadliest—fog Tarlan had ever known. Nor could he tell in which direction they were headed; he just hoped the thorrods knew where they were going.

"Low!" shouted Theeta, dipping her wings.

She led their tiny flock closer to the ground. Here the wind was just as strong, but the air was filled more with snow than ice. Tarlan clung on as the thorrods plowed their way through the blizzard, afraid they might be forced to return to Yalasti, where the elk-hunters would be waiting for him.

Never mind the elk-hunters, he thought. *Turning back means failing Mirith. I promised her I would bring the jewel to Melchior. And I will. . . .*

He was about to touch his fingers to where it hung frozen around his neck, when something loomed out of the fog of swirling snowflakes: a gigantic shape like a huge, twisted tree arching high above Tarlan's head. As the thorrods flew beneath its curve, he saw it wasn't a tree at all, but a huge, bleached bone.

More bones rose from the murk, row upon row. They were flying through the rib cage of some unimaginable beast. Tarlan felt his fingers tighten in Theeta's neck ruff, felt his frozen jaw creak open. Ice filled his mouth, but he was hardly aware of it, so astonishing was the sight.

They flew on through the vast boneyard. Far to the left, Tarlan glimpsed something mountainous that might have been a skull. Dark shadows set deep in its contours hinted at eye sockets the size of the cave he'd shared with Mirith.

Unsettling though the huge skeletons were, they did at least afford some protection from the wind. Theeta dipped lower, skimming the ground so that her wing beats raised fountains of snow. The other thorrods followed, their keen eyes scanning constantly for any sign of danger. Tarlan stared ahead, wondering what they would do if they encountered one of these unimaginable monsters still living.

Eventually they left the bones behind. Though the storm continued, the air felt a little warmer. Tarlan rubbed his hands over his body, his face, encouraging the blood to circulate. For the first time in this long flight, he began to feel optimistic.

"Look!" said Theeta.

Six figures emerged from the blizzard, running across the snow more quickly than Tarlan thought possible. They wore thick outfits made from overlapping plates of some material he couldn't identify, giving them an oddly reptilian appearance. On their feet they wore broad shoes that prevented them from sinking into the drifting snow.

"I didn't know there were people out here," said Tarlan, suddenly afraid.

"Wastelanders," said Nasheen.

"Cannibals," said Theeta.

"Madmen," said Kitheen.

Tarlan stared at the third thorrod. He spoke so rarely that, when he did, it was quite an event. He and the other birds waited to see if there would be more, but it seemed their black-breasted companion had spoken his fill.

"Well," said Tarlan. "Whoever they are—whatever they are— we're not going near them. Come on, let's—"

A cry rang out across the Icy Wastes:

"Help me!"

The voice had a liquid, purring quality Tarlan had never heard before. Glancing to his right, he saw a bulky shape battling through a deep drift of snow. At first he thought it was a child crawling on all fours, then he saw it was an animal. The creature's thick fur was striped blue and white, camouflage against the icy terrain.

A tigron!

Years earlier, he'd seen a pack of these rare and ferocious beasts from a distance, prowling the foothills below Mirith's mountain. This one looked small, just a cub.

"Help! They'll kill me!"

It was the tigron that was shouting. He could hear it, understand it. Its voice was high and wavering, and he knew instinctively it was a female. He'd always taken for granted his ability to communicate with the thorrods: Mirith had been able to do it; why wouldn't he?

But in all the times he'd wandered the mountains, watching the whitebears lumbering from their lairs, the winter rabbits grazing on the heather, he'd never heard such creatures speak. Only the thorrods.

And now a tigron.

What does it mean? Why now?

"We go," said Theeta, wheeling away from the Wastelanders, who by now had spread into a half circle and were closing in on the tigron cub.

"No," said Tarlan, gripping her neck ruff firmly. "We save her!"

The thorrods came in low, from behind. At the last moment, the Wastelanders turned. Tarlan saw their outfits were in fact plates of bone, with tufts of white fur protruding from the places where they overlapped. Scaly hoods covered their heads, the openings studded with hundreds of teeth, so that their weather-beaten faces seemed to be peering out from inside the jaws of some monstrous lizard.

The Wastelanders unsheathed long bone spears and launched them at the attacking thorrods. The giant birds dodged them effortlessly. Theeta cut low over the nearest man and raked her talons down his back, penetrating his bony armor with ease. He

screamed something in a language Tarlan didn't understand and
fell face-first into the snow.

Kitheen was making straight for another Wastelander when two
more men rose up out of the ground like the buried dead brought
back to life. They shook off the snow beneath which they'd been
hiding, presumably, thought Tarlan, as part of the operation to
ambush the tigron. Both were carrying heavy bone axes.

It was too late for Kitheen to pull out of his dive. He screeched,
cycling his wings in a desperate attempt to avoid them. The two men
drew back their axes.

Nasheen appeared from nowhere, slashing the first man's chest
open with her beak and knocking the other to the ground with her
tail. He dropped limp into a spreading pool of his companion's blood.

Three of the remaining five Wastelanders had reached the tigron
cub. The other two stood guard, swinging long ropes in circles over
their heads. On the ends of the ropes were heavy, spiked weights.

"Help!" screamed the tigron, thrashing helplessly in the snowdrift as one of the men thrust a sharp bone knife toward her throat.

"Closer!" Tarlan shouted. Reaching under his cloak, he snatched
up the bow he'd stolen from the ice fortress. As Theeta swooped low
over the snowdrift, he jumped. In midleap, he nocked the arrow into
the bowstring, drew, and loosed. The arrow pierced the Wastelander's
throat just as he was about to deliver a killing blow to the tigron cub.
With a gargling gasp, the man dropped dead in the snow.

Tarlan hit the snowdrift and rolled clear in a flurry of white powder. He staggered to his feet, spitting snow from his mouth. His hands were empty; he'd dropped the bow.

Two Wastelanders were sprinting toward him, faces furious inside their tooth-lined hoods. In a flurry of snow behind them, Nasheen and Kitheen were grappling with the remaining men. Theeta was wheeling around, still recovering from her dive, too far away to come to his aid.

Both of the men advancing on Tarlan hurled their upraised spears at the same time. His feet paddled uselessly in the soft snow as he tried in vain to dodge them.

Something heavy slammed against his hip. Air exploded from his lungs in a crisp cloud. He flew sideways, limbs flailing, skidding over an exposed patch of icy ground. Recovering, he lifted his head, expecting to see one of the thorrods standing over him. Instead he found himself looking into the face of the tigron.

"You helped me," gasped the cub. "So I helped you."

The little animal slumped against him. Blood oozed from a long gash in her flank. Enraged, Tarlan clambered to his feet, retrieved his bow, and turned to face the oncoming Wastelanders, but suddenly they began backing away from him.

"Come on!" he yelled. "Are you scared?"

They didn't look scared. Nevertheless, they continued to retreat, until they reached their companions. The four men stood back-to-back, armored plates drawn tight around their bodies, weapons held high, so that they resembled a single organism, spiked and deadly. Kitheen and Nasheen circled them, jabbing with their beaks and claws, unable to make a proper strike.

"Theeta!" Tarlan called, but she was already there, towering over him. The men had been retreating not from Tarlan but from his thorrod friend.

"Come," said the giant bird.

"I'm coming," Tarlan replied. Wincing with the effort, he heaved the wounded tigron cub onto his shoulder. "And so is she."

They left the surviving Wastelanders in the snow and struck out into the wilderness. Tarlan had no idea which way they were going, nor did he care. He just wanted to get away.

"High," said Theeta as she led the other thorrods up through the whirling clouds of ice.

Lacking the strength to object, Tarlan concentrated on keeping the tigron warm under his cloak. The cub was panting rapidly, obviously in pain, but her pulse was strong.

At last, the thorrods climbed out of the storm. The ice clouds were spread below them, a seething ocean of crystals. The air was bitterly cold and very thin, and Tarlan found it hard to breathe. But for the first time in what seemed an age, he felt safe.

"Filos," said the tigron, poking her blue-striped snout from under his cloak. "My name is Filos."

"I'm Tarlan." Though he spoke the Toronian tongue, she somehow understood him.

"They killed my pride. My family. They are bad men."

"I'm sorry."

She nuzzled him, her eyelids drooping. "You are good."

Soon the tigron was asleep. Tarlan spread half his dwindling supply of black leaf on her wound, then dabbed a little on his shoulder, which ached terribly.

The thorrods flew on. Now that they had cleared the storm, Tarlan could see exactly where they were. Behind them, the sea of cloud melted into the white mountains of Yalasti, his home. In front—very near, in fact—the clouds dissolved to reveal a world so green he thought his eyes were deceiving him.

The sun was low to his left, heralding the end of the day and confirming what he already knew: ahead, to the northwest, lay Ritherlee. Tarlan had heard of this land of pasture and plenty but had never seen it. It looked . . . beautiful.

At last everything was clear: the air around him, the thoughts in his head. Ritherlee was far from the elk-hunters, far from the painful memories of Mirith's death, far from everything that had caused him pain. Somewhere he might make a new start, and finally find his place in the world.

Somewhere he could begin his search for Melchior.

CHAPTER 13

E lodie wandered between the tents, her head tilted back, staring up at the morning sky. The clouds hung low over the forest clearing, corking it like a bottle. She felt trapped.

She'd lain awake most of the night, fretting about her decision to stay in the Trident camp. Was it the right thing to do? It didn't seem like she had any choice. And it was such a long way from home.

Yet when she thought about Castle Vicerin, and the courtly world she'd grown up in, that didn't feel like home either. Not anymore. Surrounded by the darkness, cold and alone, she felt a sob swelling within her. She clasped her hands to her chest and pressed tight, not wanting to draw attention to herself.

And if I start crying, she thought, *I might never stop.*

Just before dawn, Palenie had risen, telling Elodie as she left the tent that breakfast wouldn't wait. The princess had remained curled up on the hard ground beneath her rough fur blankets, feigning sleep. Now, as she walked empty-bellied through the dew-soaked grass, she wished she'd had the sense to eat.

The green tunic she'd put on was tight and ill-fitting. She had no choice but to wear it: during the night, her dress had been taken. *It had better come back mended*, she thought, fiddling with the laces on her tunic, *or someone's going to be sorry.*

As she emerged into one of the open spaces between the tents, Elodie heard a cheer, accompanied by the loud clashing of metal against metal. Directly in front of her, a crowd of people was gathered around two men sparring with short swords. The combatants drove each other first this way, then that, grunting every time the weapon of one struck the shield of the other.

After a moment, they stopped, and a ripple of applause went around the watching crowd. The swordsmen pulled off the helmets that had been covering their faces. Elodie saw that one was an older man with a grizzled beard. The other wasn't a man at all; it was Palenie.

"Ah, there you are," Palenie said, knuckling sweat from her eyes. "You're just in time. It's your turn next."

"I don't think so," said Elodie.

"It's valuable training," Palenie said. "I think you'll be good at it."

"I'd rather not."

The bearded man hawked up a gobbet of saliva and spat it over his shoulder. "So, you want the crown?" he said.

"Yes," said Elodie, drawing herself up to her full height. "Of course. It's mine."

"And you really think Fessan can get it for you?"

Elodie realized that this must be the man she'd overheard complaining as she left camp. "Who says I want any of you fighting for me?"

"Hah! If it comes to battle, it's me you'll want in charge. Trust me, Princess."

A squat man seated at a grindstone nearby snorted. "Ah, shut up, Stown. No one wants to hear it." He was sharpening swords, and broke off long enough to jerk his hand in an obscene gesture.

Palenie was still looking at her. "Well, Princess?" she said. "Will you let me teach you?"

A hush descended as the watching assembly waited to hear her reply.

Stown hawked and spat again, then grinned at Elodie.

"You're a disgusting pig," she told him icily. "I wouldn't put you in charge of an outhouse, never mind a battle. And I can think of a thousand things I'd rather do than play fight here."

Palenie came toward her, her brown eyes wide with concern, but Elodie turned away. She marched into the trees, keeping her head held high. Shouts erupted behind her, along with a jeer she guessed must have been Stown. *Who cares what any of them think!* Nevertheless, her eyes were stinging. These people said they were fighting for her, but only Palenie actually seemed to like her. *And I bet it's just because Fessan told her to be nice,* she thought bitterly. Still, she knew someone who treated her properly.

The instant she passed into the Weeping Woods, she felt a welcome calmness descend. Even when the whispering began, she didn't mind as much as usual. It was better than being in the camp, at least.

The voices murmured around her as she picked her way through the thick bracken, ducked under reaching branches, and jumped over moss-filled gullies, all the while heading deeper and deeper into the woods.

Scrambling over a low ridge, Elodie found her way blocked by a large boulder. Had she come this way last time? She couldn't remember.

"Don't get lost, little one," hissed a voice in her ear.

"Be quiet," she snapped back.

Looking closer, she saw the obstacle wasn't a boulder at all but an ancient carriage. It was half-buried, almost completely covered in trailing ivy and pale patches of fungus. She could just make out a shattered wheel and some kind of armored cabin, a little like the turret of a castle. Sharpened spikes protruded from the turret's base. She'd never seen a vehicle like it before.

"Don't get too close," said a voice above her.

"I told you to go away," she replied.

"Who are you talking to?" said another voice.

Elodie groaned. "I said get lost!" She whirled around.

Samial was standing right behind her. He lifted his hands as if to take her wrists. But just as before, he stopped at the last moment and backed away.

"Who do you hear?" he said.

"Oh, it's you." Elodie smoothed down the front of her tunic, trying to sound nonchalant. In truth, she was overjoyed to have found him.

"Who do you hear?" Samial repeated.

"I don't hear anybody."

"Yes, you do. I heard you talking to them."

Elodie waved a hand. "Never mind that. I've had such a horrible morning, I can't even—"

"Who do you hear?"

Elodie stared at the boy. She'd walked out of the camp to get away from people demanding things of her.

"Who says I hear anything?" she said, frowning.

"Nobody says it. But you do. I know it."

"No, I . . ." The words melted away. Elodie had been hiding the voices for as long as she could remember, but now, looking at Samial's sweet, earnest face, for the first time in her life she couldn't think of a good reason to lie.

"I don't know who they are." Her voice sounded very small in the vastness of the woods. "But yes, I hear them."

A weight seemed to slide from her shoulders, like dropping a heavy shawl. Elodie passed her hand over her brow.

"I understand," Samial replied.

"Really?" A thought came to her. "Do ... do you hear them too?"

"All the time."

Amazement flooded through her. Little wonder she'd been so drawn to this boy.

"I've never met anyone like me before," Elodie said softly.

She reached her hand toward his, but he jerked away again, pulling back as if her fingers were hot irons.

"Samial," she said, puzzled. "What is it?"

His face clouded with sadness. "I'm not like you," he said. "Not really."

Elodie let her hand drop to her side. "What do you mean?"

Samial swallowed. He closed his eyes, as if he was struggling with something. But when he opened them again, he seemed to have shaken his sadness away. "Running away again so soon?" he asked.

The unexpected question made Elodie laugh. *So you don't want to talk about it. That's fine; I understand. Maybe another time.*

She sat down on a fallen willow trunk. "Running away?" she said. "Maybe. I don't know."

Samial sat at the opposite end of the trunk. Elodie looked at him seriously. She had trusted him with one secret; why not another?

"There's something else you should know about me," she began. "It's why Trident took me from my home."

Elodie told him everything then, pouring out all she'd experienced over the past two days, everything she'd learned about herself and about her destiny. Samial listened quietly as she told her tale.

"I'm just so sick of it," she concluded. "First the Vicerins wanted to put me on the throne, and now Trident wants to do the same. What about what I want? Am I just some puppet, like Fessan said? I certainly feel like people are just yanking my strings, whether I like it or not."

Samial was sitting quietly, clearly taking it in.

"Well?" Elodie asked. "What do you think I should do?"

"'In Toronia, realm of three,'" said Samial, "'a tempest has long raged.'"

"What?"

"The prophecy. I learned it long ago, when I was . . . when I was little. Have you never heard it?"

Elodie shook her head. Samial jumped up onto the trunk. His voice lifted among the trees as he recited:

> "'In Toronia, realm of three,
> A tempest has long raged.
> By power's potent siren call,
> Weak men are enslaved.

Too much virtuous blood has spilt
In this accursed age.
When the stars increase by three
The kingdom shall be saved.

Beneath these fresh celestial lights,
Three new heirs will enter in.
They shall summon unknown power,
They shall kill the cursed king.
With three crowns they shall ascend,
And true peace, they will bring.'"

"It's beautiful," said Elodie with a shiver. "And frightening too."

"It's about you," said Samial. "I knew there was something special about you."

She turned away. The voices that had plagued her were silent. All the Weeping Woods were silent, as if waiting for her to speak.

Somehow, in strange and subtle ways she couldn't begin to comprehend, the world seemed bigger than it had been before.

"I thought it was what I wanted," she said. "To be queen, I mean. But now . . ."

"It is who you are, Princess. You cannot change it."

"Why not? Why can't I just stay here with you, Samial?"

The boy sat down again. His sadness had returned. "The woods are cold. Colder than you know."

"I don't care. I already have to sleep on the ground. It can't be much worse."

"You would still be a princess."

"Then let me behave like one! My whole life, I've never decided anything for myself, other than what jewels match my dress or how I want the maid to do my hair. Shouldn't a princess get to decide what she wants?"

"What of the throne?"

"I don't know. This isn't how everything was supposed to happen." She shook her head. "If this is what taking the throne means, maybe I don't want it anymore."

Samial sighed, the sigh becoming a shudder that shook his wiry body from head to toe. Elodie couldn't tell if he was happy, or sad, or something else altogether.

"Very well," he said at last. "You may stay with me. But you must tell Trident."

As Elodie stepped out of the trees and back into the camp, she saw that the group of swordsmen had swelled to become an entire company. And they were arguing.

One voice in particular sounded loud over the clamor. Elodie recognized it at once: It was Stown.

"Why you?" the man was shouting. "Why not any of us? A commoner should earn his leadership by proving he is worthy, not because some old man said so!"

"And who would you say is worthy, Stown? Yourself?" That was Fessan, his voice less raucous than the other man's, but no less powerful.

"Perhaps! Why not? I'll fight any man who challenges me!"

"This morning a woman bested you!" Palenie's voice rang out above the others.

"It was a tie and you know it!" Stown replied.

Elodie threaded her way to the front of the crowd. Fessan and Palenie were standing together in an open space near the grindstone. Facing them were Stown and a small band of hulking, angry-looking men.

"I promised Melchior that I would lead Trident," Fessan said, "and I mean to keep my word. He rubbed the scar on the side of his face, his expression weary. "Besides, this isn't about you and me. It is about the prophecy."

Stown snorted. "The prophecy! Trident has been together for three years now, and what has the prophecy brought us? Nothing."

"I say it will bring us everything," said Fessan. "And I will fight to see it come true."

"It's not about fighting," said Palenie. Her sword was drawn, and she turned it over thoughtfully, the blade gleaming in the morning sun, which had just found its way through the clouds. "The prophecy's beyond that. Above it. Destiny will win, no matter what we do."

"Oh, right," scoffed Stown. "So we should just lie down and not do anything."

"That's not what I mean," said Palenie quietly. Her red hair shone like her sword.

Elodie dithered, trying to pick her moment to speak. Had anyone even noticed she was there? Well, they would prick up their ears soon enough when she announced that she was turning her back on them. Then all this debate would be meaningless.

"I say the prophecy will never come true," said Stown. "Didn't you hear what the scout said? The one just back from Idilliam. He said Brutan is dead, killed by his son Nynus. You hear that? No triplets. No destiny. Just a single son bent on vengeance for being locked up these ten years past. There's a new king on the throne in Toronia now." He threw his gaze around the watching crowd, where people were shifting their weight uneasily, muttering to each other. "Fessan is too cowardly to admit it, but it's obvious—the prophecy is dead!"

"No," said a voice. "It is not."

A silver horse trotted through the middle of the crowd. People fell back, staring up at the young blond woman riding on its back. Even before the horse had stopped, the woman had sprung lightly to the ground. Apart from her cry, she arrived in utter silence: Elodie heard neither the thump of hooves nor the jangle of her horse's reins.

Fessan's eyes were wide. "My lady! What are you doing here?"

"I bring news from Idilliam," said the stranger. The low morning sun bounced oddly against her angular features, so that her face seemed carved first from marble, then from glass. "I say to you that this man is both right and wrong."

She pointed a thin finger straight at Stown. The grizzled man flinched, then squared his shoulders, looking uncertain.

"King Brutan is dead," the woman went on, "just as this man claims. His son Nynus now sits on the throne. Another truth." She turned a full circle, sweeping the crowd with her gaze. When her eyes reached Elodie, the princess flinched, just like Stown. The woman's eyes moved on.

"Fessan . . . ?" Palenie began, looking quizzically at her leader.

"But here is the mistake," the woman said. "Nynus did not slay his father. The king was killed by another of his offspring. One of three."

A tingle ran down Elodie's spine. Her heart leaped into her throat. *One of three!*

Others in the crowd had made the connection too. Some of the onlookers began to murmur.

"The triplets live," the woman continued. "The prophecy will be fulfilled."

Elodie's heart was racing. *The prophecy is real.* The woman's words seemed to tangle around her, drawing her in.

"I seek Melchior," the woman said. "Wheels are turning, but if they are not steered straight, many will be crushed beneath them. Without Melchior's guidance, all may yet come to ruin."

"Why do you ask us, Limmoni?" said Fessan.

"Do you know where he is?" Limmoni replied.

"I am surprised you do not, since you are his apprentice."

"Apprentice? To a dead wizard?" said Stown.

"Dead?" said Limmoni, tilting her head at an unnatural angle. "Do you say so?"

"Everyone says so!"

Stown nocked an arrow into his bow and aimed it at Limmoni's chest. "Now, why don't you—?"

Before he could finish, Limmoni extended her hand again, not pointing this time but gesturing with her palm held flat. The air around her wrist seemed to *twist*, then a streak of bubbling white light shot from her hand to the point of Stown's bow. In an instant, the curved limb of yew wood flashed to pale powder. Stown snatched back his hand with a yelp, as if he'd been stung. The arrow clattered to the ground.

Elodie clapped her hand to her mouth. She knew about magic from books, but nobody in the kingdom had seen a living wizard for years. Magic was as dead as the swiftdragons of the north—everyone knew that. Yet this woman had wielded it before her eyes!

"Melchior is alive," said Limmoni, slowly lowering her hand.

"He is my master. Do not speak of what you don't know."

Elodie watched as Stown retreated to the safety of his companions. She clasped her hand around the jewel, trying to still the frantic beating of her heart. She looked at Limmoni, only to find the young woman—*the wizard!*—staring straight back at her, her violet eyes boring into Elodie's own.

She tried to look away, but couldn't.

Open your hand.

Elodie couldn't tell where the voice was coming from. It wasn't in her head, nor was it outside, like the voices she usually heard. It simply . . . *was.*

Show me.

Slowly, as if someone else were commanding them, Elodie's fingers opened. The jewel drew in the sunlight and fired it back out across the clearing in a kaleidoscope of flashing rays. The green light flooded Limmoni's face, which broke into a dazzling smile. Suddenly she was standing directly in front of Elodie, seizing her hands. The princess hadn't even seen her move.

"You!" Limmoni cried. "It's you!" She stroked Elodie's cheek, her hair. "Black eyes, just like your brother. Hair of red and gold. Hair like fire."

The crowd watched in silence, but their faces were a blur to Elodie. Limmoni's presence filled her attention completely, as if the two of them were the only people in the world.

"My brother?" Elodie said, her voice shaking. "You've seen him? You know him?"

For every question she asked, another tumbled through her head. *Which brother do you mean? Are they already together, waiting only for me?*

Limmoni brushed one fingertip over the jewel. It seemed to jump at her touch. "Never let this go, Princess. Like you, it is one of three."

"They . . . they have one too?" Elodie wanted to shout, to sob. Her whole body was trembling. Limmoni's hands were cool and strong on hers.

Limmoni nodded. "Three jewels for three crowns. One day, they will come together. And so will you."

What are they like? Are they like me?

"I have met only one of your brothers," said Limmoni. Had she heard Elodie's questions? Had Elodie even asked them out loud?

"What's his name?"

"Agulphus. But he calls himself Gulph."

Gulph. "Where is he?"

"He is safe. His life has been hard so far, but he is brave and true. Unlike you, he has only recently learned that he is a prince. For many years he lived among a band of traveling players. Now all that has changed." Her hands tightened on Elodie's. "Everything has changed."

"And the other one?"

Limmoni shook her head. "I do not know. I hope Trident will find him."

She released Elodie's hands. The world swam back into focus, crystallizing around her. Fessan was standing just behind Limmoni, his scarred face grim. How long had he been there?

"Our scouts continue to search the three kingdoms for him," said Fessan. "Are you here to join us, Limmoni?"

"As I said, it is Melchior I seek. Without him, all will be lost. That is my task. I can do nothing until he is among us again."

They bowed their heads in murmured conversation. Elodie stood back as the crowd closed around them. Her head ached, full of confusion.

Gulph. A hard life.

She thought of her childhood at Castle Vicerin. How had he fallen so low, when Elodie had risen so high? And what of their brother? Why was he lost?

Among the whirlwind in her head, one thought was clear.

I must find them. I have to.

It was as if a beacon had been lit inside her. Was that what Limmoni intended—to bind her to the prophecy and her fate? No matter. She needed her brothers and her every instinct told her they needed her.

With a start, Elodie realized something else. Samial was waiting for her in the Weeping Woods. She had come back to camp to say good-bye. But how could she leave Trident now?

CHAPTER 14

P ut your hands in the fire," said the king.

The two boys clung to each other, clearly terrified. They looked much younger than Gulph, though the bounty hunters who brought them claimed they were both thirteen, the same age as him. Their faces were drawn into identical masks of fear, and Gulph had no doubt they were twins.

Or, as Nynus believed, triplets.

"Seize their hands!" shouted Nynus.

The two legionnaires holding the boys looked with concern at Captain Ossilius, who was standing near the door of the throne room. The room was long and narrow, almost a corridor, with the Great Throne of Toronia dominating one end. Tall shutters hid the windows, blocking out the sun; the only light in this gloomy chamber came from the brazier that stood near the Great Throne.

The Great Throne was very different from the sculpted gold chair that resided in the banqueting hall. It was black and gnarled, a tangle of knotted wood and twisted boughs, like the roots of some ancient tree. The age-polished wood spiraled high into the air before curling over to form a spiky canopy.

Gulph didn't think he'd seen anything more soaked in antiquity than the Great Throne. Nor had he seen anything more unsettling than the snarling face of the boy who now sat on it. Standing here beside the throne, dressed in his fine courtier's clothes, Gulph could hardly believe this was the same meek boy he'd discovered in the Vault of Heaven.

Was Nynus truly his half brother? It didn't seem possible.

Gulph looked at the twin boys cowering before the throne, their scared faces lit by flames from the brazier. They were brothers too. Yet he could see that they loved each other. Wasn't that how it was supposed to be?

He transferred his gaze to Nynus, and felt nothing but horror.

The twins were the latest in a long line of unfortunate children brought here from across the kingdom. For days on end, child after child had been marched up the narrow throne room. By the time they reached Nynus's feet, most were crying. That was the purpose of the long walk: to remind the king's subjects of their place.

Nynus's strategy was simple: to root out every child who might be one of the surviving triplets. Given the size of the kingdom, Gulph thought it unlikely to succeed—thought it was madness, actually. Yet dread grew in the pit of his stomach that, sooner or later, a child would be brought to the throne with black eyes and red-gold hair.

A child who looked like him.

Nynus would look from the child to Gulph. His eyes would grow wide. He would make the connection.

And it would be Gulph's turn to put his hands into the flames.

So far, the children brought before the king had been quickly dismissed. Either they were too young or too old, or looked nothing like each other. But these boys were different.

"You are Idilliam born?" Nynus had asked when they'd first knelt before him.

The boys had nodded.

"Born on the night the three stars appeared?"

After exchanging a glance, the boys had nodded again. Nynus had leaned forward. The throne's canopy hung over him like the claws of some monstrous beast. On his head was the crown of Toronia: a polished gold ring etched with intricate runes.

The crown that, until a few days before, had been worn by Brutan. Their father.

"And you have a sister?" Nynus said.

Without consultation, both boys vigorously shook their heads.

Nynus sprang from the throne and started pacing, pale hands clasped behind his flowing robes. He walked only a short distance before turning and marching in the opposite direction, his feet marking out the dimensions of a room he'd only recently left behind.

The Black Cell.

"You lie," Nynus said. "You were born into the prophecy. Your sister is hidden, for fear of giving you away. But we will find her, have no fear of that. As for your mother, she was a witch. It follows that you both have the power of magic. This you will demonstrate for me now."

Gulph watched helplessly as the soldiers held the boys' hands toward the brazier.

"It is a simple test," said Nynus, his voice quavering on the edge of reason. "If you are the chosen ones, your powers will deflect the flames."

Gulph wanted to cry out, to tell Nynus that these were not the boys he was looking for. That he, Gulph, was the one. Yet he held back. Nynus had threatened children with this test many times already, but never actually gone through with it.

"Do it!" Nynus snarled.

There was a madness in his eyes that Gulph hadn't seen before: an empty light, like that of a dying star. Was this Brutan's legacy? The old king must have been insane to lock up his six-year-old son in the Vault of Heaven. Was Nynus crazy too?

Am I?

The thought horrified Gulph. He too was the son of Brutan.

The blood that flowed in Nynus's veins was inside him, too.

If I were king, is this what I would become?

His hand stole to the place at his throat where the green jewel hung, safely hidden behind his velvet collar. Its cool, hard presence reminded him that he wasn't alone with his secret. Limmoni knew his real identity, and was working even now to help him. But it was days since she'd left in search of Melchior, and still he'd heard nothing.

Despite Nynus's direct order, the legionnaires still held back. The young king stalked up to them, his eyes blazing.

"Do as I command," he growled, "or I will have you flogged!"

Their faces set like stone, the two men thrust the hands of the twins into the fire. Gulph cried out, but the screams of the boys drowned out every other sound in the throne room.

Captain Ossilius began to run toward the throne.

Nynus watched impassively as the flames licked around the twins' clutching fingers. Still screaming, the boys tried to pull away, but the soldiers held them fast. Gulph thought one of the boys was crying. Slowly, horribly, the smell of burned flesh began to fill the room.

"Enough!" Captain Ossilius, reaching the brazier, pulled the boys away from the fire. They fell to their knees, sobbing and pawing the air with their poor burned hands.

"What do you mean by this, Captain?" said Nynus with icy calm.

"The test was over," Ossilius replied. "If they had magic they would have used it immediately. There was no need for them to suffer further."

Nynus paced out the dimensions of his former cell a single time, returning to face the captain.

"You may be right," he said. "Then again, you may not. Until we have the sister, we cannot be sure. Take them to the Vault of Heaven. We will keep them there until the family is reunited."

"There is no sister!" Captain Ossilius ran clenched fingers through his gray hair. He was a tall man, towering over Nynus. Gulph almost expected the captain to strike the young king.

"You forget your place, Captain Ossilius," Nynus intoned.

"These children are innocent! Show them a little mercy! You of all people know the horror of imprisonment."

Gulph couldn't take his eyes off the wailing boys. "Nynus," he said, touching the king's arm, "don't you think you should—?"

Nynus threw Gulph aside and lunged for Ossilius, grabbing his captain's badge and ripping it from his uniform. The legionnaires gasped. Ossilius didn't flinch.

"My mother will hear of this," said Nynus.

The crown tilted on his head. Nynus nudged it back into place, his pale face flushing slightly. The threat he'd made was absurd, coming from the mouth of a king.

Then again, given what Gulph knew of the Dowager Queen Magritt, perhaps it wasn't.

Captain Ossilius stood impassively, his face an unmoving mask, as Nynus summoned more men from his Legion. At the king's command, the captain's wrists were locked in iron manacles; more manacles hobbled his ankles.

You can't do that! thought Gulph, balling his hands into fists.

But of course, Nynus could.

As Nynus gave the order to take Ossilius to the Vault of Heaven, the captain's eyes found Gulph's, and held them. Startled by the intensity of his gaze, Gulph looked away.

Does he know?

As soon as Captain Ossilius had been led away, Nynus returned to his throne. His white face was furious. He gnawed at his finger-nails. His heels beat a tattoo against the ancient foot rest. The soldiers, still holding the sobbing twins, shifted uneasily on their feet, looking to Gulph in the hope he might know what to do next.

"King Nynus," said Gulph. "Shall I . . . ?"

"Take them away," said Nynus with a listless wave of his hand. "Take them to the Vault of Heaven. Do not trouble me further today."

The legionnaires looked relieved to be making their exit. When they'd gone, Gulph approached the throne. His mouth was dry. Nynus's behavior was so unpredictable these days. There was no telling how he might respond to even the most innocent request.

What Gulph was about to ask was far from innocent.

"Will you permit me to escort the prisoners?" he said, licking his lips. "It would be a great honor. They are such a valuable prize."

Nynus said nothing, merely waved his hand again. Good enough. Gulph hurried after the legionnaires, catching them in the corridor beyond the throne room.

"There's been a mistake," he said, trying desperately to make himself sound authoritative. "These are not the children we seek. They're to be released into my custody at once."

"I'm not sure," said the first legionnaires.

"We should check," said the second.

"Certainly you may check," said Gulph. "By all means return to the king and tell him you doubt the word of his chief courtier."

The soldiers stared first at each other, then back at Gulph. In perfect unison, their shoulders slumped.

"Take them," said the first legionnaire.

"I'm not going back in there," muttered the second.

The legionnaires left, leaving the whimpering twins alone with Gulph. They stared at him fearfully, their blistered hands clutched to their chests.

"You're safe now," Gulph said gently. "But you have to keep quiet, and we have to move fast. Do you understand?"

The boys nodded dumbly.

Gulph led them through the maze of narrow service corridors

that ran parallel to the main castle passageways, hoping they wouldn't meet anyone along the way. Luck was with them, and soon they were at one of the outer doors. Directly opposite, across a busy courtyard, the main castle gate stood open.

Gulph watched as an endless stream of horse-drawn carts trundled through the gate. Those leaving the castle were piled high with sacks and barrels. The previous day, Gulph had overheard the kitchen staff discussing the campaign being fought by the king's soldiers against rebel landowners in Ritherlee; he guessed this supply train was meant for them.

The Thousand Year War, he thought as he watched the long line of vehicles trundling out of the castle. *Has it really lasted as long as they say?*

The arriving carts were empty. Many were damaged, hacked by swords or studded with arrows. The horses pulling them looked weary and were foamed with sweat.

Everything's going out. Gulph looked at the tired, hungry faces of the Toronian citizens who'd gathered to watch the parade. *And nothing's coming in.*

"Go through the gate with them," he said to the boys, picking out a line of smiths and farriers walking alongside one of the departing wagons. Several young boys—their short aprons marking them out as apprentice blacksmiths—hurried behind them. "After that, you'll have to find your own way. I'm sorry. I wish there was more I could do."

"You done lots, sir," said one of the twins.

"Thank you," said the other.

Gulph held his breath as they made their escape, scuttling behind the smiths in the shadow of a hay cart. When he could see them no longer, he returned to the castle keep. He'd thought he would feel relieved, but he didn't.

Glancing up, he saw a window, high above. A woman stood there, looking down.

Magritt.

Gulph hurried inside. Had she been looking at him? Had she seen what he'd done?

Gulph spent the rest of the day waiting for a gloved hand to clamp down on his shoulder, and for a soldier from the King's Legion to march him first before the king, then back to the Vault of Heaven. Perhaps he would be put in a cell with Captain Ossilius. They would have a lot to talk about.

But nothing happened. Gulph busied himself with his duties; as chief courtier he was expected to make three security inspections a day (though never actually to make any changes to the watch), to cast his eye over the many letters that came in and out of the keep (though not actually to answer any of them), and to attend to the king whenever required. His responsibilities were vague at best, and Gulph had most of the day to himself. So one afternoon, once he had filed the unanswered letters in the castle scroll room, Gulph had rummaged through the moldering parchments, eager to find whatever he could about his fate. Finally, he'd opened a gossamer-thin scroll to reveal the prophecy written down in a faded hand. A possible future outlined in ink and paper . . . Was it really true? For now, all he could do was wait until Magritt and Nynus decided what to do with him. It was as if, now that they'd elevated him to court, they didn't know what his role should be.

Or as if they were simply biding their time.

Waiting for the chance to get rid of me.

At nightfall, Gulph made his usual circuit of the castle grounds. When he'd finished, he kept walking. The sky was black as velvet, the stars crisp and clean. Directly overhead, brightest of all, shone three stars in a perfect triangular constellation. The prophecy constellation. One green star, one red, one gold. Gulph walked with his head tilted back, fascinated by the blazing trio.

Which star am I?

The packed earth under his feet turned to smooth stone. Bringing his gaze from the heavens, he looked down at the Royal Mausoleum. This great stone building had been constructed on the very edge of the vast chasm separating Idilliam from Isur.

Thick pillars jutted at an angle from the canyon wall, supporting a circular platform on which the main structure stood. Its walls were solid granite; its roof was domed. Between carved pillars was set a heavy iron door.

Nearby was the Idilliam Bridge, a huge finger of rock extending from the city wall and stretching all the way across the chasm. The bridge was the only way in and out of the city. When he'd built the mausoleum, Brutan must have known the building would be the first thing visitors would see as they crossed the great span of stone to enter the royal capital.

So vain, Gulph thought.

A flock of crows was circling the mausoleum. Every so often, one of the birds landed on the roof to pick at what was lying there. Gulph didn't want to look, but he couldn't help himself.

The thing on the roof was Brutan's body.

Gulph watched as the crows pecked at the old king's corpse. It had been Nynus's decision to pin the body to the roof instead of placing it inside. That had been three days ago; already Brutan's remains were rich with stink and squirming with maggots.

Gulph's dinner surged up from his stomach. He turned aside, convinced he was going to throw up. Somehow he kept it down. As he straightened, the thing he'd been dreading all day finally happened.

"Here you are, Gulph." A hand closed on his shoulder. "I've been looking for you everywhere. Where have you been?"

Swallowing down bile, Gulph turned to face Nynus.

"I've being doing my duty, Your Majesty," he said.

Grinning, Nynus slapped his arm. "We're friends, aren't we? Call me Nynus!"

"Yes, Nynus."

Nynus plucked a napkin from a pouch at his belt and handed it to Gulph. "Here. You look a little green. Must be the stench from that animal on the roof!"

"Thank you, Nynus." Gulph pressed the napkin to his mouth, grateful for the chance to hide his expression. "What can I do for you?"

"You can listen—that's what you can do. I've had the most wonderful idea, and I simply had to tell someone." Nynus walked to the edge of the chasm and spread his arms. "This! This is the future!"

Gulph stared at Nynus's back. *Just one push. That's all it would take.* Given Nynus's cruel treatment of the two boys, it was what he deserved. And it would be so easy. After all, when you've killed one king, what difference does another one make?

Gulph took a deliberate step back, shocked by his own thoughts.

"The future?" he said. "I don't understand."

"This chasm is our greatest asset. It keeps our enemies at bay. Even now, Isur is filled with rebel traitors plotting to bring me down. And that's only one small part of it. The western baronies have fallen to some warlord they call The Hammer; the feuding families of the Isle of Bones have finally united, and say they want to break away from Toronia; and barbarian tribes are massing in the foothills of the Unpassable Mountains. Traitors, the lot of them."

"The Thousand Year War continues," agreed Gulph, unsure of where this was going.

"Then there's Ritherlee. Today I heard from my spies that Lord Vicerin's army has called in the laborers from the fields and handed them swords instead of plowshares. His army is doubled in size; soon it will march on Idilliam itself."

"Idilliam is well defended."

"Not well enough."

"What about the chasm?" Gulph glanced at the abyss into which he'd so nearly pushed his brother.

"It's effective. Better than an ordinary moat—there's no water to swim across!" Nynus laughed—a little shrieking sound that rasped against Gulph's ears. "But it isn't perfect."

"What's the problem?"

Nynus pointed past the mausoleum, past the swooping crows, past the rotting remains of his murdered father. Pointed straight at the Idilliam Bridge.

"That."

"The bridge?" Gulph couldn't believe what he was hearing. "What are you saying, Nynus?"

"I'm saying it has to go."

"Go? You mean . . . destroy it?"

"Yes."

Gulph stared at the ribbon of rock connecting Idilliam to Isur and beyond. He'd looked out on the Idilliam Bridge from the Black Cell, yearning for the clear passage it promised from the royal city, out to the rest of the kingdom. It was the single, vital route by which supplies were brought into the city. By destroying it, Nynus would instantly place Idilliam under siege.

Before long, the city would starve.

And I will be trapped here with Nynus and Magritt.

Nynus spun around, laughing. In that moment, his pale face bright under the light of the prophecy stars, he looked utterly insane.

CHAPTER 15

Ritherlee was overwhelming. If Tarlan had been a bird, he'd have swooped in drunken delight, basking in the heat of the sun, inhaling the myriad scents of flower and herb, and gazing down on field after field of windblown crops. It was warm and rich and vibrant, truly a land of plenty.

"It's so different from Yalasti," he said in Theeta's ear. "Different from . . . from anything I've ever seen!"

"Green," replied the thorrod.

"Yes." Tarlan laughed. "It's green all right!"

Beneath his cloak, Filos shifted her weight. Tarlan's laughter died as he stroked the tigron cub. He was worried about her: She'd said nothing since they'd left the Icy Wastes—hadn't so much as growled. The black leaf he'd applied to her wound had flaked away, revealing an angry-looking gash of red.

Tarlan felt in his pouch, hoping he might still have some shreds of the precious medicine. But the black leaf was all gone. During the fight with the Wastelanders, Nasheen had been slashed across the breast, and feathers had been torn from her left wing. Tarlan had used the last of the black leaf to soothe her pain, ignoring the increasing ache from his own injured left arm. But Nasheen's wings were beginning to labor, and she was clearly suffering. Tarlan didn't think she'd be able to stay in the air much longer. Though she made no complaint, Theeta was clearly exhausted, and even Kitheen's strong wings were beginning to falter.

As pack leader, it was up to Tarlan to make a decision.

"We're going to land," he announced. "We all need rest, and Nasheen and Filos need help."

The three birds dipped their heads wearily.

"Rest," said Theeta.

"Help," said Nasheen.

A line of low hills rose ahead. Beyond it, plumes of smoke towered into the air: There must be a village, Tarlan supposed. He could also see the tops of trees crowding the skyline. If there was a forest, his pack could hide while he scouted for help.

And after that, their search for Melchior could begin.

To Tarlan's dismay, as they crested the hills, he saw the smoke was coming from burning buildings. There was a village all right . . .

but it was on fire. People ran across the open ground between flaming barns and homesteads, shouting and screaming. Some carried pails of water; others carried farm tools, waving them as if they were weapons.

They were low now, committed to their approach. Nasheen's eyes flickered shut, then opened, then closed again.

"Nasheen!" shouted Tarlan. "Head for the trees!"

The little flock of thorrods made a clumsy turn over the ravaged village. A few frightened faces turned up to look at the huge birds, but most people were too concerned with fighting the fires.

The forest Tarlan had anticipated turned out to be just a ragged copse. Still, it would give them shelter and a chance to stay out of the sight of humans. They landed hard at the tree line and stumbled together under a thin canopy of oak and birch. As soon as they were in the shade, Nasheen slumped awkwardly, her chest shuddering as she struggled to breathe. Theeta nuzzled her; behind them, Kitheen was forcing his way through the trees toward a small stream running down from the hillside.

Sliding off Theeta's back, Tarlan nestled Filos into a clump of ferns and covered her with his black cloak. He checked she was still breathing and that her wound wasn't bleeding. Then he stood back. There was nothing more he could do for her.

He stared into the thicket. It was a poor place to hide. If Mirith were here, she would no doubt have been able to dig up all the curative herbs they needed. If only he'd paid more attention to her lessons! What was it she'd used to soothe tired limbs? Something with ground-up bones? Well, there were no bones around here and, even if there were, Tarlan wouldn't know what to do with them.

"We need help," he said.

"Help," croaked Nasheen without opening her eyes. Kitheen, having returned from the stream, spilled the water he'd carried in his beak down her throat.

Tarlan gazed at the burning village. He could just make out the heads of the people as they dashed around, trying to save their homes.

"We need help," he said again, quietly and to himself.

Theeta nudged him with one golden wing. "Theeta comes," she said.

"Yes," said Tarlan. "I think I might need you."

Side by side, they crossed the field separating the trees from the village. Tarlan kept his good hand on his bow and tried to forget about the pain in his left shoulder. Did he even have the strength to draw an arrow? He didn't know.

One of the barns on the outskirts of the settlement was still intact. A battle was raging before it: Villagers armed with rakes and scythes tried to defend their homes against soldiers wearing blue sashes over chain mail. It looked like a very uneven contest.

"What do you think, Theeta?" said Tarlan. "Should we get involved?"

"On," the thorrod replied.

Tarlan grabbed her feathers and swung himself onto her back. Spreading her wings, Theeta accelerated toward the barn, flying so low that her talons raked a furrow in the grass. As they neared the two opposing forces, she steered a little to the right, aiming herself at the soldiers.

"How do you know they're the enemy?" said Tarlan.

"Took child," said Theeta.

The faces of the combatants turned toward Tarlan and Theeta. One of the soldiers cried out and dropped the little girl he'd been carrying. Grim-faced, his comrades backed away from the farmers and formed a hasty wall against the oncoming thorrod. A woman rushed forward and scooped her up.

"Look out!" said Tarlan, as two of the soldiers lifted spears. "Go left!"

Theeta changed direction at once, her pounding wings raising clouds of dust from the yard in front of the barn. As the soldiers retreated farther, coughing and spluttering, Tarlan steered the thorrod directly into their midst and waited for her claws to come out.

But they didn't. Theeta was flying so low, and so fast, that her momentum alone knocked the soldiers aside, just as Tarlan might have scattered a line of wooden pegs with a thrown rock.

Hardly had the soldiers picked themselves up than the villagers, sensing an advantage, pressed forward with their attack. Dazed and confused, the enemy started to re-form their ranks.

As soon as they saw the thorrod lining up for a second attack, the soldiers dropped their weapons and fled. A ragged cheer rose from the villagers as Tarlan brought Theeta in to land in the meadow beyond the barnyard.

No sooner had they touched down than the woman whose child they'd saved rushed up to them.

"Thank you," she cried. Still cradling her little girl, she looked up in awe at the thorrod. "Did Lady Darrand send you to save us?"

"Uh, no," said Tarlan, untangling the complex speech of the woman. Without Mirith to talk to, he was out of practice. Animal languages were so much more straightforward. "I don't know who Lady Darrand is. I don't know anything about what's going on here. I just need—"

A trumpeting horn cut off his words. With a thunder of wheels and hooves, a chariot drawn by two white horses burst from behind the barn. Running behind it was a troop of twelve men wearing brown leather armor and carrying broadswords. Driving the chariot was a woman clad in metal armor. Where it wasn't splattered with mud, it shone as bright as silver under the Ritherlee sun.

The woman cracked a whip, urging the horses across the field to where Tarlan and Theeta stood. As the chariot skidded to a halt, she pulled off her helm. Black hair spilled down her back.

"I am Lady Sora Darrand," she said. Like the other woman, her gaze was fixed not on Tarlan but on his giant winged companion. "This village is under the protection of my family. State your business here."

"I have no business," said Tarlan. "I just want help."

Lady Darrand raised one black eyebrow. "Indeed? And yet help is what you have given. Is that not right, Amalie?"

The woman with the child nodded.

"What's going on here?" said Tarlan. Now that the attacking soldiers had departed, the villagers dropped their weapons. A man opened a faucet set in a wall and people ran to it with buckets, bowls, and barrels, filling them with water and sloshing it over the flames.

Lady Darrand pursed her lips. Tarlan felt her eyes scrutinizing him. Judging him. At last she spoke.

"This land is mine. It has been in my family for generations. For all that time we have lived in peace with our neighbors, the Vicerins. Ever since we played together as children, Lord Vicerin and I have been friends. We fought together as allies against the corrupt crown."

It meant nothing to Tarlan. Lords and ladies? Battles against the crown? None of it interested him at all, but Lady Darrand was looking at him expectantly, waiting for a response.

"Oh. So what went wrong?"

"For a young man who knows nothing of our affairs, you seem astute."

Tarlan shrugged. "I've got eyes. I can see that something bad happened here."

"Something bad. Yes. A few days ago, Lord Vicerin's daughter was kidnapped. Now his army is on the rampage, seizing land, killing livestock. Villages are being burned to the ground." Lady Darrand's expression grew hard. "And he is taking our children."

It made no sense to Tarlan. "Revenge?" he hazarded.

"No," said Lady Darrand. "Bargaining power."

"I don't understand."

"It is complicated." A shadow fell over her face. "Two days ago, my own daughter was snatched from her sleep. My own dear little Sorelle . . ."

For the first time, Tarlan found himself interested in what this woman had to say. He had no time for armies and kingdoms. But he knew what it was to be a child alone in the world.

"I'm sorry," he said.

Lady Darrand shook herself. Stern as her face was, her eyes sparkled too.

"This is a thorrod, is it not?" she said, looking up.

"Her name is Theeta."

"And your name?"

He hesitated before answering. "Tarlan."

"Such a beast would be a great advantage in battle."

"I suppose so." Something about this woman's strength reminded Tarlan of Mirith, yet he knew he had to be cautious. The little he'd seen of other humans had taught him that much.

"You say you need help. I will give you that help, if I can."

At last Tarlan understood what she was saying. "In return, you want us to fight for you."

Lady Darrand raised her eyebrow again and smiled. "As I said: astute."

Tarlan looked up at Theeta. She returned his gaze. His thorrod friend would do whatever he asked, he knew that—as would the rest of his pack.

But is it something I should ask of them?

"Do you need time to think?" said Lady Darrand.

Tarlan thought of Nasheen, suffering under the trees. He thought of Filos, who was perhaps dying. He felt the heat in his own injured arm, spreading slowly with the ache through the rest of his body.

"No," he said. "We'll help you, but you have to help us first. I have three other companions. They're just over there, in the woods. We need a healer. We've had . . . a long ordeal. Make us well, and we'll do whatever you ask."

"Your companions," said Lady Darrand, her eyes narrowing. "Are they warriors?"

"Two are thorrods." Tarlan enjoyed seeing the expression of wonder overtake her face. "The other is a tigron. She's young, but her claws are sharp." He squared his shoulders. "They are all loyal to me. They will do whatever I ask."

"They obey you?" Her surprise was evident in her expression.

"I talk to them."

She stared at him for a long time before finally summoning one of her soldiers. They conferred, then he trotted away, returning moments later with an old man. The man was so laden with packs and pouches that he resembled a walking market stall.

"My lady?" he said in a hoarse, dry voice.

"Caraway, go with this young man. Do what you can to help him and his . . . companions."

The old man bowed low. "Many of your men lie injured, my lady. Are you sure this is what you want?"

"I am sure, Caraway. Now stop wasting time and do as you are told!"

The old man flinched under the sharpness of her tongue. Lady Darrand nodded at Tarlan in dismissal, but he wasn't finished.

"This is not our war, Lady Darrand. We'll help remove the threat to this village, but that's all. As soon as your people are safe, we're leaving. Do you understand?"

Lady Darrand looked taken aback. Tarlan imagined she wasn't used to being given orders—but then, neither was he. For a moment, he thought she'd refuse. Then she stepped down from her chariot and offered him her hand. "I accept your terms, thorrod rider," she said.

Tarlan shook it.

"Lead the way, young man," said Caraway.

"I can do better than that," replied Tarlan.

Despite her exhaustion, Theeta made no complaint when both Tarlan and the healer settled onto her back. It was a short flight back to the copse, during which Caraway clung tightly to Theeta's feathers and kept his mouth shut in a thin line. In the far distance, Tarlan could see the blue sashes of the Vicerin army massing for another attack. This wasn't over yet.

As they stepped under the trees, Kitheen lunged out of the shadows, his golden beak wide, the black feathers on his breast standing erect. The old man drew back fearfully, scattering his bags on the ground.

"Easy, Kitheen!" Tarlan soothed. "Easy, everyone. He means you no harm."

Kitheen folded his wings, almost knocking the old man over.

"It's not me doing the harm I'm worried about," grumbled Caraway, eyeing the three thorrods and the cub.

Tarlan smothered a grin as he helped gather the fallen bags. Caraway opened them up and, despite his shaking hands, quickly mixed together a bewildering array of herbs and ointments. Tarlan watched in fascination. For Mirith, the art of healing had been a slow, sacred ritual. He supposed the fighting had given Caraway practiced speed.

"You first," said the old man, standing suddenly with a clay bowl in his wrinkled hands. "It's your left arm, if I'm not mistaken."

Surprised, Tarlan eased his tunic away from his shoulder. "How did you know?"

"I wouldn't be much of a healer if I didn't."

Caraway smeared a foul-smelling poultice onto Tarlan's wound. It was warm and unspeakably slimy but, within a few breaths, he felt the pain subside. The effect was so sudden, and so complete, that he couldn't help but think of Mirith again. Of witchcraft.

Of magic.

"Have you ever heard of a man called Melchior?" he said. At once he cursed himself. It was one thing seeking a wizard, quite another blurting out his name to a stranger.

"Melchior?" said the healer. He was leaning over Filos, his long fingers hesitantly exploring her injuries. "You mean the wizard? Yes, of course I've heard of him. Who hasn't?"

"Is he famous?"

"I suppose you could say that." Caraway began rubbing ointment into the tigron's flank. Almost immediately, the little cub started to purr.

"Does he live around here?" Tarlan could feel the jewel pressing into his chest, as if urging him on. Was Melchior really going to be this easy to find?

"Why do you want to know?" Caraway's eyes were keen and searching.

Tarlan shrugged. "Just curious." He stroked Filos's head.

"Mmm. Well, it's common knowledge. Melchior died years ago. His was the last magic in the world, you know. It's all gone now. All of it."

The healer's words hit Tarlan like a landslide. All the breath rushed from his body, leaving his chest tight and his mind numb.

What am I supposed to do now?

It was over. The mission he'd embarked on had proved a fool's errand. There were no wizards, and the jewel he carried was just a cold green stone, a memory of Mirith. There was no destiny waiting for him. He was just Tarlan.

Apparently unaware of the impact his words had had, Caraway turned from Filos to Nasheen. He looked very small against the huge bulk of the unconscious thorrod.

Tarlan forced himself to breathe again. To his amazement, the shock was replaced with relief. He grieved Mirith bitterly, but he was no longer bound by the path she had set for him. He was free to do as he pleased—and he already knew what that was. Once he had paid his debt to Lady Darrand, he would find somewhere safe to live with his pack, far from humans.

What more could I want? he thought.

CHAPTER 16

W e cannot wait for Melchior," said Fessan.

Elodie had lost count of how many times he'd said this. It was an argument he'd been pressing all afternoon as the debate went on in the Trident camp. Many agreed with him. But not all.

She looked at Stown, certain he would trot out his own familiar point of view. He didn't disappoint her.

"What if Limmoni finds the wizard?" Stown demanded. "You saw the look on her face when she left. I swear that girl knows where he is."

"Limmoni is determined," Fessan agreed. "But she works magic, not miracles."

"We need his guidance," said an old woman.

"We will make do without it." Fessan stood, his fists clenched.

Elodie rose from the crude wooden stool on which she'd been perched. This wasn't going anywhere and it was driving her mad. She might as well take one more walk around the clearing before the sun finally disappeared behind the trees. It might clear her head.

Palenie laid a concerned hand on her arm. "Princess, are you all right?"

"You've been on the move all afternoon, Elodie," said Fessan. "Are you staying or going? You might as well decide."

His question startled Elodie. Stay or go? Did he mean the meeting? Or Trident itself?

"I don't know," she said, picking at the hem of the uncomfortable green tunic.

"Won't she just sit down?" grumbled Stown. "It's wearing me out just watching her."

Elodie realized that in fact everyone was watching her—the whole of Trident, crowded around in a rough circle in the center of the clearing. Fessan sat among them, just another face in the throng. The only person who wasn't staring at her was the blond young man beside Fessan—Rotho, who had joined Trident just that morning. His eyes flickered around the meeting and Elodie wondered if he was as confused by what was happening as she felt.

"Very well," she said stiffly, sitting on the stool again. She glanced at Fessan. "I'll stay. But I still don't know what to do."

"Well," said Fessan, "you are in the right place. Please help us decide."

"We're not deciding anything," grumbled Stown under his breath.

Ignoring him, Fessan went on, speaking once more to the crowd at large. "Do you not see? The time is right. Limmoni said one of the triplets is already in Idilliam—in the castle itself, no less. The second"—he gestured toward Elodie—"is here among us. If we march now, we can bring two of the three together before the moon is full."

"What of the third child?" said a man.

"He will be found. He *must* be found. Regardless of that, the first triplet—Agulphus—needs our support. He is in the tigron's den, in danger as long as he draws breath. We have to go."

Stown snorted. "You really think now's the time to go against the crown? Think we're ready to go up against the entire King's Legion?"

"My father is there," said Fessan. "And he is not alone."

Elodie groaned as the bickering voices flew back and forth. Before, when she'd heard Fessan and the other members of Trident arguing, it had infuriated her as she'd felt so remote and far from home. Now it was because she desperately cared about the outcome.

Thin clouds parted, revealing three stars flickering in the twilight sky. Elodie gazed up at them, struck by how close they seemed. Not stars at all, but bright jewels hanging just out of reach.

All I have to do is stretch up, and they will be mine.

"There," said Fessan, standing and pointing at the sky. "Do you not see the prophecy stars?"

Elodie shivered. It was as if he'd been listening to her thoughts.

"So what?" said Stown.

"They are the proof!" Fessan's normally calm demeanor was cracking. Elodie could hear the passion in his voice. The scar on his face twitched. She wondered how he'd got it. Was it fighting for Trident—for her and her brothers?

"Can you not see it?" Fessan was striding in front of the crowd now. "The wheels are turning. All the pieces of this great puzzle are coming together. This is happening. It is happening *now*!"

"Fine words," grunted Stown. "But the truth is that Melchior's abandoned us. Fessan thinks he can command Trident, but he can't even command the spoiled brat he's saddled us with for a princess."

Fessan's face clouded with rage. "How dare you insult your future queen? On your knees, Stown, and beg forgiveness!"

Stown just spat on the ground.

That did it. Elodie rose once more from the stool. A hush descended as she stepped into the middle of the circle. She felt suddenly taller, just that little bit closer to the watching stars.

"Stown is right," she said. Fessan frowned. Stown's face creased into a sneer. "I was like that. When I first arrived here, I was spoiled and ungrateful. I'm sorry."

"More words," said Stown. "If I were you, little girl—"

"Princess," corrected Elodie. "Now be quiet while I speak."

The burly man looked furious, but closed his mouth all the same.

"Since I've been here," Elodie went on, "I've learned a lot about myself. I've learned that until now I've lived in a very small world. I've learned that I have two brothers, and that I want them by my side more than anything—even on the throne."

She walked across the circle to Fessan, who immediately dropped to one knee. Elodie's spine tingled. "One of my brothers is in Idilliam," she said, looking down at Fessan's upturned face, "probably in danger. I say we march to be by his side."

A murmur rippled through the crowd. Fessan stood again. His eyes were shining.

"Are there any who doubt that our queen is among us?" he shouted.

The murmur became a rumble.

"She says she will march to Idilliam!" Fessan went on.

The rumble became a roar. Rotho leaped up, his hands raised in applause, and the others followed.

"Let us draw our own courage!" Fessan cried. "I say it is not

Elodie who will march with us! It is we who will march with her!"

The combined voices of Trident crashed against Elodie like waves against the shore. It was more than a roar; it was a storm.

A storm for her.

We're coming for you, Gulph, she thought, gazing around at the cheering faces. *We're coming.*

The whole camp was in an uproar. Tents were torn down, supplies were packed into sacks and crates, horses were harnessed, fires were dampened. Fessan was everywhere, supervising the preparations for departure. Whenever he passed Elodie, he gave her a smile that seemed to say he'd always known he was right to believe in her. *I hope I don't let him down*, she thought.

Not quite knowing what to do, Elodie returned to her tent, only to find Palenie in the process of rolling up the canvas and packing away the poles.

"Can I help?" said Elodie.

"Oh, it's all right," Palenie replied, tossing her bearskin cloak onto the pile. "That's the last of it. We'll be on the road before the moon's up."

Elodie nodded. Everything was happening so quickly, and she was the one who'd triggered this avalanche of activity. It was overwhelming.

Palenie stepped over to her. "It's going to be all right." She smiled. "You were wonderful earlier. You sounded like a queen."

Elodie grinned back. "Really?"

"Really, Princess. You should have seen Stown's face. He looked like he'd swallowed something rotten."

The two girls laughed. Elodie felt warmth rising inside her, and she realized it was the first time she'd felt happy since she'd left Ritherlee. The only other person who'd made her laugh was Samial.

Samial.

"There's something I've got to do," Elodie said. "I won't be long!"

Leaving the tent, she hurried toward the Weeping Woods.

He'll come with me, she thought. *He has to.*

On the way, she passed Rotho, who was busy piling spears into a low wagon. When he saw Elodie, he put down the spear he was holding and strode over. He was lean, his shoulders broad, and the breastplate he wore gleamed in the late-afternoon sun. From his waist hung a slender blade.

"Princess," said Rotho, sweeping into an elegant bow.

He looks like a knight, Elodie thought. Perhaps Trident wasn't as ragtag as she'd first believed.

"When I heard that one of the three was fighting alongside Trident, I could hardly believe it," Rotho said. "But your speech left me in no doubt. I am honored to follow you, Princess, wherever you may lead." He drew his sword and knelt, laying the blade flat upon both palms. He held it up to Elodie. "My sword is yours."

Pride flooded Elodie. Palenie had said that everything would be all right, and maybe it was true. After all, if young warriors like Rotho believed in her, surely others would follow? Having both him and Samial at her side would ease the long road toward her brothers and the crown.

"I thank you," Elodie told him. "The honor is mine."

Rotho bowed his head once more. As he rose to his feet, Elodie hurried off toward the trees. When she glanced back, she saw that Rotho was still watching her. He raised a hand, then turned back to the wagon.

In the woods it was already dark. Elodie didn't care. After tonight, she wouldn't have to visit this fearful place again. Even the voices didn't upset her, whispering away at the edge of her awareness. Soon she and Samial would be gone from here, on the road to Idilliam. She plunged on through the undergrowth, shouting Samial's name.

When she reached the glade where they'd first met, she stopped. The prophecy stars cast their baleful light down into the tiny clearing. High in the trees, someone was sobbing.

"Samial?"

No reply. Just the murmur of the voices only she could hear.

She corrected herself: the voices she and Samial could hear.

She ran on, her hands pressing back the clutching needles of pine trees. *Down this gully, over this cluster of roots, through this screen of willow....*

She stopped. Directly in front of her, the air was shimmering. A shadow formed out of the darkness, black on black. It flowed briefly, a slick of oil suspended between the ground and the sky. Finally it melted into the shape of a boy.

Samial.

Elodie backed away, the breath leaving her mouth in short, silent bursts. Her heart thudded. What had she just seen?

It's the shadows, that's all, she told herself. *A trick of the dark.* But why then was dread tugging at her heart?

"What did you say?" said Samial, stepping forward.

She seized the jewel so tightly she nearly pulled it from its chain. "Nothing," she gasped. "You just took me by surprise."

He frowned. "You are upset? Why?"

Elodie gulped, telling herself not to be so silly. He'd just been hiding, that was all. He must have been.

"I'm going," she said shakily. "I mean, Trident is going, and I'm going with them."

"Oh." The boy's expression was unreadable. "You made your decision then, Princess."

"Yes, and I want you to come with me. With us." Elodie extended her hands. As he always did, Samial shrank away from her touch.

Why does he do that?

"I cannot leave Sir Jaken."

"We're marching to Idilliam. My brother's there and . . . Please, Samial. Trident supports me, and Palenie is my friend, but you're the only one who really understands. . . . I don't want to go without you."

"You must."

She reached for him again, but he retreated farther into the shadows. The darkness seemed to envelop him, as if he were somehow part of it.

It's just the dark, she told herself again.

But a shiver ran through her and she sat heavily on a moss-covered stump.

"There's probably going to be a battle," she said bitterly. "I've never even been near a battle. How am I supposed to know what to do?"

"You will know," said Samial.

"That's easy for you to say! You have trained for war. I thought you'd help me, but now all you want to do is skulk about these stupid woods with some stupid knight who—"

A branch snapped behind her. Elodie jumped to her feet, whirling around in fright. Her first thought was that she'd see

Stown bearing down on her. To her relief, it was Palenie.

"Who are you talking to?" Palenie said, stooping as she picked her way between the willows.

There was no point lying. "His name's Samial." Elodie turned back to her friend.

But Samial wasn't there. In his place, slowly dissolving into the empty air, was a dark cloud in the crude shape of a boy. Just before it disappeared altogether, the two pale circles of his eyes flashed once, then faded to nothing.

"A ghost!" Palenie gasped. "Look there, the trees moved!" For the first time since they'd met, Elodie saw fear in her face.

"No, he's here," Elodie cried. "He has to be. . . ." Horrified, she ran through the deserted clearing, trying to pick out Samial's fleeing form among the trees. But he was nowhere to be seen.

Deep down, in her gut, she knew Palenie was right. Samial wasn't a boy at all. He wasn't even alive—he was just a wandering spirit, lost in the borderlands between this world and the next.

She'd spent her days here talking to the dead.

Elodie felt herself shaking, not with fear but with anger. All this time he'd let her think she could stay with him in the woods. Let her believe they were friends.

"Many people died here," said Palenie, looking anxiously around at the shadowy trees. "In the War of Blood. It ended when Brutan took the crown. That's why they call them the Weeping Woods."

Elodie couldn't stop trembling. Samial had told her that his knight had fought in that war. Now she knew that he hadn't been squired to an exiled knight at all, but killed alongside his lord in these woods. She knew the truth, but it was so hard to believe. "I saw him," she insisted. "I really did."

Palenie came over to Elodie. "You saw his ghost. He was real once. Not anymore." She took her hands, her voice gentle. "Elodie, is he the only one you saw?"

"Yes." Hot tears came from her eyes as the truth about herself, about the voices, came to her. "But I hear others. I always have."

She thought about all the times she'd heard whispered conversations in the corridors of Castle Vicerin. All those voices. All those years convincing herself she was mad.

All those ghosts.

Was the whole world haunted? And was she the only one who heard the dead?

She pulled away from Palenie and rubbed her eyes. "I thought it was all in my head. . . . I thought I was . . ."

"Don't say it," said Palenie sharply. "There's nothing wrong with you, Elodie."

"Apart from hearing ghosts?"

She waited for Palenie to leave, to say she was going back to the camp to tell Fessan and Rotho and the others that their future queen was cursed. Instead, Palenie gently took her hand.

"Maybe it's a gift," she said softly. "You're a princess, after all."
She looked nervously around the trees. "Come on. We've a long
journey ahead."

As they left the Weeping Woods, Elodie refused to look back
over her shoulder. There was no point.

I never want to see him again, she thought.

CHAPTER 17

The minstrels played a rousing march. Behind them, colorful flags flapped in the wind. A line of soldiers stood at attention, polished spears pointing straight up at the sun. Gulph had expected to see more of them, but most of Nynus's army was now deployed across the chasm in Isur, laying siege to a rebel village.

Gulph wondered how the scene looked through Nynus's eyes. He supposed the young king was pleased with what he saw: loyal subjects enacting the king's command. Yet he was about to sever the only link between Idilliam and the rest of the world, cutting off the very soldiers he'd just sent to Isur.

This isn't a celebration, Gulph thought. *It's a disaster.*

Crowds had gathered near the Idilliam Bridge, ready to

watch the spectacle. Gulph wondered how many of them had been bullied into attending. Their faces were either angry or full of fear. Destroying the bridge meant isolating the city, and none of them wanted to be marooned.

"Raise the rams!" cried Nynus.

The king of Toronia was seated beside his mother on a low wooden platform that had been constructed to overlook the bridge. A black canopy shielded him from the sunlight; even so, Nynus held his hand over his eyes and kept his face screwed up.

On the bridge, a gang of soldiers hauled at ropes attached to four huge siege engines. The giant machines were relics from the War of Blood, brought at Nynus's command out of the garrison storehouses and set up on the Idilliam Bridge. Originally designed as battering rams, they'd been completely rebuilt. Now, instead of swinging sideways, the huge log rams hung vertically, their solid iron tips aiming straight down at the bridge's rock bed.

As the ropes were pulled tight, a series of gears and cranks raised heavy weights high into the air. The instant the ropes were released, these weights would drive the rams down onto the bridge.

When Nynus had first described the plan, Gulph had thought it crazy. Watching it unfold before his eyes, he found his opinion hadn't changed one bit.

"Please stop!" The voice came from a peasant man stumbling out of the crowd. Before anyone could challenge him, he'd mounted the platform and was pawing at the king's feet. Nynus stared down at him in disgust.

"Please," the man wailed. "My family. They live in Isur. Without the bridge, how will I ever see them again?"

Nynus kicked him away. Legionnaires closed in to seize the man, but he broke through their ranks and ran out across the bridge. As if his actions were a signal, other spectators surged through the line of soldiers and climbed the short flight of steps onto the bridge itself, dodging between the siege engines and racing toward the far end.

Gulph could hardly stand to watch. *They're never going to make it*, he thought.

By now, the rams were fully extended and poised to drop. The servants on the ropes waited in the sunlight, their muscles tensed, their bodies slicked with sweat.

Nynus raised his right hand.

Gulph grabbed the arm of his throne. "What are you doing?" he cried. "You can't start yet. There are people on the bridge!"

"And soon they will be off the bridge!" snapped Nynus.

"But that's . . ." Gulph stopped himself. His outrage boiled inside him. Yet angering Nynus would only make things worse for everyone.

How do you tell a tyrant not to be cruel?

At last it came to him. "You want them to love you, don't you?

Your subjects, I mean. How will it make you look if you kill these people?"

"It will make the king look strong," said Magritt. Her voice was dry and hard, like pebbles rattling in a box. "Not soft like you!"

Gulph was about to argue, but her glare silenced him. He thought back to her face looking down from the castle window. Had she seen him save the twins after all?

Watch your step, Gulph, he told himself.

"But still, my sweet," Magritt said, "our friend may have a point. Without the bridge, no food will—"

"Mother," Nynus interrupted. His pale eyes flashed. He clenched his fists like a small child about to fly into a rage. "You would question me?"

Gulph saw a flicker of fear pass over the dowager queen's face. Then she smiled. "Of course not. The king is always right."

"Yes," said Nynus, serene once more, gazing back out at the crowd. "Oh yes, I am."

Even his own mother doesn't dare cross him now, Gulph thought with a shudder. He looked back at the people running across the bridge. At least a dozen were already halfway across; many more were bunched close behind them. Perhaps his fears were unfounded. Perhaps they were going to make it after all.

Nynus brought down his hand.

One after the other, the four gigantic battering rams slammed into the rock, making contact precisely at the weakest part: where the end of the bridge met the solid bedrock on which the city of Idilliam was built. The impact was immense, beyond mere sound. The blast wave slammed against Gulph's ears and beat against his chest, turning it into a drum. His eyeballs seemed to be vibrating in their sockets.

Horrified, yet fascinated, too, he stepped off the platform to get a better look. Nynus gestured, and the rams pounded the bridge again. The young king's smile widened to demonic proportions. Gray dust rose in an expanding cloud. The ground shrugged like a waking giant. No storm had ever been this loud.

Again the rams struck. Near the middle of the bridge, a chunk of stone the size of a house broke away and plummeted into the chasm, turning end over end. Clinging to it, his face contorted with terror, was the peasant who'd first come to Nynus for help.

Gulph watched, helpless, as the poor man fell to his death. How many more would die today?

There was sudden movement on the far side of the bridge. A white horse and rider cantered out of the trees. As more slabs of rock started to collapse into the abyss, the rider spurred the horse out across the slender finger of rock, scattering the terrified people and speeding straight toward the royal party. With a gasp, Gulph recognized the rider's long hair and sculpted features.

"Limmoni!" Heedless of the danger, he forced his way through the melee, up the steps, and out onto the bridge. The air around the rams was choking, filled with dust and grit. He coughed it out, ignoring the dreadful heaving sensation as the rock rippled beneath his feet.

"Stop!" he yelled, darting between the battering rams. "Go back, Limmoni!" He knew there was no chance she would hear him; he couldn't even hear himself. He was lost inside a world of thunder. His eyes filled up with dust, blinding him. He ran on, senseless in the confusion, not wanting to stop for anything.

The section he was standing on gave way.

Falling forward, scrabbling with his hands, Gulph tried in vain to gain purchase on the crumbling rock. His knees hit something hard and suddenly he was spinning, falling, out of control. Something scraped his arm and he clutched at it instinctively. His fingers found a broken edge of stone and curled around it, stopping his descent abruptly. The jerk yanked his right arm from its socket. Normally this was a trick he could perform easily, but the sudden shock drove a hot spike of agony into his shoulder.

Howling with pain, Gulph swung from the edge of the broken bridge, his feet dangling over the abyss.

On the bridge above, one of the huge battering rams tilted sickeningly over the precipice. There were shouts of terror. "Let it go!" someone shouted, and it plunged, trailing ropes behind it, past Gulph until it was swallowed up in the cloud below.

No, he thought, *I'm not going down there too!*

He pulled against the pain, snapping his bones back into place.

Pretend it's a show! Be an acrobat, Gulph, perform for the crowd!

Throwing his legs sideways at an angle no ordinary person could have achieved, he found a foothold on the swaying stonework. Slowly, painfully, he pulled himself to safety. Shaking from head to toe, his breath ragged, he ran off the bridge and didn't stop until he was on Idilliam soil. Finally, he looked back. Devastation lay all around. The remaining giant rams had fallen silent. Before them, a huge gap had opened in the middle of the bridge.

Limmoni was on the far spur, riding headlong toward the gap. There was no horse in the world that could jump it.

Beneath the shattered bridge, the air was filled with people, falling. Their arms and legs thrashed. In the absence of the thunder, Gulph could hear their screams.

Limmoni's horse reached the end of the falling spur. As her steed's hind legs kicked backward, she stood up in the saddle. Both her hands left the reins. As she raised them high, dazzling light burst from them.

As the horse soared over the gap, not just jumping but *flying*, the light knitted itself into a glowing mesh. The mesh flew out and down, becoming a net that surrounded the falling people and gathered them up. A net of light and life.

Limmoni closed her hands together and the net rose up out of the chasm. Her expression was agonized as she fought to keep it aloft. The net drifted over the crowd, finally depositing its precious cargo safely on the grass sward before the castle keep.

The white horse touched down and galloped on. Limmoni slammed down into the saddle, looking utterly spent. The net vanished, leaving the rescued people to clamber to their feet, eyes agog at their savior.

The lights in Limmoni's hands winked out.

Just as the horse reached Idilliam and Gulph, its remarkable rider slumped sideways and fell. Gulph caught her before she struck the ground. He lowered her gently down, dumbfounded by what he'd just experienced, what he'd just seen.

"I'm sorry," she croaked. Her face was as pale as Nynus's, and her blond hair was caked with stone dust. Her voice sounded like pouring sand.

Gulph crouched over her. "Don't try to speak," he said.

"I must. I don't have much time. I have to tell you."

"Tell me what?"

"Melchior—I couldn't find him. I'm sorry."

The despair in Limmoni's eyes told Gulph how serious this was. What did it mean for him? What did it mean for his siblings, wherever they were? He stroked Limmoni's hair from her face, wishing desperately that he could help her.

"It's all right," he said. "You're all right now."

Her hand gripped his, momentarily strong but weakening fast.

"No. I'm not. That leap ... saving those people. It's broken me. My magic. I thought I was ready, but ..."

Her eyes closed and her body folded, seemingly twice as heavy as it had been before. Panic-stricken, Gulph pressed his fingers to her throat. There was a pulse, but it was very faint.

A shadow fell across him.

"Fine work stopping her, Gulph," said Nynus. He was cowering under a large parasol that his mother was holding over his head. "Although she doesn't look capable of running away."

"Are you ready to hand over your prisoner?" said Dowager Queen Magritt, one arched eyebrow raised.

"Oh no," said Nynus. "I don't think he needs to do that."

Gulph stared blankly at him. Had Nynus come to his senses at last? It hardly seemed possible.

"I don't?" he said.

"No." Nynus laughed. "I think I'll just kick her over the edge."

Gulph grabbed Limmoni protectively. "You can't do that," he said.

"He is the king," said Magritt. "He can do whatever he chooses." Beside her, Nynus grinned and tensed his legs. "But ... I have a better idea."

Nynus scowled. "You do? But she's a wizard. Don't you think we should punish her?"

"Of course, my dear. But wizards can be useful."

Magritt gestured toward the two remaining fingers of rock, each pointing at the other from opposite sides of the chasm.

"The gap is wide, but not wide enough. I suggest we keep our wizard somewhere safe until she wakes. With her magic, the task of destroying the rest of the bridge will be an easy one."

Beneath his parasol, Nynus giggled.

Gulph eyed first the queen, then her son. Any regard he'd had for them had long since vanished. Now he saw them for what they truly were: monsters.

"Somewhere safe?" Gulph said. "What do you mean?"

Magritt smiled down at him.

"Why, the Vault of Heaven, of course."

Thick clouds hid the moon and stars, except for a tiny gap hovering directly above the city. No matter how the clouds moved, this gap remained. Through it, Gulph could clearly see the three prophecy stars. They seemed to beckon him.

Standing in the darkness, Gulph prepared to do something he'd never imagined he would attempt.

Break back into the Vault of Heaven.

He flexed his muscles, preparing to make the arduous climb up one of the Vault's stilt-like legs. He'd thought he was sure of this, but the risk was huge. If he was caught, Nynus would do more than plunge Gulph's hands into a brazier.

As Limmoni had been dragged away from the half-demolished bridge, Gulph had felt Magritt's gaze burning the back of his neck. And Nynus had been cool toward him for the rest of the day. In defending Limmoni, had he gone too far?

Then he thought of Limmoni lying cold and alone in the Black Cell.

His choice was clear.

She helped me. Now I've got to help her.

The climb was just as difficult as he'd imagined. The wooden stilt was slippery, and twisted as it ascended. Only Gulph's extraordinary flexibility allowed him to reach the few handholds there were. When he reached the top, he compressed his shoulders and hips to an unnatural degree and squeezed his agile body through a tiny crack in the prison wall.

I suppose being deformed isn't always a bad thing, he thought.

Once inside, he paused, catching his breath. It was just as he remembered: dark, stinking, echoing with the wretched screams of the inmates. It sounded as if there were more prisoners here than before. No wonder: Lately Nynus had made a hobby of sentencing people to a stretch in the Vault for even the most minor crimes.

Where's Blist?

He hoped he was snoring somewhere, while the rest of the prison guards did his work for him.

Gulph crept through the gloomy passageways. Water dripped, a percussive sound to accompany the screams. At least Nynus had told him where Limmoni was to be imprisoned: the one cell that had remained empty since their escape. The little room where Nynus had spent ten years of his young life.

The Black Cell.

This way . . . around this corner . . . up these steps . . .

A torch flared. Horror coursed through Gulph as two legionnaires stepped into its light, their bronze armor glinting. He had been on the verge of running; now he stopped abruptly, his heels skidding on the greasy floor. The soldiers advanced, shoulder to shoulder, then parted.

A third figure came forward between them. Gulph saw flowing robes, a pair of gloved hands, a triumphant smile.

Magritt!

It was a trap!

His heart pounding, Gulph spun on his heels and ran . . . straight into the clutches of a third legionnaire waiting behind him. A gloved hand clamped around his throat, almost lifting him off the ground.

"No!" he gasped. "Let me go!" He beat at the man with his hands, tried to kick him, but to no avail.

"I knew you were a traitor," said Magritt, circling him like a hawk. "I told Nynus, but he would not believe me, not without proof. So I decided to give him some."

Gulph flailed in the legionnaire's grasp. "Where is she?" he croaked. "What have you done with her?"

"The Vault of Heaven is not the only secure place in Idilliam," said Magritt. "Your wizard friend is safe in the castle. Locked up, of course. But safe." She loomed over him, sneering in the torchlight. "But you, Gulph, are not so safe."

"You don't scare me!"

"Be quiet! How dare you? How dare you betray our trust, you ugly, ungrateful brat! We picked you out of the gutter, raised you up to a position of high office, and this is how you reward us!"

"You didn't raise me up! You dragged me down!"

Magritt leaned close. "King killer," she whispered.

To Gulph's dismay, his eyes filled instantly with tears. "You made me do it," he choked. "I didn't know. You tricked me."

Straightening up, Magritt snapped her fingers. The legionnaire kept his grip on Gulph's throat while the other fastened heavy chains around his arms and legs. By the time they'd finished, Gulph felt twice as heavy as he had been, and was almost completely unable to move.

"Let me see you wriggle out of that, you deformed monster," said Magritt. She walked away into the darkness, her robes billowing behind her.

"You're the monster!" yelled Gulph, throwing the words after her. But she was already gone.

The legionnaires dragged Gulph like a side of beef to one of the big communal cells. Blist himself was there, a crooked smile on his sweating face.

"Ah, the frog boy returns!" He cackled.

Blist opened the cell door, using a barbed whip to keep back the jostling prisoners. Gulph was thrown inside. The chains clanked as he landed, driving their cold metal curves into his back. The door slammed shut, the key rattled in the lock, and the footsteps of the retreating men faded to nothing.

Gulph fought to breathe against the constricting pressure of the chains on his chest. One by one, the faces of the other prisoners appeared above him, staring down out of the darkness, just as the prophecy stars had done. But there was no light in their eyes, only hatred and despair.

Gulph found a corner and shrank into it. Now he knew how a sheep felt when the wolves closed in. He curled up and waited for it to be over.

CHAPTER 18

When he'd first flown over the village, Tarlan would have said Lord Vicerin's troops boasted only a few dozen men. Now, as he flew over it again, he saw the enemy attacking afresh and in the hundreds. It seemed an extraordinary show of force.

There's more to this than Lady Darrand said, he thought. *Lord Vicerin wants to take over Ritherlee. What other explanation could there be?*

Tarlan bunched his hands in Theeta's neck ruff and shook his head, clearing his thoughts. Lord Vicerin's goal was not his concern. He and the thorrods were hired mercenaries, nothing more. As soon as they'd done their job, they would be on their way. These humans could sort out their own affairs.

"Low over the mill," he said to Theeta, tugging her to the left.

His giant steed banked smoothly, the long feathers on her wings rippling silently in the changing airflow. Her head snapped back and forth, keen eyes tracking the soldiers on the ground as an eagle might follow its rodent prey.

The mill loomed. This was where the fighting was at its fiercest. In the shadow of the slowly turning waterwheel, villagers valiantly brandished farm tools against the Vicerin attackers. What they lacked in weaponry and training they made up for in vigor; all the same, their well-armed opponents were steadily pushing them back.

"Put the sun behind us," said Tarlan.

Adjusting her trajectory, Theeta swooped down on the Vicerin squad. The soldiers looked up, their faces terrified. They raised their hands to their eyes, momentarily blinded. The thorrod screeched. Several of the soldiers screamed. Tarlan grinned.

Scary, isn't she?

Theeta plunged through the middle of the soldiers, her talons lifting men bodily into the air and tossing them aside, her beak opening and closing, opening and closing. A spray of blood blossomed, splashing Tarlan's cheek. Horrified, thrilled, he wiped it away with the back of his hand.

Having cut a swath through the Vicerin troops, Theeta flew a tight circle around the mill, narrowly missing the waterwheel as she came in for a second attack.

"They're falling back!" said Tarlan, pleased to see not the weapons of the enemy but the backs of their uniforms. "Let's encourage them."

As a line of villagers ran in to deal with the injured, Theeta chased the retreating Vicerin troops up the steep bank overlooking the mill. One soldier slipped and fell; Theeta speared him with a talon before he could get up.

The rest just ran faster.

Once he was sure this particular troop was no further threat, Tarlan steered Theeta back to the mill. The dead and wounded lay on the ground, their blue sashes turning red as the blood flowed out of their bodies.

As the thorrod flew overhead, the villagers raised a ragged cheer. Tarlan urged Theeta higher, keen to gain an overview of the battlefield. To his right, Kitheen had chased a second squad of soldiers into a tight gully that ended when it met a steep rock wall. Trapped, the men turned, only to find the huge thorrod slashing at them with his claws and beak. Tarlan pulled Theeta away. No form of prey could survive when Kitheen was in a killing frenzy.

A leisurely pass over the village reassured him that the fighting was all but over. Despite the overwhelming odds, the thorrods had turned the tide of the battle. More of Lady Darrand's own soldiers had now arrived, easily identifiable in their brown leather armor.

Together they helped the villagers rout out any last pockets of resistance. The rest of Lord Vicerin's men were in full retreat.

It was over.

A shadow passed over Tarlan. Looking up, he saw Nasheen soaring overhead. The wound on her white breast still looked bad, but she was flying straight and level, her wings beating as powerfully as they ever had. Caraway's poultice was clearly doing its job. Though she'd been awake when the fighting had started, Tarlan had ordered her to remain in the woods, partly to regain her strength, partly to keep watch over the sick tigron cub.

"Nasheen!" Tarlan called, his heart filled with joy at the sight of her. "Are you all right?"

"Filos," said the thorrod. "Awake."

Tarlan grinned. The news just kept getting better.

Soon we'll be able to leave!

"Good!" he said. "Go back to her. Keep her safe. It's nearly over here. We'll be with you shortly."

"Tired," said Theeta, gazing at Nasheen as she headed back toward the thicket.

Tarlan patted her neck. "I'm sure you are, my friend. If anyone's earned a rest, you have. Put me down."

Theeta landed in front of the mill, where the villagers were busy covering the dead with sacking and carrying the wounded away on wooden litters. Tarlan slipped down from the thorrod's back and touched his hand to her beak, aware of the awed expressions of the onlookers.

Lady Darrand's chariot appeared from behind the mill. The warrior woman was standing at the reins, a fierce smile on her face, her bloodied sword held high. When she saw Tarlan, she let out a guttural cry.

"Go to the others," said Tarlan to Theeta. "Get your rest. I'll be with you soon."

The thorrod flew off just as Lady Darrand's chariot drew to a halt beside Tarlan. He stroked the horses, sensing their stress from the battle.

"It's over," said Tarlan.

"And we are grateful to you, thorrod rider," said Lady Darrand. "This village is free of Vicerin's rats once and for all." She eyed him steadily. "I do not know what fate brought you to us, but I'm glad it did. The times are dark in Toronia. May you travel safely."

Tarlan nodded. "We will. I hope you get your daughter back."

Lady Darrand raised her helmet in farewell.

She drove her chariot onward and Tarlan started walking back to the thicket where his pack was waiting.

"Please!" a voice called. "Please, wait one moment!"

Tarlan turned. A man in a dirty cloak was hurrying up to him.

"You'll be hungry on the road," the man said. "Won't you take some food for yourself and your friends? I don't have much, but I want you to have it. You saved my home, you see."

Tarlan hesitated. He'd happily eat whatever he and his pack caught on their travels. Still, the man looked so eager that he found himself agreeing.

"Why not?" he said with a grin. "Lead the way."

"This is where I keep my supplies," the man said. They had come to a barn tucked away from the rest of the village in a shallow vale. The man opened the door and ushered Tarlan through it. "Whatever you find in here is yours."

Tarlan strode inside. The barn was gloomy. Thick dust hung in the air from the hay bales stacked by one of the walls. In the far corner was a barrel next to a stack of crates. *Must be where the food is*, he thought.

He went over and lifted the lid of the first crate.

Empty.

The next crate was empty too, and the barrel.

"Hey!" Tarlan called. "What's going on?"

The man was inside the barn now too—and closing the door.

Then movement caught Tarlan's eye. On the wall, flickering behind the hay bales, were shadows.

It's a trap....

Enraged, Tarlan raised his sword as five Vicerin soldiers burst through the hay bales. Straw showered everywhere. The man who'd lured him here threw off his cloak, revealing his blue Vicerin colors beneath. His blade clanged against Tarlan's.

Tarlan dodged and swung at him. It was too close quarters to use his bow, and the unfamiliar weapon felt slow and heavy; Tarlan grimly wished he had something more effective at hand.

A thorrod's beak, for example.

Laughing, the soldier parried Tarlan's clumsy thrust, the force of it shoving Tarlan all the way back through the door and out into the sunlight. He stumbled, looking around for Lady Darrand's soldiers. But the Vicerin soldier had chosen this barn for good reason—there was no one in sight.

I'm alone.

Recovering his balance, Tarlan sidestepped another blow, then lunged with his sword again. Another soldier fended him off, this time forcing Tarlan to his knees. Then the soldier pulled a small, curved knife from his belt and slashed at Tarlan's face. Tarlan recoiled and the blade whistled past a hairbreadth away. His feet tangled together and he fell, dropping his sword.

His vision faltered. His ears filled up with a low, dull roar.

Get up, he told himself. *Come on!*

But the man with the knife had fallen on him. He planted his knees on Tarlan's chest and all the breath whooshed out of him. He clawed in vain in the dirt for his sword, then felt cold steel at his throat.

Tarlan froze.

"Don't kill him!" came a voice from the barn.

"Why not?" said Tarlan's opponent.

"Lord Vicerin wants us to take the kids alive, remember?"

The soldier removed his knees from Tarlan's chest and grabbed his arms. Another pair of hands seized his legs. Before he could even draw breath, he was being dragged back into the barn.

"Take his bow! Tie him up and cover his head!"

A moment later, Tarlan found himself facedown in the dirt. Hasty fingers tied thick rope around his wrists and ankles. Someone put a rag in his mouth and drew a coarse canvas bag over his head. Everything went dark. He was lifted, then dropped. His body felt like a lump of dead prey.

"Theeta!" he tried to yell. But the rag turned his shout into a meaningless groan.

Something hit his head and the world went black.

Tarlan woke to the sound of creaking. His head—aching from the blow he'd received—was still covered, and his arms and legs were tied. Trussed like a mountain fowl, he was lying on a wooden floor that swayed to and fro as he struggled to free himself. Something heavy pressed down on him, hampering his movements. He remembered Mirith talking about boats. Was he at sea?

Trying to spit the rag out of his mouth, he cursed himself for being captured again. He felt hot and stifled, and yearned for the cold, clean air of his homeland.

Yalasti. Ritherlee. Is there anywhere I can really be safe?

Tarlan's fear for himself was quickly overwhelmed by a greater concern:

What's become of my pack?

The swaying stopped. Somewhere nearby, a horse whinnied. Not a boat, then, but a cart.

The weight was lifted from his body, and a hand snatched away the hood. Tarlan blinked against the sudden rush of light. Hands fumbled with the knots around his ankles. As soon as they were free, he kicked out, only to find a knife at his ribs.

"Calm yourself, bird boy," said the soldier. "Now, I'm going to remove your gag. Are you going to be quiet, or am I going to stick you?"

Tarlan glared at his captor.

"Take it off," said the soldier who'd untied his legs. "He's got nowhere to go."

As soon as the rags were unwrapped from his face, Tarlan spat out the gag and worked his jaw, gulping down the fresh air as a parched man might swallow water.

"Come on," said the first soldier. "Lord Vicerin will be happy to have another hostage."

"There's no prison built that can keep me," Tarlan snapped back. "What happened to Theeta?"

"Who?"

"The thorrod, you idiot."

The soldier's tone hardened. "Why should I care about that monster? Now shut up, or I'll put this sack right back over your head."

For all his pent-up frustration, Tarlan was too weary to put up a fight. He felt detached from his body, and the effects of Caraway's poultice were wearing off, leaving his injured shoulder feeling hot and sore. Better to bide his time and regain his strength. He'd escaped captivity before; he could do it again.

Except . . . last time he'd had the thorrods to help him.

Now he was on his own.

The cart had stopped beneath a high castle wall built from fine red stone. Slender towers punctuated the wall's gentle curve at regular intervals. Patterned blue flags flew from masts set high on their sloping roofs.

The soldiers dragged Tarlan through a small gate in the castle wall. Beyond it was a narrow thoroughfare, and then another wall. A second gate led to a yard where rows and rows of vegetables grew. Tired-looking gardeners tended the plants; none looked up as the soldiers hauled Tarlan past. But the sentry standing in the corner watched their every move.

So much food! Tarlan thought, unable to take his eyes off the bounty of crops.

Through a decorative wrought-iron gate set in an arched doorway, Tarlan glimpsed a group of children playing some kind of chase game. Elegant women stood nearby, talking as they watched over their brood. They held parasols and fanned themselves. A servant stood to one side holding a silver tray laden with goblets.

Tarlan couldn't imagine a scene more different from the simple rustic reality of the village he'd been helping to defend. And it was a whole world away from what he'd known in icy, barren Yalasti. The deeper he delved into the affairs of humans, the more complex they became. So much for keeping his distance.

At the far end of the kitchen garden was another wall, this one overgrown with ivy. The soldiers took him through a narrow door and into a dark corridor. Here, the walls were black and smelled of damp. For the first time since arriving in Ritherlee, Tarlan shivered with cold.

The deeper the soldiers led him into the castle, the more Tarlan felt the impulse to escape. He wondered if Theeta and the rest of his pack were searching for him.

If so, they'll never find me in here.

The corridor opened onto a long room lined with cells. In the middle of the room, with his back to Tarlan, a man was sitting on a stool. His clothes were fine: purple robes and white furs. But it wasn't he who caught Tarlan's attention.

There were children in the cells.

They huddled in small groups, perhaps a dozen in total. Their faces were dirty and many of them looked as if they'd been crying. So these were the hostages his captors had mentioned. Tarlan wondered if Sorelle, Lady Darrand's daughter, was among them.

Near the door, chained to the wall, lay a wolf. It looked bony, with patchy fur, and was clearly malnourished. As they entered, it sat up and whined pitifully, tugging listlessly at the chain, which was far too tight. One of the guards kicked it aside; Tarlan bit his lip, barely restraining himself from lashing out in retaliation.

The man on the stool spoke.

"Is anyone going to answer my question?" His voice was high for a man's. His head turned slowly from one side to the other. Tarlan wished he could see the man's face. "What do you think Gretiana found at the end of the path?"

The trapped children stared listlessly back at him.

"Very well—I will tell you." The man raised a scroll from his lap and read from it. "'At the end of the path, Gretiana found a cottage made of bread and bones. Green smoke rose from the chimney, and a black cat sat on the step. After wandering in the woods for a day and a night, she was right back where she had started: in the clutches of the evil witch.'"

One of the boys began to cry.

Spotting Tarlan and the soldiers, the man stopped reading and rolled up the scroll.

"Enough for today, children," he said.

A single groan of disappointment came from the cells. All the other children looked relieved. Tarlan saw one small girl elbow another in the ribs. Her companion piped up:

"Please, sir, can we go out today?"

The man who'd been reading smiled indulgently. "I am sorry, children, but you know the rules. I would love to let you play outside in the sunshine, but I have to keep you safe. No, it is better—far better—that you are protected. You have food. You have stories. Nothing can harm you here. And you are happy, are you not?"

"Yes, Lord Vicerin," chorused several of the children. The others glowered.

So that's him! thought Tarlan. He'd been expecting some kind of warlord or tyrant, not a finely dressed dandy.

"Why are you keeping them prisoner?" Tarlan demanded, unable to stop himself.

Lord Vicerin turned slowly to face him. "Forgive me," he said. "I did not hear your name."

"Never mind my name. You can't keep them here like this!"

The guards tightened their grip on his arms.

"The children are happy. Did you not hear?"

Tarlan regarded the line of anxious faces pressed up against the bars.

"They don't *look* very happy to me."

Lord Vicerin came close. His skin was smooth, and smelled faintly of flowers. "I suppose you do not know fear?"

He nodded to the soldiers, who shoved Tarlan to his knees in front of the wolf. At once, the mangy creature lurched to its feet and bared a vicious set of yellow teeth. Several of the children cried out.

"No creature scares me." Tarlan leaned in close to the snapping wolf. "It's all right," he murmured. "Everything's all right."

Just as the tigron had, the wolf seemed to understand his words. It stopped snarling. Tarlan could sense the creature's pain, its hunger. Looking into its eyes, he knew it sensed something of him, too.

Remaining still, he allowed the animal to sniff his face. It nuzzled his hair and licked his cheek. Tarlan heard one of the children gasp.

Theeta. Filos. Now you.

Finally, the wolf curled up with its muzzle resting on its paws, staring up at Tarlan intently.

I have a way with animals, he thought, marveling at how natural this new bond felt.

The scent of flowers wafted past his face, and he looked up to find Lord Vicerin standing over him.

"Well, this is a curious thing," said the lord of the castle. "What is your name? Or shall I just call you 'wolf boy'?"

Tarlan said nothing.

The guards held him still as the lord's hands lifted his black cloak. They turned it over, revealing the vivid red lining. Compared to the man's finery, the cloak looked grimy and threadbare. The hands moved up to Tarlan's neck, where they found the green jewel hanging on its gold chain. Tarlan endured the contact, though he could feel his muscles clench. He could sense the wolf quivering at his side, making ready to pounce.

You better not think about taking Mirith's jewel, he thought.

Slowly, Lord Vicerin's eyes opened wide. His fingers reached for Tarlan's face, then pulled back, as if in fear of being burned. He tried to speak, but emitted only a croak. His tongue flicked out over his lips, then retreated inside his mouth again.

"So here you are," he said at last. "Black eyes. Hair like copper. You look so much like . . ."

He raised one hand. Tarlan prepared himself for the blow.

To his astonishment, Lord Vicerin knelt. The hand he'd raised made a complex gesture in the air, then the man bowed his head. When he raised it again, his eyes were glistening with tears.

"You are come to us, Prince," he said softly. "Welcome."

CHAPTER 19

Tarlan was still in a daze when they emerged into the kitchen garden. His head felt thick and heavy. As the two soldiers escorted him between the rows of vegetables, he realized he was no longer chained. When had they freed him? He couldn't remember.

Lord Vicerin, who was striding ahead of them, reached the iron gate and unlocked it with a large key. Tarlan followed him into the garden he'd glimpsed earlier. The children had gone, leaving the expanse of smooth grass and neatly trimmed hedges empty but for a pair of extraordinary birds, each with a fan of colorful tail feathers spread wide in the sun.

Peacocks, he thought absently, dragging up a memory of a word Mirith had once used.

Tarlan's nose filled with the scent of flowers. Feeling dizzy, he stopped, bent over, and planted his hands on his knees.

"Come, Prince," said Vicerin. "This is not a day to dally."

"I'm not a prince," said Tarlan, standing up straight again. "I told you. My name is Tarlan. I come from Yalasti. You can't keep me here—I'm nothing to do with this stupid war of yours. I just want to be back with my friends."

"Friends?" Vicerin frowned. "If you are a friend of Lady Darrand, then you are involved with this 'stupid war,' as you call it, whether you like it or not."

"I don't mean her."

Vicerin's frown turned to puzzlement. He waved his hand in front of his face, banishing the expression. "It is tragic," he said, "that you know so little. It has been hidden from you, no doubt, by well-meaning individuals. But now you will know the truth."

Tarlan eyed the gate. The soldiers hadn't followed them into the garden; he was essentially free. But there would be other soldiers beyond. If only they hadn't taken his weapons.

Could I make it?

If he could only get beyond the castle gate, he was confident he could trace the route the cart had taken. If they hadn't already set out in search for him, Theeta and the rest of his pack would be waiting there.

Three things stopped him from making his bid for freedom. The first was the thought of leaving all those children locked in the dungeon. The second was his desire to free the wolf.

The third was simple curiosity.

"What do you mean?" he said. "What's been hidden?"

"Your destiny." Lord Vicerin's smile flashed on like a beacon flame, revealing large white teeth.

"I don't understand."

"Where did you get that?" Vicerin pointed to Tarlan's cloak.

"I've always had it."

"Mmm. That cloak was once the property of a man called Captain Leom. When you were a baby, he carried you away from certain death and into . . . well, I suppose some might consider it exile. I prefer to think of it as a place to wait."

"Wait for what?"

"For the time to be right." The smile broadened. "As it now so clearly is."

The dizziness came again. Tarlan pushed it away. He didn't know if he could trust what this man said. But why would he lie? And had Mirith not told him stories about how she'd found him in the forest, wrapped in the very cloak Vicerin was talking about?

His heart stirred. He'd never given much thought to his past before.

"Then there is the jewel you wear around your neck," Vicerin went on. "A very beautiful thing. Just like you, it has a destiny."

"Destiny?" The word faltered on Tarlan's lips. "What do you mean?"

"Only that you are in the right place at last, my young prince."

Tarlan's newly awoken curiosity was like an itch. All he wanted to do now was scratch it.

"What do you know about the jewel?" he demanded. "Tell me!"

Lord Vicerin waved his hand airily. "Never mind. All you need to know is that one day, that jewel will be set into a crown. The crown you yourself shall wear when you sit on the throne of Toronia."

A gust of wind blew past Tarlan's face, momentarily ridding the air of the cloying smell of grass and flowers.

"Why should I believe you?" he said. "You're just a fancy thug who keeps children and animals locked up!"

Vicerin's expression turned to one of horror. To Tarlan's surprise, he fell to his knees and held out his manicured hands, pleading.

"Forgive me, Prince!" he exclaimed. "This is a shock to you, and I have failed to explain everything. The cells you saw . . . The Darrands are snatching youngsters from all corners of Ritherlee. No child is safe. It looks barbaric, I know—and it breaks my heart to confine them—but it is truly for their own good. You must believe me."

"What about the wolf?"

"A savage beast. We hope to tame it. Wolves make good castle guards. Would you rather it was killed?"

Tarlan folded his arms, staring down at this finely dressed lord who was inexplicably crouched before him.

"Lady Darrand told me you were the one stealing children," he said slowly.

Vicerin nodded. "That does not surprise me. Her capacity to lie is matched only by her charm. The two combined make her a very dangerous woman." Climbing to his feet, he brought his powdered face close to Tarlan's. "'Too much virtuous blood has spilt in this accursed age. When the stars increase by three, the kingdom shall be saved.'"

"What? What is that?"

"A prophecy. Or part of one. You, Tarlan, are part of it. You are a triplet, one of three heirs to the throne of Toronia, sired by Brutan and hidden in the far reaches of the kingdom, awaiting your day. I say to you now that I, Lord Vicerin of Ritherlee, will bring you to your inheritance. The Vicerins will not stop until the prophecy has been fulfilled."

"Triplets?" Tarlan spluttered. His heart quickened. He couldn't believe what he was hearing. Instead of crowns and kingdoms, however, all he could think of was brothers and sisters. Suddenly, after being raised an only child and orphan, he was being told he had a family. "Where are the others?"

Lord Vicerin's hand settled on his shoulder, his face a mask of tragedy. "Alas, Tarlan, they are lost. This is why you are so important to us. To Toronia."

He led him to a tall stone tower rising from one of the castle's inner walls. A sense of unreality washed over Tarlan as they passed from the garden into a high hallway lined with dark wood panels and draped with colorful banners. Silver swords were fixed to the walls, the polished metal shimmering in the light of a dozen blazing torches.

I could run, he thought again. But his mind was too full of questions, so he stayed.

As they entered the hall, a pair of maids wearing white aprons appeared from a low doorway, as if they'd been waiting all this time for their lord to approach. Lord Vicerin snapped his fingers.

"Hot water," he said. "Clean clothes. In the top chamber. Now."

The maids scurried away, leaving Vicerin to lead Tarlan up a steep staircase. By the time they reached the top, the muscles in Tarlan's thighs felt tight and strange.

He'd never climbed stairs before.

"This will be your room," said Lord Vicerin, ushering Tarlan into a large chamber.

The room was like nothing Tarlan had ever seen. Lilac silks lined the walls; beneath the window stood a dressing table piled high with gold and jewelry. An enormous bed sat beneath a canopy supported by four oak posts, covered by embroidered pillows and coverlets. Everything smelled of flowers.

"Fit for a prince!" Vicerin pronounced, setting an ornate chair straight against the wall.

Tarlan eyed the sturdy bolts on the door—the *outside* of the door. The room bore an unsettling resemblance to a prison cell.

"It's very big," he said. He waved an arm at the other side of the room. "What's through there?"

Vicerin went over and opened the door, revealing a large closet in which rows of colorful dresses hung. As his back was turned, Tarlan started edging toward the door. He felt trapped. He didn't want this. He wanted his friends, his freedom, and the wide-open sky.

His escape plan was foiled when the maids bustled in. One carried a big bowl of steaming water, the other a stack of neatly folded linen. Behind them came yet more servants—a virtual stream of them. Between them they filled the bedchamber with plates of fruit and cooked meat, goblets of wine and water, and piles of books.

Tarlan was bemused by the sudden flurry of activity, and intoxicated by the mouthwatering smells coming from the food. By the time he'd come to his senses, the servants had left and Lord Vicerin was standing between him and the door. Which was now closed.

"Please, make yourself at home," said Vicerin. "You are safe here, Tarlan. You are surrounded by loyal followers, all of whom are prepared to lay down their lives if it will help you take your rightful place on the throne of Toronia."

"I don't want anyone to die," said Tarlan. "And I don't care who you think I am. I just want my pack."

Vicerin's eyes narrowed. "You mean your friends?"

"That's what I said."

"Well, that may be. But you are here now, and here you will stay. Your mind will change, Prince Tarlan. I will make sure of it."

Bowing slightly, Vicerin departed, closing the door quickly behind him.

The clunk of the bolts being drawn was very loud.

Furious both with Vicerin and himself, Tarlan kicked over the bowl. Hot water sluiced across the stone floor, filling the room with steam. He grabbed the nearest plate of food, intending to fling it out the window. But the slices of roast chicken and ripe berries looked and smelled so succulent that he relented.

Putting the plate on the bed, he devoured everything he could see, washing it down with copious drafts of cold water. When he'd finished, he let out a tremendous belch.

Now, how am I going to get out of here?

Tarlan lay down on the bed, his head filled with half-formed plans.

Moments later, he was asleep.

Tarlan woke with a start from a dream he couldn't remember. He rose from the bed, found his head was aching, and flopped back again. A plate rolled from a pillow and smashed on the floor.

He sat up again, more gingerly this time. His mouth tasted of stale food. His stomach felt stretched. He stood, swinging his arms, and crossed the room to the window.

Night had fallen, but the castle was ablaze with light. Everywhere Tarlan looked, torches burned. Bright windows stared back at him like probing eyes. He turned away, not wanting to be watched.

Clasping his hands to the back of his neck, he tried to stretch the tension out of his back. His fingers touched bare skin. He froze, his stomach writhing with dread. Bending, he stared into the mirror on the dressing table.

There was nothing around his neck.

Someone had been in the room while he'd slept.

The green jewel was gone.

Dread turned to fury. He grabbed one of the goblets he'd drunk from and sniffed it. Thanks to Mirith's teachings, he could detect the scents of a dozen different drugs and medicines. But he smelled nothing.

He ran to the door and yanked at the handle. It didn't move even a hairbreadth in its frame. He went back to the window and looked down, but the tower was high, and there were no ledges on the wall outside.

So he really was a prisoner here.

He held on to the anger, using it to beat down his fear. How had it come to this? How had he been so stupid as to follow that lying soldier?

It wasn't important. What was done was done. Only one thing mattered now.

Escape.

CHAPTER 20

What's wrong, Princess?" said Palenie.

"Nothing," Elodie replied.

"But you look uncomfortable. Is there something wrong with the saddle?"

"I'm fine!"

Elodie gave her horse—a sleek gray stallion called Discus—a gentle kick, urging him forward. Palenie was right, she was uncomfortable, but it wasn't her saddle or even the itchy green tunic that was bothering her. She glanced around at the Trident column.

I ought to feel pleased about all this.

Elodie knew she should be happy to be on horseback again. Back at Castle Vicerin, she'd loved riding the high-shouldered Ritherlee horses around the castle grounds.

She knew she should be honored to have a place at the front

of the column, riding just behind Fessan as he led the rebels west through the Weeping Woods.

She supposed she should be excited about the coming battle, despite her lack of training. Every step took them closer to the Idilliam Bridge and her brother.

Elodie knew all these things but could do nothing about them. All she could think of was Samial and what she'd learned in the woods.

I can talk to the dead, she thought with a shiver.

Set against this knowledge, nothing else seemed to matter.

Palenie quickened her horse's pace too, until she drew level with Elodie again. They rode together in silence for a while, before Palenie finally spoke.

"We'll be passing close to my home soon," she said.

"Oh."

Palenie pointed. "It's over there, in western Isur. Just a little village, but it's so pretty. There's a huge chestnut tree in the middle where we have dances and music. . . ." She threw Elodie an anxious glance. "One day, when all this is over, I could show you."

Elodie stirred herself. Palenie was clearly trying to cheer her up and the effort touched her.

"I'd love that," she said. Lowering her voice, she added, "Thank you, Palenie."

"What for?"

"For being here. For not telling anyone about . . . you know."

Palenie's cheeks flushed. "I'll always keep your secrets. But if you do decide to tell people, they won't think it's terrible. They'll think it's powerful and wonderful. I know I do."

"Really?" Elodie smiled at her. *I still have one friend with me,* she thought.

At the head of the column, Fessan raised his hand. The long line of horses, wagons, and foot-weary swordsmen slowed. Elodie stood up in her saddle and looked around.

They'd reached the outskirts of what had once been a village nestled in the woods. Now it was a random scattering of burned and broken huts. The trees overlooking the wreckage were charred black and devoid of leaves. The ground was littered with bodies.

"The war," said Palenie.

"I never thought I'd see something like this." Elodie surveyed the carnage with barely contained horror. "I mean, I've read about what happens in war. . . ." Her voice trailed away as her eyes fell on a cluster of corpses lying beneath a dead beech tree. Two were tiny—just infants. The third was a woman, her blackened arms draped over her babies. A mother, trying to protect her family even as they burned.

There was sudden movement behind one of the ruined buildings. Palenie's hand dropped instantly to her sword. Her whole body tense, Elodie tried to draw hers, but the hilt caught in the scabbard and the blade jammed fast.

She relaxed when she saw a small group of children coming toward them. They ran past Fessan and his pathfinders to crowd around Elodie's horse. Their upturned faces were filthy and filled with joy.

"The queen!" they shouted. "The queen is here! She's here!"

Elodie couldn't help but smile. "How do you do?" she replied. Then she whispered to Palenie: "How do they know who I am?"

Palenie was smiling too. "News travels."

A crowd awaited them in the small village square. When the Trident column arrived, they raised a ragged cheer. The people had gathered before the only building left intact: a forge, from the eaves of which hung iron horseshoes and farming tools.

The building where they make fire, Elodie thought, *and the only one that didn't burn.*

A woman rushed up to Elodie carrying a garland of flowers. Elodie leaned forward in the saddle and dipped her head so the woman could place the garland around her neck. She inhaled, allowing its scent to mask the lingering aroma of charred wood and burned flesh. The flowers reminded her of Ritherlee.

"You bring us hope of better times," said the woman, squeezing Elodie's hand. Her eyes shone. "It's all we have now. But it's enough. You're all we need, my queen."

"Who did this?" said Elodie. She was aware that she was being watched: by the villagers, by the men and women of Trident. By Fessan.

"King Nynus," the woman replied. "His soldiers, I mean. He won't leave Idilliam himself, they say."

"He must be brought down!" shouted a man from the crowd in front of the temple. "The signs have been hanging in plain sight these past thirteen years. Surely now the time has come."

"Aye," added the woman. "The three stars."

Whispered words rippled through the throng: "The prophecy . . . the prophecy . . ."

"You are one of them," the woman went on. "One of the three. Are you going to Idilliam to take the throne? Do the others await you there? Will you bring us peace? We've lost so much, so much. . . ."

She was crying openly now. Her grip on Elodie's hand had tightened uncomfortably. Elodie endured the pain. Far more distressing was the immense weight she felt pressing down on her shoulders.

"I will take the throne," she said, not knowing if it was what she wanted to say or simply what the woman wanted to hear. "I will take it soon. You will all be safe again. I promise."

"Thank you," the woman cried. "Thank you, my queen!"

They passed through the village to the mingled sounds of cheering. Children ran beside the horses, waving rags and burned leaves as if they were flags. Many people fell to their knees as Elodie passed, hands clasped to their breasts, their faces hopeful and happy.

"You see?" said Palenie with a smile as they turned onto the wide dirt track that led away from the village through the steadily thinning woods. "They already love you."

This wasn't how Elodie had imagined greeting her people. Her daydreams had always been set in a glittering balcony, from which she in a flowing gown waved to a rapturous crowd. This muddy track and the dirty faces around her couldn't have been more different, yet a glow of pride filled her—and the desire to protect. *When I'm queen I will rebuild all this*, she thought fiercely. *They will want for nothing.*

"Princess Elodie!" It was Fessan, calling from the head of the column. She trotted her horse up to meet him, conscious of the stress he'd place on the word "princess."

"Stay close to me now," he said. "I did not expect news of our march to spread so quickly."

"They were pleased to see us," Elodie pointed out.

"Yes. But not everyone will feel the same."

It was nearly evening when the Trident column reached a wooden bridge crossing a deep stream. A crowd of perhaps fifty people had gathered at the end of it; they seemed to be waiting for them.

To Elodie's surprise, Fessan didn't slow his pace as the procession drew near to the bridge. Instead, he sent outriders galloping ahead and spurred his horse to a trot.

"What's he doing?" said Elodie.

"The crown holds strong here," said Palenie. She drew her sword.

Now they were close enough for Elodie to see the faces of the people awaiting them. Most of them looked angry. A chant rose up as the outriders raced toward them:

"One true king! One true king!"

The front line of the crowd raised rakes and other farm implements to block the outriders' path. One or two even had swords. For a moment, Elodie thought the outriders would crash straight through them nonetheless. Her heart leaped into her mouth. But at the last moment, they turned aside.

"All right," muttered Fessan. "If they won't clear the bridge, we do this the hard way." He turned to the column. "Re-form!" he shouted. "Palenie, take the front!"

Jeering, several people dashed out of the crowd, throwing cabbages and rotten fruit at them as their horses wheeled and reared. Fessan barked commands, restoring order and driving the column toward the bridge. He himself dropped back to Elodie's side.

"Stay close!" he told her.

The outriders took up flanking positions on Elodie's sides, creating a protective box made of horses and armed men. Close by was Rotho, balanced expertly on a huge black charger, sword in hand.

Meanwhile, Palenie's horse had carried her to the head of the line. She held her sword high over her head, the blade glinting in the midday sun.

The column met the crowd. The angry people in the front row stood firm until the last moment, red-faced and yelling. Only when they faced a choice of moving or being trampled did they throw themselves aside. Some were not quick enough; Elodie winced as she heard their screams. Palenie led the column straight through the middle of the horde and onto the bridge. The thudding of hooves on the wooden deck sounded like war drums.

Then Elodie was among the crowd herself. Fessan and his men elbowed people away, or knocked them back with their swords. Rotho urged his great horse onto its hind legs, sending the mob reeling from its thrashing hooves. Still Elodie felt trapped and jostled. Angry faces screamed insults at her. Arms flailed, hurling putrid tomatoes and stinking greens. Something struck the side of her head, pouring down in a trail of slime. Shocked, she put a hand to her hair and found a broken egg.

Rotho gave a cry of anger. "Dare you to insult your queen?" He spun his horse at a man clutching another egg, and with a whirl of his blade, knocked it from his hand. The man turned and fled.

As Elodie wiped her hair, someone laughed. Somehow, this was far worse than being hit. She whirled in her saddle, only to see the grinning face of Stown, riding close behind.

"Enjoying your first taste of battle?" he said.

"I thought you'd be skulking at the back," Elodie retorted.

"What, and miss all the fun?"

Furious, Elodie faced forward again. Wasn't it enough to have enemies outside Trident?

"Go back!" yelled a woman from the mob.

"Any farther, you'll regret it!" cried another.

"Don't let the usurper girl pass!" a man chanted, over and over again.

"Listen to my warning!" This came from a young man with a shock of white hair running alongside the column, forcing his way through the crowd just like the trotting horses. "We know of you and your triplet kin. If any of you try to take the throne, blood will flow. Hear me now! Turn back!"

Fessan raised his sword. Elodie's heart shrank with horror. She knew violence would have to be done to take the throne, but surely it needn't be today? By striking the young man down, Fessan would just be proving his warning true.

"No, Fessan! Spare him!" she cried. Suddenly she was seeing not just a man and a sword but a village filled with burned bodies, a kingdom littered with corpses. An entire world at war.

Fessan swung his arm, leading not with his weapon's metal edge but with his elbow. Knocking the white-haired man aside, he sheathed his weapon and rode on. The column flowed over the bridge, and soon the stream, the bridge, and the crowd were dwindling behind them as the woods thinned and they galloped out into rolling meadow.

Had Fessan heard her plea? Elodie didn't know. All that mattered was that the fighting she knew would come had been postponed—for now.

That night they camped in the lee of a steep hill thick with juniper bushes. Elodie lay shivering in the tent she shared with Palenie. She could hear her friend's breath rise and fall with sleep, her long, red hair spread out in an inky shadow in the darkness. But sleep eluded Elodie. Too many thoughts filled her head—about Samial, about her brothers, about what might lie ahead. Giving up, she fumbled for where Palenie had dropped her huge bearskin cloak in a corner, wrapped it around herself, and stole out of the tent.

The cold air made her draw a sharp breath. She pulled up the tooth-fringed hood and wandered the camp until she reached the temporary corral containing the horses. She found Discus and gave him the apple she'd brought. He munched it eagerly, then nuzzled her. She pressed her forehead against his nose; then, resting her hand against the warm pulse of his neck, she gazed up at the night sky.

There they were: the three prophecy stars. She should have grown used to the sight by now, but every time she saw them her wonder only grew.

I am them, she thought. *And they are me.*

Except that wasn't quite right. It wasn't "I." It was "we," and it was "us." Would she be with Gulph soon? And what of her other brother? Wherever he was, she hoped he was safe.

"Three are stronger than one," she murmured to Discus, running her hand down his gray mane.

The night deepened, and the air grew even colder. Elodie wrapped the cloak tightly around herself. A voice called, very far away, or else it whispered very close—Elodie couldn't be sure.

Just someone crying in the night, she told herself.

Or a voice of someone dead. The thought gave her a chill.

Blowing on her hands, Elodie patted Discus's flank and headed back toward the tent. On the way she passed three watchmen, all of whom nodded to her. She had no doubt her every move had been observed.

She supposed that, once she was queen, it would be like that for the rest of her life. At least life at Castle Vicerin meant she was used to it.

"The princess throw you out?" asked one of the men. "Too high-and-mighty to share a tent?"

Elodie turned. He was one of Stown's cronies—Merrick, if she remembered rightly. She scowled at him. "What do you mean by that?"

Realization passed over Merrick's face. "Oh, it's you," he said irritably. "Thought you were Palenie. That's her cloak, ain't it? And you've got the same hair and all."

"My hair isn't red," Elodie retorted. Did they look alike? It had never occurred to her.

"Oh yes, it is. With a bit of gold. You're nearly the same, I tell you."

"Don't be daft, Merrick," said his companion. "You're just seeing double, is all."

"And being rude on top of it," said Elodie. She felt her cheeks flushing. "You could just leave, if I annoy you that much." Sweeping the cloak around her, she made her way back to the tent. Once there, she stopped. Strange sounds were coming from inside: a kind of heavy breathing, but muffled.

Palenie doesn't snore. . . .

Suddenly afraid, Elodie gripped the tent flap. Her hand was shaking; her heart scampered like a frightened rabbit in her chest. Steeling her nerves, she eased back the flap.

The starlight revealed Palenie. Her arms and legs were thrashing, thrown wide on the ground. Kneeling over her was a man. His back was turned to Elodie, so she couldn't see his face.

He was holding something around Palenie's throat.

CHAPTER 21

E lodie tried to move her arms, her legs. She wanted to cry out. But nothing happened; she was frozen beneath the tent flap. The edges of her vision blurred, leaving the shocking scene before her crisp and clear.

The intruder was choking Palenie to death. It was one of the thugs they'd encountered at the bridge, she was sure of it. Who else would dare to enter the camp and commit this horrifying crime?

Palenie arched her back and emitted a hideous gargling sound. For an instant, Elodie saw her friend's bloodshot eyes staring wildly back at her, pleading.

The sight spurred her into action. She lunged into the tent. Palenie's sword was hanging in its scabbard from the central support pole and Elodie grabbed the hilt, drawing the long blade in a single, fluid movement. The sword felt heavy and awkward.

Why hadn't she paid more attention in the training sessions?

Use both hands.

The voice sounded like Samial's. But it couldn't have been: He was far away in the Weeping Woods.

Tightening both hands around the cold hilt, Elodie raised the sword over her head, preparing to bring it down on the man's neck. At the last moment, she reversed her grip and stabbed the weapon straight into his back. The sharp tip easily penetrated his leather jerkin, his skin, the flesh beneath. There was a hideous shuddering sensation as it grated over what Elodie could only assume were his ribs.

Instantly, the man went limp. Elodie could almost see the life leaving him, rising from his collapsing body like a cloud of vapor. He fell sideways, sliding off the sword and landing face-first on top of Palenie like a sack of meal. Dark blood spread from beneath his body, glistening in a thin beam of moonlight as it soaked into the furs covering Palenie.

"Palenie! It's all right! I'm here now!"

Staring at her bloodied sword, Elodie suddenly remembered the words of the white-haired man.

Blood will flow!

She'd never imagined the first drop would be by her hand.

Tossing the weapon aside, Elodie attempted to heave the dead man off her friend. He was impossibly heavy. She tried again, fighting the bile rising in her throat, trying not to think about what she'd just done. . . .

I have killed a man!

Putting all her weight into the effort, she finally managed to roll the corpse off Palenie's body. Now the dead man lay on his back, slack face staring sightless at the roof of the tent, framed with blond hair.

The man was Rotho.

Elodie couldn't believe it. Rotho was courtly, charming, a warrior who'd said he'd been honored to fight alongside her. . . . Why would he hurt her friend?

Then she noticed Palenie's long hair spread in a wide, red fan.

Red. She looked down at the cloak she was wearing.

Palenie's.

Of course . . .

"He thought you were me!"

There was something around Palenie's neck. Elodie tore it away—a metal coil as fine as a spider's web, wrapped around the purple-bruised skin. Slipping one hand under Palenie's head, she touched the other to her friend's cheek. Her hands, slick with Rotho's blood, left long red trails on Palenie's skin.

"Palenie!" she cried. "Palenie—wake up!"

Elodie pressed her fingers against Palenie's neck. There was no pulse. She turned her cheek to Palenie's lips. There was no breath. She brushed Palenie's hair back from where it had fallen over her face.

Palenie's eyes stared past her, as lifeless as those of the man Elodie had just killed.

Her friend was dead.

Elodie stumbled backward out of the tent. Somewhere, someone was screaming. She held out her hands to the empty air. She tipped back her head and turned a slow, unsteady circle, all the while gazing up at the three prophecy stars. They glared down at her with their cold, uncaring light.

"Elodie!" The voice was Fessan's. "Elodie! What's wrong?"

She felt his hands catch her. She hadn't even known she'd been falling. His face hovered over hers, pale and shocked. Other people crowded behind him, their expressions equally startled. How had they known to come?

Elodie realized it was she who'd been screaming.

"She's dead!" she howled. "Palenie's dead and it's all my fault!"

"What? Tell me what happened!" As he spoke, Fessan snapped his fingers and pointed to the tent. Two men ran inside, leaving Fessan to lower Elodie gently to the ground.

"Rotho," she sobbed. The ground was cold and hard. All her strength was pouring out of her, encased in her tears. "It was Rotho. He . . . he . . . he strangled her."

"It wasn't your fault," said Fessan, touching his hand to her brow.

"Yes, it was. If I hadn't come . . . if I wasn't here . . . Palenie would still be alive."

"It was Rotho who killed her."

"But he thought Palenie was me! It's all my fault! If it wasn't for me . . . if I wasn't here . . ."

Elodie curled up, her arms clutched around her knees. The sobbing racked her body from head to toe.

One of the men came out of the tent, his face ashen. He handed the metal coil to Fessan.

"A garotte," spat Fessan in disgust. "I have heard these are used in other lands. This is no Toronian weapon."

Stown had come hurrying over. He looked into the tent, then he marched toward Fessan, jabbing with a finger. "You did this," he yelled. "You let an assassin among us!" He turned to the others. "For how long will we suffer this weakling as leader? Until we're all murdered in our sleep? How—"

A blow from Fessan's fist silenced him. Stown staggered back, clutching his jaw.

"Get him out of my sight," said Fessan. "Now!"

Stown was dragged away, and all around, people began to make themselves busy—except Fessan, who stayed with Elodie, stroking her head.

"Leave me alone!" she said.

"Never, Princess," he replied.

She tried to push him away, but he might as well have been made from rock. At last she gave up and simply leaned against him with her head thrown back, crying out her grief, her guilt, her pain, staring up at stars made blurs by her endlessly flowing tears.

And the stars stared back down.

Later that night—when Elodie's tears had stopped and her body had stiffened—a woman came up to Fessan and knelt by his side. They started whispering.

"What are you talking about?" said Elodie. "Tell me."

"A grave's been dug," said the woman. "We thought . . . we thought Fessan might want to say a few words."

"Are you going to do it now?"

"It must be done," Fessan replied. "We cannot stay here. And . . . she cannot come with us."

Elodie wiped her face. "Wait for me."

Rubbing the cold from her arms and legs, Elodie hurried back to the tent. Palenie's body was gone; so was Rotho's. Someone had covered the enormous bloodstain with a carpet of furs. But the tent still stank of death.

She picked up the garland of flowers she'd been given in the village, then accompanied Fessan to the hastily dug grave. She tried to listen as Fessan spoke to those watching about bravery and sacrifice, but none of the words seemed to mean very much.

All that mattered was the moment when she placed the flowers on Palenie's breast, just before her body was covered with earth. In memory of what Palenie had told her of the tree in her village, she'd found some chestnut leaves and woven them among the flowers.

"Farewell, true friend," Elodie said through her tears. "Be at peace."

It should have been her whose body was vanishing into the ground. She clenched her fists. She couldn't believe how easily Rotho had fooled her, with his bowing and compliments—she wished she could kill him all over again.

Afterward, Fessan took her back to his tent. He talked all the way there, and continued to talk once they were inside. All Elodie could do was stare at the flame flickering in the single oil lamp hanging from the tent's supporting frame.

"Elodie? Princess? Are you listening to me?"

His voice pierced her thoughts. What had he been saying? Something about rounding up Stown and his followers and ejecting them from Trident.

"I'm sorry," she said. "Please, carry on."

"I tolerated their presence for too long," Fessan growled. "I was too distracted by Stown's constant griping to notice the viper in our nest. To think I welcomed Rotho to our cause! I don't know where he came from, but we must be vigilant against others that might follow. No, *I* must be vigilant. If this tragedy is anybody's fault, Elodie, it is mine."

Then, somehow, it was morning, and Elodie was sitting astride Discus near the head of the column. The camp had been struck and Trident was marching again. To the south, on the far side of a wide open meadow, a motley band of men trudged with their heads down back toward the river: Stown and his men, heading into exile.

"Are you all right?" said Fessan, riding up beside her.

Elodie had no idea how to reply, so she simply nodded.

"Would you prefer it if I left you alone?"

She nodded again, and Fessan rode forward, signaling to the other riders to pull back a little, and give her space.

As the day grew brighter, Elodie's thoughts cleared, although her head throbbed with a deep, pulsating ache that started at the back of her neck and ran all the way around to her forehead. She massaged her temples, trying to banish the tiredness. And the grief.

The pain eased a little, but the throbbing continued. Soon she realized the throbbing wasn't in her head after all, but in the air all around her. Gradually it condensed into a sound, quite close—a sound like . . .

Horses?

"Elodie?"

She turned—and flinched with such shock that her feet jerked from her stirrups and her hands let go of the reins. She teetered on her saddle, on the verge of falling.

Samial was beside her.

He was riding on a silver horse that matched Discus stride for stride. Under the bright sun's glare, both the boy and his steed seemed to shimmer, as if she were seeing them underwater.

"Careful," Samial said with a laugh as she recovered herself. Then his grimy face became taut with concern. "Are you angry with me?"

Elodie felt she ought to be. He'd let her believe he was real, let her think he was her friend. . . . Except, she realized now, it had all been true after all. He was as real to her as the Trident soldiers marching nearby. And he'd listened to her as carefully as any friend. For all the darkness of the previous night, her heart felt unexpectedly light.

"No, Samial," she said. "I've never been more pleased to see anyone in my life!"

Samial beamed. "I have brought help," he said.

He gestured across the field, and Elodie gasped.

Gliding through the grass alongside the Trident column was an army. Silver men rode on silver horses, their armor sheer like silk, their faces hard like steel. Glass spears stabbed the sky; banners of smoke flowed through the air. Their shields glowed with a dim and eerie phosphorescence that somehow outshone the sun, yet at the same time was as dark as shadow.

The throbbing that had filled Elodie's head was the muffled thunder of their passage, the unreal sound of a thousand otherworldly hooves beating time against the skin of the living world.

"A ghost army," she whispered.

"Your army," said Samial, and a tingle shivered its way down Elodie's spine.

"Where did they all come from?"

"You know where. The voices you heard among the trees—they were the voices of these men. These men who died. In the War of Blood, Brutan promised us a truce and freedom. But he had us surrounded in the woods and slaughtered."

"Oh, Samial . . . My father was a monster."

Samial nodded. "Our restless souls could not pass on without revenge. But nor could we leave the place where we died. We were trapped forever inside the Weeping Woods."

"What set you all free?"

"You. Wherever you lead, we can follow."

One ghostly horse peeled away and approached Elodie. On its back was an old man, very tall, with a straight back and a withered but kind face. He wore battered armor and a helmet split almost in two.

"I am Sir Jaken," he said, bowing low in his saddle. "And I am honored to serve you, Princess."

As Sir Jaken and Samial took up their places again, the other riders bowed too, one after the other. The motion began at the head of the army and flowed all the way down the line to the rear, an overwhelming wave of supplication.

Elodie thought her heart would burst with pride.

Fresh hoofbeats cut through the dull rumble of the ghost army, and suddenly Fessan was back. He rode his horse in a wide circle, finally ending up at Elodie's side.

"Something strange is going on," he said. He pointed across the field, to where Elodie could clearly see Sir Jaken and his fellow knights keeping pace with the Trident column. "See there, the way the grass is moving, yet there is no wind?"

"Is that all you see?" said Elodie.

Fessan looked deep into her eyes. "You were talking, just as if there was somebody there. But I saw nobody. What do *you* see, Princess?"

Elodie gestured at the riders of Trident. "The same as you, Fessan. An army prepared to bring down King Nynus and set me on the throne in his place."

Fessan shook his head. He smiled at her. "As you wish, Princess. There is more to you than meets the eye, but I will not ask for more."

His gaze lingered on the grass for a few moments longer before he rode forward, leaving Elodie alone once more.

A cloud passed over the sun, sending a ripple of shadow through the army of ghosts. Elodie shivered.

Are you there, Palenie? There among the dead?

If she was, she wasn't showing herself.

Her friend had told her that her strange ability was a gift. *People won't think it's terrible,* she'd said. *They'll think it's powerful and wonderful. I know I do.* Perhaps Palenie was right, but for now Elodie would keep her secret—even from Fessan. Could Samial and the others fight alongside Trident? Could ghosts even fight the living? She had no idea, and if Fessan didn't believe her, it would be terrible.

Nonetheless, with an army of the dead at her side, she couldn't help feeling that she really did stand a chance of becoming queen of Toronia.

CHAPTER 22

"More venison, Prince Tarlan?"

A servant hovered to the side of Tarlan's chair. The silver platter he held was stacked high with bite-sized pieces of succulent meat. He wore white gloves and, when Tarlan glanced around at his face, he looked away as if afraid to make eye contact.

Tarlan snatched a handful of meat from the platter, savoring the feel of the juices on his fingers. Just as satisfying was the thinly disguised look of disgust on Lord Vicerin's face as he dumped the food on his plate, pushed his cutlery aside, and started shoveling the tidbits one after the other into his mouth.

The conversation around the banqueting table died away as Tarlan continued to stuff himself. He thought their table manners ridiculous, with their dainty little mouthfuls and those foolish white napkins. As for having the food presented one morsel at a time by an army of servants—what was wrong with just sitting beside an open fire and helping yourself?

Most of the other diners—who consisted of Vicerin's cousins and assorted courtiers—shared their lord's look of disdain. The only one who seemed amused by Tarlan's behavior was the young woman sitting opposite him. A little older than him, she watched Tarlan with a wry smile on her pink face. By listening to the conversation, he'd learned her name was Sylva, though he wasn't yet sure where she fitted into the Vicerin court.

"Our princely guest is clearly hungry after his years in the wilderness," said Lord Vicerin, dabbing his powdered face with his napkin. The other diners chuckled politely. "When we have made you king, you will be able to dine like this every day. What do you make of that?"

Tarlan stared at Vicerin and burped. Sylva stifled a giggle. Several of the courtiers seated nearby looked shocked. Lord Vicerin merely gave Tarlan an indulgent smile and returned his attention to his plate.

Like a snake, Tarlan thought, remembering the white asps that used to crawl into Mirith's cave, seeking the warmth of the fire. *He seems slow, but sooner or later—when you least expect it—he will strike!*

Tarlan grabbed his goblet and emptied its contents into his mouth. The others were drinking wine, but he'd refused it and asked for fresh water. As he drank, his elbow nudged the arm of the man beside him.

The man shrank away, brushing at the sleeve of his frilled coat and regarding Tarlan's own garment with an expression of horror.

Looking down at his filthy Yalasti clothes, Tarlan was glad he hadn't bothered with the finery they'd laid out for him. Partly, he found it entertaining to upset these so-called civilized folk. Mostly, he thought it important simply to be himself.

You want to turn me into something I'm not, he thought, regarding Lord Vicerin over the rim of his goblet. *Well, I have a mind of my own.*

However, something still troubled Tarlan—something that prevented him from feeling wholly himself.

"I want my jewel back," he said abruptly, thumping his goblet down on the table.

"All in good time," Vicerin replied. "I have simply put it in a safe place."

"Like you did with those children?"

One of the other diners gasped. A flicker of fear crossed Sylva's face. Vicerin's expression, however, remained serene.

"The jewel is safe," he repeated.

Sensing it would do no good to pursue the subject, Tarlan tried a different tack. "Tell me about my brothers. Or is it sisters?"

Vicerin launched into a lengthy answer full of fancy words that told Tarlan precisely nothing. Again he caught Sylva's eye; this time her smile was kind and a little sad.

"Once we have placed you on the throne," Vicerin concluded,

"we may be in a better position to determine where your siblings are. Alas, as things stand, we know nothing." He spread his hands in mock sympathy.

"I don't care about the throne!" said Tarlan, kicking his chair away from the table. "I just care about my pack. And that includes my siblings!"

Finally Vicerin's calmness cracked. Scowling, he called over a quartet of castle guards.

"The young prince has eaten his fill and is tired," he snapped. "Escort him back to his chambers."

Tarlan allowed the men to take him out of the dining hall. He'd grown used to being escorted this way: two guards in front, two behind. The men stayed far enough away to present the illusion that he was free, but Tarlan knew that the minute he tried to run, they would be upon him.

Halfway up the stairs leading to his tower room, he heard a soft padding sound. It was Sylva, falling into step beside him, having just emerged from a side passage.

"Keep walking," she whispered. "They won't care I'm here."

Tarlan gave her a curious glance and obeyed.

"My father lied to you," Sylva went on in a hushed voice.

"Your father? You mean . . . Lord Vicerin is . . . ?" Tarlan stared at her, feeling stupid. Why hadn't he seen it? "He doesn't seem to like you very much. For a daughter, I mean."

Sylva's shock turned rapidly to laughter. "You're very uncouth!" she whispered.

"What does that mean?"

"Never mind. The point is, your sister and I grew up together. I don't know about your brother, but . . . oh, Tarlan, she looks so much like you."

"My . . . my sister? You've seen her?"

"Of course! The room they keep you in—that was hers, until she was kidnapped by Trident." Her face flushed and her expression became pinched. "That was the worst day of my life. I should have done more."

Tarlan was struggling to keep up. "Kidnapped?" he said weakly. "Who's Trident?"

"Not 'who'—'what.' Trident is an organization, a band of rebels. Outlaws. They want to bring you together, all three of you. The triplets of the prophecy. After Elodie was taken—"

"Elodie?" The name flashed sudden fire through Tarlan's thoughts. He had a sister! She had a name!

Sylva showed him the smile he was growing to like. "Yes. Her name is Elodie. As soon as she was kidnapped I raised the alarm and my father's men gave chase. But the trail went cold at the bridge on the border between Ritherlee and Isur." She lowered her eyes. "In that respect, I suppose he was telling the truth. We don't know where she is."

Tarlan glanced at the guards. They showed no sign of interest in their whispered conversation. All the same, he kept his voice pitched low.

"Why are you telling me all this?" he said. "I mean . . . thank you, but won't your father be angry?"

Sylva blushed a deeper pink. "Elodie was happy here. We were happy together. Like sisters. We *were* sisters. After my brother Cedric went away to war, Elodie was all I had left. But you . . . you don't belong here, Tarlan. You don't want to be here, and you shouldn't have to stay. Nobody should be kept against their will."

They were nearing the top of the stairs. With a final smile, Sylva slipped away. Tarlan watched her pale dress swishing down a side passage and into shadow.

A sister, he thought. *And a friend.*

The guards ushered him into the room that wasn't a room but a prison cell, and locked him away for the night.

Huge wings like golden clouds cast shadows over a land ablaze with fires. On the ground, people run screaming from the flames. Tarlan rides the clouds. He wants to call down to the people that everything is going to be all right, but someone has sewn his mouth shut.

"I cry!" cries a voice high above him.

He tries to look, but someone has wrapped chains around his neck. His whole body is in chains. He can't move a muscle.

"I cry!" says the voice again. "I cry!"

Tarlan struggles against his bonds, desperate to break free from . . .

The dream dissolved. Tarlan lurched from his bed, wide awake, every muscle twitching. He tried to keep hold of the images he'd seen in his sleep—the flames, the golden clouds—but they fled his thoughts even as he tried to tighten his fingers on them.

One thing remained, however.

"I cry!"

Raucous, the voice drifted on the thin night air. Tarlan recognized it instantly.

"Theeta!"

He stumbled to the window and peered out. It was long past midnight, and most of the windows in the castle were dark. The air was cold. Moonlight edged the battlements with silver.

Three golden shadows flew in front of the moon.

"I'm here!" Tarlan cried in the secret tongue only the thorrods knew.

His heart swelled as the three thorrods flew down to the window. He'd been right all along. He had no place among humans. These were his true friends; this was his pack. And they'd come for him!

Theeta arrived first, beating her huge wings hard to maintain a steady hover just below the window. She looked up at Tarlan, her black eyes wide and glistening, soft cooing sounds spilling from her hooked beak. Behind her, Nasheen and Kitheen turned circles in silent and obvious joy. To Tarlan's relief, Nasheen seemed to have recovered from her injury. In fact, he'd never seen the three birds so energized.

And he'd never been so pleased to see them.

Without thinking about what he was doing—and without even a glance back at the luxurious room where his sister had once slept, and that had been his prison cell—Tarlan climbed up onto the window ledge and jumped down onto Theeta's back.

The yielding warmth of her feathers was a thousand times better than the expensive pillows he'd just been sleeping on.

"We go!" Theeta cried. "We go!"

"Yes," said Tarlan, stroking the back of her neck. "Yes, but . . . there's something I have to do first."

The kitchen garden was empty, the gardeners long since retired for the night. A single guard lay slumped and snoring outside the door to the dungeon, an empty bottle by his side. Beside him lay three enormous dogs.

The three thorrods landed without making a sound. Tarlan slipped from Theeta's back and told them in a hushed voice to wait for him.

"Be ready," he said. "We may have to leave in a hurry."

He tiptoed toward the door. As he approached, each of the three guard dogs raised its head in turn. They watched Tarlan for a moment, then stood with their hackles raised, growling menacingly.

"Please," Tarlan whispered. "I'm not doing any harm. Let me past."

The dogs looked confused. Their snarls turned to something resembling language, but it was crude and hard to understand. Walking slowly toward them, Tarlan kept up a stream of soothing words, wondering if living with humans robbed animals of their natural ability to communicate.

To his relief, the dogs backed away, allowing him to lift the keys from the guard's belt and unlock the door. Taking a burning torch from a wall sconce, he made his way to the cells. Behind the bars, the children slept in silence. But they were not the reason he'd come.

He went straight to the wolf. The poor, starving creature was awake and alert, watching his every move.

"I hear you," the wolf said in a growling, guttural tongue, as Tarlan fumbled through the keys on the ring, searching for one that might open the padlock securing the animal's chain. "I am Graythorn."

"I'm Tarlan." He tried a likely-looking key and grinned when the lock snapped open. "And you, my friend, are free."

The wolf stood on shaking legs and stretched. A shudder passed down his body. "Free to help you?" he said.

"I was hoping you were going to say that."

Satisfied, Tarlan made his way back to the exit. Graythorn limped after him. At the end of the passage, he stopped, remembering what Sylva had said:

Nobody should be kept against their will.

Returning to the cells, he looked again at the sleeping children. They were prisoners, just as he had been. Just as Graythorn had been. They too deserved their freedom.

"Sorelle!" he called, making his way between the cells. "Sorelle Darrand!"

A small face rose into the light of the torch: a girl, rubbing her eyes in sleepy surprise.

"That's me," she said. Her voice trembled with fear.

"It's all right," said Tarlan. "I'm going to get you out."

One by one, he unlocked the cells. By the time he'd finished, all the children were awake. They clustered around him, blinking and confused.

Tarlan made a quick head count. There were twelve of them. He cursed himself for not thinking this through. Twelve was surely too many.

"What's happening?" said a young girl. Wide eyes stared at Tarlan from a dirt-smudged face. "Who're you?"

"I'm scared of the dog," said a small boy.

"He's not a dog," Tarlan whispered. "He's a wolf. And he's a friend. *I'm* a friend, and I'm going to get you out of here. But you have to be quiet. Now, do you know how to tiptoe?"

The children nodded mutely.

"All right. Now follow me. And not a sound."

The minute the words left his mouth, the dungeon filled up with a dreadful screeching. Several of the children clapped their hands over their ears; others started to cry. The stiff hairs on the back of Graythorn's neck stood up in a trembling ruff, and the wolf started to growl.

"Theeta!" said Tarlan.

"Who is Theeta?" said Graythorn.

"You'll see!"

Abandoning all thought of secrecy, Tarlan plunged into the exit passage. "Graythorn!" he roared over his shoulder. "Round them up!"

Like a sheepdog, the wolf herded the children into a tight group, urging them along in pursuit of Tarlan. As they raced down the passage, the other thorrods added their cries to those of Theeta. The noise was shattering and immense. Tarlan knew that he alone could hear the words of warning within it, and could only imagine how terrifying it must sound to the children.

A dark shape blocked the exit: the guard, standing dazed and confused, his sword half-drawn.

"Who goes—?" he began.

Tarlan barreled into the man, sending him flying across the nearest vegetable patch. As he landed, the guard's helmet slipped aside and his head banged hard on the stone flags of the pathway. His face went instantly slack.

The three guard dogs gathered around the unconscious man, tongues lolling and tails wagging. Tarlan thought they looked immensely stupid.

In the windows overlooking the enclosed kitchen garden, torches were flaring into life. Shocked faces peered down, wondering at the commotion. Ignoring them, Tarlan slowed down, allowing the children to catch up.

"Come on!" he shouted. "Hurry!"

The thorrods were waiting for them in the middle of the garden. The three giant birds were hopping anxiously on their clawed feet, screeching out their concern.

"It's all right," said Tarlan when he reached Theeta. He stroked her beak. "We're here."

"I don't like the birds!" wailed a small voice.

Turning, Tarlan saw the children bunched several paces away. Graythorn prowled behind them, panting, his eyes fixed on Tarlan's.

"There's nothing to be afraid of. This is my pack—friends, understand?"

"Scary birds!"

"Yes, they are," said Tarlan with a grim smile. He picked out Lady Darrand's daughter from the huddle. "Sorelle—are you brave enough to be the first?"

Just as he'd hoped she would, the little girl stepped forward defiantly, her young eyes alight with the same warrior spirit possessed by her mother.

"I'm not afraid!" she piped.

"Good girl!"

Tarlan hoisted her onto Theeta's back, showing her how to bunch her hands into the thorrod's neck feathers. At once, Theeta stopped screaming and twisted her head to brush the smooth upper surface of her beak against Sorelle's arm. The little girl giggled.

"See?" said Tarlan. "Who's next?"

Within moments, he'd lifted all the children onto the thorrods' backs: two for Theeta, five each for Nasheen and Kitheen.

"Graythorn," he said to his new friend. "Your turn." But the wolf was ignoring him, his green eyes fixed on the garden gate. "Graythorn—come on!"

Now the wolf was growling. Stepping away from Theeta, Tarlan saw Lord Vicerin racing toward them from the outer yard. His long purple robes flowed behind him like a stream of ink in the night. His face was set with fury, and his sword was drawn.

Behind him ran an entire squad of castle guards.

"Stop this madness!" Vicerin shouted as he plunged into the garden. "Turn back now, and you'll be forgiven!"

"I've done nothing wrong!" Tarlan snapped back. "Unlike you! And you'll pay for it, Vicerin. You'll pay!"

Moving with surprising speed, Vicerin lunged at Tarlan, sword raised. "I'll *make* you come to heel!"

Tarlan stepped back, but tripped on the edge of the path. He staggered, off balance.

Graythorn's gray body flew through the moonlight, fur flashing momentarily silver. His jaws closed on Vicerin's arm, stopping it dead. The wolf's momentum carried both him and Vicerin to the ground.

Recovering himself, Tarlan sprang onto Theeta's back.

"Graythorn!" he yelled. "Come on!"

The wolf was standing over the screaming Vicerin, shaking his head back and forth, his teeth locked in the lord's forearm. Reluctantly he relaxed his hold and stepped back.

"But he has such a soft throat," the wolf said sadly.

"There's no time! Come, Graythorn! Now!"

The wolf jumped onto the waiting thorrod's back, leaving the bleeding Vicerin whimpering on the ground. Tarlan threw one arm around Graythorn and the other around the two children.

"Theeta! Nasheen! Kitheen!" he roared. "We fly!"

As one, the three mighty birds opened their wings and beat

them against the air. At the same moment, the guards burst into the garden, only to fall back coughing and spluttering as the air whipped up by the thorrods' departure raised a whirlwind of dust and dirt.

Within two breaths they were above the castle wall, and still climbing. Tarlan peered down past Theeta's head to see Lord Vicerin clambering to his feet, clutching his injured arm.

"You're nothing!" The lord's voice rose up, faint but distinct. "Without the jewel—you're nothing at all!"

"I don't need jewels," Tarlan shouted back defiantly. "I don't need anything but my pack!"

Theeta turned, and her great golden wing eclipsed Vicerin and the garden. Soon the entire castle was just a dark red speck in the moonlit landscape.

The rush of excitement slowly ebbed away. So did Tarlan's defiance. The farther they flew from the castle, the more he felt empty inside. He told himself that losing Mirith's jewel didn't matter compared to his freedom.

It's just a bit of stone, he told himself. Mirith had given him many more important gifts—she'd plucked him from the snows and saved his life, had shown him how to talk with the thorrods.

But it did matter. Somehow he felt that he had left a part of himself behind.

By the time they reached the village, dawn was painting the sky pale crimson. Tarlan directed the thorrods to circle in from the east. From the ground, their massive silhouettes would look spectacular against the sunrise.

"I think we've earned ourselves a grand entrance," he said to Theeta, stroking her neck.

Lookouts stationed at the village perimeter quickly raised the alarm. Despite the early hour, the villagers poured out of their houses, weapons at the ready. Barely half of the buildings had survived intact, and the looks on their faces told Tarlan they would do anything to protect the rest.

When they saw it was the thorrods approaching, they dropped their pitchforks and scythes and raised a ragged cheer. The thorrods circled once before coming lightly to earth in the middle of the central square.

As Tarlan hopped down from Theeta's back, Lady Darrand pushed her way through to the front of the joyous crowd. The instant she saw Sorelle, her stern warrior's face crumpled and she burst into tears.

Tarlan's chest swelled with pride as mother and daughter were reunited. Shouts of delight rang out as one child after another jumped down from their thorrod steeds and ran sobbing into their parents' arms.

Carrying a beaming Sorelle in the crook of her arm, Lady Darrand strode up to Tarlan and kissed him firmly on the cheek.

"My soldiers saw them leave with you," she said, "but could not help. I'm sorry. And now you have brought me the greatest gift." Even in joy, her voice was fierce. "You are a wonder, thorrod rider."

Something pushed past her legs: a small animal with blue-and-white-striped fur. Tarlan dropped to his knees and held out his arms.

"Filos! Come to me!" The little tigron bounded into his arms, purring madly. "Are you all right? How are you feeling?"

"Better now you are here," Filos replied in her tigron tongue, rubbing her head against his chest. "I belong with you."

"Your friend is as pleased to see you as I am," said Lady Darrand, smiling down at them. "Tarlan—I thank you with all my heart for what you have done. I owe you more than anyone can repay. If ever a time comes when I can honor my debt, call on me."

"I will," said Tarlan.

Her gratitude—and Filos's loyalty—warmed his heart, even as the rising sun warmed the back of his neck. Yet as he smiled back at Lady Darrand, a small voice in the back of his mind warned him not to get attached to these humans. He'd simply done them a useful service and his involvement with their affairs was over.

Now it was time to leave.

CHAPTER 23

Gulph pressed his face against the bars, wishing for the hundredth time that he could find a space wide enough to squeeze through. His shackles hadn't stopped him from making a complete tour of the cell, so he knew for certain no such space existed. But it didn't stop him from hoping.

"What do you see?" said Captain Ossilius.

Despite the wretched state of his clothes, the former officer of the King's Legion stood tall and proud. The morning sun, slicing through the prison bars, painted his filthy uniform with bright stripes. He scratched his unkempt beard and gave Gulph a wan smile.

It was Ossilius who'd saved him when he'd first been thrown in the cell. As Gulph had lain on the floor, with the leering prisoners crowding over him, Ossilius had pushed them aside. Despite his fall from grace, it seemed he could still command a certain respect;

once the others realized Gulph was in his favor, they left him alone.

As soon as he'd made space around them, Ossilius astonished Gulph by dropping to his knees.

"Forgive me," he said.

"Forgive you?" said Gulph. "For what?"

"For being taken in by Nynus and Magritt. I fear my loyalty to the crown blinded me. Now I have paid the price."

Gulph had always thought Ossilius's face was sad. Now the man looked distraught.

"We were all fooled," Gulph said.

"And betrayed."

"That too." Gulph felt sympathy for this broken man. But what could he say that would help? "That's why we're better than them. Because we believed the world was a good place."

Ossilius snorted. "And now we know the truth."

Gulph took his shoulders. "Yes. We know we were right."

"Do you think so? Let me tell you about this 'good world.' This 'good world' saw my only son taken from me and beaten nearly to death. They split the side of his face open. His crime? Defending another man from being stoned by the King's Legion. That's why I became a legionnaire myself: to try to change things from the inside. But nothing changes."

"I'm sorry. Where's your son now?"

"He escaped," said Ossilius with fierce pride. "I receive word from him now and again, through secret channels. He has raised an army of outlaws, rebels with one mind: to storm Idilliam and see the prophecy fulfilled. He believes in the tale of the triplets, you see. He has devoted his life to them. He is a strong man, my son. My Fessan."

Later, with Ossilius snoring beside him, Gulph wrestled with the idea of telling him the truth: that he himself was one of the triplets. The secret was stuck inside him, like a lump of food lodged in his throat. If only he could cough it out, perhaps he could start breathing properly again.

More than once he found himself reaching out to Ossilius, hand poised to shake the man from his slumber, lips ready to spill their secret. Each time he stopped himself. Telling the truth would be like releasing a caged animal. There was no telling what damage it might cause.

Gulph wrestled with his thoughts long into the night. He thought he would never get to sleep.

But in the end, he did.

Now, as they stood together at the mesh of bars making up the walls of the prison, looking out over the city at the damaged bridge, Gulph discovered that his new companion wasn't as broken as he'd seemed the previous night.

"Fessan will come," Ossilius hissed. "I know it. I will soon see my son again."

"He'll have to be quick," Gulph replied.

They watched in silence as another gang of laborers was marched out of the castle, their legs in chains. Men had been toiling all night to complete the work Nynus had begun but, as far as Gulph could see, the gap between the two ends of the broken bridge had grown no wider. Like the roots of a mighty oak tree, the jutting stonework held fast to the sides of the chasm, showing little sign of further collapse.

"The gap can be crossed," Ossilius insisted. "Fessan will bring woodsmen, siege engines. He will find a way." His face fell. "But you are right, Gulph. It cannot hold forever. Sooner or later the rest of the Idilliam Bridge will fall, and the city will be cut off from Toronia. Then it will all be over."

Gulph suspected it might be over already, but he clapped Ossilius on the back. "Then let's hope Fessan comes sooner."

There was a commotion at the entrance to the cell. The other prisoners surged toward the noise, then immediately fell back, creating a space around the door. The lock clicked and the door opened with a hideous metallic squeal to reveal Blist standing in full armor, a barbed whip dangling from his hand. Behind him stood six other guards, all heavily armed.

Gulph shrank back against the bars, wondering what violence was about to ensue.

"It's your lucky day!" Blist boomed. "You've all got a free pass out of this stinking hole. Are you ready to step outside?"

Muttered conversation broke out, but it died away as the guards dropped great lengths of chain onto the floor. Leg irons were set at regular intervals along the coils. This didn't look like freedom to Gulph.

"The king is impatient," Blist went on. "He wants the bridge destroyed, and he wants it done quick. So you lot are going to help."

"I'd rather stay here," growled one of Gulph's cell mates. "That bridge goes down, we all go down."

Blist cracked his whip. The sound echoed like an explosion around the cell. Gulph flinched.

"If you do"—he laughed—"you won't be missed."

Under the watchful gaze of the armed guard, Gulph, Ossilius, and the others were marched out of the cell and split into several groups. The prisoners in each group were tethered together. Gulph moved his feet, testing the weight of the irons around his ankles. They were incredibly heavy; walking was going to be agony.

"You!" A hand clamped around the back of Gulph's neck and pulled him violently around. Gulph found himself staring at a grubby man with a face like a weasel. At first he didn't recognize his assailant. Then it came to him.

"Elrick?" he gasped. "General Elrick?"

The last time Gulph had seen him was at the fateful performance in the Great Hall, when he'd first been taken from his friends and thrown into the Vault of Heaven. Memories of that awful day flooded back, not least the tearful expression on Pip's face as they'd been parted. Where was Pip now? And what of the rest of the Tangletree Players?

Gulph's stomach tightened as he contemplated the idea that he might never see his friends again.

Or worse: that they were dead.

"It's your fault I'm in here!" General Elrick was crazed, a scrawny shadow of the smartly dressed soldier Gulph remembered. Yet another loyal servant of whom Magritt had grown tired. "You and your ragamuffin friends! I'm going to kill you!"

Elrick's hands closed around Gulph's throat, cutting off his windpipe. Gulph pawed uselessly at the man's arms, but Elrick was strong. The more Gulph tried to breathe, the more his lungs protested. His breath turned to hot iron. Eyes bulging, he tried to call to the guards, but they were just standing back and enjoying the show.

Suddenly, Captain Ossilius was there, drawing back his fist and punching Gulph's assailant square in the face. There was a crunch. Elrick flew backward, his hands releasing Gulph to clamp themselves against his nose.

Gulph reeled backward, drawing in agonizing breaths through a throat that felt no bigger than a hollow reed.

"You broke my face!" Elrick yelped, tottering against the pull of the leg irons. Blood squirted between his fingers.

"Try that again and I'll break more!" snapped Ossilius. "You're a snake, Elrick. The reason you're in here is all the years you spent sucking up to Brutan. Now he's crow bait, and you're in the Vault of Heaven. I'd call that justice."

"You don't scare me," Elrick whimpered.

"I rather think I do. If you ever lay a finger on my friend here again, I will kill you. Do you understand?"

As the guards marched them past the giant brazier and away from the cell bay, Gulph gradually recovered his breath. He rubbed his aching neck. *My friend*, he thought. He was glad to have Captain Ossilius with him.

By the time they reached the Idilliam Bridge, Gulph's legs were in agony and his ankles were rubbed raw and bleeding. Walking with the chains was like wading through thick mud—except the mud had teeth.

The sun lanced down through swirling gray clouds of dust. Shadows floated in the murk: long lines of men pounding the rock with sledgehammers. The ground shook with each blow, and each blow was accompanied by a chorus of grunts. Some of the men chanted workhouse songs. It was a scene of muscle and barely contained chaos.

Prowling among the chain gangs was a figure Gulph didn't

recognize: a slender man dressed in fine robes. On his head was a ring of gold.

The crown of Toronia.

Nynus!

When Nynus drew near to them, he turned his face fully into the light and Gulph saw it wasn't just the crown Nynus was wearing. His entire face was covered by a mask, shielding him from the sun he hated so much.

The mask bore human features, sculpted from gold, their contours smoothed and simplified. The closer Gulph looked, however, the more he felt chilled. There was something wrong with the fierce angle of the eyes, something too angular about the heavy brow. The golden lips curled in a sneer, revealing ferocious teeth. It looked nightmarish.

Nonetheless, as the king strode toward the prisoners, Gulph shuffled out of the line. Nynus had thought him his friend once. If he could just talk to him, maybe he could persuade the king to let them go. . . .

Nynus drew level with Gulph. The golden mask swiveled to face him. Gulph opened his mouth to speak, but at that moment, the sun burst through the floating dust, bathing the mask with light. The gold seemed to catch fire, a dazzling explosion in the hazy air. Staring at the unwavering eyes inside the mask, Gulph saw that Nynus hadn't just retreated from the sun—he'd retreated from everything. The young king, the wretched boy he'd saved from the Black Cell, was now entirely out of reach.

Gulph shuffled back into line.

"Show me what you can break!" Nynus said. The mask muffled his voice. "If all you men work together, there is no reason we cannot break the world!"

Several of the prisoners exchanged uneasy glances at this. Nynus walked on past, showing no sign of recognizing Gulph as he did so.

I don't recognize you either, thought Gulph sadly.

At Blist's command, the guards escorted Gulph's gang to the place where the end of the bridge met the chasm's edge. To their left and right, similar gangs were hammering at the rock. Their bodies and faces were caked with dust.

A pickax was thrust into Gulph's hand. He thought briefly of using it to cut through the chains around his ankles. It was more likely he'd cut off his foot. Bracing himself, he swung the ax over his shoulder and began to hack at the ground.

The sharp metal head made little impression on the hard rock, and the blows sent painful shock waves through his back and arms. The prisoners were like ants nibbling at a mountain.

Yet, little by little, Gulph could see that progress was being made. Each time he looked up, fresh cracks had appeared in the ground. Sooner or later, what remained of the bridge would be destroyed.

A scream rang out. Gulph looked up in time to see a section

of rock break away from the rest and slide into the chasm. Four prisoners from the Vault were clinging to it, scrabbling frantically in their desperate attempts to reach safety. Back on solid ground, their companions were shouting and clawing at their leg irons.

The men's chains drew tight. One by one, the remaining members of the gang were dragged over the edge and into the abyss, where they fell shrieking to their deaths.

Gulph felt the blood drain from his face. Around him, the other members of his gang had stopped to watch too. Shared glances confirmed that they all understood the terrible situation: if one died, they all died.

Blist's whip cracked and they bent to their labors again. Smaller and lighter than the men around him, Gulph stumbled constantly as the sweating bodies of his fellow workers slammed into him. Every time he fell, Ossilius was there.

"Stay strong, little one," Ossilius said as he picked up Gulph yet again. "Fessan will come."

Gulph admired his fortitude, but there seemed little hope of rescue now. Nynus had commanded them to break the world. And that, it seemed, was exactly what they were bound to do.

CHAPTER 24

Tarlan didn't think he would ever get used to how green the world was beyond Yalasti. Flying over Ritherlee, he'd been constantly amazed by the countless subtle changes in color and tone of the landscape below him: young crops shining with sap; steep meadows edged with yellow where the soil supporting them slid slowly off the underlying bedrock; the cloudy masses of woodland leaves.

Then the broad mirror of the mighty Isurian River and, beyond it, a world that was greener still. Thick forest sprawled as far as Tarlan could see: a tangled carpet of intertwined needles and reaching branches.

Somewhere far to the north lay Idilliam and the throne of Toronia. However, Tarlan's eyes were fixed not on the far distance but on the ground.

"Fly lower, Theeta," he urged, tugging at the neck feathers of his thorrod steed. "Our scouts have got ahead of us again. I don't want to lose them."

Theeta tucked in her wings and dived toward the forest canopy. The wind blasted against Tarlan's face, blowing his long hair back over his shoulders. He whooped. The wind seemed to be blowing right through him. He was here, now, in the sky, where he belonged. Just Tarlan and his pack.

"There!" he shouted, spying movement along a narrow trail, just visible through a gap in the trees. It was Filos, her blue-and-white-striped pelt unmistakable against the overwhelming green of the forest. As Theeta and Tarlan swooped overhead, the tigron cub lifted her head and roared: a high, excited sound.

The drably colored Graythorn was harder to spot. Instinct told Tarlan the wolf would be following a little way behind Filos. A few moments of searching confirmed his suspicion. When Graythorn saw them, he too looked up, gave a single brief "Yip!" and returned his nose to the ground.

Sighting his two earthbound companions filled Tarlan with fierce pride. It also drove away his elation. He was not here to have fun in the air, and this was no child's adventure.

He was on a mission to find his sister.

The more he thought about Elodie, the more he hated the idea of her trapped inside that awful tower room in Castle Vicerin. Even a closet full of beautiful dresses couldn't disguise the fact that she'd been as much a prisoner as he had.

Where are you now? he thought. *Just what do these Trident people want with you?*

The idea that Elodie was still a captive filled Tarlan with rage.

She and his brother were part of his pack too.

It's time we were all together, he thought.

Up ahead, Filos roared again. Tarlan spurred Theeta down to meet her. Filos bounded up to them as the giant thorrod landed on the soft bracken covering the floor of the glade.

"Humans have traveled here," the tigron panted. "Lots of them!"

Sure enough, something had cut a long swathe through the low-lying undergrowth. Tarlan inspected the ground, identifying hoofprints and footprints alike. Wheel ruts carved a long, meandering line through the glade and back into the trees, where the trail widened significantly.

"It looks like an army," he said. "It must be them!"

Graythorn trotted up, tongue lolling. "We saw ashes," the wolf said in his guttural way. "Humans made fire. They left things behind. Humans are so messy."

"These tracks are fresh," said Tarlan. "Theeta—call back the others. I think we're close."

Tipping back her head, Theeta opened her beak wide. Her chest convulsed. Both Graythorn and Filos flinched—the wolf in particular looked distressed, his ears flattened against his head—but Tarlan heard nothing. This was the thorrod long-cry, a sound so high-pitched that few animals could hear it. But it traveled for miles, and it carried a single, undeniable message:

Come quick!

They didn't have to wait long. Nasheen and Kitheen—who had been scouting far and wide so as to spread the search pattern—flew in on silent wings. Theeta and Tarlan met them in the air, drawing the whole formation high enough to look out over the forest again.

The trail they'd seen from the ground was unmistakable from the air. Wide enough to be called a road, it cut a broad furrow northward through the trees. Something was moving along it: a long, snaking formation of men and horses, green flags bright against the darker shade of the leaves.

An army.

Trident.

Tarlan felt the excitement bubbling up inside him. After three days of searching, they'd found her!

"Stay here!" he called down to Filos and Graythorn. "Keep out of sight. Theeta, Nasheen, Kitheen—come on!"

"They see," warned Nasheen as Theeta surged forward.

"We'll circle in behind that row of pines," said Tarlan. "If we stay low, we can scout the terrain without them seeing us."

Theeta steered a course behind as much cover as she could find, on occasion flying so low that her wingtips brushed the ground. The other two thorrods followed, their feathers plumped so as to reduce the noise of their flight to nothing. Tarlan held his breath as they drew near, peering through the screen of woven branches that lay between them and the marching army. Where was she?

"Hie!" cried a voice directly ahead. A horn sounded, its piercing blast shocking in the silence of the forest. Two men wearing camouflaged jerkins covered in leaves ran across their path. Seeing the thorrods nearly stopped them in their tracks, but they urged each other on.

The army column came to a halt. Soldiers raced to form a vanguard. Horses spread out in a circle, their riders drawing swords and raising spears in anticipation of attack.

"No use hiding now," said Tarlan. "Let's see what we're really up against."

Urging Theeta up and over the screen of trees, Tarlan led the thorrods out into the open air above the army. Having learned from his experience with the elk-hunters of Yalasti, he made sure to keep them high and out of range of arrows. Moments later, he was glad he had: a line of archers emerged from the middle of the column, their longbows drawn and aimed directly at the thorrod flock.

"Many men," said Theeta. "Many horse."

Tarlan had to agree. Trident was much bigger than he'd imagined. Apprehension fluttered in his stomach—the thorrods had been instrumental in beating back Lord Vicerin's soldiers from the village, but this . . .

There was a flurry of movement near the front of the column. Armed men on horseback were gathering around a single rider, forming a protective cordon around him.

Or her.

"Go lower, Theeta," said Tarlan. "I have to see. Nasheen, Kitheen—stay here."

As the thorrod flew down, Tarlan spread his arms to show he carried no weapon. His mouth went dry as the bowmen tracked their descent.

Just as they drew close enough to see, the mysterious rider's face tilted back, and Tarlan found himself looking into the keen black eyes of a girl about his age.

No, he thought, *she is* exactly *my age*.

Though she wore the same green uniform as the rest of Trident, there was something different about the girl. There was haughtiness about the way she sat in the saddle. Her face glowed with a curious mix of fear and courage. Her red-gold hair—the same shade as Tarlan's—moved in the wind with a life of its own.

"Girl you," said Theeta. Normally the thorrod's voices were dry and expressionless. In those two simple words, Tarlan heard the sound of wonder.

"Elodie!" he cried. "Elodie! Elodie!"

Her name flew from his lips as if it had been bottled inside him for years. And so it had, but it was more than that: He'd been waiting to shout it his whole life.

They were close enough now to hear the creak of the longbows as the archers prepared to fire.

"I mean you no harm!" Tarlan shouted, not sure if it was entirely true. "All I want is my sister!"

Elodie's mouth dropped open. A young man with a scarred face, riding close beside her, held out his hand to the archers.

"Fast with your bows!" he told them. Then he called up to Tarlan, "Who are you?"

"My name is Tarlan! Elodie is my sister!"

A gasp rose up from the column. Tarlan felt a grim satisfaction that he'd gained their attention without getting shot. But he was painfully aware that at least fifty arrows were pointed straight at Theeta's breast.

"That is quite a claim, young man," called the rider, who despite his young age looked more like a commander than a regular soldier. "And I will grant you look like her. I am Fessan, leader of Trident, and I am loyal to the young woman you say is your sister. Can you prove what you say is true?"

"It's true." Tarlan licked his lips. He had no desire to get drawn into a debate. Only action would free his sister and take him one step closer to completing his pack.

"So you say!" cried Elodie, driving her horse out of the line. Her dark eyes were shining. "Can you prove it? Do you have one of these?"

Reaching inside her tunic, she pulled out a sparkling green jewel and held it aloft.

Tarlan's guts contracted into a hard knot. He opened his mouth to speak, but nothing came out.

It's just like mine!

What more proof did he need that he and this girl were kin?

But it was proof he could not share. His heart sank as he thought of Lord Vicerin, staring up at him as he flew from the castle, boasting that he still had the jewel. No wonder he'd missed it so badly.

"I lost it," he blurted, all too aware of how desperate he sounded. "But I *am* your brother. You have to believe me."

"Imposter!"

Tarlan didn't see who shouted, but before he could respond, an arrow whistled over his head. He grabbed Theeta's feathers and yanked her around just in time to avoid three more arrows as they shot past. He roared, a primal, animal sound. These humans pretended they loved words, but all they ever really wanted to do was fight.

"Nasheen!" he yelled skyward. "Kitheen!"

Theeta screeched as he pulled her around, ready to dive on the archers. On the ground, the troops clapped their hands to their ears. Elodie watched in silence, a rapt look on her face.

"Fast!" yelled Fessan, riding down the line of bowmen. "Fast, I said! I will see no bloodshed here today!"

Tarlan tugged on Theeta's feathers, pulling her out of her dive barely a tree's height from the ground. As she hovered, the shadows of the other two thorrods fell over them.

"Wait!" said Tarlan, raising his hand. "Don't attack yet."

Nasheen and Kitheen fell into formation, one on each side of Theeta. Their great gold wings beat the air with a slow, threatening rhythm. At the sight of them, more weapons rose from the ranks of Trident: swords and spears bristling along its length like the hackles of some threatened beast.

"Let them land!" Fessan bellowed.

Elodie whirled on the column. "And hold fast your weapons!" she shouted. "All of them!"

With obvious reluctance, the archers lowered their bows and returned the arrows to their quivers. Slowly, the entire column relaxed. Tarlan was startled to see the power his sister apparently had over this army.

"Safe now," said Theeta.

Tarlan had been worrying it was a trick, but the thorrod's certainty gave him hope. Was it worth the risk?

One look at Elodie's eager face told him it was worth everything.

"Down, Theeta," he said. "Slow and careful. Don't alarm them."

Leaving their companions circling overhead, they touched down beside Fessan. As Tarlan jumped from Theeta's back, Fessan dismounted. Tarlan stood, his whole body tensed, as the leader of Trident walked a complete circle around him.

"You have her face," he said in wonder. He opened the collar of Tarlan's tunic. "Your skin is very tanned, except for these lines. Once you wore something around your neck."

"The jewel, like I said," said Tarlan. He wanted to sound defiant, but all the anger had drained from him.

"Tell me again who you are."

Tarlan drew himself up to his full height. "I am Tarlan of Yalasti. I have crossed the Icy Wastes to be here. I am leader of my pack. And I am Elodie's brother."

"Yes," said Fessan, "I believe you are."

He turned slightly, performing the trick of talking both to Tarlan and to the watching crowd.

"We mean your sister no harm," Fessan announced. "We protect her, just as we will protect you, Tarlan. You are the second of three, and we will not rest until you and Elodie are reunited with your lost brother. We march with the strength of not only weapons but the power of the prophecy. Your arrival has doubled our hope, Tarlan—the hope that we will overthrow the cruel king of Toronia and return this realm to the peace it deserves."

He paused. Tarlan held his breath, expecting a cheer. Instead, there was an expectant silence.

Fessan spoke again, this time pitching his voice so low that only Tarlan could hear. Just for a moment, the rest of the world faded to transparency.

"Will you join us?" said Fessan.

The young man's expression was so earnest, his gaze so piercing, that Tarlan was transfixed, as if he'd been pierced by one of the bowmen's arrows. He was suddenly aware of the vastness of the forest around him, and of all the rest of the great kingdom beyond that, of the heavens above him and the hidden underworlds below. What were human squabbles over a crown compared to this?

"I don't want—" he began.

"Tarlan!"

Elodie was running toward him, filling his vision, suddenly and undeniably there before him. Her face was streaked with tears. Spreading her arms wide, she pulled him into a tight embrace that went on and on. Her chest heaved against his, hitching in breaths and letting them out in faltering sobs. He allowed his own arms to close around her back, wondering at the force that drew them in, and held her.

Eventually they parted. She gripped his shoulders, holding him at arm's length, staring with wonder into his face. Her eyes shone.

"I didn't want to believe you existed!" She laughed. Her voice sounded familiar. How could that be when they'd never met? "When I first heard about you, I was so angry. . . . Can you imagine? But since then . . ." Her face fell. "A lot has happened, Tarlan. Now that you're here . . . I feel like I've found myself."

Tarlan tasted again what he'd been about to say: *I don't want any part of your war; Just let me leave with my sister; Leave us alone.* The words were bitter to him now.

"I'm glad I'm here," he said.

"Well?" said Elodie, glancing at Fessan. "Will you?"

"Will I what?" Tarlan asked.

"Join us!"

Something broke inside him. It cracked like winter ice left too long in the summer sun. Whatever it was, it splintered into countless tiny shards that melted and flowed invisibly away.

This is what Mirith would want.

"I will," he said, "but on one condition."

"Condition?" said Fessan.

"My pack comes too."

Elodie looked puzzled. "Pack?"

Tarlan whistled. Filos and Graythorn burst at once from nearby undergrowth. Clearly they'd ignored his instruction to keep their distance. Tarlan grinned. He was pleased.

Several people cried out at the sight of the animals. One of the archers raised his bow, but lowered it again as the tigron and the wolf bounded around Tarlan's legs.

Tarlan waved Nasheen and Kitheen down. They alighted with soft thuds on the trail beside him. Reunited, the three thorrods clustered together, cooing softly in the language that only Tarlan could understand.

"Yes, we're going with them," he told his pack. "We're going with Elodie."

"You can talk to them?" said Elodie in wonder.

"Yes." Tarlan felt a swell of pride. "They're your pack too," he said.

Now came the cheer. It began at the head of the column and raced all the way to the far end. Weapons rose again, this time not in threat but celebration. Tarlan stroked Filos's back, and scratched Graythorn's ears, and stared and stared at his sister, wondering if the smile would ever leave his face.

"Two of the three are with us!" Fessan shouted, stilling the uproar with his raised hand. "The third we know is waiting for us in Idilliam. So to Idilliam we march! We march for the prophecy! We march for the kingdom! We march for the crown of three!"

CHAPTER 25

Gulph spent the morning in a daze of swirling dust and blazing light. The sun was a furnace, beating down on the back of his head through the clouds of powdered stone. His arms ached, right down to the bone; his hands were covered with huge blisters. With every blow of his pickax on the rocky ground, his body rang like a bell.

Progress was agonizingly slow. Occasionally a shelf of rock would detach itself and plunge into the chasm's dark depths. But Gulph had no sense of whether the work would take days or weeks or even years. Perhaps in the very next moment the last surviving section of the bridge would collapse and Idilliam would be cut off from the rest of Toronia forever.

Or perhaps he would be toiling here for the remainder of his life.

A bugle call cut through the haze. Gulph ignored it and focused his attention on swinging his pickax, only slowly realizing that all around him the other prisoners were stopping work.

"Take a break, lad," said Ossilius, resting his hand on Gulph's arm. Like Gulph's, his palms were oozing blood. Caked from head to toe in fine white dust, he looked like a statue come to life.

Exhausted, Gulph leaned on his pickax. The sandy air scoured his throat. He must look as bad as Ossilius, he thought, if not worse. His fine court clothes were in rags and his hands and ankles looked like raw meat.

A battalion from the King's Legion had taken up position at the outermost edge of the bridge. A smaller group of armed men appeared through the murk, escorting a robed figure: King Nynus. The smooth gold mask seemed to float in the air, not part of the young monarch's body but belonging somehow to another realm altogether.

Drawing near to Gulph, Nynus stopped.

"Take heart, you who work in the name of the king!" he cried. His voice, muffled by the mask, seemed to come from a great distance. Though he spoke to the crowd, his eyes—clearly visible as bright beads through the mask's eyeholes—remained fixed on Gulph. "Now is your chance to be free!"

Despite everything, Gulph's heart rose in his chest. But what the king said next turned his hope to despair.

"I mean free to return to your cells, of course," Nynus went on with a thin, metallic laugh. "Behold—your savior approaches!"

Two legionnaires appeared behind him. All eyes turned to them. Between them they were carrying a slim figure wearing only a torn gray shift: Limmoni. Her bare feet dragged on the stony ground. Her head lolled. Her arms were covered in bruises.

When they reached the king, the legionnaires released her. At once Limmoni fell to her knees. Gulph started forward, but Ossilius held him back.

"You cannot help," the captain said.

"But she can't even stand!"

Yet, to Gulph's amazement, Limmoni struggled to her feet. She stood before the king, her body swaying, her legs looking ready to buckle at any moment. Her head hung, hiding her face. But she stood.

"You are recovered," said Nynus. "You will finish what you started. You will destroy what is left of the Idilliam Bridge. Do this, and you will be free to leave this land, on the understanding that you never return. Refuse, and you will die."

Slowly, Limmoni raised her head. The sun, breaking through the dust, sculpted her face with light. When he saw her look of determination, Gulph's breath caught in his throat.

"I am a true wizard," she said. Her voice was cracked and desert dry, but it echoed in strange ways, seeming to come from many different directions at once. Gulph touched his hand to his ear, unsure of what he was hearing.

"Yes!" snapped Nynus. "And you will use your powers to serve the king!"

"No true wizard would ever do what you ask. To bring down the Idilliam Bridge is to bring down Toronia."

"I ask nothing of you, wizard! I command! Upon the king's order, you will destroy the bridge!"

"If it is destruction that you desire, King-of-the-Mask, then destruction will be upon you."

Limmoni raised her hand. The rest of her body was trembling, almost out of control, but her hand remained utterly still. Light flared, spreading from the center of her palm to form glowing webs that scintillated between her outstretched fingers.

The words she'd spoken seemed to linger in the air. As the light expanded from her hand, Gulph felt the echo of her voice boring into his skull. All around him, men were dropping their tools and clamping their hands against their ears. The air buzzed. The ground softened. Somewhere—perhaps everywhere—people started screaming.

One of the legionnaires was drawing his sword.

"No!" shouted Gulph. Again he lunged forward, desperate to save the young woman who'd shown him who he really was. Again Ossilius held him back.

"They'll kill you!" he hissed. "And you're no good to her dead."

Gulph shook him off, tried to run toward his friend, but the chains stopped him, yanking at his wounded ankles and dragging him down to his knees.

The light exploded from Limmoni's hand. But even as it tore a jagged hole in the air on its way toward Nynus's mask, the legionnaire thrust his sword into Limmoni's back. Gulph looked on in horror as the tip of the blade, red with blood, emerged from her chest.

At once the light winked out. The bolt of lightning Limmoni had hurled at Nynus contracted to a dazzling line—a scratch against the sky—then vanished altogether. Her face stiffened and her eyes grew wide. Blood trickled from between her lips.

Gulph clenched his fists, heedless of the pain as a dozen blisters burst on his palms.

And Limmoni continued to stand.

"Do not kill her yet!" said Nynus. He stalked up to her as she stood balanced in the dust. The legionnaire had released his grip on the sword's hilt, but the weapon was still inside her—through her. Slowly, a dark stain was spreading from the wound, turning her gray shift the color of wine.

Nynus's whole body was shaking with rage. Spittle flew from the mouth of his mask as he shrieked at the woman on whom his entire plan had rested.

"You dare to defy me?" he howled. "You had the chance to save yourself and this is how you repay me? Well then, you will die indeed!"

"I am already dying," Limmoni gasped. Each word was accompanied by a bubble of blood.

"Perhaps. But there is still time for you to take your place among the traitors of the realm. Beside the biggest traitor of them all, in fact. Legionnaires! Take her to the mausoleum. I think it's time my father had a little company!"

Gulph looked on in horror as Limmoni, still impaled on the sword, was hauled through the dust and rubble to the foot of the towering mausoleum. The rows of people who'd come to watch the spectacle of the bridge's destruction—from the highest courtiers to the lowliest peasants—fell back to watch her pass. A few called out curses and insults. Most just watched in silence.

Using the stepped stonework on the mausoleum's curved wall, the soldiers manhandled Limmoni's limp body up onto the roof. By the time they were halfway up, her slack face and dangling limbs had convinced Gulph she was already dead. But as the two men dragged her over the parapet and onto the upper dome, her eyes opened.

The person she sought out in the crowd—and with whom she locked her gaze—was Gulph. Her expression was taut and anguished. Gulph had never seen anyone look more wretched.

"Do something!" he muttered under his breath. "Make your magic! Save yourself!"

But her eyes filmed over, and her gaze dropped.

"Put the wizard in her place!" shouted Nynus. He was pacing to and fro, marking out a cell-sized patch of ground.

The legionnaire threw Limmoni down onto the sloping surface of the roof. She landed beside Brutan's rotting corpse. The crows that had been feeding on his remains flapped their big black wings and took to the sky, squawking angrily at having their meal disturbed.

Limmoni raised her arms.

"Please stop this!" she cried, her voice stronger than it had any right to be. Gulph assumed she was about to plead for her life. Instead, she went on: "Kill me if you must, but not here. Not like this. You do not understand what you are dealing with. The forces—"

Limmoni choked on the blood streaming from her mouth. Gulph pulled uselessly at his ankle chains. He couldn't believe she was still alive. Any ordinary person would have been dead long ago.

But Limmoni is no ordinary person.

"Enough!" Nynus yelled. "Take off her head!"

The legionnaires exchanged puzzled looks. The first was armed only with a pair of knives; the sword belonging to the second was still buried in Limmoni's chest.

Shrugging, the man who'd stabbed Limmoni kicked her over, grabbed the hilt of the sword, and pulled the blade with one swift movement out of her body.

Limmoni lay slumped for a moment before rising slowly to her knees. She spread her arms and lifted her pain-racked face to the sky.

Arching his back, the legionnaire raised the sword over his head. At the top of his swing, he paused. The sun flashed off the blood-covered blade.

He brought the blade down.

Gulph closed his eyes. Bending double, he clamped his hands over his belly, seized by a sudden, dreadful pain. He moaned: an incoherent cry of helpless anguish.

There was a stunned silence. Then someone in the crowd cried out.

Standing up straight, Gulph opened his eyes. On the roof of the mausoleum stood the legionnaires, one still recovering his balance after swinging his sword, the other holding something triumphantly in the air.

It was Limmoni's head.

The grief churned in Gulph's belly. He felt faint; he wanted to throw up; he wanted to scream at Nynus, at the very heavens.

What have you done?

The head became a glowing orb of dazzling light. It expanded, swallowing the legionnaires and reducing them instantly to dark smears that dissolved into the air like ink into water.

The light hovered: a pulsing, blinding bubble. Then it exploded.

The blast slammed into the crowd. People fell, screaming, clutching at each other. A tall statue of an ancient king fell sideways, crushing a group of courtiers. Dust rose in vast, billowing clouds.

By the time it hit Gulph, some of the shock wave's energy had dissipated, but it was still powerful enough to knock him off his feet. As he struggled upright, the ground beneath him bucked like an unbroken stallion. At his feet, the chains coiled and uncoiled like angry snakes.

Clouds rolled over the mausoleum, throwing the great circular building into shadow. Gray ash rained down from the clouds. Soon, the entire structure was covered.

Gradually the dust settled. Those who had fallen rose unsteadily to their feet. The injured called out for help. Looking around, Gulph saw Ossilius lying awkwardly on his side, a tangle of chains piled over his legs. He pushed the chains away and helped the man stand.

"What happened?" Ossilius said.

"They killed her."

Saying it aloud made it real. A lump rose in Gulph's throat. It was over. Limmoni was gone.

On the mausoleum roof, something moved.

Despite the horror of everything he'd seen, Gulph felt himself grinning. Gripped by a ferocious excitement, he watched as a figure clambered out of the ashes. She was alive! Somehow—through some magic he couldn't comprehend—Limmoni had cheated death.

But the figure was not Limmoni.

"What passes?" said Ossilius. He repeated the phrase over and over again. It filled Gulph's head. "What passes? What passes?"

The figure rising from the ashes was tall and broad: a man. Its body was skewed sideways, as if the bones in its back were not properly aligned. Its head was misshapen. Light showed through holes in its chest. Its flesh—clearly visible through tattered rags that had once been clothes—was rotten and squirming with maggots.

Its eyes were empty sockets.

Slowly, with stiff, shuddering movements, the figure raised its arms to the sky. Half the fingers on its twitching hands were naked bones. As it turned its head, the exposed tendons in its neck stretched like bowstrings.

"What passes?" whispered Ossilius.

"It is Brutan," said Gulph, saying the words but not believing them. *My father.*

On the mausoleum roof, the animated corpse opened its mouth and emitted a long, keening cry that was devoid of all humanity.

King Brutan of Toronia was risen from the dead.

Act Three

CHAPTER 26

W hat's happening?" said Elodie. "It looks like the end of the world."

She tapped her heels against Discus's flank, urging him forward to the front of the Trident line, where Fessan was consulting with his lieutenants. Two of the three men seemed no older than Fessan; the third had a thin white beard and a weather-beaten face, and looked as if he'd seen action in every battle of the Thousand Year War. They all wore light helms and breastplates; they all looked uniformly grim.

As the view opened up further, Elodie gasped. Idilliam rose before them, a gigantic city built from gray stone and partly veiled by a rising cloud of dust and smoke. Surrounding it, festooned with turrets, was a sloping defensive wall. Behind the wall rose a dizzying sprawl of buildings, some of them many stories high. Castle Vicerin would have fit inside it a hundred times over.

No, thought Elodie. *A thousand.*

Though she couldn't see the streets themselves, it was clear from the pattern of the roofs that they all radiated out from a central point. It was just as clear what occupied that center: Castle Tor.

The castle dominated the skyline, a brooding mass of stone ramparts and fierce battlements. Crimson flags shuddered in the wind. A thousand windows stared back at Elodie like brooding black eyes. It was a hulking, alien place, and it filled her with dread.

So why does it feel like coming home?

Outside the city wall, perched on the edge of the chasm, stood siege engines, though they were oddly configured; their battering rams appeared to be pointed at the ground. Nearby was a circular building. Its domed roof was cracked and slumped, as if a giant had trodden on it. This was the source of the smoke.

There was movement around the building, but it was too far away for Elodie to make out the detail; they might as well have been ants as people. Nor was there any way to get nearer. Idilliam lay on the opposite side of a vast chasm, and the only way across was a natural bridge of rock spanning the abyss from one side to the other. That was no surprise to Elodie; everyone in Ritherlee—perhaps even everyone in Toronia—had heard of the Idilliam Bridge.

What surprised her was something nobody could have anticipated.

The bridge was broken.

Something echoed behind Elodie, like the memory of hoofbeats. She glanced back to see Samial, who'd shadowed her on the final leg of the journey to Idilliam, riding up on his ghostly steed.

"There has been a battle," said Samial. His horse champed restlessly at the bit. Behind him, the ghost army seemed to swell as, one by one, the phantom knights gathered at the edge of the chasm, forming ranks beside the Trident troops.

There was a rumble like distant thunder. At the far side of the broken bridge, part of the mausoleum wall collapsed into the chasm, raising fresh clouds of dust.

"It's still going on," Elodie murmured to him. She turned around. "Fessan, what's . . . ?"

She stopped, puzzled, as Fessan raised something to his eye: It looked like a square of leather rolled into a tube. Wrapped into the leather at each end was a glass disk.

"Fessan—what are you doing?"

"Hush, please, Princess. I am counting."

"Counting what?"

Fessan stared into the strange device for a moment longer, his lips moving silently. At last he sighed and handed the leather tube to Elodie.

"Counting our enemy. Here. Perhaps you will see something I do not."

Fessan turned away to consult with his lieutenants while Elodie put the tube cautiously to her eye. She found herself looking into a long, dark tunnel. At the far end was a tiny scene: Idilliam and Castle Tor reproduced in perfect miniature. It looked incredibly far away.

"I don't see what . . ." she began.

"Turn it around," said Samial.

Elodie obeyed, and was startled to find the castle looming over her, impossibly huge. Crying out, she shrank back in the saddle, waving her free hand to fend off the huge stone battlements that appeared to be surging toward her.

"It is a spyglass," Samial explained. "It brings the world closer."

Elodie experimented with the tube, bringing it down from her eye, then replacing it. Finally understanding its purpose, she used it to scan the scene of devastation on the far side of the chasm.

The movement she'd detected was that of hundreds of people—perhaps thousands—retreating in panic from the circular building. At the same time, soldiers were pouring out from gates in the city wall and forcing their way through the crowds. Within the chaos, groups of men stood unmoving. Elodie wondered why they weren't running like the rest. Then she saw their legs were in chains.

"What's happened here?" Elodie said, returning the spyglass to Fessan.

"We're not sure," Fessan replied, "but it gives us an advantage. The enemy is in disarray, their backs are turned. This is the perfect time to strike."

"Strike?" said Elodie. "I don't see how we can."

"She's right," said the youngest of Fessan's lieutenants, a tall youth with a mane of black hair and a wild look in his eye. "The plan's in tatters, Fessan. You said we'd be able to just ride straight in, but there's no bridge. So much for the surprise attack."

"Plans are flexible, Ghast," said Fessan briskly. "Bridge or not, we must press our advantage home. Timon—do you agree?"

"I do," said the man to his left, whose barrel chest was so big he wore a pair of overlapping breastplates instead of just one. "But how are we going to get across?"

"Siege engines," said the older man, stroking his white beard.

Fessan nodded. "My thoughts exactly, Dorian."

Ghast frowned. "I don't understand."

"The advance party," Fessan explained. "They have been here for two days now, felling trees and constructing trebuchets. We will adapt their engines and use them to bridge the gap."

Elodie had been listening eagerly to the exchange. "Trebuchets?" she whispered to Samial. "What are they?"

"Giant catapults," Samial replied. "Simple machines of tree

trunks and ropes. They will hurl rocks at the city wall. I saw many during the War of Blood."

"Hurl rocks? How does that help us build a bridge?"

Samial shook his head. "That I do not know."

The debate between Fessan and his lieutenants was growing more heated.

"Even if it works, it will take days to cross the chasm," said Ghast, echoing Elodie's doubts. "And you still say you want to surprise them?"

"It won't take that long," insisted Fessan.

"Assuming we do get across, what happens when we get to the other side?" said Timon.

"Whatever destroyed that building wasn't natural," said Ghast. "There's evil in that city, you mark my words."

Dorian stroked his beard again. "I say we act now. But before we advance, we must scout ahead," he said.

"And how long will that take?" said Ghast.

Elodie could hold back no longer.

"Dorian's right!" she said. They turned to her in surprise. "We're just wasting time. My brother's in that city, remember. No matter what evil is there, we have to find him. And if we stand around all day arguing, it'll be too late."

Fessan's eyes gleamed. "A voice of reason at last," he said. "Thank you, Princess Elodie. How do you suggest we proceed?"

All four men were staring at her expectantly. Could these experienced soldiers really want her advice? And was this the right moment to tell them about the ghost army that stood along-side Trident? *Wherever you lead, we can follow*, Samial had said. But what if she promised Trident allies, only to learn the ghosts couldn't fight in this battle? Would she lose their support? They could declare her mad after all and not worth fighting for. She wished she had told Tarlan about the ghosts and asked what he thought she should do.

Nonetheless, ghosts or not, Elodie found that she did have a plan.

"Have the siege engines brought out of the woods," she said. "While that's happening, send out the scouts. By the time the engines are set up, we should have all the information we need."

Samial smiled at her and Fessan looked impressed. "A sound strategy, Princess," he said.

Elodie felt her cheeks tinge. She imagined Palenie's surprise; Elodie might not have taken to her friend's swordfighting lessons, but she wasn't hopeless in a battle. She stared across the chasm and frowned. "I just don't know how the scouts are going to get across."

"They will fly!"

The voice was accompanied by a great gust of air as Tarlan brought his thorrod mount over the cluster of Trident soldiers. Discus reared; Elodie held tight to the reins as her hair blew wildly in Theeta's wake.

Elodie's stomach turned into a bundle of knots. She could still hardly believe that her brother had dropped out of the sky and into her life. The idea of losing him again after just a few days was unbearable.

"No!" she cried up to her brother. "It's too dangerous."

"I'm from Yalasti," Tarlan replied. "I'm used to danger, Elodie." He gestured to Idilliam. "Besides, we need to get Gulph out of there."

She knew what the set of Tarlan's jaw meant; after all, she'd seen it reflected back at her in a mirror enough times. He'd made up his mind.

"Then be careful!"

"Don't worry," Tarlan told her. "I'm coming back. I promise."

With a whoop, he tugged at the thorrod's neck feathers. The giant bird rose vertically, the down draft from her wings nearly knocking Elodie from her saddle. The other two thorrods followed him out over the chasm in close formation. The tigron and the wolf emerged from a nearby thicket of trees, ran to the edge of the abyss, and watched them depart, ears pricked.

Elodie stared as the three birds dwindled. Seen against the enormity of Idilliam, the massive thorrods looked no bigger than insects.

"I hope he knows what he's doing," she murmured.

"They will return."

A hand closed around hers. It was icy cold, but its grip was firm and confident. It belonged to Samial.

Elodie gasped. She clasped her fingers over the boy's smooth, cold skin.

"So that's why you always pulled away," she said slowly. "So I wouldn't realize that you're—"

"Dead," Samial finished. He smiled. "Living people hate the cold. You would have fled." Elodie smiled back. "You're right. But now, I want to stay."

Fessan's voice rose above the murmuring that had begun in the ranks.

"It is decided!" he announced. "We will restore the Idilliam Bridge and cross to face the enemy. Our queen has commanded it!"

Silence fell. Everyone turned to Elodie. Slipping her fingers from Samial's, she guided her horse alongside Fessan's. Her gaze swept across the sea of faces, living and dead, each looking back at her. She turned to face Idilliam, where her brother Tarlan and his loyal thorrods were just specks of dust against a tableau of war. Above them rose the indomitable heights of Castle Tor. Somewhere over there was Gulph.

She felt that the past few weeks had been designed to bring her here, to this place and this moment in time. *I don't know if it was an accident or the prophecy*, she thought. *But here I am.*

"I say Fessan is right," she said. "Have we come all this way just to turn around and go back into the woods?"

"No!" roared the surrounding soldiers.

"Then we attack. We mend what is broken and we take what is ours. We attack, Trident. WE ATTACK!"

Her words were like sparks igniting Trident into flame. The column—which up to that moment had been resting in a long straggling line stretching far back into the forest—surged into action. Shouts rang out and swords were drawn.

Elodie's whole body was tingling. She urged Discus out of the way as teams of horses hauled six enormous machines out from the cover of the trees. The trebuchets. They looked like great hunched beasts, poised to spring on their prey. The horses dragged them on sleds—there'd been no time to make wheels, she supposed—and even before the teams reached the bridge, they were foaming with sweat.

Fessan ordered the soldiers of Trident into line behind the trebuchets. The bridge was wide enough for them to ride thirty abreast and still leave ample room on either side. Elodie was glad of this: The Idilliam Bridge had no parapet, and anyone straying too close to the edge risked certain death in the chasm below.

But it was a very long way across.

Ready as she was to lead her army into battle, Elodie could hardly believe it was happening. It was less than a month since she'd been living her pampered life in Castle Vicerin, only vaguely aware of the harsh world beyond, believing the crown would simply be handed to her.

So much had happened since then.

Ahead, barely visible as tiny specks against the gray stone of Idilliam, were Tarlan and the thorrods. Beyond the city wall was Gulph.

Beside her, floating in the air as if riding on an invisible bridge, rode the ghost army. Among them was Samial.

This is exactly where I'm meant to be, she thought.

Elodie straightened her back and lifted her chin.

A bugle sounded. She dug her heels into Discus as the army picked up its pace.

Trident rode out to battle.

CHAPTER 27

With a groan, the rest of the mausoleum wall collapsed. Roof tiles clattered like giant hailstones into the rubble. A fresh wave of dust blasted out over the screaming crowd. Gulph twisted his face away, clawing the powder from his eyes.

Looking back, he saw Brutan, the undead king, descending the sloping field of debris.

He could scarcely accept what he was seeing. How could that monster have been his father?

Brutan's movements were slow and jerky. With every step, he studied his juddering legs like he was seeing them for the first time. He stretched his arms and flexed his fingers, naked to the bone, as if testing their strength. It was impossible to tell where his torn robes ended and his tattered flesh began.

When Brutan reached the ground, he stopped. Sunlight streamed through his perforated flesh. His head swiveled in little jerks on creaking tendons. With each jerk he paused to survey another part of the scene: the wide root of the broken bridge, on which the upturned battering rams had fallen silent; the crowds of peasants pressing against Nynus's soldiers, who were holding them back; Nynus himself, wearing his mask, seated on a raised platform between the mausoleum and the city wall.

How can he see it all? Gulph wondered. *He hasn't got any eyes.*

Even as he thought this, flames lit up inside the undead king's empty eye sockets. Brutan unhinged his jaw and emitted a dry, penetrating scream. The scream went on and on, grating against the inside of Gulph's skull. Fresh ash fell, shrouding Brutan in a cloud of gray.

"Ossilius!" Gulph yanked on the chain to get his friend's attention.

Ossilius shook his head as if coming out of a dream. "I did not think the old stories true."

"Stories?"

"From the dark times. Stories of wizards." He stopped to rub his eyes, as if he didn't trust what lay before them.

"What did the stories say?"

"Wizards are not magical in themselves," Ossilius told him. "They only carry their magic for as long as they walk the world.

When they die, the magic remains. If it does not pass to the next wizard in line, it finds another host."

"Brutan!"

Ossilius nodded. "That is what Limmoni was warning Nynus about before she died. But he was too arrogant to listen. Too arrogant and too stupid."

Brutan was taking uncertain, but gigantic, steps toward the crowd. His mouth was still open, except now there were words wrapped up in his howls.

"Where . . . are they?" he bellowed. "My wife! My son!" He took another faltering step. "Where is the one who murdered me?"

He continued to move toward the crowd of peasants. They tried to retreat, but ranks of men from the King's Legion were in the way. A second wave of soldiers emerged from gates in the city wall; upon seeing Brutan, they immediately halted their advance.

Let them through! Gulph thought, all too aware of the panic growing in the trapped crowd.

With each step he took, Brutan seemed to grow stronger. He swung his arms like a bear, his bony fingers hooked like talons. His shoulders were hunched. In life, he'd been an imposing figure. In death—or undeath—he looked unstoppable.

"My killer!" he roared. "I will kill you!"

"Bring him down!" shrieked Nynus, almost simultaneously. His voice sounded thin and shrill against that of his father. Gulph wondered what expression he wore beneath that hideous gold mask. Behind the young king, the expression of Dowager Queen Magritt was unreadable: fury or terror or both.

Swords drawn, a trio of legionnaires pushed through the peasants and lunged at the lumbering corpse. One hacked at Brutan's chest; his weapon sliced through the undead king's shredded flesh and stuck fast between his ribs. Brutan turned away, tugging the sword from the man's grip. His hand shot out and grabbed the legionnaire around the neck. The soldier screamed, but the sound was instantly cut off as Brutan began to squeeze.

The legionnaire's companions dropped their swords and backed away, their faces filled with horror. Brutan's bony fingers clamped tight and blood jetted from the man's throat. His feet drummed briefly against the ground, then his entire body went limp.

Gulph held his breath, waiting for his undead father to drop his victim. But he didn't.

Instead, Brutan maintained his grip on the man's throat. Gray ash lifted from his arm. At first Gulph thought it was the wind, but then he saw the ash was moving of its own accord. It flowed down Brutan's arm to his fleshless wrist, squirmed between the bones of his hand, and swarmed over the face of the legionnaire.

Wherever the ash touched the man's body, decay instantly set in. The skin bubbled; bones snapped and jutted, piercing the flesh from within. The once proud uniform shriveled to rags.

"It spreads," said Gulph, horrified.

"May the stars help us," said Ossilius.

Flames ignited in the dead man's empty eyes.

Brutan opened his hand. Moving with unnatural speed, the thing that had once been a soldier of the King's Legion threw itself on its former companion and clamped its hands around the man's throat.

One, two, three, counted Gulph, watching as thin gray mist writhed from the undead man to the living one. The fresh victim twitched and struggled, but there was no escaping the dark magic. Within moments, he was a moving corpse too, turning on his horrified comrades.

Meanwhile, Brutan was busying himself with another legionnaire. Just a few breaths later, three undead men stood swaying beside Brutan in the swirling ash, red fire burning in their gaping eye sockets.

They lunged out at the terrified crowd and went to work. Gulph's guts contracted.

"We have to get out of here," he said, bending to pull at the chains. The other prisoners in the gang—most of whom had been watching mesmerized, like him and Ossilius—were now trying to free themselves too.

"There's no time," Ossilius replied. He was rooted to the spot, his eyes fixed on the chaos ahead.

"We've got to work together!" Gulph raised his voice. "Everyone—we have to break these chains!"

Nobody listened. Panic had infected the prisoners, just as it had infected the crowd of peasants. Glancing up, Gulph was faced with a wall of people rushing toward him as they tried to outrun the undead. Those who fell, or were too slow, were instantly pounced on and killed, only to rise again as the enemy. Few escape routes remained open: the rubble surrounding the mausoleum blocked the road to the west, and the chasm made it impossible to run south. Their only choice was to go straight through the gangs of prisoners who'd been drafted to destroy the Idilliam Bridge.

It was like a human tidal wave. Gulph tried to fend off the screaming people as they stumbled past. A fat peasant woman with a long scratch on her face cannoned into him, knocking him sideways. As he threw out his hands for balance, a pale-faced courtier trod on his fingers.

"Here!" Ossilius, come to his senses again, pulled Gulph upright and thrust a hammer into his bleeding hands. "Strike as if your life depends on it." Shouldering aside a charging tradesman, he added, "Which it does!"

Gulph started to hammer at the chains still holding him down. Ossilius did likewise. The other prisoners looked on in bewilderment. Gulph grabbed a fallen pickax and tossed it to the nearest man.

"Come on!" he shouted. "Strike together! It's our only chance!"

The ringing of metal on metal added new music to the tumult. Gradually the flood of people eased, making it easier to work.

It also means the enemy is one step closer, Gulph thought grimly.

Sure enough, one by one, Brutan's growing undead army emerged from the dust clouds, their red eyes burning like angry coals.

A ragged cheer signaled the splitting of the chain a little way down the line. The freed men immediately dropped their tools and ran. Gulph redoubled his efforts, pounding at the links that trapped him and Ossilius.

Just when he thought it was hopeless, with a *chink*, the metal gave way, freeing them both. Gulph kicked it aside. The manacles themselves remained tight and heavy around his swollen ankles, but at least he was free!

As he ran with Ossilius in the direction of the city wall, Gulph scanned the crowd for faces he recognized. Where were his friends? Where was Pip? Perhaps the players had escaped over the Idilliam Bridge before it had been breached.

Please let it be true. . . . Let them be safe!

"We need to hide," shouted Ossilius, steering Gulph toward an isolated tower. "We are still wanted men. Nynus won't forget that."

A woman screamed close by. Very close. Gulph swerved to avoid a squad of legionnaires hurrying through the dust. Were they charging into battle or retreating? He couldn't tell. He stumbled, recovered, and found himself face-to-face with Dowager Queen Magritt.

She was standing stock-still, her pure white dress seemingly unmarked by the flying dirt and debris. Her hands were pressed against the sides of her head. Her mouth was wide open. She was the one who was screaming.

And she was staring straight at Gulph.

Except no. She was looking past him. Gulph spun on his heels.

Brutan was there, lunging out of the murk. His eyes blazed like miniature red suns. His grisly hands groped. His black tongue lolled against his rotting lips.

"My killer!" he roared. "I will kill you!"

"Not me!" Magritt screamed. "Not me!"

She backed away, her long dress obscuring her feet so that she seemed to float through the dust.

"Kill you!"

"Not me!" Magritt pointed both hands at Gulph. "Him! He killed you! He is the one who placed the poisoned crown on your head! Kill him! Kill him!"

Without slowing, Brutan made straight for Gulph. Gulph tried to move his feet, but the manacles were heavy and the pain in his ankles had deepened to a burning agony. He tried to take in a breath, but his lungs were clogged with stone powder. He could barely even stand.

A soldier thrust at Brutan with his sword. The undead king

swatted him aside like a fly. The man's sword slid across the ground to land at Gulph's feet. He stared at it. He'd never used a sword in his life. He didn't think he had the strength even to pick it up.

Ossilius seized the weapon. Pivoting on his heels, he swung it around in a tremendous arc, its blade aimed squarely at Brutan's exposed neck.

Brutan tilted his head, twisting his neck to such an alarming degree that Gulph was sure it would roll from his shoulders and onto the ground. Ossilius's blade grazed Brutan's skull, sending bone chips and a cloud of wriggling maggots flying in a wide spray.

As Ossilius recovered from his swing, Brutan grabbed the blade of the sword. The sharp metal edge sliced through what little flesh remained on his fingers, but the bones were strong. The undead king tossed the weapon aside and closed his free hand around Ossilius's throat.

"No!" Gulph yelled, surging forward. He would not see his friend and protector become one of the undead. While there was breath in his body, he would not!

But Brutan released his grip almost immediately, tossing Ossilius aside like a doll. The captain landed on top of the fallen soldier and lay there groaning and clutching at his throat.

As Brutan came on, Gulph backtracked. The manacles scraped together and he fell. Magritt was nowhere to be seen. Only he and Brutan remained. The thing looming over him looked nothing like the father he'd dreamed of when he was a little boy. He scarcely looked like a man. Yet here they were, father and son, reunited at last.

Brutan lunged. A dark shadow fell over Gulph. Dust rose, a sudden whirlwind.

He fell back and waited for the end to come.

CHAPTER 28

The closer he flew to the city of Idilliam, the more astonished Tarlan became. He'd grown up in a land of icy mountains and frozen valleys, where the biggest settlements were no larger than the village he'd helped save with Lady Darrand. Castle Vicerin had been big enough to take his breath away.

Castle Tor was something else entirely.

It was a mountain all its own. Towers built upon walls built upon ramparts . . . The rambling stonework rose like a termite mound from the surrounding maze of streets and buildings. How many people lived here? Thousands? More? Tarlan had no words to describe such numbers.

He just knew that Idilliam was vast beyond his comprehension.

"Never mind the buildings," he muttered. "Concentrate on the people."

"Dead," wailed Theeta as they swooped down toward the crowds. "Not dead."

Tarlan strained his eyes as they flew lower. What did she mean?

Theeta repeated her words over and over again, confusion clearly locking her thoughts into a never-ending spiral.

"It's all right, Theeta." Tarlan stroked her head; the soothing movements seemed to steady her nerves.

Scant breaths later, his own nerves were jangling.

Dead! he thought as he watched lumbering creatures stagger through mounds of rubble. *Not dead!*

It was a battle, but a battle like none he'd seen before. Backed against the main city wall, a dwindling cluster of soldiers wearing bright bronze armor and carrying crimson shields were trying to hold their ground against an onrushing wave of . . . What exactly *were* they?

Living corpses!

Tarlan could think of no other way of describing them: these stumbling things draped in ragged cloth and trailing strips of torn flesh behind them.

"How can this be?" he said, simultaneously fascinated and horrified.

"Theeta not know," said the thorrod miserably.

"Dead," called Nasheen, swooping in from the left.

"Undead," cried Kitheen, soaring on the right.

"I thought the Icy Wastes were bad," said Tarlan. "But this . . ."

He steered the thorrod flock in a wide circle over the melee, keeping high enough to avoid any arrows or missiles that might be hurled their way. But both armies seemed unaware of their presence.

Cries rose from below.

"Brutan! Brutan has returned!"

"The undead king!"

"Brutan!"

Father! Tarlan's thoughts reeled. The sight of the undead warriors was shocking enough. Hearing his father's name left him breathless, as if he'd been punched in the belly.

You're supposed to be dead! He remembered the grave delight Lord Vicerin had taken in explaining how his father—the evil king of Toronia—had been murdered.

"Lower!" he barked.

"Danger!" said Theeta.

"Fly lower, Theeta!"

Cawing anxiously, the giant bird banked toward the crowd, pumping her golden wings against the clouds of dust rising up from the ground. It was like descending over boiling mountain rapids; in the gloom, the battling figures teemed like angry fish.

Ahead was a patch of clearer air. *Strange.* Tarlan directed Theeta to head toward it. A man stood there, the still center of a circle of chaos. As they drew near, Tarlan saw it was not a man but the remains of one: another of the undead army, but taller and broader than the rest. Where his eyes should have been, red flames licked.

And he knew who it was.

He knew not because of the scraps of fine embroidery that still clung to the corpse's royal robes. Not because of the tarnished gold chain around his neck. But because, despite everything, this shell of a man still carried himself like a king.

The thing that had once been Brutan was bearing down on a boy lying sprawled on the ground. Nearby lay two men. But it was the boy who held his attention. Tarlan's shock at the dead king was driven from his mind as he stared unbelieving at Brutan's next victim.

The boy was about his age.

He was oddly proportioned, as if his body had been made from parts that didn't quite fit together.

His eyes were black, like Tarlan's and Elodie's.

His hair was a striking blend of red and gold.

Like Tarlan's.

Gulph! It must be!

"He's going to kill my brother!" he shouted.

Kicking his heels into Theeta's back, he drove the thorrod into a steep dive.

"Dive!" he yelled at Nasheen and Kitheen. "Dive now!"

Wings pumping in perfect unison, the three mighty birds powered down toward the undead king. Tarlan felt the sun burning the back of his neck, saw the great shadow his flock cast over the ground, a shadow that seemed to solidify into a thick, menacing darkness as they bore down on their target. As they neared ground level, the thorrods' wings raised whirlwinds from the dust.

Sensing their approach, Brutan spun around with blinding speed. He leaped, his gore-spattered arms thrashing at the air. Instinctively, Theeta dodged aside. At the same time, she lashed out with her talons. One claw made contact with Brutan's shoulder, slicing off something that looked like raw steak. The undead king spun backward, mangled arms flailing.

Nasheen and Kitheen, having peeled off to each side, were hovering over the hordes of undead warriors closing in to support their leader.

"Go around!" shouted Tarlan desperately. "Go around!"

As Theeta wheeled in a tight circle, he saw the boy staring up at them, his mouth a round O. His torn and filthy shirt had fallen open to reveal a green jewel on a gold chain.

Tarlan felt a surge of satisfaction. He was right! He'd found his brother at last!

Our brother, he corrected, as his thoughts flew instantly to Elodie, on the opposite side of the chasm.

"We're coming for you!" he shouted, not knowing if the boy could hear. It didn't matter.

I'm coming!

To Tarlan's relief, Nasheen and Kitheen's combined attack with claw and wing had succeeded in driving back the undead army, although he suspected the respite was only temporary. They should make the most of the lull—and act before Brutan could recover.

"We have to pick him up," he said to Theeta, lining her up for another pass. "Can you do it?"

"Pick him," she agreed.

As they swooped in for a second time, a fresh line of soldiers burst through the dust clouds. But these men were alive: soldiers of Idilliam, pushing home the advantage the thorrods had given them. Leading them was a curious figure: a thin young man wearing a strange gold mask.

On his head was a golden crown.

"Nynus!" hissed Tarlan.

All the stories Tarlan had heard—everything he'd been told— crashed together in that single moment. Here was his father, dead and yet not dead. His brother, the third of the triplets. And his half brother, the young madman who'd committed murder to seize the crown.

In a moment of clear and perfect serenity, a single thought blossomed in Tarlan's mind:

I am exactly where I am supposed to be.

"To the Idilliam Bridge!" Nynus screamed. The gold mask muffled his voice only slightly, and Tarlan could hear every shrill word. "A new enemy is upon us. Beat them back! They must not cross!"

For a moment, Tarlan was confused. What was Nynus talking about? His enemies were already upon him. Then he understood. The young king wasn't talking about Brutan and his undead army. He was talking about an attack from beyond the borders of the city. An attack coming from over the bridge.

He was talking about Trident.

"They don't know!" he said. "They don't know about the undead. They're not marching on one army. They're marching on two!"

"Warn them," said Theeta.

"Yes! We have to warn them. But first we're going to save my brother!"

Theeta's wings were a blur as she carried Tarlan down to the spot where his brother lay. The scene rushed at him: Brutan bearing down on the boy once more; the boy himself, cowering beneath his father's outstretched hands.

"Now!" yelled Tarlan. "Now, Theeta! Now!"

But they were too far away, and Brutan was too fast. Aghast, Tarlan watched as the undead king's skeleton arms reached down toward his brother.

Then, to his utter amazement, the boy vanished.

CHAPTER 29

The farther they ventured onto the Idilliam Bridge, the more exposed Elodie felt. Here they were, an entire army, balanced on a narrow finger of rock jutting over a seemingly bottomless chasm. The longer they remained out here the more vulnerable they would become.

We can't stop now, she thought. *Gulph needs us.*

Trident took up the entire width of the bridge, yet the ghost army was there too, their mounts matching the strides of the living horses hoofbeat for hoofbeat. Now that they were close to the Idilliam end of the bridge, she no longer needed Fessan's spyglass to see what was happening in front of the city. A battle raged there, with legions of troops clashing inside clouds of white powdery dust. Maybe the fighting was about Nynus's seizing power; maybe it was something else. It didn't matter. Trident was here to end it, once and for all.

But what would be the cost?

She glanced again at the ghost army, marching across thin air. *How many more ghosts will there be by the end?* she thought with a shudder.

"Halt!" cried Fessan, raising his hand. "All halt!"

Discus tossed his head and champed at the bit as the Trident column slowed and stopped. Elodie patted his neck to soothe him. No wonder he was restless. Immediately ahead yawned the wide gap between the broken roadway on which they'd been walking and the far side of the bridge. Mist swirled, obscuring the immeasurable depths of the canyon below.

"It's a long way across," Elodie said.

"We will bridge it," Fessan replied. "Trebuchets!"

Elodie fell back as, all around her, the machinery of Trident unfolded. One by one, the six giant catapults were brought forward. Their wooden frames creaked as they were maneuvered into place. Elodie held her breath, imagining the stone spine of the bridge creaking too.

Please let it hold....

But the bridge showed no signs of strain. Soon the six trebuchets were lined up at its broken end, each loaded with a large rock. White-bearded Dorian, who was standing in front of them, brought his arm down in signal.

In perfect unison, the trebuchets were released. Their gigantic tree-trunk arms swung up and over, launching the six huge rocks on trajectories that took them over the break in the bridge to land on the opposite side. Around each one was tied a heavy rope; the ropes trailed behind as the rocks arced through the air.

All the rocks fell heavily on the far side, sticking fast where they'd landed—except one, which spun away over the edge of the bridge. The rope it had trailed snapped taut, dragging the trebuchet that had fired it off its makeshift supports.

"Back! Back!" yelled Dorian as the enormous catapult slid sideways across the bridge. Soldiers scattered from its path. With an animal groan, the big siege engine toppled over the edge and plunged into the mist.

Elodie waited to hear the sound of it crashing to earth, far below. But the sound never came.

"Five is enough!" shouted Fessan. "To work!"

A group of men wound handles on the trebuchets, pulling the ropes tight. A second group made their way hand over hand across the gap, their feet dangling over the bottomless abyss. Elodie's heart rose into her mouth as she watched. When they reached the far side, they pulled on the ropes that had carried them there.

Slowly but surely, the uplifted tree-trunks of the catapults began to lower themselves across the divide.

"Elodie!" cried a voice from the open air to her left. It was Samial. "Look out!"

Instinctively, she shrank down into her saddle. A scant breath later an arrow flew through the air, narrowly missing her.

Where did that come from?

More arrows flew. Shouts followed them. Bowmen raced through the ranks to the end of the bridge. At least half were cut down before their arrows were out of their quivers. Elodie stared across the gap. All the men who'd crossed over were lying dead, their bodies skewered with arrows.

Her chest clenched with horror. *It's my fault. I shouldn't have made them attack!*

On the other side of the bridge, marching out of the misty air in which the distant castle was shrouded, came the soldiers of Idilliam.

"Retreat!" cried Fessan, drawing his sword and waving it so that it flashed in the sunlight. His horse reared, drawing on his panic. "They have us! Retreat!"

Confusion spread back through the line. There was no room to turn, and no time to re-form. Shields lifted up as the arrows of Idilliam showered down on the soldiers of Trident, but already too many lay dead on the ground.

So this is what it means to be queen, she thought wretchedly. *When you make the wrong decision, people die.*

An arrow grazed the back of her hand. She snatched it in, rubbing her knuckles.

His hand, she thought, *it was solid . . .*

In a rush, an idea came to her.

Now, she thought with utter clarity. *The time is right!*

Ignoring the rain of arrows, Elodie urged Discus through the confusion to the edge of the bridge.

"Samial!" she shouted. "Samial!"

He was there in an instant, his expression grim.

"What would you have us do?" he said.

"You can touch me," said Elodie breathlessly.

"Yes, but . . ."

"Can you all do it? To all of us?"

"I do not understand. . . ."

Elodie bit her tongue, forcing her thoughts to slow themselves.

"Could a ghost lift up a man? Support his weight? Carry him?"

"Of course. But still I do not—"

"That's all I needed to know! Bring your army, Samial. Have them gather beneath the gap in the bridge. Tell them to come close together—as close as they can"—Elodie glanced back at the Trident soldiers, who'd locked their shields together to form a protective skin—"and have them hold their shields over their heads."

"But why . . . ?"

"Do it now!"

Spurring Discus away from the brink, she rode to where Fessan was trying to marshal his troops. The scar running down the side of his face blazed white against his flushed cheeks.

"Fessan!" she shouted. "Fessan! You must listen!"

"Why are you still here?" he cried. "We must get you to safety!"

"There's no time and you know it. Now listen to your queen!"

Fessan's mouth snapped shut.

"That's better," Elodie went on. "There's a way across."

Fessan shook his head. "'I'm sorry, but I can't—"

"You can and you will. Listen to me! We're not alone here. Another army marches with us. A spirit army." She pointed at the gap where even now Samial and Sir Jaken were urging their comrades into a dense cluster of horses and men. "You can't see them, but I can. They are the ghosts of those Brutan betrayed in the War of Blood. And they have come to help us!"

Fessan's eyes strained. "I see nothing," he said.

"But you did. You did see something. That day when we were riding through the meadow. Don't you remember? You saw the grass moving by itself. . . . You knew something was there, didn't you?"

As she finished, the ghosts raised their shields above their heads. The sun passed straight through them, yet at the same time it seemed to reflect back off their phantom forms. To Elodie, it looked as though a sea of silver had formed itself between the two broken ends of the bridge.

"I see nothing," Fessan repeated. Yet his expression told Elodie he wasn't sure.

"I'll prove it!" she said.

Sliding down from Discus's saddle, she ran toward the end of the bridge. Horses jostled her on every side as she pushed her way through to the narrow space on the very brink of the chasm. Here, she stopped.

On the far side, some of the Idilliam bowmen pointed and shouted. Arrows whistled past her, but Elodie ignored them.

I've got to show him, she thought. *I've got to make him believe me. It's our only chance.*

"Elodie!" Fessan shouted. "What are you doing?"

Closing her eyes, bunching her fists, Elodie leaped off the edge and out into space.

She flew, her feet dragging through empty air. In the space of a single breath, all her fears rose at once.

I was wrong. I've been wrong all this time. Samial isn't real. The ghosts aren't real. There is no ghost army; there are no voices.

I'm just a stupid, spoiled, crazy girl who deserves what I'm about to do.

Die . . .

With a dull thump, her feet landed on something solid. Opening her eyes, she looked down at the flat, silvery surface of an upraised shield. On the shield were a cross and a picture of a lion. Through the gap between the shield and its neighbor, she saw the face of an old man gazing up at her.

The old man winked.

An arrow dropped nearby, falling straight through the ranks of the phantom knights.

It fell into the abyss.

Elodie did not.

"Follow me!" she shouted to Trident, in a voice that didn't feel like her own. "Come with me now!"

Without looking back, she strode out across the ghostly bridge. Ahead, the Idilliam archers lowered their bows and looked on, slack-jawed. To them—and to the men and women of Trident—it must have looked as though she were walking on empty air.

She wondered how long it would be before they started shooting again.

Then Fessan was following. He threw a shield and a sword forward to her.

With a sudden chill, she realized they were Palenie's.

"I will follow you," Fessan said. He glanced back. Tracking his gaze, Elodie saw a mass of soldiers dismounting and stepping out onto the ghostly bridge. "We will all follow you, my queen."

The arrows began to fall again, but Elodie and Fessan raised their shields against them and pressed on.

"And you are just one," Fessan added. "Imagine what Toronia might become when we have three."

Palenie had been right. Beneath the grime and sweat of battle, Fessan's eyes shone with wonder.

As they drew closer to the other side of the divide, an arrow slammed into Elodie's shield. The impact drove a wave of shock through her arm and into her shoulder. She recoiled, the excitement she'd felt draining rapidly away. The arrows were real; the men waiting for them were real.

War was real.

Even as she thought this, the rain of arrows abated. Elodie risked a glance around her shield; were they bringing fresh archers up through the ranks? To her surprise, she saw the Idilliam men in disarray, scattering and raising their arms to the sky as if to ward off attack.

With a unified set of shrieking cries, the three thorrods plunged down onto the Idilliam soldiers, clawing at the backs of those who ran, plucking up those who remained and hurling them into the chasm. On the back of Theeta—the one with a gold breast to match her wings—rode Tarlan. His expression was one of absolute amazement.

"You're flying!" he exclaimed, pulling his flying steed down to hover beside Elodie.

"Not exactly," she replied. "What did you see?"

Tarlan shook his head, then seemed to compose himself. His face became worried.

"You're heading into danger," he said.

"I could have told you that."

"That's not what I mean. It's not just Nynus we have to face.

There's another army. An army of . . . Elodie, they're not even alive. They're dead, but they walk."

"Ghosts?" said Elodie.

"No. Not ghosts. Walking corpses. The undead." Tarlan glanced at Fessan, who was listening intently. He took a deep breath. "King Brutan leads them."

Cold dread crawled through Elodie's bones.

"Our father is dead," she whispered.

"He was," Tarlan replied, holding her gaze. "Now he's something else."

A strange silence seemed to fall. For a moment, it was as if she and Tarlan were alone on the bridge. She searched her brother's eyes, hoping desperately that he was mistaken. But she knew he was speaking the truth.

"There's more," Tarlan continued. "I saw our brother, Elodie. I saw Gulph."

The coldness spread into Elodie's arms, her legs, her chest. Her heart.

"Are you sure?"

"I'm sure. He had a green jewel, like yours. Like mine . . ." Tarlan looked suddenly, desperately sad. Then his expression became fierce. "We must go back for him."

"Yes!" Elodie started forward, only to find her way blocked by the huge flapping wings of the thorrod. "Let me pass, Tarlan!

Let us all pass! We have to get into the city, don't you see?"

Tarlan shook his head. "This isn't going to work. You haven't seen what I've seen. The undead . . . our father . . . they're too many." He looked out across the sea of faces watching them. "If you cross this bridge, you'll die."

"No!" Elodie cried. "I won't come this far only to turn back. I'm no coward, Tarlan, and I don't believe you are either. If we leave Gulph now we might lose him forever!"

"Not Gulph. He'll survive."

Anger flared inside Elodie. "How can you possibly know that?"

"He's safe for now," Tarlan insisted. "I saw him . . . Elodie, there are strange powers at work in Idilliam. I saw our brother . . . I saw Gulph . . ."

"What? What did you see?"

"He became invisible."

Elodie gasped. The soldiers close to them had heard too, and murmurs of surprise rippled over the clink of bridles, the shouts of the enemy, the thin roar of distant fighting.

"Even so," she said, "we have to go to him."

Now anger flashed in Tarlan's eyes. "I'm telling you, none of your army will make it out of there alive. Is that what you want?"

Before Elodie could snap back in reply, Fessan had stepped between her and the hovering thorrod.

"We haven't time for debate," he said. "We must press forward across Elodie's bridge while we can. If the prophecy is meant to be, your brother will live."

Theeta reared in the air. Fessan stood unmoved in the blast from her wings. Tarlan glared down at him, his black eyes darkening even further. "Be very careful how you speak about my brother!"

Fessan turned to Elodie. "Princess, you have led us this far. What do you say? Command it, and I will obey."

Elodie looked from Fessan to her brother and back again. This was worse than when she'd had to decide between staying in the Weeping Woods with Samial and going with Trident. She felt the weight of her whole life pressing down on her.

Why are these decisions always down to me?

She brought down her shield. Its metal rim scraped against the blade of her sword.

Palenie's shield. Palenie's sword.

For what had Palenie died if not for this? Why were they here, if not to find Gulph and take Idilliam, the realm of the crown?

She looked her brother in the eye.

"Our father is not the only one with an undead army," she announced.

Tarlan's eyes widened. He stared first at Elodie's face, then down at her feet. "I don't understand," he said.

"You will, but in the meantime"—Elodie raised her sword—"*Trident attacks!*"

CHAPTER 30

S lowly, Gulph clambered to his feet. Equally slowly, he backed away from the swaying corpse of his father. The undead king stood with his arms outstretched and his ruined head cocked to one side, as if he were listening for something. Inside his exposed rib cage, unspeakable things squirmed. The red flames in his eyes pulsed.

Gulph took another step backward. Why had Brutan stopped? Those giant birds had beaten back the front ranks of his army, but the king himself had remained unchallenged. So why wasn't he closing in on Gulph, seizing his throat like he'd done to the others?

Why was Brutan now turning away from Gulph?

His feet struck the outstretched arm of a fallen soldier and he glanced down, anxious not to fall over his manacles again. He saw the dead man's clutching hand, the pale soil . . . and nothing else.

I can't see my feet.

Stunned, Gulph raised his arms. His eyes saw only empty air. He ran his fingers down his sleeves, staring at the place where his hands should have been.

His hands weren't there.

An undead warrior lurched past Brutan, heading straight for the fallen Captain Ossilius. But Ossilius was already standing, lifting up a shield he'd found on the ground and using it to fend off his attacker's blows. At the same time he looked around wildly.

"Gulph!" he shouted, staring right at the place where Gulph was standing. "Gulph! Where are you?"

Gulph thought back to the boy who'd been flying with the giant birds. Just as they'd swooped in, the bird he'd been riding had reached out its claws . . . then suddenly retracted them. Gulph hadn't gotten a good look at the boy's face as he'd flown past at speed, but he was sure the lad's jaw had been wide open in surprise.

He can't see me—none of them can! I'm invisible!

He spat. His mouth felt full of sand, although nothing came out. His head felt hot and dry. He'd felt like this before, back in the banqueting hall of Castle Tor, shortly after he'd . . .

. . . after I killed my father.

A moment of crisis.

An animal urge to run from danger.

To disappear.

He remembered the look on Pip's face as they'd met in those dreadful moments following the king's death. The look of surprise, as if she'd not noticed he was there.

He'd felt that way then, experienced that same peculiar desert feeling in his nose and throat.

The undead warrior was still raining blows on Ossilius. Little by little, he was being beaten back.

"Hey!" shouted Gulph. "Over here!"

As Ossilius's attacker looked up, Gulph grabbed a stone—so strange to see it floating in front of him, carried in invisible fingers—and hurled it at the warrior. It went straight through the undead creature's cheek, making a hideous squelching sound as it pierced its rotten flesh.

The warrior lifted its head and gave an unearthly shriek. It started lumbering toward Gulph, its red eyes blazing. Gulph held still . . . then saw in horror that his hand was materializing before his eyes. The bones of his arm appeared, then his veins and surrounding muscle. Finally his skin and clothes came into view.

Gulph shuddered. It was a hideous reminder that, underneath, he too was just a walking bag of flesh.

And entirely visible once more.

Disappear, disappear, he thought frantically, but nothing happened.

The warrior opened its mouth to scream again, then paused.

Its swollen tongue rolled and it spat out the stone Gulph had thrown. Gulph fought back the urge to be sick.

Then, with a loud crack, Captain Ossilius's sword sliced through the undead creature's neck. The thing's head lolled, then rolled to the ground. The rest of its body lumbered away, its arms waving blindly.

My father!

Gulph looked around with renewed fear. In saving Ossilius, had he left himself exposed?

To his relief, he saw that Brutan had retreated, forced back by a column of legionnaires. For the moment at least, they were safe.

"You!" Ossilius cried as he staggered toward Gulph. "The prophecy! At last I understand!"

"I don't know what you mean," said Gulph uncertainly.

"I do!"

"Whatever you think you know, it isn't true. I'm just—"

"You are one of the three!" Grinning, Ossilius fell to his knees and clasped Gulph's hands—both now back to normal. "Oh, how I have waited for this day!"

"You have?"

The grin became a look of sober respect and humility. "I am your servant, Gulph. I always have been. It's just that neither of us knew it until now."

"How did you know?"

Ossilius smiled. "It is not every young man who can make himself invisible."

Gulph looked at his hands. "Oh. That."

"There is little enough magic left in this world, Gulph. But you carry its legacy. Your mother was a witch, you know. When I think of your brother and sister . . . What powers might they have?" He shivered. "What powers might you have if the three of you are brought together?"

More legionnaires rushed past them as a small band of the undead closed in.

"Here," said Ossilius, ushering Gulph behind the broken remains of a stone wall. "This will shelter us for a moment longer."

"I just can't believe you're really on my side," said Gulph as they crouched behind the shattered stonework. "I mean, I'm just a traveling player. I was never meant to be king."

"But you were. You remember I mentioned my son, Fessan? He helped me keep my faith in the prophecy over the years. The day he left Idilliam to raise his rebel army was the day I renewed my vow to bring the triplets to the throne. Everything I have done since then—*everything*—has been toward that glorious end."

"I knew you were never really on Nynus's side."

Ossilius stared at the ground. "Do not be so quick to praise me. I helped Magritt and Nynus bring down Brutan. I truly believed it was an opportunity to rid the kingdom of his evil, once and for all."

"You did what you thought was right." To Gulph's relief, when Ossilius looked up again, he was smiling.

"And I believe now that it *was* right," he said. "Magritt and Nynus's plot was terrible, but it ended with you placing that poisoned crown on Brutan's head. *'They shall kill the cursed king. . .'* It set the prophecy in motion. I should have known from that moment who you truly were."

Gulph shuddered to remember the dreadful scene in the Great Hall, but he couldn't deny the truth in Ossilius's words. Limmoni had told him much the same thing. "All I know is that, if it wasn't for you, I wouldn't be here. I'm glad to have you as my friend, Ossilius."

"Just as I will be glad to have you as my king."

The sound of battle was coming closer again. The legionnaires who'd marched past them moments before were retreating before a fresh wave of the undead. Standing tall among the fearsome, flame-eyed warriors was the unmistakable figure of King Brutan.

"One enemy escapes, but there are more!" the undead king shrieked in his hideous, scratching voice. "Where is Nynus? The Vault of Heaven was too good for you! I should have killed you when I had the chance!"

Brutan was making for a knot of legionnaires near the base of a nearby tower. As he approached, swinging a sword he'd wrestled from one of his undead cohorts, the soldiers fell back, revealing none other than Nynus himself cowering against the stonework.

"Stay back!" Nynus screamed through his gold mask. "Help me! Somebody, help me!"

But nobody came. Gulph watched sadly as Nynus's own men fanned away from him. Their loyalty had been driven into them by cruelty and force. Now, in the face of death, they placed far more value on their own lives than on that of their king.

Gulph couldn't take his eyes off the mask and the gold crown perched above it. What had happened to the skinny, book-loving boy he'd befriended in the Black Cell?

All that remained was a monster.

"Defend him!" The voice was that of Dowager Queen Magritt. "Defend my son! Defend your king!"

Gulph saw her—or thought he saw her—floating ghostlike in her white dress at the periphery of the battle. Her voice came and went on the wind. Unlike her soldiers, she wanted her son to live.

But not enough to risk her own life.

"I have to help him," said Gulph.

"No!" said Ossilius at once. "He brought this upon himself!"

"I don't care. I can't see him die like this."

"You can't help!"

"I'll make myself invisible. They won't see me."

Shaking off Ossilius's restraining hand, Gulph raced across the battlefield. The leg irons dragged along the ground, slowing his progress and chafing his bleeding ankles, but some things were more important than pain.

As he ran, he tried to summon those strange feelings of *hotness* and *dryness*. Nothing happened. He tried again.

Make me invisible! he thought, desperately trying to invoke whatever powers had granted him the extraordinary ability. *What good is magic if I can't use it?*

The trick continued to elude him. No matter how much he tried, his body remained resolutely visible.

A pair of undead warriors leaped out from behind a low wall. It was too late to stop, so Gulph threw himself into the air. Somersaulting above their heads, he flipped his legs over in time to land safely on the ground.

Glad my circus skills are still useful.

Ahead, a line of legionnaires had blocked his view of Nynus. Squeezing through their ranks, he burst into the arena that had formed at the foot of the tower. On one side stood the men of Idilliam; on the other, somehow understanding that their king required them to hold back, stood the undead.

Nynus was pressed against the tower wall, his pale hands splayed wide against the gray stones. His gold mask, with its curious blend of beauty and horror, stared with inhuman grace at the nightmare striding toward him.

From a balcony high above, at the top of a flight of stone steps winding its way up the tower's exterior, Dowager Queen Magritt looked down, her face a mask of its own.

A mask of anguish.

Step by step, King Brutan bore down on his whimpering son. His ravaged boots raised dust in his wake. A broadsword swung from his fleshless hand. His burning eyes projected red fire across the wall of the tower.

When he reached Nynus, Brutan stopped. He placed his free hand on top of the mask. Naked bone rattled against gleaming gold.

"Die," he said simply, and thrust the sword into Nynus's chest.

Up on the balcony, Magritt screamed.

Withdrawing his sword, Brutan turned and marched back into the ranks of the undead.

Nynus slithered down the wall, leaving a trail of red blood on the stones.

Gulph rushed over and clamped his hand against the wound in Nynus's chest. With the other he pried the mask off the boy's face. Sunlight bathed Nynus's pale skin, but for once he didn't flinch. Blood bubbled at the corner of his mouth. His eyes, wide with fear, flicked from side to side.

"It's all right," said Gulph, knowing it wasn't. "You're going to be all right."

Nynus coughed, and a fresh gout of blood poured from between his lips.

"Too late . . . for me . . ." he gasped.

"Don't say that," said Gulph.

He heard the clash of swords nearby, and turned to see Captain Ossilius, alone in the arena, fighting back a straggling contingent of the undead. None of the other soldiers came to his aid.

"Help him!" Gulph yelled. "Why don't you help him?"

His cries had no effect. The rotting warriors pressed forward, forcing Ossilius against the tower wall. Gulph was about to shout again when a loud bellow brought the enemy to a sudden halt.

"To me! To me! To arms!"

In the distance, Gulph could see Brutan standing on a mound of corpses, waving his gruesome arms, summoning his troops to some new conflict near the Idilliam Bridge. At the sound of his voice, the undead warriors turned their backs and left the arena. Exhausted, Ossilius collapsed against the wall.

The ensuing silence was sudden and immense.

"Why?" said Nynus. His voice was less than a whisper, less than a breath. Gulph bent close, struggling to hear.

"Why what?" he said.

"Why . . . help . . . me?"

Gulph closed his eyes. He opened them.

"I can't help you, Nynus," he said. "You're dying."

Pale fingers closed on his.

"You're . . . here . . ." Nynus croaked. "That's . . . enough . . ."

"I wouldn't be anywhere else." Gulph had to force the words out, so tight did his throat feel. Tears broke from his eyes.

Nynus's grip tightened. "But . . . why . . . ?"

Gulph's tears were flowing freely now. Something was building inside him: a sob, or perhaps a scream.

Nynus deserved to know the truth.

"I've no choice but to help you," he said. "And I'm glad to. I'm your brother."

CHAPTER 31

Twenty more paces and Elodie would be at the end of the floating platform of ghosts. Ahead lay the other end of the fractured bridge. Twenty more paces and she would pass smoothly onto Idilliam soil. Into the city of her birth.

The spirit shield on which she was balanced shifted beneath her feet. Fessan, walking close beside her, caught her before she fell.

"You should be farther back in the ranks," he said. "I would not have you on the front line."

"I wouldn't be anywhere else," said Elodie. She wished she felt as brave as she sounded.

At her feet, the deck of shields parted and Sir Jaken poked his head through. Beside him, looking anxious, was Samial.

"You must hurry," said Sir Jaken. The sun shone both on his

cloven helmet and through it. His ghostly skin shimmered. "As long as we are holding you up, we cannot fight for you."

"I understand," Elodie replied.

"What?" said Fessan. "What do you understand?"

"That we're running out of time."

The shields closed again. Elodie forced aside the fear she felt of what they might find at the other end, and stepped forward with new vigor.

Twenty paces became ten. There was an eerie movement in the swirling dust that covered the end of the bridge. A cloud within a cloud.

"Archers at the ready!" Fessan called over his shoulder.

He dropped to his knees, pulling Elodie down with him. Around and behind them, twelve rows of Trident foot soldiers followed suit, allowing the men farther back in the column to aim their bows over their heads.

An army emerged from the dust cloud. Elodie clamped her mouth shut against a cry of horror. Hearing Tarlan's report of undead warriors and a resurrected king was one thing. Seeing this mass of rotting, shambling corpses filling the broken bridge from one side to the other was quite another.

"Loose!" yelled Fessan.

A volley of arrows flew over the front line. Elodie ducked

instinctively as they arced over her head. She held her breath as the arrows struck home, impaling the walking dead.

But the dead came on.

"Second wave! Loose!"

The second volley had no more effect on the oncoming corpses than the first. Bristling with ineffectual arrows, the hideous figures continued to lurch toward them, ragged lips peeled back from skeleton teeth, eye sockets burning with red fire.

"Stand!" Fessan shouted. "Let them come!"

Elodie's legs were shaking as she rose. She gripped her sword— Palenie's sword. It was impossibly heavy. Her mind was empty but for the thudding of her heart. She'd forgotten even the little she'd learned at the camp and on the road.

The ghost bridge trembled as two loping forms barreled through the Trident ranks: Graythorn and Filos, racing to take up positions on either side of Elodie. As their warm bodies pressed against her legs, she felt a surge of hope.

The air sang as the thorrods flew over her head.

"Stay close to her!" shouted Tarlan from on high.

The wolf and the tigron bared their teeth and growled in unison. *So he talks to them as well as the thorrods,* she thought. *Like I can talk to the dead.*

She laid a hand on the tigron's head. Tarlan had said they

were her pack too, and she felt the strength of their loyalty.

A massive figure charged through the ranks of the undead. Taller and broader than the rest, this walking corpse was dressed in the remnants of a king's robes. His hands were naked bone; the flesh of his face had shifted hideously to one side, exposing the pale shelves of his skull. His eyes blazed.

Elodie couldn't breathe.

For the first time in her life, she was face-to-face with her father.

Brutan's jaw gaped. An unearthly shriek came out.

The undead charged.

"For Toronia!" roared Fessan, raising his sword to the sun. "For Toronia!"

The battle cry rose up from the rest of Trident. Elodie held up her sword, trying to ignore the way her hands were shaking.

Brutan's undead army rushed onto the bridge of ghosts. At the last moment, those Trident soldiers still kneeling lifted the spears they'd been concealing. The first wave of corpses ran straight onto their sharp points, impaling themselves. To Elodie's horror, however, they didn't die, simply hung there with their ribs split and their arms thrashing.

At her side, Fessan swung his sword in a wide arc. Its blade cut clean through the neck of an oncoming undead warrior. The creature's head flew over the side of the ghost bridge and into the chasm. But its body came on. More men fell on it, their blades steadily taking the thing apart until it was just chunks of flesh and bone spread twitching across the deck of upturned shields.

Elodie's stomach churned with revulsion, but the ghastly sight was encouraging.

These things can be killed after all!

Summoning all her will, she brought her body under control. None of that mattered. She was here with a sword in her hand and a task before her.

If killing you means taking you apart, she thought grimly, *then so be it. . . .*

As Fessan warded off the blows from another warrior, Elodie thrust her blade at the nearest corpse. Her first strike cut off the creature's arm; her second removed its head.

A scream left her throat, whether of terror or exultation, she didn't know. As the decapitated body of the first undead warrior staggered away, a second loomed over her. She brought her blade around, instinct telling her to use the momentum of her previous thrust to guide it. At the same time, her feet danced, adjusting her balance.

"*There is a thing*," Palenie had told her on the march. "*We call it 'battle rage.'*"

"*So you feel angry when you fight?*" Elodie had asked.

"*It is beyond anger*," Palenie had replied. "*Anger is red.*"

"Red? Then what color is this 'battle rage'?"

"It is white."

At last Elodie understood what her friend had meant. As her blade connected with her latest foe, a pure, clean fury coursed through her veins. As her enemy's head tumbled, it filled her with something brighter than the sun, and far beyond any ordinary rage.

It filled her with white.

By now the front ranks of both armies were locked together in close combat. Elodie's ears filled with the overwhelming percussion of metal clashing on metal, with the screams of injured men, the hollow shrieks of the undead. Brutan was clearly visible over the sea of heads: a mighty bellowing monster using his broadsword like a scythe, cutting through everyone who stood before him.

Let him come!

"Look out!" The foot soldier beside Elodie grabbed her shoulder and pressed her down, just as a bloodied blade sliced the air above her head. The soldier jabbed his sword into the belly of her attacker, but not before the undead warrior's flayed fingers had closed around his throat. With inhuman strength, the awful creature lifted the man bodily off the ground and hurled him into the abyss.

The corpse bore down on Elodie, its teeth chattering. She tried to bring her sword to bear on it, but the very shove that had saved her made her lose her grip on its hilt.

Weaponless, she screamed.

With a flash of blue-and-white fur, Filos leaped past Elodie and buried her teeth in the corpse's throat. Biting down, the tigron worried at the creature's neck until its head hung loose like a rotten melon. At the same time, Graythorn bit deep into its ankles. As Filos released her hold, the undead warrior went down like a felled tree.

From a gap between the ghostly shields, a sword like molten silver finished what the tigron had begun, removing the thing's head with a single, clean swipe.

"Thank you!" Elodie picked up her sword, not caring if the animals had understood her.

But even as she started beating her way forward again, she saw more of the Trident soldiers thrown into the chasm, just like the man who'd saved her life. Slashing an undead warrior aside, she saw once more the junction where the ghost bridge met the real one.

It was farther away than before.

They're beating us back!

Tarlan flew past on his thorrod steed. The three birds had been attacking the enemy's rear guard, attempting to relieve the pressure at the front. Now they returned to where the fighting was most fierce.

"Do what they do!" Elodie yelled to Tarlan as Theeta swooped down. "Send them into the chasm!"

Tarlan nodded his understanding. Reaching the lowest point of her dive, Theeta grabbed an undead warrior in each claw, snatching up the living corpses as an owl might pluck a pair of mice from the ground. With a smooth movement, the giant bird flung them far out into empty space. Elodie watched with fierce approval as they fell dwindling into the canyon depths.

They couldn't be killed. But they could be thrown aside.

Brutan bellowed his rage at this new attack. To Elodie's shock, the undead king's voice was very loud: He was much closer than she'd realized. Slicing her sword through the neck of another enemy, she turned to see the undead king just a few paces away. His hand was closed around the neck of a Trident soldier, who hung limp in his attacker's clutches. Elodie waited for Brutan to throw him over the edge of the bridge, just like all the others.

Instead, the undead king held on.

With mounting revulsion, Elodie watched as the Trident soldier's eyes sank into his skull. His skin turned black and peeled away from his flesh. The color leached out of his green uniform and the cloth turned to rags.

In the creature's empty eye sockets, red flames flickered into life.

Brutan released his new recruit. At once, the undead Trident soldier rushed at Elodie, screeching through the ragged hole where its mouth had been. The thing swung its blade and Elodie ducked. Recovering herself, she spun and brought up her shield, ramming it hard into the creature's belly. Using all her strength, she shoved the undead soldier toward the edge of the ghost bridge. A cloud of red and gold fell around her as she pushed: her own hair, severed by the blow that had nearly taken off her head.

Just as she thought her strength was giving out, Filos and Graythorn were at her side. As if they knew what she was trying to do, the two animals thrust their heads against the undead soldier's legs. Together, the three of them finally succeeded in propelling the creature into the chasm.

Catching her breath, Elodie tried to look back over the battlefield. All she could see was a confused mass of swords and bodies grappling endlessly in the dust. She clambered onto a pile of Idilliam helmets to get a better view.

It was worse than she'd feared. Trident had been pushed back to the midpoint of the ghost bridge. The army of undead continued to stream out from Idilliam, a never-ending flood of living corpses. Everywhere she looked, men were falling. And every man that fell meant another undead warrior to swell Brutan's ranks still further.

We can't win this, she thought desperately.

"Get down!" It was Tarlan, bringing Theeta into a hovering position just above her head. "Don't make yourself a target!"

"It's hopeless!" Elodie shouted. "There are too many of them."

"That's exactly what I told Fessan! But he wouldn't listen!"

Elodie ignored his reproach, just as she'd ignored his warning to keep her head down. "We have to fall back."

"At least we agree on one thing."

The helmets Elodie was standing on shifted beneath her feet. She remembered how fragile the spectral bridge was.

And, as she planted her feet firmly again, how strong.

"Tarlan!" she exclaimed. "You're right!"

Forcing her way back through the Trident ranks, she located Fessan. The young man was splattered with blood from head to toe, but, apart from a few scratches, none of it appeared to be his own.

"We have to retreat!" Elodie shouted over the noise of the battle.

Fessan shook his head. "This was our only chance."

"Listen to her!" called Tarlan, bringing Theeta in over their heads. "The battle is lost!"

"No," Elodie shouted up to him. "That's not what I mean! Fessan, tell me—what will the enemy do if we retreat?"

Fessan ran his hand down his brow, smearing it with blood and sweat. An undead warrior rushed him through a gap in the front line; he cut the screaming creature down with one swift blow.

"They will follow us," he said wearily.

"Exactly! They'll follow us and fall right into our trap!"

"What trap? Princess Elodie, you must—"

"A trap made of ghosts!"

"Ghosts?" yelled Tarlan, leaning over the thorrod's beating wings. "Elodie, what are you talking about?"

"What did you think we were standing on?" she yelled back.

Tarlan looked startled for a moment. Then he grinned.

He understands, Elodie thought with relief. *Of course he does!*

Another wave of warriors pressed against the nearby Trident ranks. Metal clashed against metal.

"Speak your plan, Elodie," Fessan said. "But please, you must be quick."

"Wait," said Elodie, her heart racing. Cupping her hands to her mouth, she shouted, "Samial! Samial!"

"Who's Samial?" Fessan asked.

"You'll see," said Elodie, "or rather, you won't. Listen—we're standing on a bridge made of ghosts, yes?"

"I can hardly believe it, but yes," said Fessan.

"If we retreat, the enemy will follow us onto the bridge."

"Yes, but—"

Samial appeared, slipping between the fighting men with a strange, unsettling grace. Theeta cawed and reared up as if she could sense his presence.

"You called me, Elodie," Samial said.

"Yes, I did," she replied.

Fessan was furiously organizing a cordon of soldiers around them. The enemy was massing closer and tighter than ever. They were running out of time. He turned back to Elodie, bewildered. "Who are you talking to?"

"Samial. My friend. He's here."

"Now shut up and let my sister explain," Tarlan growled.

"Samial," said Elodie. "We're going to retreat. The instant we're back on the solid part of the bridge, I want Sir Jaken and his fellow knights to leave."

"Leave?" said Samial.

"Yes. If the ghost bridge gives way while the enemy's still on it, they'll fall into the chasm. Can you do it?"

"Of course," said Samial. "When will you retreat?"

Elodie stared at the swollen ranks of the enemy.

"Now!" she said.

But before Samial could move, something bellowed nearby. A dark shadow emerged from a roiling cloud of dust. As the air cleared, Elodie found herself staring into the twisted, inhuman face of her father.

Brutan's skeleton fingers stabbed out of the mist and closed around her neck. She tried to scream, but no sound came out. Graythorn growled and lunged at Brutan's legs, but the undead king kicked him away. Filos was nowhere to be seen.

"Back, beast!" yelled Fessan, raising his sword. Brutan swatted him down as if he were no more than a fly.

Weakening, Elodie sagged in Brutan's iron grip. His face floated over her, more bone than flesh. His eyes were furnaces, scorching her with their heat, blinding her with their light. Her neck grew cold, then colder still, and an unspeakable tingling began at the base of her skull.

This is not death, she thought in panic. *This is undeath.*

She was about to join her father in the realm of the unliving.

Brutan's fingers squeezed.

Help me! Someone help me!

The world slipped away.

Something slammed into Brutan, knocking him bodily to one side. His fingers opened and Elodie slipped free. Through blurred vision she saw the snapping beak of a thorrod, a smear of gold feathers, Tarlan's angry face. Theeta thrashed her wings, driving Brutan back, until Brutan's broadsword came up and sliced clean through one of her claws. The giant thorrod reared up, shrieking with pain. Tarlan slithered down her flank but somehow managed to cling on.

Elodie was falling backward. She let herself go. Anything to get away from the monster that had once been her father. She heard a plaintive growl, saw Filos racing toward her through the throng. She steeled herself, ready for the impact as she hit the shields below her.

The impact didn't come. As Elodie's vision cleared, she saw a sea of shocked faces—ghost faces, Samial's among them—rise past her. Except they weren't rising; she'd fallen over the edge of the spectral bridge, and was falling still, through thin air and cold cloud and into waiting darkness.

Falling into the chasm.

The cloud enveloped her and her world turned white. She felt weightless and free. It was gone, all of it: Tarlan, Samial, Fessan, the battle, her destiny. Now, at the end, it was just her, alone, falling.

How many breaths until I hit the bottom? One . . . two . . . three . . .

Fingers closed around her wrist. She cried out, thinking it was Brutan. But these fingers were warm. They tugged, yanking her arm around with sudden, welcome pain.

"Climb up!" It was Tarlan, shouting through a storm of feathers.

Twisting her body, Elodie tried to grab hold. But Tarlan's fingers were slipping, and she was already beginning to fall again.

"For your life, try!" Tarlan yelled.

Elodie plunged her hand into the mass of feathers below Theeta's pounding wings and grabbed hold. The thorrod extended her claws—one of which was just a bleeding stump—and Elodie used them to climb, just as she might have stepped up into a carriage back at Castle Vicerin. Finding new purchase on her upper arm, Tarlan hauled her the rest of the way to safety.

"Thank you, Tarlan!" she gasped as she collapsed onto Theeta's back. From the bird's labored breathing and the erratic rhythm of her wings, she could tell Theeta was in great pain. "And thank you, Theeta."

The injured thorrod cawed in return.

"She says, 'You're welcome,'" said Tarlan.

Theeta climbed steadily out of the chasm, finally breaking through the clouds to give them a heart-stopping view of the battle on the bridge.

The Trident forces were in full retreat. Most had now reached the relative safety of the finger of rock jutting from the Isurian side of the chasm. The undead army was in close pursuit but, even as they surged across the deck of shields, the ghosts broke away, tumbling them into the abyss. They plunged into the mist, shrieking. As the last men of Trident regained solid ground, the ghosts followed them. The spectral bridge was completely dissolved.

It worked, thought Elodie, exhausted.

On the Idilliam side, at the very edge of his domain, Brutan stood roaring in triumph. Surrounding him, extending behind him all the way back to the city wall, was his army of undead warriors. Thousands of eyes flamed red; thousands of voices raised their screeches to the sky.

Brutan, the tyrant king, ruled Toronia once more.

"Time to go," said Tarlan, tugging gently on Theeta's feathers. The giant thorrod circled away from Idilliam and back toward the forest of Isur.

Elodie had no hesitation turning her back on the undead, but seeing Trident so badly defeated was a bitter blow. Was this the end result of their great march through the forest? Was this all their dreams had amounted to?

"We'll come back!" she said. "Our brother is there, Tarlan. We'll come back for him. He's ours, and we're going to take him back. But that's not all."

"It isn't?" said Tarlan.

The wind blew through Elodie's battle-slashed hair. It tangled briefly with her brother's, making a single, streaming red-gold pennant.

"No. We're going to take back the crown as well."

CHAPTER 32

Gulph felt his brother's body grow slack in his arms. Nynus's pale face turned gray and his eyes closed. A thin gasp left his lips.

"Nynus?" said Gulph.

Despite all the cruelties enacted by the young king, Gulph pitied him. And loved him too. The gold mask lay abandoned in the dust; only the boy remained. With a father like Brutan and a mother like Magritt, was it any wonder he'd lost his way?

His eyes flicked briefly to the crown that still rested on Nynus's head.

Or was it being king that finally brought you down? he thought with a tremor.

In the end, it didn't matter. Gulph simply didn't want him to die.

A tremor passed through Nynus's body. His eyes flickered, fixing on Gulph's face.

"B-brother?" he croaked.

Gulph's heart lifted. Was he rallying? Would he live?

But the pool of blood in which Nynus lay was widening with every shallow breath he took, and the wound in his chest gaped and pulsed as he fought to keep a grip on his life.

"I'm here," Gulph replied.

Nynus raised a trembling hand and touched Gulph's chin. "Triplet?"

Gulph nodded. "Yes."

Nynus tried to move his head, failed, and let out a shuddering groan.

"I should have . . . seen it. I always thought . . . fate brought you, Gulph. To Idilliam. To me. Fate . . . had brought me a friend."

"I was your friend." Gulph's tears flowed down his face and onto Nynus's fingers. "But I am your brother, too."

Nynus smiled. His mouth was full of blood. "In the Vault . . . in the Black Cell . . . I used to wish for a brother."

"Wishes can come true, Nynus."

Nynus's eyes closed again. His body grew very still. But when Gulph held his cheek near to his brother's lips, he felt the faintest of breaths.

"We cannot stay here," said Ossilius.

He picked himself up from where he'd been slumped against the tower wall and staggered over to Gulph. His uniform torn and splattered with blood, his lined face caked in white stone powder, the former captain of the King's Legion looked as if he'd aged twenty years. He pointed toward the Idilliam Bridge.

"Whatever battle was fought there is over," he went on. "Soon Brutan will turn his attention back this way. We must find a place of safety, if we do not wish to join the ranks of the undead."

Through the swirling clouds of dust, Gulph saw the creature that had once been his father striding to and fro among his corpse-warriors. His sword was raised above his head; his roars of triumph echoed off the towering city walls.

A small group of legionnaires stumbled past, headed for a nearby gate that would lead them back into the city. Several of them were wounded; all looked grim and battle weary. Elsewhere, the last straggling remains of Nynus's army were fleeing into the shadows.

Brutan had won.

"You're right," said Gulph. "But I'm bringing Nynus with me."

Ossilius frowned, clearly unhappy with the idea. "All right," he said. "But you have to let me carry him. You hardly look able to carry yourself."

"You're not exactly in good shape," said Gulph. "And I'm stronger than I look. Besides, he's my brother."

Between them, they lifted Nynus off the ground, and Ossilius helped settle him into Gulph's arms. The young king's body was limp, but seemed to weigh almost nothing.

"Where are we going?" said Gulph.

"The postern gate," said Ossilius. "There are secret ways under the city known only to the King's Legion. If we can get to them before—"

"PUT MY SON DOWN!"

The cry was so shrill and sudden that Gulph almost dropped his precious cargo. Through his tears, he saw a figure in white descending the stairs that circled the outside of the stone tower. At first he thought it was a phantom; then his vision cleared and he saw it was Dowager Queen Magritt. Having fled up the tower to escape the battle, she was returning once more. Her face was contorted in agony, or anger, or both. But what held Gulph's attention were her eyes.

They were the eyes of someone insane with rage.

"PUT HIM DOWN!"

Reaching the ground, Magritt flung herself toward Gulph. Her fingers were claws. Her white dress fluttered around her like the wings of a gigantic insect. Her every breath was a scream.

Wrong-footed, Gulph took several stumbling steps backward. Then Magritt was upon him, trying to reach over Nynus's unmoving body to scratch at Gulph's face.

"PUT HIM DOWN!" she screeched. "OH, PUT HIM DOWN!"

"I'm trying to help him," said Gulph. "He's my brother."

Magritt's arms dropped to her sides. One by one, she drove her fingernails into her palms. Beneath each tiny dagger a spot of blood bloomed.

"Brother?" she said with quiet menace.

"Yes!" Gulph felt strength returning to his exhausted body. He took a step forward, driving Magritt back. "He's my brother. Do you know what that means, you evil hag? It means I'm one of the three. And I've been under your nose all this time. The prophecy said King Brutan would be killed by one of the triplets and so he was. By me. And you're the one who made me do it, Magritt! You're the one who brought me here. You brought all of us here, to this place, right here, right now. Even Nynus. Even your son!"

As Gulph spoke his name, Nynus lurched in his arms. The young king's back arched and a thin spray of blood left his mouth.

Everything left Nynus then, all life fleeing his body as he finally succumbed to his wounds. Gulph felt the change, felt the limpness turn to nothingness, felt the essential soul that had been the king depart its mortal shell.

In his brother's warm embrace, Nynus died.

The crown slipped from his head. It hit the ground at Gulph's feet, spinning in the dust.

"NO!" screamed Magritt. "YOU KILLED HIM!"

Seizing the dagger from the belt of her dead son, she plunged it toward Gulph's throat. Frozen, he watched the blade descend and prepared to meet his brother in death.

So much for destiny, he thought. *I die and Toronia falls. Who takes the crown, I wonder? The undead king or the evil queen?*

The blade kissed his neck. Magritt froze, the look of shock on her face slackening to one of vacancy. Her eyes rolled back in their sockets.

Looking down, Gulph saw a bloodied sword blade protruding from her chest. Ossilius had stabbed her, just as Limmoni had been stabbed. Unlike Limmoni, however, Magritt had no magic to sustain her against her wounds. Slipping off Ossilius's sword, she collapsed like a broken doll. She was dead before she hit the ground.

"I should have done that a long time ago," said Ossilius, wiping his sword on his ruined uniform. "I had thought I would feel triumphant to see that harridan dead. But there is no victory here."

Gulph dropped to his knees and gently placed Nynus's body next to that of his mother. Both looked as if they'd found peace. He hoped it was so.

"There's no time to bury them," Gulph said, casting another look toward Brutan. Slowly but surely, the army of corpses was drawing nearer. "There's no time for anything."

Standing unsteadily, he took a hesitant step toward Ossilius. His foot struck something heavy lying on the ground. He looked down. It was Nynus's gold crown.

The crown of Toronia.

Gulph stood in the dust, feeling very small and very lost and very alone.

Ossilius picked up the crown and blew the dust from it. He turned it in the sunlight. His eyes were very bright.

He sank to his knees.

"My king," Ossilius said, holding out the crown.

Something rose up inside Gulph: a shout, or a storm. He tried to swallow it down, but it just kept coming. It rushed out of him, a silent howl, an invisible breath in which were mingled despair and hope in equal measure.

He looked out through the clearing air at the ruins of the battlefield. Brutan and his undead army had won the day. The Idilliam Bridge was broken. Cut off from the rest of Toronia, he and Ossilius—Gulph's only friend—were trapped on this great island of rock with no hope of escape. Death surrounded them. Sooner or later, death would find them. What could there possibly be left to live for?

"I don't know what to do," he said.

"Yes, Gulph, you do," Ossilius replied.

With trembling hands, Gulph took the crown. The instant his fingertips touched the cold metal, the shaking stopped. The crown felt heavy—as heavy as all the world. If he put it on, it would crush him.

"Go on," said Ossilius. "It is yours."

Slowly, with infinite care, Gulph lowered the crown onto his head. It was just as heavy as he'd imagined. Yet he bore its weight. It felt good to be wearing it, but it was more than that.

It felt right.

"Come on," he said, extending his hand to Ossilius. "We have work to do."

EPILOGUE

Halt here!" said Fessan as they entered the clearing in the last light of day. "Rest! We will go no farther today!"

The stumbling soldiers of the Trident army obeyed without question. Battle-weary, and more exhausted still from having trekked into the Isurian forest, they threw down their packs and arms and fell to the ground. Nobody bothered to erect tents or set fires; they were glad simply to set their backs to the soil and fix their eyes on the darkening sky.

"Do you sleep?" said Elodie to Samial as the ghost army faded into the trees. The dead boy frowned.

"I don't know," he said. "Sometimes my thoughts grow thin, as if they are preparing to leave this world for another. But they always come back. The night is a comfort."

"Then go into the forest with the others, Samial, and find your comfort."

"I will not be far away. Whenever you need me, Elodie, I will be there."

Twilight fell. One by one the stars came out. Three shone brighter than the rest, casting their eerie light across the forest glade. Beneath their gaze, a few of the survivors began to stir, preparing food, tending wounds, making repairs to equipment. Muted conversation drifted through the darkness, a constant undercurrent of whispered sound.

On a boulder near the edge of the clearing, away from the others, sat Fessan. His chin rested on his fist, his elbow on his knee. His face was downturned, deep in shadow, his expression unreadable.

Behind Fessan hulked three giants: the thorrods, nested together in a scrape they'd made in the bracken. Nasheen and Kitheen slept, their gold beaks buried deep in the thick feathers on their breasts. Theeta sat a little to one side, her head upraised and alert.

Nestled against her flank were Filos and Graythorn.

"It's all right, Theeta," said Tarlan, grimacing as he bandaged the stump where her claw had been severed at the root.

Elodie returned from the edge of the clearing carrying a bowl. She handed him a rag soaked in water from the spring they'd found nearby. "How bad is it?"

"Bad enough. Hold her while I tie this."

Setting aside the bowl, she supported the thorrod's leg while Tarlan pulled the dressing tight. Throughout the procedure, Theeta uttered not a single sound.

Fragments of conversation floated past them from across the clearing:

". . . should never have come . . ."

". . . disaster . . ."

". . . it's all over . . ."

Once his work was done, Tarlan rocked back on his heels and stroked Theeta's wing.

"Sleep, my friend," he said.

Obediently, the huge thorrod closed her eyes and tucked her head out of sight.

"If only we could hide from the world so easily," said Elodie.

"We're not hiding," Tarlan replied fiercely.

"Then what are we doing?"

Lifting his head, Graythorn began to growl.

"Hush," said Tarlan. "Rest now."

Still growling, the wolf rose to his feet. Tarlan rubbed the back of the creature's neck; the hackles were standing at attention.

"What is it?" said Elodie.

Graythorn took three steps toward the edge of the clearing. Staring deep into the shadowy trees, he snarled.

Tarlan jumped up. "Who goes there?" he shouted.

At the sound of his cry, Fessan looked up. Several men ran to Tarlan's side. Their faces were lined with exhaustion, but their swords were drawn and their hands were steady.

Elodie stood alongside her brother. All three thorrods had woken and were staring along with Graythorn into the forest.

Something moved among the trees.

"Stop!" Tarlan called. "Identify yourself!"

The movement coalesced into the figure of a man. He stepped slowly out of the shadows, every footstep a slow, deliberate act. He was old and bent and bearded, dressed in a shabby yellow robe and leaning on a knobby staff of oak. His long hair was tangled with holly. Behind him trailed a garland of ivy.

"Hold fast your weapons," the old man said. "I come in peace."

"So you say!" said Tarlan.

Moving through the light of the prophecy stars, Fessan pushed past the soldiers to stand at Tarlan's side. He stared at the old man. His mouth worked, but no sound came out.

"Do you not know me?" said the old man. His eyes twinkled.

"I do," said Fessan, finding his voice at last. "By the crown of Toronia, I do."

Elodie looked from one to the other. "Who are you?"

"Will you tell them," said the old man to Fessan, "or shall I?"

"If somebody doesn't tell me what's going on . . ." began Tarlan with an angry snarl.

"Melchior!" blurted Fessan. He dropped to his knees, bowing before the old man. "It is Melchior. He has returned."

"I have," the wizard replied. His pale blue eyes sought out Tarlan and Elodie. "And it would seem I am just in time."

Driving his staff into the ground, he placed one bony hand on Tarlan's shoulder, and the other on Elodie's. His movements were swift and sure.

"What do you mean?" said Tarlan and Elodie at the same time.

"The wheels of the prophecy are turning. One triplet has slain King Brutan, two others stand united." Starlight flashed in the wizard's eyes. "My friends, we have much to do. The battle for Toronia has begun!"

Turn the page to read an excerpt from

◆ BOOK TWO ◆

THE LOST REALM

The stakes are rising even higher for the triplets. Gulph is trapped inside the burning city with an army of zombies. Elodie and Tarlan's army is in tatters, and retreat is the only option.

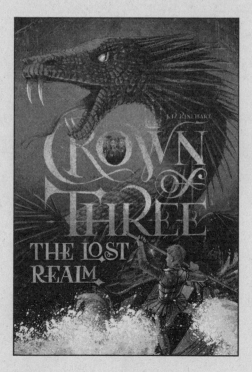

Will the three survive long enough to take the throne?

To the postern gate!" shouted Captain Ossilius. "It's our only chance!"

He swung his sword, killing two undead warriors simultaneously. Gulph dodged past his friend, kicking out at the bodies, once, twice, tumbling them end over end down the steep stone stairs, where they scattered the oncoming enemy soldiers like bowling pins.

"That should buy us some time," he gasped. "What's a postern gate?"

"Our last chance."

Together, Gulph and Ossilius climbed the rest of the way up the stairs, ran along the battlement, and plunged down a steep ramp into a small, enclosed courtyard.

Here they halted, leaning against each other as they fought for breath. Gulph felt small against the burly, gray-haired captain, and wondered if he would always be as skinny as he was now.

Never mind growing up, he thought, massaging the aches from his crooked back, *I just wish I'd grow straight.*

"So where's this last chance of yours?" he said, stepping away from his companion, who was still struggling to breathe. Ossilius ran a hand through his gray hair and ushered Gulph over to a break in the wall.

"Look," he gasped, pointing through the shattered stonework toward a squat tower built into the city wall.

"I can see what looks like a door," said Gulph. "What are those things on either side of it? Statues?"

Ossilius nodded. "That's the postern gate."

Gulph stared skeptically at the stretch of ground lying between them and their destination. Swarms of undead warriors were fighting their way through ranks of terrified citizens, and thick smoke shrouded the scene, making it hard to see exactly what was happening. But Gulph could hear the screams clearly enough.

All the people of Idilliam wanted was to flee, but even as they tried to escape they were seized and made undead. This was the horror: The enemy didn't kill you.

The enemy made you like itself.

"Every time we lose a soldier," whispered Gulph, "they gain one. How can we ever win?"

For a brief moment the smoke surrounding a nearby tower cleared, and King Brutan himself strode into view. Flesh hung from his bones; his blood-streaked clothes flapped in tatters; his eyes burned red with fire.

Gulph closed his eyes, trying to remember how Brutan had looked when he'd been alive. But all he could bring to mind was the look of betrayal on the king's face when he, Gulph, had placed the poisoned crown on his head.

I didn't know it would kill you, Gulph thought. *I never imagined it would make you a monster.* He shook his head, correcting himself. *No—you already were a monster, weren't you?*

Brutan's left hand closed on the neck of a man; with his right he snatched up a peasant woman. He lifted them both off the ground and squeezed his skeleton fingers. They struggled briefly, then their eyes closed and their bodies went slack. Their skin turned white; their flesh sank in on itself.

When their eyes opened again, they were filled with flame.

Gulph watched, aghast. He'd seen this happen many times during their headlong run across the battlefield; still, it never failed to repulse him. What made it worse was the knowledge of who Brutan really was.

You're more than a monster. You're my father.

A fresh wave of city dwellers burst from a breach in the wall: ordinary people clutching bags and boxes and clumsy wraps of cloth.

Gulph gripped the rubble of the broken wall, silently urging them on, wondering what meager possessions they'd managed to collect, and where they thought they could flee to.

"They don't know about the bridge," said Ossilius.

Gulph held his breath as the first of the refugees reached the edge of the chasm. It encircled Idilliam as a moat surrounds a castle—except this moat was bottomless. One man led his children to the brink and stopped, staring dumbstruck at the ruins of the bridge that had once connected the city to the rest of Toronia. . . .

"They have nowhere to go," Gulph groaned. "There's no escape. They're trapped here. We're all trapped."

He lifted the golden crown he'd carried across the battlefield. His fingers were cramped from clutching it. Now that he had the crown, he couldn't imagine ever letting it go—yet part of him wanted to cast it into the chasm.

"Just this morning Nynus was wearing it," he said. He shuddered, remembering what Nynus had done to take the crown—and to try to keep it. He'd tricked Gulph into killing Brutan and come up with the insane scheme to destroy the bridge and isolate Idilliam. "Nynus was no better than his father," Gulph said. "*Our* father."

"Gulph—Nynus is dead."

"But the crown is still here! Was it the crown that made him do all those terrible things, Ossilius? What will happen to me if I put it on? If I try to rule? The prophecy says that I'm one of the three.

That it's my destiny to rule Toronia. But what if I turn out to be just as much a monster as Brutan or Nynus?"

He stared at Ossilius, his eyes wide, the crown held between both hands. Ossilius looked solemnly back.

"It is just a crown, Gulph. A piece of metal. What you do with it is your choice and yours alone."

Gulph stared at the gold band. What did it matter now, anyway? For a brief moment, just after Nynus had died, when Ossilius had picked up the crown and handed it to him, Gulph had believed everything might turn out all right. But the dead had taken over Idilliam and there was nothing left to rule.

"It's time to go," said Ossilius. Gently, he removed one of Gulph's hands from the crown and placed a sword in it. "Are you ready?"

"I don't think I was ready for any of this," Gulph replied. But he followed Ossilius as they crept through the hole in the wall, heads lowered, and began to cross the battlefield. In the shadow of the nearby tower, Brutan had closed his bony fingers around the throat of a boy of about thirteen—Gulph's age. The undead king hoisted the lad into the air and studied his face with blazing red eyes.

"Are you my son?" he bellowed. "Are you the one who killed me?"

"Leave him alone!" Gulph hissed, but when he started toward the horrific scene, Ossilius pulled him back.

"It is too late," Ossilius insisted.

The boy's whimpers were cut off as Brutan squeezed. A moment later, his life had ended and his new, undead existence had begun.

"Revenge!" Brutan roared as he marched on. "I will have revenge on my son and my treacherous people!"

"I have to do something!" said Gulph, shaking Ossilius's hand from his shoulder. "I don't care if it's hopeless. These are my people. I should be fighting with them!"

He started off through the smoke, but Ossilius caught him again. "I understand, Gulph. I do. But this is not the time for you to fight. This is the time for you to hide."

Gulph stopped struggling and stared at him, dumbfounded. "*Hide?* What kind of king hides when his people need him?"

"The kind of king who wants to stay alive."

"A cowardly one, more like."

Ossilius shook his head, exasperated. "You know already that you cannot win this battle, Gulph. But you can make plans for the future. You can gather allies and arms. If you lie low now, one day you will rise again."

Gulph looked into the face of the man who was old enough to be his father, perhaps even his grandfather. He couldn't imagine a more loyal companion. And yet . . .

"The Legion was my life," Ossilius pressed. "I know when to fight, Gulph. And I know when to make a tactical retreat. Believe me when I tell you that time is now."

"But my friends are out here somewhere. Pip and Sidebottom

John and the others. I won't leave them behind. I won't leave anyone behind!"

"Do you mean the troupe of performers you arrived with? Gulph, we cannot risk it."

Gulph looked out at the legion of undead. He knew his friend was right. What chance did the two of them have? If they tried to find his friends, they'd only die in the attempt.

"All right," Gulph said reluctantly. "Let's go. But we'll take whoever we can save with us."

They ran on, hugging the city wall as they tried to circle around the worst of the fighting. The billowing smoke was acrid; Gulph could barely see through the tears streaming from his eyes.

"Look out!" shouted Ossilius as a rotting warrior leaped out from behind a mound of bodies. Gulph folded his legs, tucked in his body, and rolled away from the warrior with an agility that would have drawn a round of applause from an audience.

Once a Tangletree Player, he thought giddily, *always a Tangletree Player.*

As he sprang upright, he realized he had dropped his own sword, but spied a short sword lodged beneath an enormous stone that had fallen from the wall. He grabbed the hilt, yanked it free, whirled, and slashed his attacker across the chest. There was no blood, just a spray of bone shards and dust. The undead warrior came on, grinning its skeletal leer through hanging strips of flesh.

Gulph bent his knees and threw himself into a clumsy backflip. He landed on top of the stone and drove the sword into the warrior's skull. At the same instant, Ossilius sliced the thing's legs off at the knees.

The warrior's dismembered remains collapsed, twitching and hissing with their strange semblance of life.

"Keep moving!" Ossilius cried. "The longer we stay out in the open, the more danger we're in."

Gradually, they forged a path toward their goal. *I haven't abandoned you, my friends,* Gulph thought as he ducked and wove through a shrieking knot of undead. *I'll come for you. If not today, then tomorrow. If not tomorrow, then the day after that. I'll come for you. I promise!*

"Help me."

The voice came from behind the stone. It sounded like a girl, surely no older than Gulph.

"Pip?" He peered into the shadows, his heart suddenly racing. "Pip, is that you?"

But the face that peered up at him was not that of his oldest friend. This girl was much younger. Her cheeks were streaked with blood and her blond hair was matted with filth. She was shaking all over.

"Come with us," said Gulph without hesitation. He stretched out a hand but the girl just stared at it, too terrified to move.

"Gulph, hurry!" called Ossilius from ahead. "We cannot afford to stop."

"Wait, Ossilius!"

The captain appeared through a billow of smoke. His brow was furrowed, but as soon as he saw the little girl his face softened. He plucked her gently from her hiding place and they hurried on.

"It's all right," said Gulph to the girl as they ran. "You're safe now."

He hoped it was true.

Ahead, the ruined mausoleum loomed out of the smoke. Built by Brutan as a towering monument to death, it was now a mountain of broken stone. As they clambered over the rubble, Gulph shuddered, remembering the unearthly power that had brought this mighty building crashing to the ground.

Limmoni's power.

Broken roof tiles crunched beneath his feet—perhaps the very tiles on which Limmoni had stood when she'd been executed. The order to take her life had been the final command of Nynus's short reign as king of Toronia. A bloody reign indeed.

Will mine be any different? Ossilius had said he thought so, but Gulph wondered if he'd ever be sure.

"There!" Ossilius cried. "The postern gate!"

Gulph blinked away stinging soot and saw the tower they'd glimpsed from a distance. Set into its base was a large stone door, flanked by the statues Gulph had noticed. On the left was a man with the head of a bull; on the right was a snake-headed woman.

"So you mean the door?" said Gulph. "Where does it go?"

By now they'd run clear of the fighting. Perhaps the smoke was keeping people—and unpeople—away.

"The postern gate is the back door to the city."

"You mean it just leads to more fighting? What good will that do us?"

"We will not be going through the door."

"But I thought . . ."

Ossilius was off again, dodging through the smoke with the little girl held tight against his chest. Gulph followed, reaching the tower just a few paces behind the grizzled captain.

No sooner had they stopped than a man emerged from behind the bull-headed statue. He wore the uniform of an Idilliam soldier and was brandishing a long sword. Gulph couldn't tell which part of his body was trembling more: his arms or his knees.

"Stay back!" the man cried.

"At your ease, soldier," said Ossilius. He lowered the girl to the ground and held out his hands. "Do you know me?"

The man squinted at Ossilius's grimy outfit, then his eyes widened. "Captain Ossilius? Of the Legion?" Lowering his sword, he made a clumsy salute. "What are your orders, sir?"

Gulph spotted more movement behind the statue. "Come out," he said. "All of you. It's all right. We won't hurt you."

Two more figures appeared: a woman wearing a baker's apron and a man whose face Gulph recognized.

"You were with us in the Vault of Heaven," Gulph said, staring at the manacles still locked around the man's ankles.

"Never saw you," retorted the man. "I'd have remembered a little freak like you."

"Shut up, Slater," said the soldier. But his tone remained fearful.

"Shall I strike him, my king?" said Ossilius mildly.

Slater's eyes narrowed. The eyes of the others grew wide.

"No," said Gulph at once. "He's just afraid."

"'King'?" said Slater suspiciously. "What d'you mean, 'king'?"

Ossilius dropped slowly to one knee. "This is Agulphus, son of Brutan, born one of three. This is a child of the prophecy stars, who has slain his father and taken back the crown. See, he holds it now, in waiting for the time when the three shall be brought together to take the throne as one. If you would join his quest, kneel with me now and show your allegiance."

The soldier's jaw dropped open. The woman gasped. The little girl, crouched beside the kneeling Ossilius, stared up at Gulph with uncomprehending eyes. Slater snorted and looked away.

Gulph raised the crown he'd been carrying this whole time, but which the little crowd seemed only now to see. The crown was suddenly very heavy.

Is this what power feels like? I never knew it weighed so much.

Slowly, with infinite care, he placed the crown on his head.

"The prophecy!" cried the woman, sinking to her knees and clasping her hands in front of her apron.

"My lord," said the soldier, pressing his closed fist to his bronze breastplate. "My liege. I—Marcus of the King's Legion—am yours to command."

Slater looked back, seeming to see Gulph for the first time. His expression melted slowly from insolent to amazed.

"Can't be true," he said. "Can't be."

"It can," Ossilius replied. "It is."

"Suppose I might follow a king," Slater said after a moment's consideration. "If he had somewhere to lead me."

"As it happens," Gulph replied, "I do."

CHRISTOPHER ROWE, apprentice to Master Benedict Blackthorn, has learned to solve complex codes and puzzles. He can create powerful medicines, potions, and weapons . . . with maybe an unexpected explosion or two along the way. But when a mysterious cult begins to prey on London's apothecaries, the trail of murders grows closer and closer to Blackthorn's shop. Can Christopher discover the key to their terrible secret before his world is torn apart?